S0-AHH-925

Dear Reader,

Welcome to another fun-filled month of Duets!

Duets #29

Award-winning author Kristin Gabriel returns this month with *Beauty and the Bachelor,* the last book in the delightful CAFÉ ROMEO trilogy, about a coffee shop that doubles as a dating service. *What better place to find both lattes and love!* And talented Gwen Pemberton delivers *Counterfeit Daddy,* the tale of a sexy bachelor hero who poses as a family man in order to impress his gorgeous female boss!

Duets #30

Author Julie Kistler teams up this month with Colleen Collins to serve up BEDS & BACHELORS, two linked stories about a romantic but unusual B & B in San Francisco. Every bedroom has a movie theme! Julie's tale, *In Bed with the Wild One,* is a romp about a mousy heroine who sets off to have an adventure with the bad-boy hero. Then B & B owner Kate encounters her very own fantasy man in *In Bed with the Pirate.*

I hope you enjoy both Duets volumes this month!

Birgit Davis-Todd
Senior Editor, Harlequin Duets

The innkeeper grinned at Tyler.

"I've got the perfect themed bedroom for you. The Wild One. You get to sleep under Marlon Brando's picture. Cool, huh?"

"The Wild One?" Tyler looked bemused. "I can't wait."

An eavesdropping Emily couldn't wait, either. She knew that movie. Leather jackets, motorcycles. Bad attitude. She tried to contain her growing excitement. *Wow.*

She continued to peek as he signed the register. He was *so* sexy. He had this hard-edged, smoky attitude that just screamed sex and lust and bad, bad things. Perfect for a good girl like her.

The minute Tyler disappeared up the stairs, Emily moved to the desk. Maybe there would be a Mata Hari room with her name on it, she mused. Or Xena, Warrior Princess. "I'd like a room, please."

"Only one left, I'm afraid." The innkeeper beamed. "But it's just perfect for someone like you. Pollyanna..."

"Pollyanna...?" *Sheesh.* Emily might have known. Tyler was The Wild One and she was Pollyanna. And never the twain would meet....

For more, turn to page 9

In Bed with the Pirate

He was the swashbuckler of her dreams....

Kate zeroed in on Toby's tight black leather pants, roaming up his molded calves and muscled thighs, until her gaze landed on the flowing red silk shirt he wore.

Beside her, Kate's mother snorted. "Young man," she snapped. "You *seem* to have forgotten something."

A knife between his teeth? A sword in his hand? Kate's mind went into overdrive.

"Yes, ma'am," Toby answered. "I don't have my shoes."

Even that simple statement suddenly made Kate wish it were *her* bed he kept his boots under. *What was going on with her?* Suddenly Toby wasn't Toby any longer. Where before she'd caught glimpses of the pirate in him, she now saw the sinewy, plundering, sex-starved marauding swashbuckler in the flesh.

And in her imagination, she was his woman, the object of his fiery passion. And what would the pirate's woman say at this magical moment...?

"Want some coffee?" Kate squeaked.

For more, turn to page 197

HARLEQUIN DUETS

ISBN 0-373-44096-0

IN BED WITH THE WILD ONE
Copyright © 2000 by Julie Kistler

IN BED WITH THE PIRATE
Copyright © 2000 by Colleen Collins

Visit us at www.eHarlequin.com

Printed in U.S.A.

JULIE KISTLER

In Bed with
the Wild One

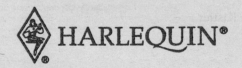

HARLEQUIN®

TORONTO • NEW YORK • LONDON
AMSTERDAM • PARIS • SYDNEY • HAMBURG
STOCKHOLM • ATHENS • TOKYO • MILAN • MADRID
PRAGUE • WARSAW • BUDAPEST • AUCKLAND

Dear Reader,

Welcome to the world of Beau's B & B! When Colleen Collins and I put our heads together to come up with a concept for a linked Duets volume, even the conversation was hilarious. We had so much fun, I can hardly remember who came up with what. I'm pretty sure the matchmaker angle was Colleen's and I think the cat was my idea. But the eccentric B & B with the goofy, movie-themed rooms... Well, that could have come from anywhere.

But then I drove poor Colleen bananas when I kept changing the name of my hero's bedroom. It only became "The Wild One" after we met with our editor, Malle Vallik, in Chicago. The three of us tripped out to dinner in 103 degree heat, ending up at a gorgeous restaurant where we laughed ourselves silly and probably embarrassed our waiter to death. Oh, well. We had fun! The best part is that this BEDS & BACHELORS concoction ended up exactly the way I'd hoped it would—funny, romantic, sexy and a little crazy. Many thanks to Colleen, Malle and Birgit Davis-Todd for making this such a pleasure to work on.

Enjoy!

Julie Kistler

To Colleen and Malle,
who were the most fun and entertaining
collaborators anyone could wish for.

1

"EMILY, IS THAT YOU? Sneaking in late? Surprise, surprise!"

Emily Chaplin stopped in her tracks. It just figured. This Friday morning in June was the first time in her entire goody-two-shoes life she'd ever been late for anything. And now she was caught red-handed, tiptoeing her way down the hall to her office, by Alissa Bergman of all people, the snoopiest, most competitive lawyer in the firm.

Emily wavered there, unsure whether to respond to or just ignore Alissa. She'd figured if she hid behind sunglasses and kept her head down, dodged the law firm's main reception area and took the stairs, surely she could sneak into her office before anyone saw her.

No such luck.

Of course, when you were among the lowly associates at Chaplin, Chaplin & Chaplin, Attorneys-at-Law, all competing to make partner someday, your co-associates watched your every move, eager to rat you out to the senior partner. They all knew the big guy was a stickler for associates making their quota of billable hours each and every day. It didn't help that the big guy also happened to be Emily's father. And he rode his family members harder than anyone.

"Emily, Emily," Alissa murmured, making a little *tsk-tsk* sound. "I heard you were out with Kip Enfield from the eighth floor last night. Had a late night, did we? Did the Kipster get lucky?"

Emily stiffened. "As *if*."

As a matter of fact, she did blame Kip for the fact that she'd overslept and missed her ride in to the city. But not because they'd had such a hot time. *Au contraire!*

Kip was just the latest terrible fix-up in her never-ending series of them. Her father the senior partner, her mother the judge, her older brothers, all four of whom were lawyers—they all insisted on matching her up with eligible but insufferable young attorneys. It didn't matter that the men bored her silly and sent her running back to the bathtub and a book about sexy spies and hard-boiled private eyes. Her well-meaning family members kept roping her into these horrible dates, no matter how much she protested.

Was it her fault the lawyers they set her up with were as limp as old noodles, while the men in the books were exciting, dark, dangerous and very, very stimulating? They saved the free world, they uncovered conspiracies, they fought off bad guys in dark alleys. They grabbed life in both hands and didn't let go.

Whereas Kip Enfield... "Gag me," she said out loud. He was the worst, the absolute worst. He wasn't just stultifyingly dull—no, he was pompous, irritable, and el cheapo to boot. Dinner with Kip had stretched out endlessly while he droned on about the wine and the beef and his fine palate. After all that torture, he'd made a big point of tipping only two percent because he didn't like the service. *Exactly* two percent—which took him about half an hour to figure out. Emily had to run back at the last minute on a pretext, unable to stand the idea of leaving such a pathetic tip.

So by the time Kip pulled his Beemer up the circular driveway of the Chaplins' suburban home, she was more than ready to dump him. Except that he insisted on coming into the house—dying to sip the senior partner's brandy out of the senior partner's snifter, no doubt—and she couldn't get rid of him no matter how many hints she dropped. Hours later, after several attempts to kiss her, paw her and cajole her into a little horizontal bingo, Kip finally consented to leave. She'd practically wept with relief.

After that fiasco, she could hardly help it if she'd slept for a full nine hours, just as a defense mechanism. At least her dreams were entertaining, unlike Kip Enfield.

"I'm never dating another lawyer as long as I live," Emily declared. "In fact, I may never date *anyone.* I've got that last-straw feeling."

But first things first. Pulling off her sunglasses, she focused on a point over Alissa's shoulder and lowered her voice. "Is that Daddy, rounding the corner to your office, Alissa? Uh-oh. And you're here in the hall, chatting with me. That can't look good."

It was a complete and total lie, but Alissa was out of there so fast she barely left a vapor trail.

With a small smile of satisfaction, Emily turned on her heel and ducked inside her own office, safely closing the door behind her. Trying to work up some enthusiasm for the day ahead, she took off her jacket and neatly hung it up, parked herself behind the desk, and then stared at the mountain of paperwork for five minutes. *Ugh.*

Finally she cracked open the Bentley file on the top of the stack. As the minutes dragged by, she fiddled with a pen, chewing on the end, staring into space, scribbling notes here and there about the tax implications of one small subsection of a client's proposed reorganization plan. It was so dull she almost nodded off right there at Part B(11), subparagraph 3(a)(iv).

"Okay, maybe I should listen to my voice mail," she decided. Maybe someone fun might have called. But who did she know who was remotely fun?

Maybe a distant relative, or even better, an old boyfriend, who desperately needed her to fly to Istanbul or Zanzibar tonight. *Yeah, right.* All the Chaplins, even the distant ones, were so boring they made the Bentley file seem exciting by comparison. As for old boyfriends...well, she had one or two, but the only thing they'd be calling for was help on their taxes.

Okay, so maybe Sukie Sommersby, her goofy sorority sister from college, might call out of the blue. Sukie was always getting into trouble. The last time Emily had heard from her, Sukie had just woken up with a new husband in a Vegas hotel and needed info on quickie divorces.

"Why don't I ever wake up with new husbands in

Las Vegas?'' Emily asked out loud. Hoping to hear something, *anything* exciting or different, she pressed the button for her voice mail.

Bad idea. There were three messages from Kip to tell her again how much he'd enjoyed last night, two from her oldest brother Rick—the doofus who'd set her up with Kip—wanting to know how it went, and one from her mother, the bankruptcy court judge, who had a new clerk she thought might be a good match for her daughter—not to mention at least one annoying message from each of her three other brothers, all of whom offered unwanted advice on her career, her car or her love life.

She felt like screaming. And that was before she heard the voice mail from her father, who had apparently called every ten minutes between eight-thirty and ten, demanding to know when the hell she was going to put in an appearance and reminding her that being a Chaplin did not bring her any special privileges at Chaplin, Chaplin & Chaplin.

''Sukie Sommersby would never stand for this!''

Without pausing to think about it, Emily stood up and grabbed her purse and briefcase, heading for the door in a blur. She called to the secretary, ''I'm taking my laptop and one of the Bentley files out of the office, and I won't be back for a while. I've got my cell phone in case anyone needs me.''

As if anyone would need her for anything truly important. She was a tax lawyer, for goodness' sake. Her life was occupied with subparagraphs of footnotes to the tax code. It was as boring as boring could be.

As she hit the street, turning her face into the bright light of the Chicago summer, Emily's mood only grew gloomier. What was the problem? Sure, the stale routine of her normal life was getting her down, but she was out of the office, wasn't she? And the good thing about getting to work so late was that it was almost time for lunch.

"Café Allegro," she murmured. Maybe that would make her feel better. After all, didn't she eat lunch at Café Allegro every day? And didn't she order the same tall glass of iced tea with a sprig of mint and the same low-fat grilled-chicken salad? Day in, day out.

It was calming, familiar and serene. Just what she needed. Right?

But her feet seemed to get sticky and slow as she wound her way down Ontario Street. She made it right up to the cool brass door of Café Allegro. But when it was time to walk in, Emily found herself paralyzed, stuck, unable to take even one more step forward. It was as if the weight of her same old routine had suddenly settled on her shoulders like a five-hundred-pound gorilla.

She pulled her hand away from the door. She wheeled. And she took off down Ontario Street as if the odious Kip Enfield himself were stalking her. She didn't stop until she hit a dark, vaguely grimy coffee shop, a place that smelled of fried onions and greasy hamburgers. The Rainbow Rest-O-Rant.

Not what anyone would expect from Emily Chaplin—which was exactly why she was going in.

Clutching her briefcase, Emily veered into the dingy

restaurant. It was mostly empty, so she had no trouble finding a booth. Scooting in, she decided this place was definitely nothing like Café Allegro. The two eating establishments were less than a block, but a whole world, apart.

She grabbed some paper napkins out of the dispenser on the table, wiping them quickly over the bench seat and the top of the table. It wasn't the grime that bothered her, though. For some reason, she found herself pondering who had carved all those initials and messages into the wood, wondering how much Marco really loved Missy, and whether Tootie and BoBo were really Friends 4-Ever.

Her reverie was broken abruptly when a rather hard looking waitress wearing a name tag that said "Jozette" slapped down a plastic menu in front of her. The woman didn't bother to smile, just raised a painted-on eyebrow as she poured coffee into one of the cups on the table. "You know whatcha want?"

"Uh, no. Not exactly. I think I need a minute." Emily peered down at the menu, unwilling to actually touch it. She might be taking a walk on the wild side, but she wasn't insane. She noted that someone seemed to have spilled ketchup on all the important parts of the lunch section, making it impossible to read. "Do you have any specials?" she asked hopefully.

"No, I don't got any specials. What do I look like, freakin' Café Allegro?" snapped Jozette. "I also don't got all day. My chili is growing legs back there." When Emily still didn't come up with anything she wanted to eat, the woman stalked off. "Lemme know when you decide," she snapped over her shoulder.

Sheesh. Life got tough when you ventured outside your comfort zone.

Using another napkin for protection, Emily flipped her menu over, looking for inspiration. Idly she tried a sip of the coffee. *Whoa.* The stuff was so strong she rubbed a finger across her front teeth to make sure they were still there. She opened four sugar packets and five little creamer cups and sloshed them in. Better. Not really drinkable, but better. Meanwhile, she distinctly made out the words "banana split" behind a smear of something brown—syrup?—on the back of the menu.

Well, why not? I've never had a banana split for lunch.

She scanned the premises, prepared to signal Jozette that she was ready to order, but the surly waitress was nowhere to be found. After a moment, Emily gave up looking for her, content to wait until Jozette wandered back on her own. Emily was in no hurry.

Closing her sticky menu, she set it aside and pulled out the newest Trick McCall novel, which she just happened to have in her briefcase. She'd bookmarked the spot where she'd had to stop last night. It had really been annoying to leave her book and her bubble bath to go out with that stupid Kip Enfield, just when Trick had been beaten to a pulp by a couple of hoods who'd double-crossed him. But Trick McCall didn't go down without a fight.

Emily scanned the page eagerly. *Trick tried to sit*

up, but the pain in his gut was like a bucket of hot lead.

A few people drifted in, a few people drifted out, dishes clattered, coffee was poured, and life went on in the outlying areas of the Rest-O-Rant. Nobody passed near her, and Emily stayed intent on what she was reading.

"Damn," Trick swore under his breath. He couldn't pass out. Not yet. Not before he knew where Rico and the Ice Man had stashed the loot...

"You have to come up with the money," a low, heated voice said fiercely. "Listen to what I say, Slab. We're past desperate here. We're right over the brink into disaster."

Wait a minute. Slab? There was no one named Slab in this book. And that hadn't been a voice inside her head. That was real. Out loud.

Confused, Emily looked up from the page, toward the source of the intriguing voice. Her gaze slid right through the gap between her booth and the next, snagging when it caught the face of the man who'd spoken. And what a face...

She swallowed. She felt her cheeks suffuse with heat.

Whoever he was—this man who was teetering on the brink of disaster—he looked *amazing*.

She didn't know who or what he was, his name, what he was doing there, any of those important details. It didn't matter. All she needed was one glance at that gorgeous, dangerous face, all hard angles and stormy shadows, the hint of stubble, the carelessly cut dark hair that brushed the collar of his battered leather jacket. And she knew him down to her bones.

She had an overwhelming desire to toss aside the adventures of Trick McCall, private eye, and toss herself over the divider into *his* booth.

"You pay up now, Slab," he muttered, "or we'll both be in too deep to shovel out."

Pay up? In too deep to shovel out? This sounded an awful lot like the book she'd just been reading. How very exciting! Easing herself up and around to one side, trying not to make any noise, she craned her neck enough to get a glimpse of this Slab person through the shabby fronds of a plastic plant attached to the top of the divider. *Holy smokes.* She could see where Slab got his name. The man had shoulders the size of a minivan and a face like a hunk of concrete.

"But, Tyler, I ain't got the dough," Slab responded, sounding higher and whinier than she would have expected from someone that large. She couldn't completely make out his next words, but it was clear he was offering excuses.

So the gorgeous one's name was Tyler. First or last? Who cared? Tyler. She tried it on her tongue and decided she liked the feel of it.

"Yeah, well, if you don't fork over some cash like yesterday, I'm the one who'll take the heat," Tyler returned. "You owe me, Slab. You owe me big-time."

"I could knock over another bank," the big lug offered cheerfully, and Emily caught her breath.

Knock over *another* bank? Who were these people?

"Keep your voice down, will you?" After that command, Tyler dropped his own volume as well, and Emily had to really concentrate to get any of their conversation. Darn it, anyway. This was fascinating.

Tyler said something about "the Feds." Was it, *you know the Feds are on our tail?* Or, *who knows if the Feds have the details? Good show the Feds let you out on bail?* She chided herself for jumping to conclusions. For all she knew, he'd just said that Joe Fezz didn't pay retail.

He added in an ominous tone, "You never know where they have wiretaps and informants parked. Let's be smart about this."

Okay, so she was right the first time. Slowly Emily slid as far down into her seat as she could go. She was only five-four, but she wasn't taking any chances that they might catch a glimpse of her and take her innocent eavesdropping for something more sinister. Who knew what these two were involved in? Just because Tyler was a major babe was no reason to think he wasn't a hoodlum.

She tried to remember what she'd heard so far. Let's see...Tyler needed Slab to fork over some cash that was owed to him or dire things would happen. Slab didn't have the money, but was willing to rob a bank to get it. And not just rob a bank. Rob *another* bank. And the FBI was apparently sniffing around.

If she had any sense, she would run, not walk, out of the Rainbow Rest-O-Rant. But she couldn't help herself—she leaned in closer to the divider so she could make out more of their soft, tantalizing words. Slab mumbled something she couldn't catch, but Tyler's words came back fast and furious.

"Listen to me," he whispered angrily, "don't even think about any more bank jobs. You got caught the last two times, and that means you better retire already."

Ooh, this was getting good. Slab had a criminal record but was none too bright and wanted to do it again, while the awesome Tyler was trying to keep him away from more criminal activity.

Maybe he was some kind of counselor, she mused, like for some ex-con twelve-step program.

"Do you know how much you're already into me for?" Tyler went on. "I trusted you, Slab. I know—that makes me every bit as stupid as you, but I trusted you. And now you need to do right by me. You said you could come up with the money. Or we both know I'm out on the street."

That made no sense for a counselor. A loan shark, maybe? She ventured another glance through the slats. World's best-looking loan shark?

But Jozette, the world's crankiest waitress, chose that moment to come back. After stopping to refill the coffee at Tyler's table, trading chitchat and good-natured insults and making it very clear they were old pals, she finally sauntered around to Emily's side of the booths. Quickly Emily pretended to be absorbed in her book so that Jozette didn't shout, "Hey, I think we got your FBI snitch right here!" or something equally scary.

As quietly as she could manage, Emily ordered the banana split she'd completely forgotten. She waited impatiently for Jozette to vamoose so she could go back to listening. Meanwhile, the men in the next booth were still arguing in the same hushed, urgent tones.

"Look," Slab said finally, half-rising in his seat. "There's only one way. I'm gonna have to get out of town."

"Are you nuts?" Tyler retorted.

She felt sure she heard something about Slab not being allowed to leave the jurisdiction—or maybe both of them—and then the name "Fat Mike," which sounded very familiar. A local mobster? Emily quickly added these clues to the others she'd already amassed. Couldn't leave the jurisdiction...if Slab were out on bail and unable to leave the area, would that make Tyler his bail bondsman?

"I gotta do it, Ty," the big guy continued. "It's the only way! I gotta go to Frisco."

"Slab, keep it down, will you?"

No, no, Emily wanted to plead. *Talk louder!* But no one cared what she thought.

Slab mumbled something about "real loot, plenty to make us even," and then "stashed in Frisco." That was followed by a string of words that went right past her, and Emily leaned her whole head into the plastic plant to try to pick up more of it.

"Money...stashed," Slab whispered, as something akin to a wistful smile crossed his blunt features.

"Sweet Shanda. Best time I ever had was with Sweet Shanda."

Emily started to get excited. This was kind of like charades. And she thought she had it! Slab had hidden his money in San Francisco with an ex-girlfriend named Shanda.

Tyler's next words were very low, but the intent was unmistakable. "If you go to San Francisco," he said, "Fat Mike will kill you. And maybe me, for good measure."

Emily shivered. Had he really said "kill"? As in, *dead?* Nobody would really kill someone who looked like Tyler, would they? And waste all that potential?

But the gigantic man shook his head, his voice rising as he argued. "I owe you, man. And Fat Mike will get off both our backs if I come up with the dough. I'm going, and I'm gonna get it."

"Forget it—"

"Damn it!" Slab bellowed, pounding a huge fist on the table and making the coffee cups bounce. "I'm going to get my stash!"

There was a long pause from their booth, as Tyler seemed to bide his time before speaking. "Sit down," he said finally, in a dark, curt tone that didn't brook objections. Slab sat. Emily could feel the reverberations all the way over on her side.

Angry words went back and forth, a "get a grip" followed by "I gotta do what I gotta do," with Tyler getting colder and Slab becoming more and more agitated. Leaning across the table, the big guy distinctly brought up "Sweet Shanda" again and then something about the money had better be where he left it or he would "tear her apart with my bare hands."

Emily felt chilled to the bone. Eavesdropping on criminals was one thing, but when they started contemplating taking women apart with their bare hands, it was going too far.

Finally the big guy raised his entire bulk from the booth, pushing himself to his feet with some effort. "I know what I gotta do," he bellowed.

After mumbling a few more things Emily didn't catch, he stomped his way out of the coffee shop, apparently determined to assault some poor woman named Shanda in San Francisco in order to recover ancient ill-gotten gains.

Tyler sent a wary glance around the place, clearly wondering whether anyone had overheard the outburst. Emily noted that, except for her, the diner's few patrons appeared to be very good at minding their own business. And unless Tyler happened to lean forward and look in just the right place, he wasn't going to see her, either. There were some benefits to being small.

Emily tucked herself even farther down into her bench seat, just to be sure, as she wondered what she should do next. Frankly, she was appalled. Had she just heard criminal activity being planned, and if so, as a lawyer and thereby an officer of the court, was she obligated to pull out her cell phone and report it to the police? Would they believe her if she did? And what would that mean for Tyler, the scowling, handsome ne'er-do-well who had done his best to dissuade the evil Slab from his crime spree?

Her head was spinning. Maybe she should at least call her mother the judge. But she was a bankruptcy judge. What would she remember about criminal law? Plus then Mom would know Emily was out eating banana splits in seedy dives and not at work. And then Dad would know, too, and she'd end up the first Chaplin in three generations to be fired from Chaplin, Chaplin & Chaplin.

Besides, she wasn't absolutely sure there was anything wrong in what she'd heard. For all she knew, Slab had done his time, was completely reformed, and wasn't allowed to leave the area because…well, there had to be some decent explanation. And if she started calling police and judges, she'd just make a fool of herself, making a mountain out of a molehill of stray words and overheard bits and pieces. Who knew anything for sure?

"Damn it." Tyler interrupted her frantic thoughts as he, too, rose to his feet. He threw some money on the table, muttering under his breath. "I have to go after him."

So maybe he was a bounty hunter? A bounty hunter with a heart?

Whatever he was, Emily gulped and hid behind her book as he crossed around the booths and passed right by her. She peeked over the cover, absently noting how well his weathered jeans wrapped his tight bottom, how wide his shoulders were under that leather jacket, how fearsome the expression on his handsome face…ooh, green eyes. She hadn't been able to tell before, but now she could. Definitely green. Not the color of emeralds or grass or even a Christmas tree. What *was* that color?

One thing she'd say for him—he might be involved in a mess, but he was hot.

As she watched his every move, he cut near the counter where Jozette was just emerging with Emily's banana split, and then he bolted up a set of stairs tucked in beside the rest rooms.

As the waitress ambled over and shoved the ice cream in front of her, Emily narrowed her eyes at the stairs. What was up there? And what was Tyler doing?

But before she'd had a chance to piece together a theory, he came barreling back down the stairs. "Jo?"

The waitress turned away from Emily's table. "Yeah, babe. Whatcha need?"

He cocked his head, indicating he wanted to talk to her by the counter. She hotfooted it over there, which said volumes about how much more she valued Tyler's business than anyone else's.

As the two of them talked, Emily set her book down, absentmindedly picking up her spoon. With an overflowing scoop of banana, ice cream and hot fudge camouflaging her, she gazed in their general direction, wondering what in the world they were discussing.

"I'm telling ya, lay off," Jozette said finally, in an aggrieved tone that was loud enough for Emily to hear.

"I wanna do this. I got a credit card—it ain't like real money—and you're good for it. I know you, Tyler. You'll pay up the minute you get back from San Francisco."

Tyler tried to protest, but Jozette cut him off, laying a hand on his arm with a gesture that seemed downright friendly. "Ty, listen. I never did pay you what I owed you. Somebody's gotta follow the big jerk and make sure he gets back in one piece. I can't, so you gotta. Least I can do is get you on an airplane."

After a long pause, he said reluctantly, "Yeah, okay. Get me an aisle seat, will you? I'll just go upstairs, you know, pack a few things. Be back in a sec," he called out as he headed for the stairs. He turned back. "And Jo—thanks."

Going to San Francisco, Emily sang in her head, leaving out the part about wearing flowers in your hair. And Jozette was apparently paying his way, which implied some relationship between Mr. Cool and the hard-bitten waitress. There was no way she would believe the two of them had, well, a *thing*. It was more as if he had done Jozette some major favor in the past—kind of like the Godfather or something.

Very curious. Biding her time until the tantalizing Tyler came waltzing back down those stairs, Emily decided that she could honestly say she'd never been confronted with anything remotely this intriguing in her entire life. Crimes, misdemeanors, mystery men, hidden loot, bank robberies, felons on the lam...

"You come to work late. You eat lunch at a new place. You break your cosmic routine. And all hell breaks loose," she whispered.

Emily smiled. What fun!

———

2

___

TYLER O'TOOLE TOSSED his toothbrush and a couple of extra T-shirts into a beat-up duffel bag.

"Damn it all to hell." The last thing he wanted was to run to San Francisco to play baby-sitter for a loser like Joseph "Slab" Slabicki. But what else was he going to do? "Worst client I ever had," he said darkly.

And he'd had some doozies in his short and unproductive legal career. So when he said Slab was the worst, that was going some. His clients were mostly lowlifes and petty thieves. Sure, they deserved a defense as much as anyone else. If only they paid better.

And if only their problems would quit sucking him into legal problems of his own. He'd already had the ethics committee of the bar association breathing down his neck—twice—over the way he'd handled a couple of cases for lesser lights in Fat Mike's organization. Allegations of jury tampering and money laundering. Right. As if his clients had the cash to pay off jurors or launder money. That was way too liquid for his flea-bitten legal practice.

"Lie down with dogs, get fleas, and don't even get a bone. Yeah, Ty, old boy. Real smart. You know, you might want to think about making some changes in this so-called life of yours."

Excellent idea. As soon as this was over.

He threw a few more things into the bag and zipped it up, aware he had to get done and get out of there if he had any chance of pulling this off. Sure. All he had to do was follow Slab to San Francisco, find the mope before he did anything stupid, keep him from getting killed or arrested, and get them both back to Chicago in time for Slab's preliminary hearing on Monday.

Because if he didn't, Fat Mike would be out the dough he'd put up for Slab's bail. And then there would be hell to pay.

Not to mention more scrutiny from the ethics committee over just how involved he was in Slab's flight from the jurisdiction. Fugitive from justice. Aiding and abetting. Yeah, it sounded just great.

And then he was getting squeezed from the other side, too—the Feds investigating Fat Mike, who were none too subtle about pressuring potential witnesses into cooperation.

"This is a lose-lose situation," Tyler muttered, making his way back down the stairs to the coffee shop. And a fool's errand. But it was also his only shot at keeping the wolf—and Fat Mike—from his door.

"Hey, Jo," he called as he hit the bottom step, "do you mind watching my place for a couple of days while I'm out of town? Only open it up for a search warrant, okay?"

"No prob, Tyler. I got you covered." She glanced down at the counter where she'd scribbled some notes.

"You're leaving from O'Hare. I got you on a two-o'clock flight."

"Terrific. Thanks again." He paused. "I should be back by Monday. I'd *better* be back by Monday."

And with that, he picked up his bag and headed to the street to look for a cab. He hoped he could cover the fare to the airport.

EMILY SAT THERE over the melting remains of her banana split, listening, thinking, planning.

"The only thing I can do is follow him," she whispered, growing more sure with every word. "I'm a lawyer, aren't I? And it sure sounds like he's going to need one."

After all, if Tyler was dangling from the precipice of legal troubles, maybe she could help him, keep his creepy friend from taking any old girlfriends apart with his bare hands, *and* get the adventure of a lifetime while she was at it.

It sounded a lot better than sitting in Chicago with Kip Enfield and the Bentley file.

Emily dropped a twenty-dollar bill on the table and grabbed her things. She still had time to catch him. And she'd always wanted to say, *Follow that cab!*

SHE SAW HIM JUMP OUT of a taxi and head into the terminal at O'Hare just as her own cab was pulling up behind it. On the trip to the airport from the city, she'd had plenty of time to rethink her impromptu plan, but she hadn't. In fact, she was more set on it now than she'd ever been. It was only for the weekend, after all.

He'd said very clearly he'd be back on Monday. And didn't lots of people throw together last-minute weekend plans?

Besides, hadn't she begged for something wild and new to happen? What more could you ask for?

"Sukie Sommersby would do it," she repeated to herself as she followed him into the terminal. As he approached the ticket counter, Emily quickly ducked behind a large family and their immense pile of luggage, to stay out of Tyler's sight line.

Pretending to be absorbed in a cartful of golf bags, she added, "Sukie would do it in a New York minute. Sukie would be waking up in Vegas with him tomorrow, no regrets. And then she'd be calling me to tell me all about it."

"Who are you talking to?" demanded the father of the family she was using as cover. He strong-armed the cart she was hiding behind, sharply wheeling it away from her. "Are you touching my bags?"

"No, no. I wasn't touching anything. I, uh, twisted my ankle and was just resting for a moment." She gave him a weak smile, which didn't seem to satisfy him.

She wanted to demand, *Do I look like a terrorist?* but she kept her mouth shut. *Harrumph.* She was wearing a beautifully cut navy-blue suit, a silk blouse and her grandmother's pearls. Hardly the sort of person who planted bombs in other people's golf bags.

Oh well. She pretended to limp as she darted behind a convenient pillar, just to allay Mr. Cranky's fears. It provided a better angle to spy on Tyler, anyway. From that vantage point, she saw him take his ticket from the agent at the counter and disappear down Concourse C.

"For once in my life," she said with determination, "I'm not going to be the one on the other end of the phone. I'm going to be the one in the middle of the adventure."

Now all she had to do was buy a ticket on his flight to San Francisco—two o'clock, the waitress had said—and keep shadowing him wherever he went when he got there. She would scope out whatever it was he was involved with, and she would step in to save him when the proper time arose.

Good plan, she told herself. It was just the sort of thing Trick McCall would do. Sukie, on the other hand, would be seducing him off to Paris for croissants in bed. But Emily preferred to stick with Trick on this one.

So she hit an ATM for as much cash as she could carry, tried not to look like a drug dealer when she paid for her ticket in cash, and then made a beeline for the gate.

Tyler was already there, moodily staring into space, and he didn't seem to notice as she skirted around behind him and buried her nose in her Trick McCall book. Either she was very good at this surveillance stuff, or he was very bad at picking up on it.

Actually, things were working out so well she wondered if she should pinch herself. But surely this was kismet, destiny, fate, with her plans neatly falling into place to show her that this adventure was meant to be.

When the gate attendant called his row, Tyler

strolled onto the plane, apparently none the wiser. Emily watched him go, drinking in his reckless, easy grace, the harsh angle of his jaw, the cool green of his eyes, offset beautifully by thick, dark lashes. Yes, she was definitely doing the right thing. She couldn't just let someone like that pass her by and not do her best to save him.

Her assigned seat was near the front of the plane, so she was one of the last people to get on. She didn't want to appear obvious, so she didn't look for Tyler, didn't allow herself to scan the rows or anything. No, she just settled in and fastened her seat belt. But even though she couldn't see him, Emily knew he was back there somewhere. He wasn't going to get away from her now.

And then the plane pulled away from the gate. A small smile curved her lips, and she felt a tingle of anticipation and exhilaration. Too late to turn back, which meant she was actually doing this. She couldn't believe it! She had never done anything this outrageous in her life, and she was loving every minute.

"This your first flight?" The man next to her, a hearty, blustery type with bloodshot eyes and a boozy aroma, leaned in closer. "Fear of flying, huh, sweetie?"

Emily blinked. Men like this never came on to her. Why in the world would they start now? "Uh, no," she managed. "Why would you think that?"

"You seem a little nervous," he said, patting her

hand, glomming on, squeezing warmly. "Kinda jittery. White knuckles. Poor baby."

Eeuw. She snatched her hand away. "I'm not nervous. I'm just anxious to get to San Francisco." She couldn't help embroidering the truth, hoping to put him off. "Y'see, I'm a lawyer. Criminal law. I have a really important case. A murder case. My client murdered a guy who sexually harassed her. We're claiming justifiable homicide."

"Okay, I get the picture." Mr. Boozy turned his attention to the stewardess, intent on snagging an early cocktail, and Emily leaned back and shut her eyes.

There were no bumps, no turbulence, nothing. And it was taking forever.

While Mr. Boozy tossed back miniature bottles of every color and type, Emily did her best to be patient. She finished off the Trick McCall book before they were even past Iowa. After that, she took a nap, thumbed through the magazine, filled in the crossword puzzle, gazed out her window. She even pulled the odious Bentley file out of her briefcase and worked on that for a while. But this waiting stuff was driving her bananas.

She was simply gazing at the back of the seat in front of her when the flight attendant held out a napkin and a bag of pretzels. "Would you like something to drink?" the woman asked pleasantly.

Although Emily waved off the stewardess, the guy next to her made up for her and then some. He had about ten empty bottles lined up on his tray, with a tiny

Scotch, a tiny bourbon and four or five wines in different colors. He wasn't just drinking, he was having a one-man tasting party.

With a jaded eye, Emily watched him plow through his liquor supply. At least he was a fairly quiet drunk. Then he turned to ask her if she wanted to try the cognac and knocked the whole uncapped bottle off his tray and into her lap. With cold, potent-smelling liquid seeping into her thigh, Emily realized those tiny bottles held a lot more than she would have thought.

The icky man did his best to blot at her with his napkin, but it didn't help. So, for two hours, she sat there, stuck in her puddle of brandy, willing the plane to get its tail fin to San Francisco on the double so she could get out of there before she started shoving little bottles down Mr. Boozy's throat.

Finally, blessedly, they were there, their gate was hooked up, and she gathered her heavy briefcase and her purse and bolted off the airplane as if there were no tomorrow.

A traffic jam behind her clogged the jetway, and she decided she surely had time to nip into the rest room and splash some water on her cognac-soaked skirt. She was in and out in record time—not that it really helped the cognac problem—but her gate had cleared by now, and Tyler was nowhere to be seen.

"What now?" Emily chewed her thumbnail, glancing up and down the concourse for a glimpse of that familiar leather jacket. Where could he have gone?

Hotfooting it in the general direction of ground

transportation, she wished she wasn't wearing pumps or hauling that stupid, cumbersome briefcase with the laptop in it. Was she gasping with exertion? Or starting to hyperventilate?

And where the hell had Tyler disappeared to?

Huffing and puffing, Emily took a decisive turn toward the taxi arrow. Tyler seemed like a cab kind of guy, didn't he? Rather than a limo or a shuttle, she thought a taxi would definitely be the best bet—

"Taxi, miss?" When she was almost at the curb, a man suddenly appeared out of nowhere and reached for her briefcase.

Emily whirled in his direction, skidding to a stop, bumping into the cab driver, as she saw—*oh, my God!*—Tyler pop up like a mirage right in front of her.

She'd not only found him, she'd practically fallen on top of him.

The cabbie said, "You share cab, miss, yes?" and wrenched her briefcase out of her hand. He'd already tossed it into the trunk of the taxi, so there wasn't much she could do but get in. Oh, God. She was supposed to be following the mysterious Tyler, not sharing the back seat of a cab with him!

Tyler waited, staring right at her, holding the door as she scooted inside. No chance of being inconspicuous now. She tried hard to manage her entrance with a modicum of grace, but it was impossible with those stormy green eyes staring a hole in her. She was flushed and breathless and she smelled as if she'd just taken a dip in a distillery vat. What kind of impression was she going to make? Besides idiotic, of course.

"Where we goin'?" the cabbie asked as Tyler folded his long, lean body in after her, stowing his duffel bag on the floor at his feet.

Tyler glanced her way, clearly giving her the first shot.

"I, uh…" She trailed off, tongue-tied. "I'm thinking."

He shrugged. "Okay, well, I need to go to North Beach. Take Stockton—I'll tell you where to stop."

Emily couldn't believe it, but she actually had the presence of mind to murmur, "What a coincidence. That's exactly where I'm going."

As the driver merged with traffic, sailing off into a sunny San Francisco afternoon, a long pause hovered over the back seat. Tyler's gaze measured her, held her, as she waited for him to say something. Finally he offered, "You don't look like the North Beach type."

"Oh, really?" She had no idea what that meant. She'd never even heard of North Beach. Did he expect her to be carrying a towel and suntan lotion? "Well, you never know, do you?" she asked brightly. "Maybe I've got my swimsuit in my briefcase."

Now she saw the spark of something else in his eyes. Humor? "There's no beach at North Beach," he told her calmly. "Are you sure you're going to the right place?"

"Oh, I'm sure. I was just joking. About the swimsuit, I mean."

Again silence hung between them. He shrugged. "Okay, if you're sure."

She wished he would stop staring like that. Miserable, Emily pulled on the hem of her soggy skirt and retreated into the far corner of the seat.

Still he was awfully close. Too close. And so very sexy. Even in repose, he had this hard-edged, smoky attitude that just screamed sex and lust and bad, bad things. It was like sitting two inches from a bonfire. She knew she shouldn't touch, but she was mesmerized, bewitched by the dancing flames.

You know what happens if you start playing with fire, a panicky internal voice reminded her. *You come away with third-degree burns.*

Ooh. Bad thing to think about. Very, very bad.

Her mind suddenly filled with images of Tyler and heat and flames. She pictured him glistening with sweat, stripping off his clothes one article at a time as the torrid temperature overpowered them both.

Now she was definitely hyperventilating.

As she fanned her face, the rest of the trip into San Francisco became a blur. She had no idea what was outside her window; all she saw was Tyler.

Stop this, she commanded herself. *Do something. Say something.*

But what? Okay, so she hadn't planned to introduce herself quite this quickly. She could roll with the punches, couldn't she? Surely this was her golden opportunity to cross-examine him, to get him to tell her more about whatever this was she was horning in on.

And then she would say, *Hmm, sounds like you need my help,* and somehow make it all sound natural and reasonable.

Except she hadn't exactly figured out how to do that yet.

She mulled over various openings, but before she'd so much as asked for his name, the taxi swooped up one hill and down another, and Tyler leaned forward.

"This is it. Pull over here," he instructed, and the cab slammed to a stop.

"Okay, we got North Beach," the driver shouted. He jumped out to open the trunk and retrieve Emily's briefcase as Tyler unwound himself and his duffel bag from the back seat.

Emily got out more slowly, not exactly sure how she was going to maneuver Tyler into showing her where he was going. For her to follow, he had to lead the way. But he was standing there waiting, doing the gentlemanly thing and allowing her to go first.

"No, no, you go ahead," she said suddenly. "I'll take care of the cab. My treat. You just go right ahead and get on your way."

His dark brows lowered. "Why would you want to do that?"

"I—I'm practicing random acts of kindness," she blurted. Well, that was as good an explanation as any.

He studied her for a moment, but finally accepted the favor, probably deciding it was easier to let the crazy lady have her way than fight with her. *Phew.* As Emily thrust bills at the cabbie, her quarry ambled across the street and up to a charming little Queen Anne house on the opposite corner. Mostly painted pink with some white trim, the house had a faintly purple conical tower in one corner. The sign out front read "Beau's B and B." And Tyler marched right in the front door as if he owned the place.

This was a surprise. Although Emily thought the B and B looked delightful—the only remotely Queen Anne house around—it was not where she would have expected Tyler to land. Everything else on the softly sloping street was strictly Edwardian, mostly three stories, with squared-off angles and bay windows. But whatever it was, at least Beau's B and B was a legitimate place to stay, and she wouldn't look incredibly weird filing in behind him.

As soon as she got rid of the cabbie, Emily gathered her purse, her briefcase and her courage, and took off across the street to Beau's B and B. Her heart pounded as her hand closed around the brass knob on the front door. *Get a grip, Emily,* she chided herself. *You just spent half an hour in a car with him.* How much scarier could sharing a bed and breakfast be?

So she opened the door.

The inside of the B and B was even cuter than outside, with a small pine desk tucked inside a cozy vestibule in the front hall. There was a Tiffany-style lamp on a three-legged table opposite, casting a soft, rosy glow into the hall. A dark-haired woman—a very *pretty* dark-haired woman—stood behind the desk, smiling and laughing as she put Tyler on the register.

Emily took a good look at her, a little in awe of the casually eccentric way the woman was dressed, and how at ease she seemed to be around Tyler. Her hair was short and kind of spiky, as if she'd just washed it, tossed her head, and left it that way. And she was wearing a scarlet silk T-shirt under a crazy quilt vest—an outfit that was just as unique and striking as the rest of her.

This woman was exactly the sort of person Emily had always secretly wanted to be, but had never come close to. How annoying. She hated her already.

Emily dawdled by the door, trying to be inconspicuous. She pretended to be occupied looking at the array of colorful and exotic postcards pinned to the wall, taking in bright pictures of Zanzibar and Pago Pago, but mostly she was eavesdropping on Tyler and the beautiful innkeeper. It only took about a second to pick up that these two were old friends. *Sheesh.* Jozette at the Rainbow Rest-O-Rant and now the offbeat proprietor of Beau's B and B. Did he know every unattached woman in the western hemisphere?

"Aw, c'mon, Kate," Tyler grumbled. "You know I don't have a reservation. How long have we known each other? Have I ever had a reservation?"

"No," the brunette returned cheerfully. "But I keep hoping you'll surprise me." She cocked her head to one side, fixing him with a mischievous gaze. "Are you going to pay me this time?"

"You can take it out in trade," he said in a low, husky voice, and Emily just about fainted where she stood. *Take it out in trade?* What kind of trade was he talking here?

Now she really hated her. *Lucky dog,* she thought. But the innkeeper, the vivacious Kate, didn't seem to take the offer seriously. She just laughed at Tyler, shaking a finger in his direction, while a huge yellow tabby leaped up on the desk from out of nowhere, right smack in between the two of them. The cat landed with a clatter, knocking over a ceramic pencil cup and scattering pens and papers every which way.

"Whoa." But after the momentary surprise, Tyler leaned in and began to scratch behind the cat's ears. "Hey, big bad Beau, it's been a long time. You still remember me, pal?"

Beau, after whom the B and B was apparently named, responded with a loud, rusty purr that Emily could hear all the way over by the door. She took that for a yes.

"I guess rascals and rogues have to stick together," Kate noted dryly. "You and that cat are two of a kind. Beau, get down from there."

The cat ignored her, whipping her with its tail, giving her a dismissive glance from brilliant green eyes— eyes that were the exact same shade as Tyler's.

"I've got it. Leaves on an apple tree," Emily said out loud. The apple tree outside her bedroom window when she was a kid. She'd finally placed the color.

Tyler, Kate and even the cat turned at her words. *Oops.* Emily could feel her face suffuse with rosy heat.

"Sorry," she mumbled. "Just thinking out loud."

"About apple trees?" Tyler shook his head. She could see the questions forming on his lips. *Who are you, anyway? Why are you following me? And who gave you a day pass from the mental ward?*

Oh, yeah. She was making a great impression.

Kate smiled kindly. "I'll be with you in just a sec," she told Emily. And she winked, as if to say, *I get the apple tree thing.*

Oh, dear. Here she was ready to dislike Kate on sight, and the innkeeper was acting like a co-conspirator. Emily focused on the postcard from Pago Pago, trying to sort out her jumbled thoughts.

Meanwhile Kate turned her attention back to Tyler. "Hey, Ty, I've changed things since the last time you were here. You were in the Gone With the Wind room last time, right?"

He nodded.

Kate sighed. "I loved that room. But I had to re-decorate. A couple of guests set the bed on fire trying to recreate the burning of Atlanta."

"That's, uh, too bad," Tyler choked, disguising a chuckle by concentrating on the cat. He stroked his fur and tried to maneuver the stubborn little animal into a position where he could get picked up. Undaunted, Beau stood his ground, bonked his head into Tyler's chest and purred even louder.

Emily was enchanted. This was the first time she'd seen him really smile, let alone laugh, plus he was act-ing all sweet and tender toward the yellow cat. It was a whole different side of him.

"Okay," Kate went on, chewing the end of a pencil. "Let's see. I know you like the Pirate and Kismet rooms best, but they're full. So I guess I'll put you in the new one."

"And that is…?" he asked warily.

"You'll love it. After I decided Gone With The Wind was too dangerous, I switched to my next favorite movie," she explained. "Turns out it's perfect for you. The Wild One. Yep. You've already got the leather jacket and everything. And you get to sleep under Marlon Brando's picture. Cool, huh?"

"The Wild One?" Tyler shook his head. "The Pirate and the red one—what is it, Kismet?—are bad enough. I can't wait to see what you've done to this one."

Emily couldn't wait, either. She could feel her eyes growing rounder at the mental images The Wild One evoked. She knew that movie. Leather jackets, motorcycles. Bad attitude. She gulped, trying to contain her growing excitement. *Wow*. It *was* perfect for Tyler.

But he didn't seem to notice. He just scooped up his key and his duffel bag and went down the hall. As soon as he left, his best pal Beau went after him, skidding off the desk and showering pens and paper clips to the four winds.

As Emily watched Tyler's well-shaped, jean-clad derriere disappear up the stairs, her mouth went dry. But his departure didn't really dampen her enthusiasm. Once again, she thanked the Fates that had landed her in the midst of all this. Pirates and Kismet and The Wild One? This place was great!

She stepped up to the desk, eager to see what room awaited her. The way things had gone so far, maybe this would be perfect, too. Maybe there would be a Mata Hari room with her name on it, she mused. Or Xena, Warrior Princess.

"So, you're checking in?" Kate inquired.

"Right. If you have a room." After buttoning her suit jacket so it more completely covered the stain from the cognac spill, Emily hurriedly ran her hands through the basic brown strands of her chin-length bob. She hoped she wasn't too much of a mess. After all, she had to look respectable enough to get a room.

"One room left," Kate told her.

Emily smiled. See? Her luck was holding.

"Will you need help with your...? Oh." Her host glanced over the desk and then back up at Emily. "No luggage?"

"Lost," Emily replied quickly. "I think my bags got sent to, uh, Pago Pago by mistake."

"Okay. Well, if you need me to call the airline and track that down for you, you let me know," Kate offered sympathetically. "Usually lost baggage shows up in a day or two, but it never hurts to call. Just leave the tracking number and I'll be happy to take care of it."

"Tracking number. Right."

Kate leaned forward, sniffing loudly. "What is that

smell? Smells like, I don't know, brandy or scotch or something. It's really strong, isn't it?"

Emily stiffened, but Kate didn't appear to notice, or to pinpoint the source of the overpowering, boozy odor.

"I wonder what Beau got into now. I hope he didn't knock over the decanter in the parlor." She frowned. "You wouldn't believe the things that cat thinks it's funny to dip his tail in."

"It's not the cat."

Kate paused. "No?"

"No. It's me."

"You?"

"A man on the plane spilled one of those tiny bottles of booze—cognac, I think—on me." Emily gave a delicate whiff of her own. "Oh, dear. It really is potent, isn't it?"

"Well, it could be worse. I mean, it'll come out. Don't you think?"

"I hope so." Eager to change the subject, Emily pulled out her purse. She reached for a credit card, but put it back on the double. No credit cards as long as she was on the lam—too traceable by well-meaning family members. Her dad and brothers were bad enough, but her mother...*sheesh*. Once Judge Patience Burr-Chaplin found out her only daughter had skipped town, she was going to have a fit. And she wouldn't rest until she located Emily.

"The least I can do is make it tough for her," Emily murmured under her breath. With a faint smile, she added, "Do you need me to prepay? I have cash. I hope that's okay."

"Oh, sure. That's great." Kate looked up expectantly. "And how long will you be staying?"

Emily paused. How long would she be staying? The first answer that occurred to her was short and succinct.

As long as Tyler.

3

BUT SHE DIDN'T SAY THAT. "I'll be staying through the weekend, I think. Have to be back in the office on Monday."

"Great." Kate beamed at her. "You'll be in the Pollyanna room."

"The Pollyanna room?" she echoed. Pollyanna? But she was hoping for... "Isn't there anything else?"

"Sorry," Kate replied. "Pollyanna is the only room available. But I'm sure you'll like it. It's very lacy and feminine—just right for someone like you."

"Someone like me...right."

Which was exactly what she was trying to avoid.

"I'm really sorry." The innkeeper lowered her voice to a conspiratorial tone. "I completely understand. I think Pollyanna is kind of lame, too. But my mom made me add it. She thinks the other rooms are too— oh, I don't know—slutty or something. Mothers." She rolled her eyes. "Can't live with them, and they won't let you live without them."

"I hear you."

Kate edged the register book in front of her and then stooped down under the desk. From down there, she called, "Hang on. I have to get a pen off the floor—

that darn Beau!'' Straightening, she handed over a felt-tip. "Okay. Now I'll need you to fill in your name and address.''

The register. The very one Tyler had signed a few minutes ago. With heightened anticipation, Emily pulled the book closer, eager to read whatever he'd written about himself.

But it was just a blank page. Darn it. Emily's registration was the first one on a new page, and she was going to have to very conspicuously turn the page back if she wanted to read his information.

"Is there something wrong?" Kate inquired.

"Oh, no. Well," she said, improvising, "this pen is dried out. Do you have a different one?"

As Kate once again ducked under the desk, Emily grabbed her chance, flipping the page back, squinting at the slash of rotten handwriting to make out "Tyler O'Toole, Chicago, IL," and then several blank lines.

Quickly she put the register back the way it was, just in time for Kate to pop up with a pencil. Emily took it and scribbled down her own name and address.

Okay, so he wasn't terribly good at filling out forms and he hadn't given her much to go on. At least she knew his last name now. Tyler O'Toole.

Speaking of last names...she glanced down at her own. Was it wise to use her real name? Or smarter to go with a fake one just in case her mother started looking for her?

While Kate was occupied tidying up the pencil cup, Emily erased her last name and penciled in the first cool name that popped into her head. "Bond," she wrote. *Emily Bond.*

After spinning the book around to read the name, Kate smiled. "Nice to meet you, Emily." Then she turned to pull an old-fashioned key off a hook. "Okay. Pollyanna is the first room on the right at the top of the stairs. There's a doll on the door—that's how you'll know it's Pollyanna."

"Pollyanna and baby dolls," Emily murmured, feeling more disappointed by the minute. It sounded like her room when she was twelve. As the youngest child and the only girl in the Chaplin family, she'd had to endure all kinds of smothering, fussy stuff. "I'll be sure to look for the doll."

Handing over the key, Kate began to list a few other B and B procedures, something about when she wanted breakfast, and did she like coffee or tea, and would she want afternoon snacks, and checkout time. But Emily just nodded at appropriate times, not really paying attention. She was too busy watching Tyler slip back down the stairs and head this way. Beau nipped at his heels, but Tyler grabbed the big tabby in the crook of one arm and then deposited him with Kate.

Hanging on to the squirming cat, she interrupted her welcoming spiel to ask him, "On your way out so soon?"

He nodded, edging toward the door.

On his way out? But he couldn't be yet. Emily needed to follow him, but it was difficult to do that in the middle of registering. How blatant would it be if she ran out now, without even looking at the Pollyanna room, just dropping everything and racing after him? Pretty blatant.

Beau gave a howl and Kate dropped him. After landing with a big thud, the cat immediately attached himself to Emily's legs, winding around, meowing, giving her a plaintive stare from those infuriating green eyes.

"I—I guess he likes me," Emily murmured.

So why was he bumping her with his head and nudging her closer to Tyler? Was the cat actually telling her to go for it?

"Now, now," she said sweetly, trying to disengage herself. But Beau was a stubborn little beast, and he rammed his whole weight into her, pushing her after Tyler.

Tyler's moody gaze swept the two of them. Was that suspicion she read in the clear green depth of his eyes? Or interest? Just before he cleared the door, his hand already on the brass knob, Tyler stopped. He turned back.

"The airport, the cab..." he said slowly. "Do I know you?"

"Um, no." Suddenly reckless, taking her opening where she could get it, Emily asked, "But would you like to?"

"Would I like to what?"

He gave her an odd look, but it spoke volumes. It was the same one that said, *Who gave you a day pass from the loony bin?*

She hated that look.

And then he shook his head, frowned at her, shoved

open the door and took off for parts unknown, leaving her holding the key to the Pollyanna room.

Emily closed her eyes and tried not to feel like an absolute doofus. The first time in her life she'd gone for coy and flirtatious, and it had flopped big-time. *Let's not try that again.*

"Emily, I'm sorry to have to say this." Kate bit her lip. Clearly she was trying to be kind. It was written all over her pretty face.

"You don't have to say any—"

"Yes, I do. I can't help but notice that you seem sort of, well, smitten with Tyler."

Smitten? *Smitten?* But that wasn't it at all! Tyler was part of an adventure, a caper, an escapade. She hardly wanted to date him or bring him home to meet Mom and Dad—although the expression on their faces would have been priceless when they got a load of Tyler.

Emily shook her head, getting back to the business at hand. She didn't want anything like that from Tyler. No, she wanted to skate on thin ice with him, to dance on the brink of danger. *Smitten* had nothing to do with it.

"You seem to have the wrong idea—" she began.

But Kate interrupted. "I'm so sorry, Emily, but I think it's better you should be warned up front. Forewarned, forearmed, all that, you know? It's just that Tyler and I, well, we go back a long way."

Forewarned and forearmed? Tyler and *I?* Emily backed away from the desk. "Are you trying to say you and Tyler are a couple? I have always been very respectful of—"

"No, no, nothing like that." Kate waved her hands anxiously. "It's not that Tyler is taken or anything like that. And certainly not by me. Far from it. Well, we had a couple of…I mean, years ago, we did…never mind." She gave Emily a wry smile. "Let's just say I know him pretty well. And I have some experience with this matchmaking business. You know, running the B and B." She inclined a thumb at the wall of postcards. "Those are some of my success stories."

"M-matchmaking?" Emily sputtered. "But I don't need—"

"That's what everyone thinks," Kate confided. "But you'd be surprised how many otherwise perfectly sensible people will walk right past the perfect person for them." She shook the wayward tendrils of her short-cropped hair. "Luckily, I have really good instincts about people, and I am an excellent matchmaker, if I do say so myself."

Looking at all the postcards, Emily had to agree.

"It's my experience as a matchmaker that's telling me this." There was that kind, half-pitying expression again. "Frankly," Kate said, "you and Tyler…I just don't see it. Not a good match."

"But I'm not interested in being matched up with him," Emily insisted. What was it with her? Did she have "please find me a date" stenciled on her forehead? Everyone in the world seemed to think she was so pitiful she needed to be fixed up with a guy, any guy. And that was the last thing she wanted.

"I know, I know. Everyone says they're not interested in getting matched up. And don't get me wrong,"

Kate interjected. "Tyler is a great guy. And you seem very nice. But I don't think he's at a place in his life where he'd be looking for someone like you. I mean, I have to be honest with you. Since he and I had our couple of nowheresville dates years ago, the only women I've ever seen him with have been hookers and strippers."

Emily's jaw dropped. "Hookers and strippers?"

"Oh, no, not to date or anything," Kate assured her. "It was business. You know, in his line of work, it comes up."

And what line of work would that be?

But Kate was continuing with her friendly warning. "Really, trust me. He's not your type." She perked up. "On the other hand, I do have a sweet, nice, stable guy staying in the Pirate room. A nice, stable divorce lawyer. I think he'd be perfect for you—"

"A lawyer? No. No lawyers. Ever."

Even if she had been interested in dating, which she wasn't, that bit of info would've been enough to put her off. *Yech.* Her brain manufactured an image of the pompous, self-important face of Kip Enfield, and she shuddered. If she never saw another lawyer, it would be too soon.

"No lawyers? How funny," Kate mused. "Tyler always says the same thing."

But Emily was rewinding the tape of their conversation, back to the part about the hookers and strippers. Trying not to sound too nosy, she ventured, "Okay, so you said that women from the wrong side of the tracks come up in Tyler's line of work. Why would that be, exactly?''

Kate blinked.

"I mean," Emily tried again, "what line of work is it that these bad girls come up in?''

"Sorry." Kate pressed her lips together. "I do apologize, Emily, since I brought it up, but I feel very strongly about maintaining my guests' privacy." She clapped the register shut with a quick thump. "I'm sure you understand." Kate turned and ducked behind the desk, stowing the registration book securely in a drawer. "Where did I leave that...? Oh, here it is." She held up an envelope. "Better go pay the bills. Right now."

And Kate beat a hasty path down the hall to the parlor door. She turned around long enough to call out, "Remember, the Pollyanna room is the first right at the top of the stairs."

"Got it." Oh, she had it all right. She understood perfectly. Kate was not going to tell her anything useful about Tyler at all. Blast it, anyway.

Lugging her briefcase, which seemed to be getting heavier by the minute, Emily decided that with Tyler already off the premises, there was nothing to do but get upstairs and see what this Pollyanna room was all about.

"I'll relax and then I'll formulate a plan," she said out loud, taking the stairs as rapidly as she could manage. When she almost tripped on the top step, she glanced at her sensible pumps. "The first thing I'm going to do is get out of these shoes. And the second…'' She crinkled her nose. ''The second is take off my skirt.''

She felt better already, having a plan.

''Okay, find the door with the dolly.'' That was easy enough. The golden-haired doll in Edwardian clothing was fastened to the door with a pale pink ribbon around her waist, and she held out her arms in welcome. A dead giveaway that this was the Pollyanna room.

But Emily couldn't resist. She passed it by, long enough to tiptoe down the hall to locate The Wild One. A small silver trophy was the marker for this door, for reasons she didn't quite understand.

Fingering it gently, Emily wished again that she could see inside that room. ''The Wild One,'' she breathed. ''That is majorly cool.''

Oh well. As she traipsed back to her own door, she decided that the good news was that The Wild One was right next to her room. It shouldn't be tough at all to keep an eye on Tyler—if he ever came back.

Safely inside the Pollyanna room, Emily kicked off her shoes and took a look around. As promised, it was pretty. There was a canopy bed, dripping in white lace and ruffles, with a pastel-colored movie poster of Hayley Mills as Pollyanna hanging next to it. Under the poster sat a white wicker rocking chair, and in the rocker, someone had placed a fluffy teddy bear wearing what looked like a vintage christening gown.

Tall bookshelves took up most of the outside wall; they overflowed with exquisitely costumed dolls in velvet frocks and feathered hats. There was even a small wicker tea table with child-size chairs pulled up around it, and an antique armoire pushed up against the wall Pollyanna shared with The Wild One. Delicate bunches of violets had been painted on the doors of the armoire, making it an even more lovely piece.

"Oh, pooh." Emily sat down on the bed, curling her hand around the carved wood bedpost. She'd only been here five minutes and she'd already fallen under the spell of the Pollyanna room. "I actually like it here."

Somehow, Beau the cat had sneaked into the room with her, and she bent to pet his head absently. Apparently deciding that was an invitation, Beau hurled himself into her lap.

"Whoa." He was one heavy cat. She tried to be friendly, but he began to sniff and paw at her cognac-soaked skirt, and Emily got the hint. "I was going to change it," she told him. "Everyone is a critic."

So she slipped off her jacket and skirt, even her panty hose, tossing them onto the bed. Much better. Beau immediately curled up on the pile of discarded clothing and began to lick his paw.

"I'm glad you're happy, Mr. Kitty. But what do I wear now?"

While hanging out in her silk blouse and underwear was comfy for right now, it had its disadvantages in the long run—like the fact that she couldn't leave the room.

"Aha!" Emily announced, stooping and dragging her laptop out of her briefcase. After carefully moving the tiny tea set, she opened her computer on the small wicker table, managing to squeeze herself into one of the junior-size chairs. "Let's do a little E-commerce," she muttered, booting it up and searching for the nearest decent clothing store. It took a few minutes, but she hit pay dirt eventually. "Ooh, this one's good. Based in San Francisco, and they even deliver."

She clicked on an image of a plain white T-shirt, and then a pair of khaki pants. "And let's see. Maybe a pair of sneakers and some socks."

All it took was quickly verifying the inn's address, keying in her credit card info, and then sitting back and waiting for her new clothes to arrive.

"I love technology," she said brightly. She felt so smart, so hip, so *now,* coping with the various challenges of her impromptu adventure.

But what now? She had to do something while she waited. Of course, she was keeping an ear peeled for any activity next door in The Wild One, but so far, nothing. She'd already read her book, and she had no intention of working on that stupid Bentley file. Not here. Not now.

But the Bentley file did remind her that she'd sneaked away from work in the middle of the morning, and left not so much as a note to explain her hasty departure. A quick check of her watch told her that in Chicago time, her parents would have expected her home for dinner about an hour ago. They probably would assume she had a date and refrain from calling out the National Guard for at least a few more hours, but she had to do something.

"E-mail." It was the only solution. So she sat there at her laptop, composing a good cover story for her nosy, overprotective family. "Hmm…how about Sukie Sommersby?"

A few cheerful E-mails detailing a frantic call from Sukie were a cinch to come up with. "Sukie had another emergency," she typed, "so I'm off to Miami for the weekend. Don't worry—everything is fine. You know Sukie! See you on Monday."

She was just sending the last note when Beau bolted from his perch on the bed and went racing to the armoire. He began to howl—not just meow but *howl*— and to purposefully scratch his nasty little claws against the beautiful wood.

Emily hustled over to try to pry his paws off the cabinet. "What is it you want, Beau? You can't want to go inside the armoire, can you?"

He spun around suddenly, bounding to the bed and leaping on top of her clothes, and then just as suddenly dashing back to the armoire, where he started the caterwauling and scratching act again. He repeated this mad dash two or three times.

Emily was struck with a very odd thought. "Beau," she said out loud, "this can't really be your way of telling me to hang up my clothes, can it?"

It was the best theory she could come up with. So she dutifully shook out her jacket and hung it, not quite shutting the armoire doors as she toted her skirt into the adjacent bathroom to rinse off as much cognac as she could. She was still carrying the dripping skirt when she noticed Beau seemed to have disappeared.

"Where did he get off to?" she mused. But there was no Beau to be seen. Shrugging, she hung the skirt in the bathroom, and then searched under the bed and behind the rocker. Nope. "Okay, so he must be stuck in the armoire."

But when she opened the doors this time, she noticed a wide crack all the way around the back wall. And she could see daylight through there.

What was this? A magic armoire with a secret passage at the back? Emily's heart beat faster.

"Beau?" she called. "Did you go through the crack?"

Peering closer, she couldn't help but give the partition a little push, and then a little look.

And before she knew it, she'd shoved it open wide, climbed through the back of her armoire, and scrambled out the front of the one next door. There she was, standing in the middle of The Wild One in her underwear!

"This room is so cool," she whispered, her eyes wide. Cool wasn't the half of it. The bed frame was shiny chrome, while the spread was black leather, stretched taut against the frame. The footboard looked like the front grill of a motorcycle, and it actually had handlebars that twisted back around the corners. "Yowza."

It made her want to take a ride on that bed and see where she ended up.

"Yowza," she said again, although that was not a word she could ever remember uttering before in her entire life. She whirled around in the room, drinking it in. Decorated completely in black-and-white, it had a big poster of Marlon Brando in his motorcycle gang

attire from the movie, a black-leather director's chair
near the front window, a dresser that looked more like
the counter at a fifties diner, and a big silver trophy
sitting on its own special shelf. Beau was curled into
a half circle in the director's chair, and he lifted his
head long enough to fix her with those infuriating, all-
knowing green eyes.

Emily swallowed, fingering the handlebars. This was
like all her fantasies come true. It was adventure and
excitement boiled down and turned into a bedroom.
And she absolutely loved it.

"Okay, get a grip," she ordered herself. "You
wanted to know more about Tyler, didn't you? This is
your chance to snoop around, handed to you on a silver
platter—by a yellow cat."

She shook her head. Whether Beau had led her here
or not, the reality was, she was inside Tyler's room,
and she might as well make the most of it. She chewed
her lip, glancing around.

"The duffel bag," she declared. It was tucked neatly
under the leather chair. "Look in the duffel bag."

But she barely had her hand on the zipper when she
heard the sound of the side window scraping open behind her. She spun around in time to see a huge, bulky
man vaulting in over the windowsill. Sensing danger,
Beau leaped over her head and skidded under the bed.

Suddenly her little adventure had gotten scary. Very
scary.

Oh, God, what now? The intruder was even bigger
and uglier than that Slab person she'd seen at the coffee
shop. He had muscles and bulges everywhere, includ-

ing his neck, and he looked mean enough to pop a
blood vessel just for fun. He also had a dull, vacant
squint to his eyes—in her experience, the mark of the
terminally stupid.

Not good. Not good at all. Emily could feel sweat
drizzling down the neck of her blouse as she frantically
wondered if she could scream and if anyone would hear
her and how she would explain what she was doing
here. She edged along the wall, hoping to make a break
for it. But the thug advanced, blocking her path to either the open armoire or the door, and there was nowhere to go.

"Hey, you," he bellowed, pointing a meaty finger
at her. "Don't move."

"I'm not moving," Emily returned quickly. "Not
even a toe."

"Yeah, well, you move a toe and I break it." His
thick lips twisted into a menacing grin. "That's what
I do, you know, like, what I get paid for. Breaking
stuff. So don't tempt me, huh?"

"Not tempting. Not doing anything." She held herself so still she could hear a rushing sound in her ears.
She licked dry lips. "You know, I think you have the
wrong room. Could I help you find the right one,
maybe?"

He narrowed his piggy little eyes, giving her the
once-over. "I ain't got the wrong room. I know
O'Toole is here. I wanna know what he's doing in
Frisco. Is he helping Slab? Or looking for him, huh?"

"O-O'Toole? I actually don't know what he's doing
in town."

"You look like a smart girl to me," the big bruiser growled.

Yeah, well, you don't look very smart to me. But she kept it to herself.

"So don't be a dumb bunny, huh?" He marched his massive bulk nearer, where that fat finger could poke her right in the collarbone. "I'm an old friend of Slab. Associate, you might say." He pronounced the word ass-*o*-cee-*ate*." "So now I need to know where Slab is. You know, for ol' times. And where the stash is. And you're going to tell me, huh, cutie? Now."

"S-Slab? S-stash?" she stuttered. "I wish I could help, really I do. But unfortunately for both of us, I have no idea. I'm really very sorry, so incredibly sorry."

She had only the vaguest notion of what she was chattering on about as she eyed his trousers, trying to figure out if she could get her knee anywhere near the big gorilla's, um, tender parts. Not likely. Plus he would probably break her kneecap for even thinking about it.

"Will you please shut your trap?" he roared. "I am loosing my patience with you."

"I think you mean 'losing,'" she said helpfully. "Not 'loosing'—losing."

His face contorted with rage as she realized it was probably not the best strategy at this juncture to point out his grammatical problems.

When, thank God, the door crashed open, Emily practically shouted with relief. She might be in her underwear, and she might be in his room, but she was awfully glad to see him.

Tyler.

HE BARELY HAD A CHANCE to register that some over-size lunk was manhandling a half-dressed woman. Was it that goofy little brunette from the cab? Before Tyler knew what hit him, she broke away, catapulted herself into him, and knocked him backward onto the leather bed.

He tried to catch her. Fat chance. "Oof" was all he could get out as he toppled back onto the bed, taking her with him. He was underneath, she was on top, and they each made a bad move and then another in a vain attempt to get off the damn slippery leather bedspread.

After about a second of wrestling around, it became impossible to tell whose limbs were whose. Her legs and arms seemed to be all tangled up with his body in ways that were really not a great idea for strangers.

"Your elbow is in my ribs," he tried. "And will you get your hand off my—?"

Her hand flew off his crotch and settled on his hip as she cried, "*My* hand? Do you realize where *your* hands are?"

Yes, he did. He was about to break into a cold sweat over it. Why wasn't she wearing any clothes? It wasn't his fault if one of his hands had landed on the back of her thigh, just under the silky curve of her skimpy pant-ies, and the other one was lodged somewhere under her shirt, slipping over her slick, naked flesh, unable to get a decent hold.

"If you would just...oh, forget it!" She attempted to sit up, winding a bare leg around his abdomen, somehow managing to brush him in any number of intimate places. Without thinking, he rolled the other way, but the tail of her blouse got caught under his arm. When he rolled, the fragile fabric pulled, popping buttons every which way.

Tyler stopped dead. He gulped, looking straight down into a whole lot of pale, creamy skin. The fact that she was wearing a wispy scrap of a bra only made her exposed curves look that much more tantalizing.

Across the room, the window frame screeched and splintered as the burglar barreled out in a hurry, not bothering to be neat about it. Funny, but Tyler had almost forgotten about him.

Meanwhile, he couldn't take his eyes or his hands off all that skin. But he had to get himself out of this before it got any worse—if that was possible.

Savagely dragging his lower body out from under her, Tyler found his head pointing toward the open doors of the armoire. He could see all the way into the Pollyanna room through the gaping hole in the back.

"What?" He stared down at her. "You broke into my room through the armoire, dressed like *that?* Are you stalking me or something?"

"Ha!" she retorted. She scrambled to a sitting position, vainly attempting to hold the sides of her blouse together. "Of all the nerve! You may be gorgeous, in a menacing and disreputable sort of way—which is not at all my type, for your information—but my motives toward you are completely honorable and virtuous and have to do with helping out a fellow human being who is clearly in trouble with a capital *T*. This has nothing to do with some insane stalker thing."

He had no clue what she was babbling about. "Who are you? What are you doing here?"

But she ignored his questions. "I'm the one who deserves some answers. I have just been threatened by a criminal, and I think you owe me an explanation. Who was he? And what does he want with you? He said something about you and Slab and a stash and how he breaks toes for a living!"

"Toes?" he echoed, mystified. "Legs, maybe. But who breaks toes for a living?"

"Don't change the subject." As she leaned in closer, her voice dropped to a softer, more intimate tone. "You're in trouble, aren't you? But I can help. You can trust me. I'm a lawyer."

He laughed out loud at that one.

"Why are you laughing? Okay, so I don't look much like a lawyer at the moment." She spared a rueful glance for her tattered blouse and bare legs. "But I am. I swear it!"

Tyler laughed even harder.

Apparently trying to make him stop guffawing at her, she bent nearer, grabbing his shoulders in her small hands. "Listen to me," she said, but her voice dropped into a huskier, less self-assured range as a tangible, shocking kind of electricity flowed between them. One of her hands slid to his jaw. "I was trying to…"

Her hazel eyes glowed with something that had very little to do with honor or virtue, and her gaze seemed to have caught and stuck on his mouth. He knew why. He suddenly had the crazy notion that all he had to do was lift his head about an inch, and he would find her sweet, soft lips melting into his kiss.

Why not? She was half-naked and she was in his bed.

His mouth grazed hers, and he could already feel her hunger, her eagerness.

He reached for her.

4

"WHAT'S GOING ON?" a loud, frightened voice from the doorway demanded. "It sounded like there was a train wreck up here!'"'

It was Kate. She stood there like the wrath of God, wielding a shaky hammer as if she planned to use it on someone's head. And she was not alone.

Verna, the inn's normally low-key cook, was backing her up with a cast-iron fry pan, while a third person—a stunned-looking kid hauling a stack of packages—lurked behind the two women, angling for a better view.

The cavalry had arrived.

Tyler sighed, shoving his bed buddy behind him for protection. No half-naked hot kisses just yet.

"Emily?" Kate peered into the room. "Is that you?"

She didn't answer, but her expression gave a clear message. *Caught.*

Well, at least now he knew her name. Emily, huh? Yeah, that fit. Pretty, sweet, a touch old-fashioned. All the things that drove him nuts.

"Well." Dangling her hammer, Kate seemed lost for

words. "Emily, you're a faster worker than I thought," she said finally.

Emily attempted to wiggle out from behind Tyler. "It's not what you think," she tried. "I was just—"

But Tyler clapped a hand over her mouth, not ready to let her spill all the details about the thug and the break-in just yet. No need to scare Kate. And no need to get them both kicked out of the B and B.

"Come on, Kate, give us a break," he said, trying to put on his most charming voice. "We were just having a little fun. It's your fault—you're the one who made this place so romantic. Kismet, pirates, wild ones—we lost our heads."

Glowering at him, Verna slapped her skillet against her hand. He'd never thought Verna was a particularly intimidating woman. Okay, so she always wore black and looked like a beatnik, but she was harmless. Now, however, she seemed a lot fiercer.

"What about the window?" Verna asked grimly.

"The window?"

"How did it get that way?"

Under his hand, Emily struggled to answer, but Tyler kept a firm grip. "We steamed things up a little. You know." And then, God help him, he winked at Verna like some goofball Romeo on the prowl. "Sorry. I guess I got carried away when I opened the window to let in some air."

"I'll say," Verna bit off under her breath.

Kate's brows drew together in consternation. "Tyler, this is so unlike you."

"Yeah," he allowed. "Sorry."

"Are you going to fix the window?" Verna prompted.

"Oh, don't worry about it. I can fix the window later," Kate cut in. "It's just the latch. Tyler, let me know when you go out for dinner, and I'll take care of it then. Right now, we'll just leave you to your, uh, romp. Won't we, Verna?"

She backed off, shooing Verna in front of her, but the boy with the boxes got caught in the shuffle.

"Excuse me," he tried to say, bobbing away from Verna's frying pan. "I'm looking for Emily Ch—"

"That's me!" Ducking out from under Tyler's grasp, Emily asked, "Are you from the Gap? Are those my clothes?"

Tyler was beginning to think his baffled and confused state of mind was going to be permanent. Emily had delivery boys from the Gap running over with packages of clothing? *Huh?*

"I have to get my purse," she told the wide-eyed kid. "Go next door. The room with the doll on the door. I'll meet you."

And before Tyler could stop her, she'd scrambled off the bed and through the armoire to find a tip for the delivery boy.

With a particularly nasty oath, Tyler let himself fall backward onto the black leather bedspread. He stared at the ceiling. What in the hell had just happened here? His room had been broken into by a crazy stalker with wide hazel eyes and the cutest, softest mouth he'd ever seen, and then again by a moronic hood who was probably going to come back in five minutes and try again. And he'd let both of them escape unscathed.

Rousing himself, Tyler slid the window back down and flipped the lock. It was wobbly, but it should do until Kate could do a real repair job. Then he crossed to the armoire.

Emily was safely on her side, in that girly paradise called the Pollyanna room. As he watched, she handed the delivery boy a few bills and backed up with her boxes. But how long would she be content to stay put?

With a grim smile, he pulled the panel closed from her side, snapped his own side shut, too, and slid the bolt to keep it that way. For good measure, he grabbed the heavy silver trophy off the shelf and propped it against the secret door.

"Tyler!" she shouted, banging against the back of the armoire from her side. "I still need to talk to you. I can help! Please let me help."

"Go away, Emily," he returned calmly.

"Let me in. Please?"

"No."

Whistling loudly to block out her pleas, he strode out of The Wild One and locked the door securely behind him. He had business to attend to, and he had no time for pretty little distractions, no matter how sweetly her bottom curved or what delights she had spilling out of her unbuttoned blouse.

"A lawyer," he said derisively. "Yeah, that's just what I need."

As far as he was concerned, there would be no more visits from Miss Emily tonight.

THERE WAS NO WAY she was standing still for this. Who did he think he was, anyway?

First he'd laughed at her, then he'd almost kissed her, and now he'd locked the door on her! He simply refused to listen even though what she had to say was of vital importance to his own well-being. What a jerk!

"Oh, God. He almost kissed me," she whispered, slumping onto the edge of the bed, remembering every second of that intimate encounter. She lifted a weak hand to her lips. "And I almost kissed him back."

She didn't even want to think about what might have happened next. But it was too late. Her imagination was running away with her. She would have wrapped her arms around him, he would have pulled her underneath him, and they would have played all kinds of naughty Wild One games.

It was true. She would've done anything he wanted at that moment, on that bed, with him. She could protest to everyone who would listen that she wasn't interested in him that way, that she didn't want to seduce him or sleep with him, but one roll around a leather bed, and she could think of nothing else.

"I want his hands on me," she whimpered. "I want my hands on him. I want to peel off every article of his clothing and lick him from head to toe."

This was pathetic. Emily Chaplin, daughter of the senior partner and the esteemed judge, did not think about licking handsome strangers, let alone say it out loud.

She gulped. Until now.

Okay, well, that was neither here nor there. Didn't

happen. Not going to happen. She repeated both those sentences a few more times. *Didn't happen. Not going to happen.*

He was The Wild One and she was Pollyanna and never the twain would meet.

She felt better now that she had identified this weakness in herself—identified and dealt with it. So she had a small problem. Did that mean she had to abandon her whole quest, her once-in-a-lifetime, footloose-and-fancy-free escapade?

"Absolutely not!" she told herself. "I'm here and I'm in this thing, and I'm going to stay until I solve the puzzle and save Tyler's adorable butt."

It probably would have been better to leave the "adorable" out of that equation, but she felt sure it was just a tiny oversight. The important thing was that she was back on the case. She'd heard his door slam and his footsteps bang down the hall a few minutes ago, so she could logically assume that he had once more taken off into parts unknown in North Beach. And she needed to get a move on if she wanted to catch up.

Quickly pulling on her new T-shirt, khaki pants and sneakers, Emily yanked her arms into her suit jacket on the way down the stairs. She certainly hoped she could get out of there before she ran into Kate or the cook again. How embarrassing to be caught in bed with Tyler five minutes after she'd assured Kate she wasn't interested in him.

But luck seemed to be with her this time. She didn't

see another soul. After snatching a map of the area out of a rack near the front desk, she was ready to go.

North Beach, straight ahead.

Thank God. Outside, with a silky San Francisco breeze wafting through her hair and cooling her fevered brow, her head felt much clearer, much better able to cope with the overpowering Tyler O'Toole.

Surely all that sex and sin malarkey was just a momentary reaction to The Wild One room and its leather and chrome delights. Now that she was out in the world, she wasn't susceptible to him at all. Right?

It was dusk as she followed her map down Columbus Avenue, and that gave a romantic glow to the parade of cafés and bistros, delis and pastry shops. She didn't want to look like a tourist, but she couldn't help staring at the hustle and bustle of customers of all colors and shapes and sizes. Her senses were on overload as her ears filled with the sounds of opera on one corner and jazz on the next, and her nose inhaled the wonderful odors of fresh-ground coffee, garlic, cheeses, fresh tomato, and a whole lot of other things she couldn't identify.

Her stomach growled loudly enough for her to hear it over the recorded aria drifting from a nearby Italian restaurant. Suddenly she remembered she hadn't eaten since that banana split at the coffee shop so many hours ago. It felt like months.

As she gaped through the window at the mouthwatering wares inside a deli, a man carrying a huge salami almost knocked her down. When she backed up to avoid the salami, a woman lumbering along the sidewalk with a fully dressed mannequin—dressed like a pirate?—got her from behind. Stumbling away from the mannequin, Emily tripped over two men at a sidewalk table who were smoking cigars, drinking cappuccino and arguing at the top of their lungs.

Bohemian, eccentric and colorful, North Beach was great, even if there was no hint of a beach. After the quiet B and B, this extravaganza of sounds and smells was a bit overwhelming, but it was also the perfect setting for an offbeat adventure.

Starving, her stomach rumbling, she managed to navigate a crowded coffee bar and nab a cup of latte and some chocolate biscotti. The latte was better than anything she'd ever tasted in her life. Look what a little hunger could do for you!

As she kept an eye out for any sign of Tyler, sipping her latte, she stumbled over a lingerie store where she picked up a few pretty items, and wandered past everything from bookstores to massage parlors. She stared openmouthed at some of the boutique windows, where they had the kinkiest clothes imaginable on display. A bikini made out of plastic Easter grass? Or was that Astro Turf?

"Hey, you! You interested in some bargains?" A woman at a makeshift stand parked in the alley motioned to her, drawing Emily away from the Easter grass. "I'm closing up for the night. I got some great stuff here, and I'm slashing prices so I don't have to drag it home."

Discounted merchandise in the alley? Emily glanced one way and then the other, looking for the catch. This sounded like a real swindle, like someone selling stolen watches out from under his overcoat, or hot VCRs on the back of a truck. And the saleswoman had so many piercings in her head she probably whistled like a tea-kettle every time she drank a hot beverage.

But still…the colorful piles of clothing and jewelry *did* look interesting, and too unique to be stolen.

"Did you make these?" Emily asked, holding up a sequined red jacket in one hand and a pair of lavishly embroidered bell-bottoms in the other.

"It's vintage," the Amazing Pierced Lady replied. "I pick up all kinds of ratty things at thrift shops and then add all the good stuff, recut them, you know, spruce them up, make them cool."

Ratty things from thrift shops, repackaged and sold in an alley? Her mother would kill her if she ever found out she'd bought secondhand clothes. But come on! These things were great. The workmanship was first-rate, and all the handiwork was beautiful.

"I'm going for it," she said to the saleswoman. "When am I ever going to see anything like this again?" She mulled over a tie-dyed pile—did she want the halter or the crop top?

"I'd go with the halter," her fashion advisor offered. "The cropped stuff just doesn't make it without a pierced navel."

Emily was willing to concede that point. She reached for the tie-dyed halter top and an embroidered denim miniskirt, holding them up to check the size. They looked like they would fit perfectly. "How much?"

But the saleswoman had more sales in mind. "Did

you see these?'' she inquired, coming up with a box of shoes that had been set off to one side. "These are my bestsellers. If you take the halter and the skirt, I'll throw in the shoes and take fifty dollars for the whole bunch.''

Ooh, the shoes were to die for. Ms. Pierced had apparently taken some clunky wooden platform sandals from the seventies, and then carved and painted monkeys and palm trees into the wood. One of a kind was an understatement. Emily had to have those sandals. Without further ado, she located her size and went for her wallet. But as she peeled off a fifty-dollar bill and handed it over, she happened to glance in the other direction.

And there, on the other side of the street, Emily caught sight of a very large man, shaped something like a chunk of concrete. He was tooling down the sidewalk, headed somewhere in a big hurry.

"Oh, my God," she said under her breath. "That's Slab!"

As Ms. Pierced dutifully stuffed the clothes and shoes into the bag with the lingerie, Emily grabbed her purchases and rushed out of the alley, not wasting a moment. Even though it was growing darker, the street was brightly lit, plus Slab was a very easy person to tail—he was so huge he could hardly just fade into the crowd.

Still, he had long strides, and she was huffing a little by the time he turned into a crumbling, garishly painted building with a flashing neon sign. It was something called The Flesh Pit. Charming.

But Emily was game. Calming herself, she squared her shoulders and followed him right in the open door, undaunted. Or at least she pretended to be undaunted. The ground floor appeared to be a tattoo parlor, with various tough-looking people loitering around and lots of bizarre designs on display on the walls. In the back, there was a staircase with a big arrow pointing to the second floor. Above the arrow, the words "Live Entertainment" flashed on and off in red lights.

Slab was disappearing up those steps, his massive frame blocking out all but "ment." Since raucous music, jeers and catcalling drifted down from upstairs, Emily could only guess that whatever was going on up there was even worse than down here.

Okay, so she was scared. It wasn't her fault if she stood out like a sore thumb in this tattooed, pierced and generally tough crowd. No wonder so many people were staring at her. She had to face it—she was dressed more like Suzy Suburbs than someone who should be scanning the tattoo chart downstairs at The Flesh Pit.

Gathering her courage, Emily traipsed nonchalantly over to the staircase, fully intending to follow Slab right into the bowels of hell—or whatever it was up there—if that was what it took. After all, Tyler was looking for Slab. She had found Slab. No way she was going to let him go. Not when producing him would certainly show Tyler that she meant business and deserved to be allowed to help him on this caper.

The music and noise above her intensified with every step. She got as far as the upstairs landing, where a couple of brawny bouncers stepped into her path.

"Where ya goin'?" one of them demanded, crossing his beefy arms over his chest.

"In there?" she asked hopefully, pointing to the smoky, dimly lit room behind him. She could barely make out a scantily clad woman gyrating around a pole on a raised area with footlights, while clusters of men yelled and hooted from small cocktail tables. It looked pretty vile from here. She had a feeling it would be even nastier close up.

Was that Slab's silhouette over by the stage? The shoulders were vaguely shaped like a refrigerator. Who else could it be?

"I don't think you need to go in there," the bouncer told her, giving her a cynical once-over. "You don't look like our kind of customer."

"I can pay the cover charge."

"Yeah, I'll bet. What are you, writing a book?" he asked with a sneer. "Or maybe looking to save the strippers, drag 'em off to some halfway house? We've seen your kind before." He tapped a square, poorly lettered sign attached to the stand behind him. It said We Reserve The Right To Exclude You If We Don't Like How You Look. "Consider yourself excluded, doll." He shook his head. "Don't make me get tough with you."

"Hmm." Emily frowned at the stage. She wouldn't have thought the things that woman was doing to that pole were humanly possible. "She's certainly… talented, isn't she?"

"Yeah." Big Bruiser actually cracked a smile.

"That's Shanda. She's our headliner. She knows what to do."

Emily's ears perked up. She'd heard that name before. Coffee shop. Slab. His voice echoed inside her ears. *Sweet Shanda. Best time I ever had...* "You did say Shanda, didn't you?"

"Yeah, sure. She's a major star in the strip game. Shanda Leer. You heard of her?"

"Shanda Leer?" As in chandelier. Good heavens. But this Shanda Leer had to be the mysterious girlfriend Slab had left Chicago to see. How many Shandas could there be running around North Beach?

Emily felt the thrill of discovery. She'd not only found Slab, but Shanda, too! Putting her miles ahead of Tyler. Now he would have to admit that he needed her help. Just wait until she got back to the B and B and made him beg her to tell him what she'd discovered.

As she contemplated just how she would hold Tyler's feet to the fire, there was a brassy, musical flourish of sorts inside The Flesh Pit, and Shanda slithered offstage after an enthusiastic hand from the rabble. Slab's large shadow rose from its place near the stage and skirted the tables, moving toward a back exit.

Emily had to get in there, too. She made her move, but the bouncer stopped her before she'd gone two steps.

"I'm sorry, doll, but you'll have to step aside," he told her. "We got real customers coming up." He inclined a fat thumb down the stairs, and Emily absently glanced that way as she plotted her next move.

Uh-oh, speak of the devil. Tyler was just planting his foot on the first step, a really cranky look on his fabulous face. Even if she had wanted to see him now, which she didn't, she also didn't want to face the indignity of being turned away at the door while he marched right in, smirking at her.

So she relied on the first rule of female avoidance tactics: the ladies' room.

"Excuse me," she asked politely, leaning in over the bouncer's podium, "but do you have a rest room I could use?"

"Yeah. Over there. Behind the stairs. Second door on your left."

Emily beat a quick path down the hall he'd indicated, but it wasn't pretty. There was one bare bulb screwed into the ceiling, and only a trail of grimy linoleum to lead the way. She pushed open the swinging door marked Girls and barged right in. Empty. It probably didn't get a whole lot of use except by the strippers themselves.

So she frowned into the mirror, trying to give herself enough time to think up a way into the main room of the strip joint. Since there was a back exit, perhaps there was also a back entrance, like a stage door. Or what if she changed into the halter and miniskirt she'd just bought on the street? Would her looks be more acceptable to the bouncer?

While she pondered, she realized she really did look like Sweet Polly Purebred in her plain white shirt and pearls under the navy jacket. Or maybe it was the hair.

"I should've changed it years ago," she said darkly,

fingering the obscenely boring medium brown strands of her chin-length bob. Sure, her hair was shiny and neat, but not very va-va-va-voom. She fussed with her bangs and tucked the sides behind her ears. "Maybe some barrettes or clips or something."

As she fluffed and fussed with her hair, she found herself glancing absently at the air duct over the mirror. How very strange. She could swear there were voices coming through the filthy grate.

Was that Slab's distinctive high-pitched whine she heard? She couldn't be sure, but it certainly sounded like him.

Emily dropped her bag of clothes and her purse and boosted herself up onto the sink, teetering there, grabbing the top of the first stall for balance, as she leaned in closer to the vent to hear better.

Definitely Slab, she realized with a certain triumph. His voice was unmistakable. The words were muddled, but he was pleading with somebody about something, and denying all over the place, that much was clear.

A woman's voice cut in, telling him to "cram it." Shanda? No way to tell. She didn't sound too sweet, that was for sure.

And then another, lower, more irritated voice joined in the conversation. "Tyler," she whispered. After eavesdropping so shamelessly at the Rainbow Rest-O-Rant, Emily recognized his inflection immediately.

It was gross to press her ear and her clean hair into the dirty duct, but she had to hear more.

She caught Tyler's acerbic tones, something about jumping bail and Fat Mike, and then demanding a list of who exactly knew Slab was back in San Francisco and who else had claims to the money.

"Wow," she murmured. This was simply riveting.

Tyler's voice grew louder and more intense. "Somebody looking for you busted into my room at my friend's place," he said angrily, "and tried to rough up an innocent bystander."

Emily knew who that referred to. Her. She winced, not feeling all that innocent.

"I can't help it—" Slab began, but then there were choking sounds, as if someone had grabbed the big guy and stopped him in midsentence.

"You tell your friends to stay away from Emily, do you hear me?" Tyler ordered in a savage tone.

Yikes. Tyler was defending *her*, and with physical violence. Emily didn't know whether to be flattered or scared out of her wits.

The female voice interjected, "I'm real sorry your little tootsie got in the way, Ty. But it's got nada to do with me."

Little tootsie? *Oh, God, she means me.* And Tyler didn't even correct her. What was a "tootsie," anyway? Was that like a girlfriend, or more of a slut-type person?

"Shanda, he told me he left the money with you. Do you think I'm the only one who's going to come looking for you?" Tyler asked impatiently. "You're involved whether you like it or not."

"He didn't leave no money with me!" she insisted. There was a *thwack,* as if somebody had gotten slapped. "You big dope! Why'd you go around telling people you left your stash with me?"

"I didn't. I swear!" Slab protested. "Yeow! Stop it, Shan. Quit hittin' me!"

The two of them argued back and forth for several minutes, with more smacking noises and more cries of "ouch!" and "yeow!" in Slab's distinctive whine. It sounded as if Tyler tried to intercede and pull them apart a few times, but Shanda kept up the assault.

Sweet Shanda? Not so you could notice. For being the best time Slab had ever had, Shanda was one tough cookie.

"I guess I didn't need to fly to San Francisco to protect *her*," Emily murmured. "Slab was going to take her apart with his bare hands, huh? Sounds like vice versa to me."

But their tiff was cut off by the sound of splintering wood, as if a door had been forced open, and heavy footsteps that boomed right over Emily's head. Now another angry voice joined the fray.

"Slabicki!" the new person growled. "I heard you was back in town."

From this set of noises, Emily could conclude that this was all happening one floor up, in whatever was on the third floor of The Flesh Pit over the bathroom. As she kept her ear pressed to the register, she heard Slab and the third man trade insults, plus another set of feet stomp around.

How many people were up there?

As if he were right next to her ear, Tyler muttered,

"Damn it all to hell. This is just what I need. More mopes. The damn place is crawling with mopes."

"Who you calling a mope?" the third man demanded. "Who are you, anyway?"

"I'm nobody," Tyler retorted. "I'm not even here."

"Yeah, well, you're in my business now!"

And then he pounded across the floor, and there was the sickening sound of a fist meeting a face.

Tyler's face? She gasped, almost pitching right off her perch on the sink. Not Tyler's face!

She knew what she had to do, and she leaped off the sink so fast she skidded into the first stall. It didn't matter. Her mind honed in on one thought and one thought only.

Save Tyler.

5

EMILY RACED out of the rest room and up the stairs before she had a chance to think better of it. A bizarre cocktail of bravado and excitement flowed through her veins, catapulting her up those stairs, and all she could think of was that Emily Chaplin was ready to kick some butt, baby. As she got closer, the sounds of shouting and thrashing got louder, but she wasn't frightened. The idea that there might be danger at the top of the stairs only spurred her on.

When she got there, she knew she was in the right place. The door had been smashed completely off its hinges, leaving a gaping hole opening into a lavishly decorated apartment. Not her taste—very purple, pretty darn tacky—but hey, it was plush. Since there were full-size posters of Shanda Leer, exotic artiste, mounted on every possible surface, it was easy to guess who lived there.

Although Emily slowed down and proceeded cautiously as she approached the door, no one glanced her way. They were too busy.

Near the doorway, Slab and some guy were rolling around on the floor, grunting and socking at each other. Clutching a skimpy robe around her inflated curves, wearing a pair of spike heels and not much else, Shanda was sort of squealing and trying not to trip over the two of them.

"Stop it! Stop it!" she cried. "You're gonna wreck my place. You stop it right this minute!"

At the moment, the other guy was getting the best of Slab, pummeling his head into the carpet and creating a minor earthquake. With a shriek of distress, Shanda secured a rickety end table loaded with framed photos and glass knickknacks, all of them shaking with the force of Slab's head hitting the floor.

Shanda and her knickknacks could fend for themselves—Emily had a more important mission. Steering past the wrestling match on the floor, she went straight for Tyler on the other side of the living room. He was holding up a chair like a lion tamer. Except the lion in this case was a short, stocky man with a twisted face. Tyler's attacker wore a black pin-striped suit right out of a gangster movie, and he sliced a wicked-looking knife through the air in front of him, making a vicious *snick-snick* sound.

Knife? Her heart was in her throat as she scanned Tyler from stem to stern, looking for wounds. But all she saw was a thin slash in one sleeve of his leather jacket and a slightly puffy area on his lower lip where he'd presumably been punched. She sighed with relief. All in one piece. No major damage. She'd arrived in time.

"Put down the damn chair and fight like a man!" Mr. Pinstripes bellowed.

Since Tyler had a definite height advantage, Emily

would have put her money on him in a fair fight, but the presence of the knife changed the odds somewhat. She wasn't taking any chances.

Weapon, weapon! She didn't have a weapon, she reminded herself, then decided she'd figure something out on the way.

Hugging the wall, she snagged one of her new shoes out of the bag and held it in front of her. The men were too intent on macho posturing to notice one small woman brandishing a shoe, so it wasn't hard at all to sneak up behind the pin-striped creep, rap the back of his nasty little head hard with the wooden base of her sandal, and watch him plop to the floor like a ripe tomato falling off a vine. The knife clattered beside him.

"Yes!" she cheered. "I knew I could do it!"

"Emily?" Tyler yelled. "What the hell are you doing here?"

"Rescuing you," she returned sharply. Seizing the knife, she stuck it and her sandal back into the bag with her new clothes and undies. But she stopped, gaping down at the man on the floor. "I didn't kill him, did I?"

"Nah. He's moaning." Tyler grabbed her hand, backing away. "In fact, I don't think you hit him hard enough. He's starting to come around. Let's boogie, shall we?"

"I'm with you."

Hanging on to Tyler for dear life, she hopped over Slab, who was lying apparently unconscious in the doorway. The two of them headed straight for the stairwell, not even stopping to breathe or synchronize watches. Tyler let her lead the way down, and she took the steps at a dizzying pace, trying to ignore the sound of pounding footsteps coming after them from above. By the time they hit the ground floor, shoving open a thick door that opened into an alley, she was gasping for breath.

Over the sound of approaching sirens, she shouted, "Rescuing good guys and escaping from bad guys is a lot less strenuous in the books."

"We haven't escaped yet." Tyler's expression was grim. "He's not going to let us get away that easily. I suggest we—"

But a flashlight caught them where they stood in the alley.

"You folks okay down here?" a cool voice called to them.

"Oh, yes, Officer." Emily straightened, putting on her perkiest I-am-a-Chaplin smile, rolling her pearls between her fingers so that the cop with the flashlight would be sure to notice she was a woman of quality and not some alley cat. "We were just wondering what all the commotion's about. Did someone trip a fire alarm?"

"Nah. Place is busted. Bunch of underage kids getting tattoos. Plus we tripped over a domestic disturbance upstairs. You didn't see anyone come out this way, did you?"

"No, sir, we didn't," she said with all due innocence. With Tyler's hand in hers, she strolled nonchalantly out toward the sidewalk. "Oh, my, look at that."

She lifted an eyebrow Tyler's way, assuming he'd want to stay clear of the authorities milling around The Flesh Pit. "That's a lot of policemen, isn't it, dear?"

"Quite a lot, darling," he returned smoothly. "Makes a body feel safe, doesn't it?"

"Indeed."

Luckily, all the cops seemed to be flooding into The Flesh Pit through the front door, and nobody paid them any attention when they curved around the building and blended in with pedestrian traffic.

"I suggest we make tracks," Tyler whispered in her ear.

"Agreed."

Zigging and zagging, they sped up one street and down another, through an alley or two, across a courtyard, doubling back and branching out, finally zipping in the front and out the back of a Chinese restaurant.

"Couldn't I just steal one little pot sticker off a tray?" she begged. "I didn't have any dinner. I'm starving. I deserve something for my rescue effort, don't I? I mean, I was awesome, wasn't I?"

"Yeah. Awesome." Tyler scanned the street one more time, for what she guessed was any sign of a pinstripe. "But we don't have time for pot stickers just yet. Let's make sure we've ditched Mack and his knife before we start celebrating."

"Mack? Is that really his name?"

Tyler's gaze was sardonic. "Are you kidding? How would I know his name? I'm not even sure what your name is."

"That's not true. You called me Emily," she said logically. "I heard you. Ergo you know my name."

"Yeah, but it could be a fake."

She smiled up at him, slowing down as he pulled her across the street. "Do I look like someone who would use a fake name?" she asked with a laugh. "I mean, come on."

"Emily, I don't know anything about you except that you have a strange habit of popping up when I least expect it. Plus I checked you out on the register." Tyler backed up into a quiet, shadowy park, an oasis of green in the bustling neighborhood. "Emily Bond, huh?" He paused, circling an arm around a tall tree, and she could see the dubious gleam in his eye even in the dim light. "That's convenient. What are you, James Bond's cousin? Sister?"

Uh-oh, she'd forgotten about that. "Don't be silly. Emily Bond is a perfectly normal name. There are a lot of people named Bond in this world besides James."

"Maybe. But you're not one of them. The Gap boy said he was looking for 'Emily Ch—.' Since when does Bond start with *Ch?*"

"Maybe he made a mistake. Maybe my middle name's...Charity." Emily skipped right past him, out into an open area of grass. Over the tops of the trees, she could see the twin spires of a nearby church, illuminated so that they seemed to float there, up in the sky. The glow they cast down into the park was both beautiful and eerie at the same time.

"Emily." Unexpectedly, he was right behind her,

and she spun around, almost losing her balance. But he caught her and pulled her up against him. He leaned in so close that his warm breath tickled her ear when he whispered, "I know."

"W-what?" Closing her eyes, allowing herself to melt into him just a tiny bit, she tried her best not to be intimidated.

So what if it was dark and private and incredibly romantic here in the park? So what if they'd just had an amazing escape and she was light-headed from lack of food and too much adrenaline and the heady, unbelievable triumph of bashing a jerk over the head with a shoe?

Out of your league, her inner good girl told her sternly. *Having the best time of your life,* her inner bad girl countered.

"What do you think you know?" she asked him finally, staring up into those moody green eyes, letting her gaze wander over that tiny, swollen ridge on his lower lip.

Soft, insistent, husky, the sound of his voice spun down her spine, weakening her already thin resistance. "I know you're lying to me," he murmured, tipping up her chin. "I know you're following me. I just don't know why. But you're going to tell me, aren't you?"

So he thought he could seduce her into spilling her guts? She lifted one finger to trace the bruise on his lip. "Does it hurt, where he hit you?"

"Emily, stop trying to distract me." But he was the one who opened his mouth slightly, just enough to touch the tip of his tongue to the side of her finger, making her tremble and catch her breath. "You do know you're playing with fire, don't you?"

"Yes," she whispered. "Oh, yes. I'm counting on it."

And he licked her finger again. She felt she had to hang on or she'd fall down, right there in the middle of the park. That tiny touch of his warm, wet tongue against her cool flesh was enough to send her tripping over the edge. Too much excitement, too many reckless emotions in a too-long day. And he was too good at this.

She wound her arms around his neck, lifted herself into his embrace and pressed her mouth into his with all the energy and passion she could muster.

His arms fastened tight and hard around her, pulling her up into him, fitting her curves to the hard angles of his long body. The sensual assault of his lips and tongue was hot, relentless, delicious. He tasted like danger and joy and sin and nothing she'd ever imagined in a man or in a kiss.

If this mind-numbing desire was what she thought she'd wanted, she must have been out of her mind. It was incredible. Addictive. And terrifying.

A hungry little moan escaped her lips, and she couldn't believe that sound came from her. "I want you," she murmured, breathless, trembling.

"And I want to know what this is all about."

His harsh tone was like a splash of cold water. She pushed away. "That again?"

"What do you really want, Emily? What are you doing here?" When she made no reply, Tyler smiled.

It was a very dark, crooked smile. "Did you really think I'd take this any further when I know you're still lying to me?"

"I am not!" Emily was furious. Humiliated, dripping with desire, and furious. "Okay, my name is Emily Chaplin. I lied about Bond. Big deal. I sort of ran away from home for the weekend and I didn't want my mother to find me." A new thought occurred to her. "Shoot. I wasn't supposed to use my credit cards, either. But I forgot when I did the Gap thing."

"Which is why the delivery boy knew your real name."

"I didn't say I was good at this. Yet." She sighed. "Okay, so I already told you I'm a lawyer. That's true. You also know I'm from Chicago because I was on the same plane you were. What else do you need to know?"

"No, I didn't know you were from Chicago," he said tightly. "So you spotted me on the plane and decided to follow me off? You *are* a stalker."

"No, I did not follow you off the plane!" Actually, she'd followed him *on* the plane, which was even worse. "I didn't see you during the flight at all," she said, sticking to a grain of truth. "Not until I went to get a cab, and there you were. You remember, the taxi driver grabbed my briefcase and asked if I wanted to share. I came to San Francisco on a whim, I admit that. But I'm not a stalker. And I didn't have anywhere better to go, so when you said you were going to North Beach, I thought why not? And then the B and B was so wonderful, it just seemed like fate. Like kismet. It even has a Kismet room! So I stayed."

That sounded plausible, didn't it? And less bizarre than the real story.

"So that's when you started following me, after you came to the B and B? You're saying you just stumbled into this when that guy came through my window?"

She avoided the direct question. "My motives were really very good. I wanted to help you. I could tell you were in trouble and I wanted to help. That is the absolute truth," she swore.

"Little Ms. Emily Chaplin, lawyer from Chicago." He ran a careless hand through the dark strands of his hair. "And let me guess—you've never done anything like this before in your life, and you decided this was your big chance to attach yourself to a bad boy in a leather jacket and get a ride to the wrong side of the tracks, am I right?"

"No." She hesitated. "Okay, well, kind of. I mean, yes, I've never done anything like this before. But no to the rest of it."

"Listen to me, Emily," he told her, putting even more distance between them, stabbing a finger in the air. "I am nobody's walk on the wild side. Do you hear me?"

"I hear you. But you're being ridiculous." She rushed to catch up before he left her in the park all by herself. "I'm not asking for a walk on the wild side. I'm telling you, you need my help."

He flashed her a very unpleasant look.

"You can deny it all you like," she persisted, "but

we're a good team. Where would you have been tonight without me? Sliced and diced in Shanda Leer's living room?''

"I was doing fine."

"Oh, yeah, right. I saved your adorable butt, Tyler O'Toole, and you know it." *Oops*. She was supposed to leave out the adorable part.

His lips curved with amusement.

"Well, it's the truth," Emily insisted. "And you owe me."

He stopped without warning, and she crashed into him before she could put on the brakes. But his hands bracketed her shoulders, holding her steady. "What exactly do you think I owe you?"

The first thing that flashed into her mind was a roll on the leather bed in The Wild One?

Best to keep that thought to herself.

"You at least owe me dinner," she decided instead. "I really am starving." In more ways than one. Love, sex, food...she had an abiding hunger for all of them. Best to keep that to herself, too.

"Okay. Dinner it is. Come on." His long strides sent him down Columbus Avenue ahead of her. "I doubt ol' Mack or anybody else will think to look for us in a restaurant. At the very least it'll waste a few hours, and then maybe it will be safe to go back to Beau's." He regarded her with a speculative look. "And we can talk, you and I. How about we make a deal? For every question you answer about yourself and what you're doing here, I'll take a question, too. What do you say?"

"Deal," she answered without a moment's hesitation, positive she had the best of that bargain. The life of boring Emily Chaplin was an open book.

The life of mysterious Tyler O'Toole was better than any spy novel.

TYLER REFILLED her wineglass, congratulating himself on an excellent strategy. After the kiss-and-tell in Washington Square had backfired, he'd switched to Plan B—ply her with pasta, a nice, smooth Chianti, a little more Chianti, and eventually she'd tell him anything he wanted to know.

He now had her entire résumé and then some, including a blow-by-blow account of her trip to The Flesh Pit. Meanwhile, he'd relied on dodging, obfuscation and evasion, and she hadn't learned one thing about him. Nice girls were so easy it wasn't even a fair fight.

"What do you do for a living?" she'd asked.

"Nothing at the moment."

There was a pause. "And what did you do when you still did something?"

He'd shrugged. "This and that."

Her eyes had narrowed. "What did whatever you did have to do with hookers and strippers?"

That took him by surprise. "Who told you I had anything to do with hookers or strippers?"

"Kate."

He'd made a mental note to have a talk with Kate. To Emily, he'd offered another shrug. "Let's just say I have a weakness for underdogs. I offered help when they needed it."

"Like me!" she'd said happily. "Like me with you."

And as neatly as that, they were successfully off the subject of him and back to her.

Of course, that still didn't explain why she had decided that she needed to attach herself to him. She wasn't terribly coherent on that part. Could she be more deceptive than he thought? Nah, she was a terrible liar. So the bit about concluding that he was in trouble and needed her help must be true. Because she'd liked his looks in the back seat of a cab, or because she'd been captivated by Beau's B and B, or because her curiosity had been aroused when the thug came through the window. Insane, but true.

"How exactly did you think you could help me?" he inquired, trying not to notice how erotic it was when she sucked the marinara sauce off her spaghetti like that.

"Legal help," she said immediately. "Clearly you're in a jam."

"You always operate on so little information?" He shook his head, latching onto a hunk of bread to keep his hands busy. Otherwise he'd be tempted to reach across the table and brush that little smudge of sauce off her chin. "Or did you just have a burning need to work on a merit badge?"

"Oh, I get it." She gave him this cornball smile, all cutie-pie Midwestern girl, and he started to melt in spite of himself. "Merit badge. 'Cause you think I'm a real Girl Scout. Pretty funny."

"Yeah. Pretty funny."

Actually, not funny at all. Could she really be as genuine and sincere as she seemed? Or was she snowing him down to his shoes?

Tyler took a big swallow of wine, watching her, weighing her, mentally taking her apart and putting her back together.

The bottom line was there was just something about Emily. Something about the sparkle in those round, trusting hazel eyes, about the perfect Little Dutch Girl hairdo that seemed to frame her face and make her eyes even bigger, about the bright, uncomplicated radiance of her smile. About the way she attacked her clams with the same gusto she'd kissed him with in Washington Square.

That was something, all right.

And if he didn't watch himself, he would be falling for her crazy, mixed-up charms. Big-time.

"Great time for that," he muttered under his breath. "You are on the verge of losing your office, your practice and your kneecaps. Sure, great time to fall for Susie Sorority."

"What did you say?" she asked politely.

"Nothing."

"I thought you said something about Sukie Sommersby. Now that would be a coincidence." Emily laughed, shaking her not-quite-golden brown hair.

Tyler found himself distracted by the way the candlelight played across the fall of her shiny hair.

"Sukie and I go way back."

"Sorry. Don't know anybody named Sukie."

But Emily was off and running, doing this riff on

the adventures of her old college chum, who seemed to have lived quite the roller-coaster life. Waving her hands for emphasis, giggling, trying on and discarding goofy accents to sketch the various personages who drifted through Sukie's madcap escapades, Emily was irresistible.

Her performance also gave him a pretty good idea of why she thought it was acceptable to jump on a plane to San Francisco and then run off on a wild-goose chase once she got there. Because it was what Sukie would do. Damn Sukie. And what kind of name was Sukie, anyway?

Oh, well, at least the collected stories of the life and times of Sukie Sommersby gave him a chance to watch Emily lick the cream out of a cannoli.

There were few pleasures in life to top that.

TYLER FELT ABOUT TEN YEARS older by the time he took her back to Beau's B and B. Given how giggly and clingy Emily was getting, he probably shouldn't have poured quite so much wine down her. Or had the last few glasses himself.

Good thing he'd found her credit card when the bill came. Not only did he verify that her name really was Emily Chaplin, but he didn't have to wash dishes to get them out of Caffe Fiori. By himself, he couldn't afford the first bottle of Chianti, let alone a second one.

"Okay," Emily told him as he opened the front door for her. "I want you to say it. You say, Emily, you saved my adorable butt and thank you, thank you, I need you on the team, you are my partner now."

"I'm not going to say that."

Emily stopped in the doorway. "Why not? Didn't I bonk that guy on the head for you? Didn't I pick up the tab at the Caffe Fiori because you were temporarily without funds?"

"Yes, you did." Sighing, Tyler scooped her up and lifted her over the threshhold. "But that just made us even, you know. I saved your adorable butt, too—from Sluggo who came through the window, remember?"

"Yes, but that was your fault, too," she argued. "Sluggo was after you, not me. And why are you calling him Sluggo?"

"He just looked like a Sluggo."

"I don't think so," she shot back. "Brutus. I would call him Brutus."

"Does it matter?" He lowered his voice as he carried her down the hall. "Let's try to be quiet, okay? We don't want to wake Kate or the other guests."

"Oh, Kate. She's nice, isn't she?"

"Very nice."

"I really like her." Emily smiled mistily. "I like everybody."

"I'll bet you do, with two bottles of Chianti in you."

"Tyler, I'm not that drunk," she said severely, wiggling until he put her down. "Don't patronize me."

"Never."

"Oh, yeah, right." She put a hand on the rail to steady herself, and he could tell she was concentrating on the tiny lights along the floorboards to guide her. She navigated her way up to the second floor all by herself by sheer force of will. "All you do is patronize me. Don't think I didn't notice that you didn't give me a straight answer all night. I was honest with you. But you? Ha!''

''Emily, come on,'' he said, poking through her purse until he located her key. He unlocked the door for her, ushering her into the Pollyanna room.

''You come on. I deserve better.'' After tossing her purse, her shopping bag and then her jacket onto the bed, each one with a satisfying whack, she faced him down. ''I really do.''

''I'm not going to argue with you on that one. You do deserve better.''

''Well, then...''

But he shoved all the junk off the bed and tipped her backward. ''Get in, Emily.''

''Tyler, this is important. In the morning, you will take me with you, right?'' Her expression was dead serious and her gaze steady. ''Promise?''

''Yeah, okay.'' He backed away from the bed. ''I'm afraid *not* to let you tag along,'' he teased. ''Or you might conk me on the head with your trashy sandals, too.''

''Exactly,'' she declared. She sat up, unbuttoning her pants.

''Maybe you should wait on that,'' he began, but she wasn't listening.

She kicked off her shoes and socks, and then started to shrug out of the khakis, still bubbling with enthusiasm. ''This is going to be great, Tyler. We'll find Slab and Shanda again, before he can take her apart with his bare hands to find the stash. But I don't think that will be a problem, do you? Because she seemed pretty capable of taking care of herself. I am a lot less concerned about her than I was at the beginning." With a finger to her lips, she stage-whispered, "I'll bet she spent his money."

"What?" How did she know Slab's name? Or Shanda's? Or anything about a stash? Was that something she'd overheard from the rest room at The Flesh Pit? And why was she undressing in front of him?

"Tyler, I don't want you to worry." Her hands moved to the hem of her T-shirt, and she edged it up over her rib cage, displaying every intention of taking that off, too.

This time he put a stop to it himself, knocking her hands away from her shirt. "Don't you think you should leave that on?"

"Well, I was planning to sleep in it, but I have to take my bra off first." She rolled her eyes. "Men. Why would I sleep in my bra?"

"Oh, I don't know," he said sarcastically. "Maybe so I don't dream all night about you in here without one?"

"Would you? That is so sweet." And she gave him that moony smile again, the one that made him think she needed a keeper—but not him, of course.

"Yeah, yeah. Just go to bed, will you?"

"Tyler, I want you to know everything will be okay," she said dreamily, falling back into a stack of frilly pillows. "We're going to do this together, and we're going to make sure you are not out on the street, that Fat Mike doesn't lay a hand on you, that Slab shows up for court on Monday, and you can pay Jozette back every dime you owe her."

As this speech progressed, he grew more and more still. It took a minute, but he found his voice. "How the hell do you know all that?"

"Oh." She hesitated, lifting her head, squinting as she attempted to focus. "You said it. I couldn't help but overhear." She giggled. "Don't you remember, at the Rainbow Rest-O-Rant? What a dump!"

"The Rainbow...? In Chicago?"

"Uh-huh." She yawned and reclined further into her pristine white bedclothes. "I had a banana split. Slab made the coffee cups bounce. Where did you think?"

"What I thought was..." He set his jaw. She'd followed him all the way from Chicago. Not from a cab at the airport, not because she liked the B and B, not even because a burglar had piqued her interest. All the way from the beginning—which put this into a totally different category. "I don't know what I think."

But her eyes were already closed. Emily had drifted off into never-never land.

Quietly seething, he left her there on the bed in the Pollyanna room, carefully locking the door behind him. Back in the relative safety of The Wild One, he stared at the newly repaired window, wondering just how much of a sucker he was.

Again and again, she'd kept to her story. *I could tell you were in trouble and I wanted to help. That is the absolute truth.*

Was it possible? Was Emily really as innocent as she wanted him to believe?

No one could really be that naive or that crazy, could they? To follow some guy she'd never met all the way from a third-rate coffee shop in Chicago to San Francisco on a whim?

It didn't make sense.

But what might make sense was a different scheme. Say she was a rookie cop or even a fledgling investigator for either the FBI or the ethics committee to the bar association. Say she got assigned to him, she did some surveillance, and she trailed him from Chicago to California, all by the rule book.

So maybe she got in over her head once she got here. Maybe she liked him more than she was supposed to. Maybe she drank too much and had some fun and totally screwed up her assignment.

Maybe she was the world's worst undercover investigator.

Now *that* made sense.

He stripped off his own clothes, splashed some water to knock some sense into his head, and stretched out on The Wild One bed. But he wasn't interested in sleeping. He had some thinking to do.

Who was Emily Chaplin? What did she know?

And how much trouble was she going to cause him?

6

WRAPPED IN WHITE LINEN and lace, Emily tossed and turned. She wasn't exactly awake, but she wasn't asleep, either. She felt itchy and uncomfortable, a little constricted, a lot woozy. And why was her head full of buxom strippers who had tattoos and Tyler lying on a black leather bed wearing nothing but a smile?

"Mmm," she mumbled into her pillow, enjoying the image. "Tyler..."

But when she moved her lips she realized there was something wrong with her mouth. She tasted like garlic. Old, used-up garlic.

Rousing herself, Emily padded into the bathroom to brush her teeth. She had a vague recollection of where she was and what she'd been doing, but things were still awfully fuzzy. Blearily she squinted into the mirror over the sink, giving her reflection a hazy once-over.

"Yuck," she said out loud. Her hair was a disaster area, and she was wearing nothing but a rumpled white T-shirt with her grandmother's pearls. Somehow she doubted Grandma Burr would approve. "Maybe Grandma had more of a sense of adventure than I think."

Unlikely. Fumbling with the catch on her necklace,

she dropped the pearls near the sink, and then scanned the basin and the marble top. No toothbrush. The best she could do was swish some water around in her mouth and rub a finger over her teeth. But she still reeked of garlic and wine. Way too much wine.

"My head hurts." She stumbled back a step. No medicine cabinet. No helpful pain relievers, either. "But wait."

A ray of clarity penetrated the fog. There should be aspirin in her briefcase. And a tiny toothbrush and tube of toothpaste, too—emergency supplies for client meetings after lunch.

"Fabulous," she murmured, locating what she needed in the dark, savagely brushing her teeth, knocking back the aspirin and climbing into bed with a glass of water.

After sticking the cup on the wicker bedside table, she dropped into her Pollyanna bed, but she was still uncomfortable. Frowning, she sat up. With one tug, she pulled her T-shirt off up to her neck, unhooked the damn bra and tossed it on the floor, and then readjusted the T-shirt.

"Much better," she said drowsily, conjuring up the forbidden mental pictures she'd been enjoying. Tyler, black leather, nothing but a smile. "Oh, yeah."

OVER IN THE WILD ONE, Tyler was restless.

He'd shoved that stupid leather bedspread onto the floor, yanking out the black sheets around the edges enough to give him some room to breathe, but he still kept staring at the ceiling, wide-awake. Or glaring at the armoire with its secret passage into Emily's room. Or glancing at the window, wondering whether Sluggo or Mack the Knife planned return appearances anytime soon.

"Damn it," he muttered to himself. As near as he could figure, and from what he'd been able to gather from Slab before the brouhaha broke out, the mopes who'd been bothering him were ex-cohorts of Slab's who thought they were entitled to a share of whatever ill-gotten gains Slab had hidden in San Francisco. And they didn't plan to let it go easily. They wanted their money, and they wanted it now.

And because Emily kept showing up where she wasn't supposed to be and barging into what didn't concern her, the bad guys undoubtedly thought she was involved in this, too. Plus Mack the Knife had a personal score to settle, given that she'd hammered him over the head with her shoe.

The memory of that altercation came flooding back, and Tyler laughed in spite of himself. The way that guy had crumpled to the floor was a picture, all right. Who'd have figured Emily to pack such a potent left hook?

But he sobered quickly. Because of that hook, Emily had put herself in a bull's-eye. It was mostly her own fault, but it was still a fact.

No matter where she fell on the spectrum—from total innocent to really bad undercover agent—stooges like Sluggo and Mack didn't play around. It was only a matter of time before they came gunning for Emily. And what the hell could he do about it?

Because of him, Emily had imbibed way too much wine, and she was probably passed out in a stupor right now, totally unable to defend herself.

He got up to check the new latch on the window. It seemed fine. And he didn't see any suspicious shadows down below on the street, as if anyone were watching or waiting.

He went back to bed.

He got up to make sure the armoire was secured, that the trophy was in place and the hooks were fastened. All fine.

He went back to bed.

He got up and re-examined the window and the armoire and the entire security system. Nothing out of the ordinary.

But the silence in this room was deafening. Where was a siren when you needed it? Or a storm or a cat fight or a garbage truck, or even a drunk staggering home in the wee hours singing, "You Picked a Fine Time to Leave Me, Lucille"? It was too damn quiet out there, and in here.

Unable to shake his uneasy feeling, Tyler pulled his jeans back on, got a drink of water, paced for a while, and stood at the window, gazing out into the dark, mysterious San Francisco night.

Maybe he should take a gander into the Pollyanna room, in and out, just one little glance, to make sure she was okay. He knew she was fine—of course, she was fine—but it couldn't hurt to double-check, could it? He'd be quiet, he'd be quick, he'd slide open the armoire, take a peek, verify that she was sleeping peacefully, and have the whole shebang back together before she even knew he was there.

Gliding along the hardwood floor, Tyler removed the silver trophy and set it on the floor. It only took a second to undo the latches, to slowly edge the panels open, to ease himself ever so carefully through the opening, and then take one tentative step into the Pollyanna room.

Moonlight spilled in through the white lace curtains, streaking across the bed, illuminating Emily's cheek against her pillow and the pale line of her bare leg where she'd kicked off her covers.

She looked like an angel. All warm and cozy, sleeping sweetly, probably spinning mental pictures of the ballet or the opera or the new Donna Karan line or whatever pampered suburban rich girls with a fistful of credit cards dreamed of.

Clearly she was fine, just fine, so he'd completed his rounds and it was past time to—

When out of the blue, something landed on his head. "Ow!" he yelled. "What the hell?"

It was furry, yellow, and it had claws. As he spun around, trying to catch it and get it and its damn claws off his head, some scrap of stretchy fabric on the floor tripped him, and he almost fell down. As he staggered, the cat smacked him in the face with its fluffy tail, bounded down his shoulder and took off under the bed.

"Damn cat!" he swore. He grabbed whatever it was that had tangled up his foot, jerking backward when he recognized it. A sliver of silk, the color of champagne.

Emily's bra. It was still warm from her hot little

body. He stood there, dumbfounded, clutching Emily's bra, grasping it so tight the hook embedded itself in his palm.

"Tyler?" Sounding dazed but conscious, Emily lifted herself on one elbow in the four-poster bed, linens pooling around her waist. "What is it?"

"Nothing. Sorry. I was just..." He dropped the bra like a hot potato. "I got to wondering whether you were safe. You know, with Sluggo and Mack on the loose and probably looking for us. So I came over to check. But Beau must've been hanging out on top of the armoire, and he jumped on my head." He hesitated, aware how stupid all this sounded. "Sorry."

"S'okay." She peered at him, obviously confused and three-quarters asleep. "D'ya wanna come in?"

"Come in?" he echoed. What the hell did that mean?

Yawning, she scooted over to one side of the bed and threw back the covers on the other. "Come in," she repeated. "Do you want to come in?"

His mouth fell open. She was inviting him into her bed as if it was nothing? The way she would offer a cup of coffee to a vacuum cleaner salesman?

"I don't think I should," he muttered. "That's probably a really bad idea."

He wondered if she was aware of exactly what she was offering. Sure, too much Chianti, a very long day, and she was opening up, relaxing, letting down her hair. But even so, he would have bet everything he had left in the world that Emily did not normally invite anyone into her bed on the first date.

Not that you could really call what they'd been through tonight a date. A foiled burglary, a knife fight at a strip joint, escaping a police raid, a walk in the park, dinner and two bottles of wine at a quaint Italian restaurant. Well, that was as close to a date as he'd had in a good long time.

He squinted at her face in the dim room. Did that soft, out-of-focus expression mean that she had a platonic sleepover in mind? Or was that more of a sly, come-hither look?

It didn't matter. It suddenly seemed to him that whatever she intended, he could, if he wanted to, take advantage of her as easily as walking across the room. He knew that. With every bone in his body. Every aching, bruised, vulnerable bone in his body.

All he had to do was get in that bed, cuddle up, strip off her teeny-weeny little T-shirt, and make love to her until the sun came up. It was what his body wanted. And it was there for the taking.

But, damn it all to hell, Emily was the last woman on earth he could possibly take advantage of. He just couldn't do it.

"Oh, come on." She dropped her head back down to her pillow, but she patted the open side of the bed. In a voice muffled by sleep and her pillowcase, she mumbled, "You said you were trying to make sure I was safe. Don't you think I'd be safer if you were here?"

As long as he behaved himself, she had a point. He had to admit it. Damn it, she actually had a point.

In The Wild One, all he did was worry about

whether Emily was all right. But in Pollyanna, with her literally at his fingertips, he might be able to relax. Or at least that was what he told himself.

A small, nagging voice chided, *Yeah, you're really going to be able to relax here,* sidled up next to her. But he ignored it.

"I'll keep my pants on," he muttered.

The bottom line was that it was very late, they were all alone, and Tyler could better protect her if he was right there with her. Besides, what harm could it do? She was already making soft, snoozy little noises, lost in sweet dreams, smiling to herself and hugging her pillow.

He'd never been all that noble, but he swore he would start now. So he found himself bunking down right next to her, bunching up the bedclothes between them so nothing was actually touching anything else, and then just lying there, watching Emily sleep.

"Mmm..." She made a contented little moan, her lips curving with pleasure.

Tyler gritted his teeth, stiff as a board on his side of the damn bed, drowning in ruffles and frills. This room, this bed, were so cutie-pie he could spit. He snatched a pint-size, heart-shaped pillow out from under him and pitched it across the room.

Why was she making those noises? What in God's name was she dreaming about, anyway?

"Mmm, Tyler..." she whispered. "That feels so good. Right *there*."

She was dreaming about *him?*

At that moment, he was holding himself so rigid he

could have bounced a dime off his abs. This platonic bodyguard stuff was insane, preposterous, and probably going to cause him permanent bodily harm.

"I'm never going to make it through a whole night like this," he said darkly. Good thing it was already well into morning. What would surely turn out to be the longest morning in history.

THERE WAS SOMETHING breathing in her ear. The puffs of air were warm and rhythmic, and they tickled. "Mmph?" she mumbled, brushing at it.

But it wouldn't go away. And she couldn't move away, not with that hard, heavy, muscled arm thrown over her chest, the hand brushing her T-shirt, gently cupping her breast. And an even heavier leg nestled between hers.

She slid her foot up the pant leg. Jeans. Soft jeans. Hard man underneath.

Oh, my god.

What was she doing with a man in her bed?

Tyler. It had to be Tyler.

She sneaked a peek over her shoulder. His eyes were closed, his lips parted slightly, and the sharp angles of his cheekbones, his jaw, his elegant nose, seemed softer in sleep. He looked so drop-dead gorgeous it took her breath away.

She'd never woken up to anything this fabulous before, not even Christmas morning.

But when had he gotten into bed with her? When had she let him? What exactly happened last night?

Frantic, holding herself stock-still so she wouldn't

wake him, Emily carefully eased his hand off her breast and set it a few inches lower where it could get into less trouble. At the moment, however, pretty much everywhere was a danger zone. All she was wearing was a thin T-shirt and a lousy pair of bikini underpants. She tried to look on the bright side—at least she was wearing *something*.

Her brain racing, she tried to pull together some coherent memory of what she'd done, what *they'd* done. The Flesh Pit—yes, she remembered that. The altercation with the pin-striped, knife-wielding guy—okay, yeah, that was clear. And then what?

A kiss in the park. Yummy. Scary, but yummy. Tyler asking questions. Her magic, refillable wineglass.

"Oh, my head," she groaned. It felt like someone had wrapped her in wool and then started pounding hammers on her temples—which made it even harder to think.

The sad truth was she had no recollection whatsoever of how she'd gotten back to the B and B or what Tyler was doing in her bed, although that didn't take much imagination. She'd already come on to him in as many ways as she knew how, so she'd probably just attacked the poor guy. Jumbled images of him naked, slithering around the chrome-and-leather bed in The Wild One, suddenly filled her mind, making her even more sure she was right.

But that didn't work. They were wrapped up in *her* bed, not his.

"Oh, no. Maybe we did it both places," she murmured with growing horror. "I'm a slut. I slept with the man of my dreams—twice—and I don't even remember!''

See what happened when you started to act like Sukie Sommersby? Wasn't that what she wanted, to wake up with a handsome stranger in the middle of a moral quagmire, just like Sukie?

Not so fun when it really happened, was it?

Meanwhile, her head hurt like blazes and his hand had crept back to her breast again. ''Maybe I'm dreaming.''

Right. And that ridge of solid male flesh pressing against the front of his jeans and the back of her bottom was just her imagination?

Keep your eyes shut and don't move. Let him wake up first and deal with it.

It was a plan. Emily squeezed her eyes shut and settled back into him. And the fact that it felt wonderful and natural and as if she was born to fit right there was of no consequence.

Absolutely none.

HE COULD HEAR HER HEARTBEAT. Erratic, racing, alive, it sounded like a beacon in the misty gray morning.

Her skin was so soft, her hair silky and smooth as he nuzzled her neck and her ear. His fingers glided under the edge of her T-shirt, teasing, testing, and his knee slid up between her thighs. She was warm, relaxed, sweetly yielding. Now this was what he called a great way to wake up.

Somewhere nearby, he could smell coffee brewing and bread baking. Mmm…he breathed in the delicious mingled aromas of steaming espresso and blueberry muffins and Emily in the morning.

What?

Tyler jerked awake, tumbling backward and off the side of the Pollyanna bed. Once again, he tripped on her lingerie, and he bent and lunged for it.

"Damn it, Emily!" he shouted. "Could you keep your damn bra off the floor?"

She blinked, wide-awake, staring at him. "Excuse me?"

"Your underwear is on the floor again. It's a hazard." He flung it at her and turned on his heel.

"Where are you going?"

"Out."

"But, Tyler," she tried, clasping ruffled sheets to her front as she tripped out of the bed after him. "Can you at least tell me what we did last night? You know, you and me? Did we—I have to know—did we do it?"

That was all he needed—Emily overcome with guilt and amnesia and who knew what else. He practically leaped through the back wall of the armoire and into his room, this time banging his bare foot on the trophy he'd left in the middle of the floor last night. He found a particularly colorful curse to throw at the trophy as he pitched it out of his way.

Behind him, he could hear Emily rustling around, trying to find clothes, he supposed. Great. Now she'd be popping through the armoire and complicating his life even more than it already was. He thought of taking a cold shower so he could forget everything that had just happened, but he was afraid Emily would hop right in with him.

"What I need," he said suddenly, "is to get out of this freaky place and get a really strong cup of coffee. Maybe two or three."

First he shut and latched the secret panels to keep her out for a little while longer. Then, with one hand firm against the door of the armoire, he shucked his clothes and pulled on clean ones. It wasn't easy undressing and re-dressing with one hand, but he just didn't trust her.

And then he paced to his window, wrenched it open and scrambled out over the sill. If Sluggo could do it, he could, too. Besides, it was quicker and more direct this way, instead of navigating through the house where people like Kate and Verna might want explanations.

So he stretched over to the drain pipe, got a fairly secure footing between that and a trellis full of clematis, and methodically climbed down the side of the house. As he dropped to the sidewalk, he heard another window scrape open above his head.

"Tyler!" Emily cried. "Wait! I want to come with you."

"Oh, no, you don't," he muttered, picking up his pace. "Oh, no, you don't."

EMILY WATCHED HIM DISAPPEAR into the foggy morning, feeling every bit as frustrated and annoyed as he looked.

If she could only see where he was going, she could get dressed on the double and follow. But the last she saw was a glimpse of his dark head whipping around a corner and out of view. There was nothing she could do.

She lumped herself down onto the edge of the bed, trying to focus. "Okay, so we didn't make love. Because if we did, first, that is something neither I nor my body would forget, and second, he wouldn't be so cranky."

Yes, she felt that was a persuasive line of reasoning. The more pressing question was whether that conclusion was a relief or a disappointment.

"It's a relief," she snapped. "Okay, so it's time I admit I really, really want to sleep with him. But not while I'm unconscious!"

No, she wanted to savor every second.

"But what a guy," she said wistfully, changing her train of thought and jumping to her feet as she leaped to the next conclusion. "There I was, sloshed to the gills, eminently seducible, and he didn't go for it. What a great guy."

Or should she be insulted? Maybe he wasn't attracted to her at all.

She raised a weak hand to push her bangs off her forehead. "Life is so confusing when you throw away the rule book."

Her nose picked up the scent of freshly baked blueberry muffins, and she decided food might help her brain work better. It couldn't make it work any worse.

She vaguely recalled Kate giving breakfast instructions when she'd checked in. So she pulled open her door, hoping she remembered right, gratified to find she did. There was a silver tray with a basket of muffins, strawberry preserves, a pot of coffee, cream, sugar and a pretty china cup.

"Heaven," Emily announced, taking the lid off the coffeepot and inhaling deeply. "Absolute heaven."

As she pulled herself up to the wicker tea table, munching away, she plotted her next move. Now that Tyler had stomped off into the fog, she had all the time in the world to plan and ponder and get it right this time. If only she could remember more of what had happened.

Emily drank her coffee, ate a muffin and a half, and then marched herself into a long, extremely hot bath. As the water sluiced into the claw-footed tub, with steam rising around her, she found that there were bits and pieces of conversation hovering at the fringes of her conscious mind.

"I think we agreed that we would be partners," she said slowly. "And that he would include me on the deal from here on. Plus he was worried that the guy with the knife was still after us, which would explain why he stayed with me last night."

But not why he would run off at the first light of dawn.

Still she distinctly remembered something like *I saved your adorable butt, Tyler O'Toole, and now you owe me, so you have to take me on as a partner.*

No, that wasn't it. All she'd gotten out of that was dinner—on *her* credit card.

Something after that. Later, much later. *In the morning, you will take me with you, right? Promise?*

And she could swear he said yes. She had this fuzzy, half-baked recollection of telling him that they were in it together, and that he shouldn't worry, because...

Clunk. It came back in one fell swoop. "Because I would make sure he wasn't out on the street, that Fat Mike wouldn't lay a hand on him, that Slab would show up for court on Monday, and that he could pay Jozette back every dime he owed her."

Emily sat up straight in the bathtub, sloshing water onto the floor. "Did I really say all that? Oh, my God. I did. I even mentioned the Rainbow Rest-O-Rant. He knows." She sank deeper into the water, trying to drown her humiliation. "He knows I followed him from Chicago. He thinks I'm a stalker again."

She had to find him. She had to explain. Reaching for the towel, she made rapid plans to track him down and make him listen to reason. But she stopped in mid-plan.

"Hey, wait a minute. If he thinks I'm a stalker, why did he sleep next to me like my guardian angel all night?"

That didn't make any sense at all. But then, Tyler seemed to be operating a few peas short of a pod, anyway. He was a guy, which made the workings of his mind mysterious enough. On top of that, he had some strange profession that he refused to talk about, but it involved hookers and strippers and hoodlums. He had very loyal friends like Jozette the waitress and Kate the innkeeper who fed him and let him stay over. He had a fondness for underdogs. And he didn't have any money whatsoever.

Except for being uncommonly good-looking, he didn't add up to anything she could make heads or tails of.

Emily took her time finishing her bath, using all the little bottles and soaps so kindly laid out as part of the hospitality at Beau's B and B. But by the time she was clean and brushed and ready to go, she still hadn't really come up with her next move.

And then it hit her.

The Flesh Pit. No matter what he thought of her, whether he'd decided she was a nut or an annoyance or a babe in the woods who needed to be protected, sooner or later, he would be back at The Flesh Pit.

"I've read enough mysteries in my time," she said out loud, "to know that the sleuth always goes back to the place where he last saw his target."

Slab was his target. Slab had been lying on the floor at Shanda's apartment above The Flesh Pit the last time they saw him. And Tyler would be heading back there for clues as soon as he got his head together and got back on course.

"Oh, yeah. I'm right!" Emily shook a fist in the air. "I am *so* right!"

And this time she wasn't going to stand out like any sore thumb at the strip joint, either. This time she had the proper—or improper—wardrobe, baby.

Quickly Emily found the shopping bag that held her purchases from last night. The new underwear was going to come in handy, plus she sifted through the other items she'd bought from the lady in the alley. Perfect.

All that was left in the bag was…a big honker of a

knife. "I forgot all about that," she said, sinking to her knees, dangling the thing from her fingertips. What was she going to do with Mack's knife?

Where she was going, venturing back into the lion's den, aka The Flesh Pit, a weapon might actually come in handy. But where could she hide it on her person so she could take it with her? And if she did hide it, could she get arrested for being in possession of a concealed weapon?

With a certain amount of distaste, she wrapped it in a washcloth and stuck it down in the bottom of her purse. And then she was on to happier tasks—like dressing up in her new clothes.

Finally, decked out in a tie-dyed halter top, a denim miniskirt embroidered with flowers, and the cutest pair of monkey-and-palm-tree wedgie sandals in the Bay Area, she was ready.

It might not be Mata Hari. Not even Wonder Woman.

But Emily Chaplin was ready for anything.

7

EMILY HAD HER HAND on the doorknob, ready to step out of Beau's B and B, when she got caught.

"Emily? Good heavens, is that you?"

She turned back to see Kate emerging from the kitchen, balancing a tray with someone else's breakfast. Dressed as uniquely as ever, Kate wore a silky white poet's shirt with billowy sleeves, a pair of sapphire blue leggings, and a deeply fringed purple vest.

"Yes, it's me." Self-conscious, Emily held her arm and the shoulder strap of her purse in front of the neon swirls on her halter top. "My baggage never arrived, so I bought some more things last night. Different things. Different from the khakis-and-white-shirt look, I mean. What do you think?"

"I think you look like someone else." Kate's gaze swept up and down her. "Someone with a very creative fashion sense."

Translated, that statement probably meant Emily looked like a goon. Well, she wasn't dressed any more weirdly than Kate, Emily thought defiantly. Okay, so maybe she was showing more skin. But her outfit was no more bizarre or eccentric than three-quarters of the inhabitants of North Beach.

"I was in the mood to change my look."

Kate raised an eyebrow. "I can see that. Where did you find that outfit, anyway?"

"There was this woman with a table in an alley..."

Now she was undoubtedly going to get lectured about the folly of buying from con artists or thieves or something. She was so tired of everyone telling her what to do, when, and with whom. She was an adult, and if she wanted to do business with people who had studs in their lips and noses and hung out in alleys, she could darn well do it.

"Oh," Kate said, breaking into a smile. "I know her. She does beautiful work. You should see what she can do with silk. I bought a hand-painted scarf from her a few months ago that was to die for."

Emily blinked. No lecture? "So you don't think it was a stupid thing to do?"

"Why would I think that?" Kate shrugged. "She only comes to North Beach a few times a month. You got lucky running into her."

"That's me—lucky." Emily straightened her shoulders. She *was* feeling lucky—and confident and full of energy and enthusiasm. She felt like a whole different person, the kind of woman who could carry off monkey-and-palm-tree sandals and take no prisoners while she was at it. Ever since she'd undertaken this very strange mission, she'd felt so alive, so focused. Speaking of which...

"Kate, you wouldn't happen to know where Tyler is, would you?"

"Tyler?" She shook her head. "Haven't seen him

this morning.'' Her eyes sparkled with matchmaking fervor. ''You two seem to be hitting it off, though.''

Emily said dryly, ''Hitting it off? I don't think that exactly captures our relationship.''

Kate's lips curved into a mischievous smile. ''I don't know. You're awfully cute together. And after seeing the two of you all wrapped up and cozy on the bed in The Wild One, I'd say you have something going for you. Chemistry, if nothing else.''

''Chemistry?'' Emily repeated in surprise. ''Really? You think Tyler and I have chemistry?''

''Don't you think so?''

''Well, yes. I mean, Tyler could have chemistry with a mailbox.'' She sighed. That boy had chemistry to burn. ''But I thought you thought I was the totally wrong person for him.''

Her smile widened. ''I'm not above a little reverse psychology, now and again.''

Emily crinkled her forehead with confusion. ''Do you mean reverse psychology because you told me we weren't a good match but you really thought we were? Or because you're telling me now we have chemistry when you really think we don't?''

''Emily, sometimes you think too much.''

''Yes, I know, but—''

''Sorry, gotta go,'' Kate interrupted, heading for the stairs. ''This tray's getting heavy. And I want to deliver this breakfast while it's still warm.''

''Yes, I know, but—''

''See ya!''

Emily was left to ponder the possibilities of reverse

psychology all on her own. It didn't get her anywhere. All she could think of was how odd it was that Kate thought that she and Tyler were cute together. She and Tyler. *Together.*

Now there was a picture. Not just together for five minutes, tangled around each other without any clothes, the way they were in her fertile, fervid imagination. Not just together for a weekend while they teamed up like Dick Tracy and Tess Trueheart to foil the bad guys. But together for…forever.

"I am not thinking this," she said slowly. "I am not."

But she couldn't help it. This was all so new, this deciding whether she and someone else made a good couple. A couple? She shuddered. She'd never even been that good as a single. So how could she contemplate doubling the confusion and stumbling into couplehood, especially with someone as complicated as Tyler?

"I didn't start this to find a guy," she whispered. "I swear I didn't."

And she certainly never would have gone looking for someone like Tyler. Not the least eligible, he was secretive, moody and undomesticated.

He was also gorgeous, sexy as hell, smart as a whip, funny, loyal, and his fondness for underdogs evidenced a warm, kind heart.

Now that she'd found him, could she honestly let him go?

THE FLESH PIT WAS HOPPING.

As she approached, Emily saw no sign of Tyler, but

there wasn't much opportunity to look. The first-floor tattoo parlor was jammed with people, so crowded that would-be customers had spilled outside, and now they were pushing and shoving to get back in. She thought she caught sight of a black pinstripe in the melee, giving her a momentary flicker of anxiety. But it must've been something else, because she couldn't find it again and didn't see the man they'd dubbed Mack, either.

"Back up!" shouted a heavily illustrated man who elbowed his way out to the sidewalk. "Everybody will get in sooner or later. Make a line." And then he started to unceremoniously herd people into some semblance of order.

Emily got squashed in behind a pretty teenaged girl wearing a pile of makeup, from wavy, sunset-colored eyeshadow to deepest mulberry lipstick. Or maybe those were tattoos.

"What's going on?" Emily asked her.

"Guest artist," the girl mumbled, straining to get a look over the top of the line. "He is, like, a total master. He does things with indigo and henna that you wouldn't even believe. Today only."

"But I just want to get upstairs, to the strip joint. Can I sneak past the line?"

At the very mention of such a thing, the crowd seemed to growl and turn on her.

"No cuts!" a tough-looking kid yelled around the metal bar poking through his lip.

"Wait in line like everybody else!" someone else chimed in.

"But I just want to go—"

"I don't think they believe you," her line buddy confided, flapping her glowing orange eyelids. "No offense, but you don't look like the strip-joint type."

How disappointing. She'd done her best. Meanwhile, they all thought she didn't look like the strip-joint type, but she *did* look like the tattoo-parlor type? That was a pretty subtle distinction in her opinion.

"Besides," the girl continued, "I think the Pit, you know, the upstairs part, is, like, closed, so how could you really be going there? That's why they think, like, you know, you're just scamming for a way to cut in line."

Emily's head was spinning with all the "likes" and "you knows." She tried to pick out words she recognized. "You're saying the strip joint is closed? But it was open last night."

"Uh-huh. But Shanda, who owns it, is, like, out. You know, gone." She nodded sagely. "I heard they had that yellow stuff, you know, like tape, all blocking off the Pit upstairs and everything."

"Police tape?" Emily asked slowly.

"Yeah, like that. Totally closed off, you know. Totally no entrance." She lifted pencil-thin eyebrows. "Scary, huh?"

"Yeah, scary." Emily began to have a terrible feeling about this. She remembered Mack the Knife, bonked over the head with the very shoe she was wearing, crumpling to the floor. Injured? Dead? Under her breath, she whispered, "Oh, no. What if I killed him?"

Tyler had sworn that the mean little man was

breathing and coming after them. But what if he was wrong?

"Don't panic," she ordered herself. "You're not thinking straight."

"Did you say, like, something?"

Emily found a wan smile. "Um, no. I was just wondering whether you knew why there was crime-scene tape all around upstairs. What crime was it? And was it upstairs, upstairs? Or just the second floor?"

"I dunno." Waving a hand patterned with rust-red dots and lines, the girl called out to a guy a few people ahead of her. "Guppy, do you know what, like, happened at the Pit upstairs? Somebody OD or get busted or what?"

"Busted, man." He shook his head sadly. "Shanda and her boyfriend. Busted."

Hearing nothing about murder, Emily relaxed a little.

Busted meant arrested. She chewed on her lip, considering. Shanda and her boyfriend. Had Shanda and Slab been carted off to the pokey last night when all the police were here? Or maybe Shanda and the man with the knife? Did that mean everyone was alive and accounted for, just in jail?

And where was Tyler? If not at The Flesh Pit, then where?

"Here's the list of what the artist is doing today." Wearily the tattoo-parlor owner strolled down the line, handing out hastily photocopied sheets with designs on them. "Decide ahead what you want."

Emily pretended to scan the sheet, but she was deep in her own thoughts. Finding Tyler at The Flesh Pit had been her only inspiration. Otherwise, she'd just have to walk all the way back to Beau's B and B and wait for him. It was a long walk, especially with all the ups and downs around here. Especially in wooden platform sandals. And what if he never came back?

"Excuse me," she asked the girl with the hennaed hands, "you didn't happen to see a guy hanging around here, also interested in getting upstairs, did you? A really good-looking guy, tall, great shoulders, partial to a leather jacket, dark hair, green eyes, probably wearing jeans and a T-shirt. A *really* good-looking guy."

"You mean *him?*"

"Who?"

"Him." She inclined one rust-painted thumb over her shoulder. "The babe coming out the front door."

Emily whirled. Oh, goodness. It *was* him! And he was headed straight for her.

Her first thought was that her deductions had been right on the money and he *had* come to The Flesh Pit and she deserved a gold star. "Good for me."

But then he stopped. His jaw dropped.

Her second thought was that he was really mad at her for some reason and maybe she should've thought this through.

"Emily?" he demanded. "Why in the world are you dressed like that?"

Now everyone in line was staring at her.

She had to think of something. "Maybe I like it," she ventured.

"You like it?" He started moving again, cutting through the crowd, setting one fist in the small of her back and resolutely steering her out of line. He looked furious.

Yeah, right, we have chemistry and make a cute couple, like lightning and a rod make a cute couple.

He glared at her. "That outfit is so not you, Pollyanna. So let's start over. Why are you dressed like that? Is this some tactic? Are you on the prowl?"

"On the prowl?" She kind of liked the sound of that. "Actually, I just wanted to fit in."

"Fit in? Fit *in?*" Tyler narrowed his eyes. "Trust me, Emily. In that outfit, you definitely stand out."

She really liked the sound of that. Especially when his eyes couldn't seem to tear themselves away and his gaze left a little trail of heat and fire every place it touched. "I stand out? You think so?"

"Oh, Lord, she's taking it as a compliment." Muttering under his breath, he started to walk away.

"Wait! Where are you going? Did you see Slab or Shanda? Do you have any leads?"

She hustled her wooden wedgies to catch up, but he just kept marching down the sidewalk.

"Tyler, listen to me. We need to talk."

"I don't think so."

"I do." As he waited for traffic to clear enough to cross the street, she maneuvered herself in front of him. "Okay, listen. I know that I let it slip that I overheard you in Chicago, when you and Slab were at the restaurant, and that I tailed you all the way here. I remember that I, uh, mumbled something about that as I went to sleep last night."

He paused. "And?"

"And I'm sorry."

"That's it? That's all you have to say?"

She rolled her eyes. He wasn't going to make this easy, was he? "Tyler, I'm sorry I lied. But I'm sure you can understand that I didn't want you to think I had totally lost my mind." Weaving through cars stopped at the light, she scrambled to keep up. "I mean, I am fully aware that it's bad enough to attach yourself to a total stranger who's in the same B and B you're in, but to glom on to someone in the next booth at a coffee shop in Chicago and jump on a plane to San Francisco...well, that might sound a little abnormal."

"*Might* sound a little abnormal? How about completely, out-of-your-mind, around-the-bend deranged?"

"But it was fate. Kismet! I didn't have a choice."

"You're starting that fate and kismet crap again?" Turning to face her, he raked an impatient hand through his hair. "Do you really expect me to believe that you accidentally came into the Rainbow at the same time I was there, just happened to be there, just happened to overhear, and you followed me all the way out here?"

She mulled that over. "Well, yes. Because that's what happened."

"Emily," he said slowly, darkly, "if you are any kind of investigator or agent for any kind of law enforcement body, now is the time to tell me."

"What?" She stepped back, almost falling off the curb and into the path of a little red convertible, but he caught her in time. "Me?" She began to laugh. "That's what you thought?"

"Who else would do what you did?"

Who else, indeed? How could she say *I promise I'm just crazy, not a secret agent?*

"Tyler, I swear," she began. She raised her right hand just the way she'd done the day she was admitted to the Illinois bar. "I swear that I am a plain old tax lawyer. My name is Emily Chaplin. I am an associate at Chaplin, Chaplin & Chaplin. My mother is a bankruptcy judge. My four older brothers are all lawyers at Chaplin, Chaplin & Chaplin, and my father is the senior partner. You can check all of this out. We are the most boring family on the face of the earth, and there is not one investigator or agent among us because that would be far too interesting."

"God help me," he grumbled, "I think I believe you."

"Well, of course you believe me." Emily sent him her sunniest smile. "Why else would you have bunked in with me last night?"

He set his jaw into such a fierce line she feared for the safety of his teeth. "Bunked? Is that what you're calling that little exercise in sadomasochism? Bunked?"

"Well, okay, if you insist," she said kindly, not exactly sure why this was such a hot button. "I will rephrase. Why else would you have slept with me last night?"

"That was not sleeping," he growled.

"It certainly was."

"Oh, no," he returned, "it wasn't. I didn't sleep at all."

She started to say, *No wonder you're so grouchy— you're sleep deprived,* but she bit her tongue. "If you weren't sleeping, then who was that curled up behind me like a kitten this morning when I woke up? You were sleeping. You might as well admit it."

"Oh, Lord, this is why I hate lawyers."

"See? We have something else in common. I don't like them, either." But Emily decided to take a different tack. "Look, the point is, you slept in my bed even after you knew I had followed you from Chicago. Why? Because you believed me, and you agreed that you and I and this mission—it's all kismet. Well, that and the fact that you were trying to protect me from Mack and Sluggo—although I still think he looks more like a Brutus." As he began to walk out into the street, she went on, "Not that I needed to be protected, mind you. Everyone always thinks that about me, and it is simply not true. I can protect myself."

"Uh-huh." He gave her a cynical smile. "Which is why you're standing in the middle of the street."

Emily glanced around. "Why are we standing in the middle of the street?"

"Because we're waiting for the cable car. I can't afford a cab."

"I can." But the cable car screeched to a stop, clanging its bell, and she had to hop on if she wanted to stick with him. Besides, she discovered she was expected to pay their fares. "Where are we going, anyway?"

"Fisherman's Wharf."

"Really?" She settled in beside him on the wooden seat, enjoying the quintessential San Francisco moment of riding on a cable car. "But isn't this a strange time for sight-seeing? Shouldn't we be looking for Slab and Shanda? I mean, it's already halfway through Saturday, and you have to have him back in Chicago by Monday morning."

"I'm aware of that, although I wasn't aware you were."

"It's not my fault if you and Slab were talking so loud." She brightened. "Although now you have me as a witness that you weren't conspiring to help him flee the jurisdiction. I mean, I distinctly overheard you trying to convince him to stay. So at least that's one offense they can't charge you with." She smiled. "See? I can be useful to have around. I can testify on your behalf. Pretty useful."

Tyler lifted one dark eyebrow but said nothing.

"Do you want to tell me the rest? I've formed a pretty good idea of what's going on, but not exactly," she tried, figuring she might as well keep going as long as she was making headway. "What was all that about Slab having a stash and Fat Mike and the Feds being on your tail?"

"Emily, I am not talking about this with you. You want to tag along and pay for things, fine." He glowered at her. "But don't think I'm letting you get any more involved than that. For one thing, it's dangerous. You saw Sluggo. You saw Mack and his knife. Do you think they care if you're Emily Chaplin of Chaplin, Chaplin & Chaplin?"

"I can pro—"

"No, you can't."

"Tyler, I don't want to fight with you." The cable car dinged again, and he rose to leave, so she did, too. She felt they were just getting to the crux of the matter, and she had no intention of giving up. "We can make this work if you would just stop trying to be so grumpy."

"Make what work?"

"This. Us." Distracted, she looked around for the first time. Fisherman's Wharf. It was so cool. Amid the crush of tourists and souvenir shops, she could smell sea air, hear the cry of gulls above her head. She wished she had time to act like a tourist herself for a few minutes. But Tyler was already marching away from her down the pier.

Once again, she had to play catch-up.

"Will you please stop and talk to me? Or at least tell me where we're going?"

He stopped. He turned. "Emily, there is no *this* and no *us*. I don't know what you think happened last night. But nothing happened. I kept my pants on and my hands off and nothing happened."

She gazed up into his sweet green eyes, just the color of the leaves on the apple tree growing under her bedroom window when she was a child. "I know that," she said finally, placing her hands gently on the sleeves of his jacket, holding him still for a moment.

"So what is this all about?"

"A lot more than sex." That should have been obvious to him, but she guessed she had to fill in the blanks. She fingered the narrow gash in his sleeve, not sure how to say what she wanted to say. "Actually, the fact that we didn't have sex last night is part of what convinces me that I'm right. You cared enough about me not to."

He glanced away. "That's not why I didn't…make a move."

"Tyler," she whispered, "I really like you—as a body, yes, but as a person, too. I feel a connection to you. And even if you won't admit it, I know you feel the same way."

"Emily, I—"

"No, don't wreck it by saying guy stuff about me misunderstanding or this not being what I think it is or whatever you're planning to say to brush me off." She lifted her chin. "I know what I know."

He sighed, tipping his head down so that it rested on hers, raising his hands to frame her face. "You don't know anything. But I'm going to give it to you straight. Your mother is a judge and your father is a senior partner at some fancy law firm and you and I live in different worlds. Do you think I like it that I can't even pay your fare on a cable car?"

"Oh, Tyler, that is so silly," she countered. "I have plenty. You wouldn't even believe how much—my grandmother left me this obscene trust fund because I'm the only girl in the family. I didn't earn it—why should it matter to me?"

"An obscene trust fund?" he repeated. "It's even worse than I thought."

"You just don't get it, do you? Do you know how many men I know with money? A ton. And I don't want to sleep with any of them. And don't," she warned, "start that stuff about Pollyanna taking a walk on the wild side. That is so not true, and insulting, too."

"Yeah, well, I can't see what else you see in me."

She searched his features for a clue. "You're joking, right? You're poor, so you have nothing to offer? What is this, 1912?"

"Emily, it isn't just the money." He broke away, dropping his hands from her. "This isn't a good time for me. My life is a mess. I can't do this."

She bit her lip. "You know, you're right. Your life is a mess and this isn't the best time to be throwing extra complications at you."

"Good. You agree."

"Uh-huh." She took his hand and started to tug him down the pier in the direction they had been traveling. "Which is why you want us to go wherever it was you were heading, follow whatever clue it was you found at The Flesh Pit, and run Slab or Shanda or the money to ground."

"That is actually not a bad idea." He shook his head. "I can't believe I just said that."

"You'll get used to it," she said cheerfully. "Here's the plan. We'll do exactly what it was both of us originally intended, which is to locate this mythical stash of money and get Slab back to Chicago with it. And once we're there, with your problems neatly solved, when you see how well you fit into my life, you can stop moaning about different worlds and all that nonsense." She paused. "So what clue did you find? Where are we headed?"

"How did you know I found a clue?"

"Like, duh. Why else would you be taking cable cars and hiking down piers?" She waited impatiently. "I suppose you could be planning to toss yourself into the bay because you're so bummed about our doomed love affair, but I don't think so."

He actually cracked a smile at that one.

"Come on, 'fess up. Did you talk to Slab? Or Shanda? Did one of them tell you something?"

"Neither of them was there," he said coolly, jamming a hand into one jacket pocket and leaving it there. "There was police tape all over the place—I'm guessing from last night's 'domestic disturbance'—but the door was still bashed in, so I just ducked under the tape and looked around."

"And you saw something? What did you see?" she prompted.

"This." He pulled his hand out of his pocket, revealing a small photograph. "It was on the table near the door. Shanda had framed pictures of herself with baseball players, politicians, even one with Clint Eastwood. But also this. I took it out of the frame."

Eagerly Emily scrutinized the photo. But all she saw was Slab, looking very broad in a Hawaiian print shirt, grinning behind Shanda, who was squished into teeny white shorts and a tank top, both of which emphasized her unnatural curves. They were posed against the side of an ordinary-looking boat—what she thought might be called a cabin cruiser—docked at a pier.

"Okay," she concluded, "so it's a picture of Slab and Shanda with a boat. So what?"

"Look at the name of the boat."

"Sweet Shanda," she read. "That's very nice. Somebody—presumably Slab—liked her well enough to name a boat after her. Although why, I couldn't tell you. She seemed like a real snot to me."

Tyler's gaze measured her. "Do you remember exactly what Slab said to me in Chicago, about where he left the money?"

"Hmm..." Emily happened to have an excellent memory for details. She cast her mind back to the Rainbow Rest-O-Rant. "He said he'd left the money with his dear, darling Shanda and that he was going back to get it and he would take her apart with his bare hands if he had to."

"Wrong." Tyler smiled. "He said he left the money with *sweet* Shanda, and he would take her apart with his bare hands if he had to. Sweet Shanda. Not Shanda the girlfriend, but *Sweet Shanda* the boat."

"It's a boat? He hid the money on a boat?" Emily turned to Tyler for confirmation.

"I think that's exactly what he did."

"Then what are we waiting for? It shows the pier number right there, over Slab's ear. Come on!"

"Hold on a sec," Tyler interceded. "If it were still at that pier, Slab would've already found it. When I was there, he was grilling Shanda about stuff he'd left behind, and she told him she'd thrown out or sold everything of his. But I think she just moved the boat. Look on the back.''

"There's a number.'' Emily glanced up quickly. "But that doesn't mean that it's a pier number. It's low enough that it could be anything from her IQ to what she charges for a lap dance.''

Caught off guard, Tyler laughed at the zinger. "Why, Emily, you're not as kind as you look.''

"I try.''

"Anyway, it's worth a look to see if that's where *Sweet Shanda* is docked, don't you think, partner?''

"Well, then,'' Emily said with a smile, liking the sound of that partner thing, "I guess we're going boating.''

8

EMILY BLINKED. There it was, bobbing gently in the water, floating right in front of her. It looked bigger in person than it had in the picture. Or maybe on film it had just been dwarfed by the enormous Slab standing in front of it.

But it was definitely the same boat. And it still had *Sweet Shanda* painted in a swirly script on the hull. The rest of the paint was peeling and the boat seemed to have faded into genteel disrepair, but the words *Sweet Shanda* looked practically new.

"The one thing she's kept in good shape is her name," Emily commented. "Why am I not surprised?"

But Tyler was ahead of her. Carrying his jacket over one shoulder, he was already on board, poking around into the life preserver bin, examining corners and crevices for any likely treasure trove. When he moved to try to jimmy open the door to the lower level, he turned back. "Are you coming?"

"Well, okay." But Emily hesitated. She didn't have a whole lot of experience with boats.

"Just get on, will you?"

"I'm coming. Where you lead, I follow," she said lightly.

Tyler had the door open by the time she gingerly picked her way across the deck in her wedgies, and she followed him down the steps to what she would have called the cabin area. It was mostly just an open room, full of accents and gewgaws, done up in knotty pine, fake thatching and coils of rope, à la Gilligan's Island. There was a funny little kitchenette and counter built into one corner, a big bed draped in a ghastly red velvet spread on the opposite side, a tiny standing-room-only bathroom, and a couple of cabinets and closets. Not exactly a posh yacht from a James Bond movie.

Besides, there was a musty, neglected feeling to this place, as if no one had taken *Sweet Shanda* out for a ride in a good, long while. "Poor Slab," Emily murmured. "He said this was the best time he ever had. And now look at it."

Tossing his leather jacket onto the counter, Tyler immediately opened the kitchen cabinets and drawers, even going so far as to jab at the garbage disposal.

Emily sat on the edge of the bed, but jumped back up and dropped her purse when it undulated underneath her. "Waterbed," she exclaimed. "Didn't expect that."

Tyler didn't respond; he was busy pulling cleaning supplies out from under the sink.

"You really think he would hide bundles of money somewhere obvious like under the sink?" she inquired.

"This is Slab we're talking about. There's no telling where he would put anything."

"Okay, well, maybe." Considering, Emily chewed her lip and scanned the ceiling and the walls as Tyler moved on to the closets. He tossed some blankets and pillows out onto the floor, but didn't seem to find anything of interest in there.

She didn't really know what she was looking for. Some panel or board that looked different? There was always a mysterious hidey-hole or a secret passage in the books, and if you turned the right andiron or pressed the right bookend, voilà!

In the absence of andirons and bookends, she felt her sleuthing possibilities were dramatically reduced.

"Maybe if I had a crowbar," she said out loud.

"Crowbar?" But Tyler was gazing at the ceiling. "Uh-oh."

"Uh-oh?"

But his expression said it all. With a sinking feeling, Emily realized she heard it, too. Footsteps. Heavy footsteps. Up on deck. She gulped. They had company.

She could see that she and Tyler were thinking along the same lines. No way to jump overboard from a cabin with no windows and only one door. No way to make a stand or prepare an ambush when they had no weapons and the heavy footsteps likely did.

Before she had a chance to say a word, Tyler grabbed her and shoved her into the closet, up against a life preserver.

"Don't you think this is the first place they'll look?" she whispered, clutching his shirt so she could pull him in with her.

But he backed in far enough to scoop up some blankets and a pillow, and he wedged them between him and the door before he slowly, quietly, slid it shut. Emily got the idea. Camouflage. If anyone opened the door, they would see extra bedding, not people. Of course, all they had to do was move the protective cover, and she and Tyler would be dead ducks.

Better not to think about that.

Right now, she concentrated on trying not to breathe or make a sound. There wasn't enough room in the minuscule compartment to stand up, plus she had the hard edge of a life preserver stuck in her back. So they crouched uncomfortably, forced to find a way to fit various body parts into the same cramped space, doing their best not to touch anything too intimate.

Tyler's arms crept around her. He eased her over into his lap, a centimeter at a time, so that he could balance them both more steadily and not risk anyone getting clumsy and creating any thumps or scuffling noises. She understood that. But this way, she and her miniskirt were sort of half riding his knee, with his hands sliding over her bare back and his mouth an inch from her neck. She could feel his hot breath puff against her collarbone. And it tickled.

Oh, dear.

It was very stuffy in here. Very close. Very hot.

She began to see stars in the periphery of her vision. She told herself it was because she wasn't getting enough oxygen. But she knew better.

It was because Tyler's hands grazed her waist, her back, her leg. Because she could feel his warm, muscled chest and the steady jump of his heartbeat through the thick cotton of his T-shirt. Because she couldn't stop herself from closing her eyes and hanging on tighter and leaning in closer, rubbing her cheek against the top of his head, her mouth against his soft hair.

In this situation, one little halter top and a brief miniskirt weren't nearly enough protection. Too many parts of him were touching too many parts of her, and she didn't know what to do.

What if I faint and fall over and whoever is out there hears it and I give us away? she thought desperately. *What if I don't faint and I have to be conscious for every single second of this torture and whoever is out there never goes away and I'm stuck here forever, with him but not with him, intimate but not intimate enough?*

She wanted to scream.

She didn't. Instead, she stayed where she was, scrunched into the smallest closet she'd ever seen, perspiring, strung out, on the verge of a panic attack, clinging to Tyler for dear life.

Clump. Clump. Clump.

They're coming down the stairs. She read the same thought in Tyler's eyes.

A male voice that sounded familiar jeered, "Guess we beat 'em to it, huh? Clear sailing, huh?"

Sluggo, she mouthed to Tyler. He nodded.

And then another man laughed snidely. Could it be Mack? Were the two thugs in cahoots? "First we gotta find the stash. Then we go sailin'."

It certainly sounded like him. Great. Both bad guys, together and in one place. Double the fun.

"Let's start with the floor, huh?" the first one put in. "You got the crowbar?"

Oh, sure, *they* had a crowbar. Huddled in the closet, she winced when she heard the crack of splintering wood. *Sweet Shanda* wasn't going to be worth much when these guys were done with her.

This was followed by huffing and puffing and a great deal of cursing, some of it in combinations and phrases Emily never knew existed. Wow, they certainly knew how to separate the men from the boys when it came to swear words.

As their labors progressed with more grunts of effort and even more swearing, the men's voices began to rise. "It's got to be there!" hollered the one they had identified as Mack. "Jimmy, what the hell is wrong with you?"

"It ain't my fault, boss," a third voice chimed in. "I pulled out half the floor by now. And it just ain't here."

"Could be in the wall," Sluggo announced. "Maybe like a safe or somethin'. You want we should start smashin' in the walls?"

"What's the matter with you? There ain't no safe here."

His words were followed by an audible slap. Now she was sure—that had to be Mack the Knife. The snarly, ill-tempered attitude fit him to a tee.

"You half-wits got taken for a ride," he bellowed. "Again! You said you followed O'Toole and his girl-friend here. So where did they go? Why ain't they here?"

Emily got a queasy feeling in the pit of her stomach. *We were followed?*

Outside, Mack continued his tirade. "Why do you suppose they ain't here and we are? 'Cause they led us here for nothing, while they're probably rolling in our dough at the real stash right now."

No, we aren't that smart, Emily thought. *We were too busy worrying about our love lives to notice that we were being tailed.*

"This boat thing was just a...what do you call that? Like a...what the hell do you call that?"

Red herring? Emily supplied inside the closet. *Ruse? Misdirection?* But she had no compunctions about letting them suffer without her vocabulary help.

"They played us for saps," Mack said finally. "Again."

Sluggo began to mutter dire threats, kicking something as he did. "I oughta've strangled that broad when I had the chance."

Emily swallowed.

"All right already." It was Mack again. "Let's be sure about this. We didn't look under the bed. Move the damn bed. It would be just like Slab to hide his stash under the bed so he'd know it was there every time he made it with what's-her-name."

"Shanda," the one they'd called Jimmy responded helpfully. "I'd like to make it with her. Don't run across girls who own their own strip joints very often. Made in the shade, I'll tell you."

"Yeah, yeah. Just move the damn bed, will you?"

"Uh, boss?"

"Yeah, yeah. What?"

"The bed—it's a water bed. It don't move."

"Yeah, well, stomp around on top of it, then. Just in case the loot's inside it."

Somebody guffawed as somebody else followed the order. There was the odd sound of a large body sloshing itself against rippling water, again and again.

"Go, Jimmy!" Sluggo began to wheeze with laughter. "Body surf that bed, baby!"

Oh, great. Now they were playing games while they trashed the place.

Meanwhile, Emily's leg was going to sleep. Yet if she moved it even a fraction, she would be rubbing it up and down Tyler's thigh.

So why not rub it up and down Tyler's thigh for real? Why not tune out the nonsense on the other side of their cozy little closet and do what she really wanted to do?

This was a nightmare. How much longer could she bear listening to those stooges and their idiotic conversation, all the while yearning for Tyler, breathing with him, melting into him? She suddenly had a mental image of him as a burger sizzling on a grill, and she was nothing but a big hunk of cheese.

"Hey, boss, what's this?" The water-bed surfing noises broke off, and Jimmy's voice rose, sounding utterly mystified. "It's a purse, boss. Right here by the bed. Whose you think it is? It's got a funny clasp, though. I never could do this girly stuff. Do you want me to bust it open, boss?"

If her entire body hadn't already been on red alert

inside the closet, Emily would have cried. Her purse. She'd left it by the bed. *How stupid are you, Emily?*

"And there's a jacket over there on the counter, too!" Sluggo yelled.

Okay, so she wasn't the only one. Was it a good thing that Tyler had also blown it? Or did it really matter whose fault it was, now that discovery was imminent? She hugged his head, bracing herself.

"Whose ya think this stuff is, huh?" asked Sluggo, as obtuse and thickheaded as ever.

"Whose do you think? It's that damn O'Toole's," Mack growled. "See the slash in the sleeve? That's where I cut him. And the purse has gotta be the girl's. Leave it alone, Jimmy. We don't need it open. We know whose it is."

"So where are they?"

"Here somewhere. Check the john. No?" There was a pause, and Emily could only imagine three pairs of beady eyes surveying the cabin, looking for any hole big enough for two bodies to crawl into. "I think I got it."

Clomp. Clomp. Clomp.

The foorsteps grew louder, nearer. The closet door was yanked open with one lurching jerk, and a pillow and three blankets fell to the floor.

"Lookee what we got here," the man they'd called Mack the Knife said with an oily smirk. He looked exactly the same as Emily remembered him—before she hit him over the head with the shoe, of course. Oh, and this time he was holding a gun. That was a new wrinkle. "So, kids, you want to come out and play?"

"Not really," Emily tried. But it was way too late for that.

Delicately she stood up as she stepped forward, carefully disentangling herself. But Tyler emerged right behind her, draping an arm protectively around her.

Mack backed up, waving them out of the closet and into the center of the room, near a gaping hole in the floor. Sluggo stood there, over the chasm, leaning on what appeared to be a sledgehammer. The third man, Jimmy, held the crowbar. She thought she recognized him, too, as the person who had been pummeling Slab last night.

"Now ain't that cute?" Mack announced in a smug tone. "Don't they make a cute couple?"

Cute couple. She hoped she never heard that again as long as she lived.

"Bet you kids was havin' fun in there, huh?" Sluggo's grin made him look even less intelligent, if that was possible. He chuckled, trying to sound sleazy and ripe with innuendo. He succeeded.

Emily felt as if she needed a shower just getting a hint of what was on Sluggo's dirty mind. She would have lifted her chin and stood tall, but it was tough when she was wearing so little clothing. She tugged down on the hem of her miniskirt.

Mack circled around behind her, looking her up and down. Things just kept getting grimmer by the minute. "So, you was letting us do all the dirty work? And then you two was gonna waltz out and take whatever we found, am I right?"

"Uh, no. We got here first, but we weren't, uh, packing heat,'' Emily responded politely. Tyler elbowed her when she said ''packing heat,'' but heavens, it was in all the books. What was she supposed to call it? ''Anyway, we were unarmed, so we decided discretion was the better part of valor.''

Sluggo wrinkled his ugly brow. ''Huh?''

She tried again. ''We decided we'd wait until you left.''

''Why didn't you say that the first time, huh?'' Under his breath, the big brute muttered, ''Shoulda strangled that broad when I had the chance.''

''Yeah, yeah,'' Mack interrupted. ''But here's the real question, boys. What do we do with Romeo and Juliet?''

''Who?''

''These two!'' Mack said impatiently. ''Them. What should we do with them?''

''Maybe throw 'em into the bay, huh?'' Sluggo volunteered.

''Nah. I think I'd like a little chat with 'em first, see whether they got took for a ride like us with this boat crap.'' Mack jiggled his gun at Tyler. ''So, O'Toole, did Slab send you here? He tell you the money was here? Or was this your idea?''

''Oh, this was my brilliant idea.'' Tyler cast a jaded glance at the hole in the floor. ''Guess it didn't work out too well.''

''Yeah, well, we still got some places to look,'' Sluggo said sullenly.

''Maybe we should all go find Slab and ask him,'' Emily suggested. ''He seems to be the only one who really knows. And maybe he's in more of a mood to share now."

Tyler elbowed her again, but she didn't care. It was worth a shot if it would get the Three Stooges and their gun and sledgehammer and their crowbar off the boat and far, far away.

"Nobody's gonna be askin' Slab nothin'," Sluggo muttered. "'Cept the cops. Him and Shanda got busted."

"Busted?" Tyler echoed.

Emily murmured, "Oh, right. The girl at the tattoo parlor told me that."

"You knew? And you didn't tell me?" Tyler's expression was fierce, and Emily was guessing it was not good news to hear that Slab had been arrested. "This changes everything."

"But why?"

"Emily, you're a lawyer, you're supposed to know this stuff!"

"She's a lawyer?" Mack interrupted. "Hey, you ever do any interstate trafficking in stolen goods? I got some charges pending, and I swear, my attorney ain't doing nuthin'."

"I got a couple of extortion raps," Jimmy cut in eagerly. "Maybe you could help me out?"

Everybody waited for Sluggo to join the party.

"Don't look at me," he said after a moment. "I been clean ever since I got out of the joint the last time."

Apparently he wasn't counting yesterday's breaking and entering or today's criminal destruction of property. How convenient.

"So, you think you can help us?" Mack prompted.

"I'm really very sorry, but I'm a tax lawyer." Emily threw up her hands. "I'd help if I could, but all I can do is look at any tax problems you might have."

"Big help," Jimmy muttered. "Okay, I vote we toss her into the bay."

"Let's not be hasty!" she said. "You wouldn't want to add anything really nasty to those legal problems you already have, would you?"

"I can't believe you didn't tell me," Tyler said under his breath.

"I didn't know it was important."

"What kind of lawyer are you?"

"A tax lawyer!" she told him. "What do you want from me?"

"Will you stop the bickering already? Come on, guys, we got work to do, and I'm tired of foolin' with these two. They don't know any more than we do." Mack edged away far enough to pick up a length of rope. "Let's tie them up and throw 'em..."

She held her breath, hoping "in the bay" wasn't going to come next.

But he ended his sentence with "...back in the closet."

"The closet?" Emily cried. "Please don't put us back in there!"

"You'd rather they dump us overboard?" Tyler whispered. "Shut up, will you?"

Mack ignored both of them. "We'll finish up here, see if we can find the money without them drivin' us nuts."

"Can I tie 'em up, boss?" Sluggo asked with obvious enthusiasm.

"Yeah, sure, knock yourself out." Handing his gun over to Sluggo, Mack motioned to Jimmy to pick up his crowbar and follow him up the stairs. But he turned back to offer some final instructions. "Be sure and take her shoes away. Oh, and make it hurt, will you? That crazy dame practically gave me a concussion last night with one of those."

"Can do." Sluggo gestured with the gun. "The shoes," he ordered.

"But I—"

"Emily, lose the shoes," Tyler hissed at her.

Giving in, she bent to undo the straps as Mack resumed his conversation with Jimmy. "I still say the dough's gotta be here somewhere. Slab loved this stupid boat. Soon as I saw it, I thought, yeah, that's where he would've stashed the loot. That Slab, always a romantic. Let's see what we can find, you and me."

The two of them toddled up to the deck, leaving Emily and Tyler to Sluggo's tender mercies. *Great. Just great.* She had no choice—she handed over her darling monkey sandals when she would much rather have bashed Sluggo with them. And Tyler, too, for that matter. *What kind of lawyer are you?* still sort of rankled. Sluggo tossed her shoes down the hole in the floor, and she felt like weeping. Or crawling after them.

"You," Sluggo commanded, giving Tyler a shove, "put your arms around her, with your hands behind her back."

"Behind her...?"

"I always wanted to do this," the creep said with a leer. He tucked the gun into his waistband and then slammed Tyler up next to Emily, front to front.

When he'd said he was going to tie them up, she had envisioned them hog-tied separately, like the hostages in the bank robbery movies. Or maybe like the secret agents, who always seemed to end up plunked down on chairs, facing away, hands together, where they could figure out how to untie themselves.

But this...

"Long as you gotta be tied up and in the closet, you might as well enjoy it, huh?"

"Enjoy it? You've got to be kidding." She felt her face flame as Sluggo the maniac jerked her arms around Tyler's waist, lashing her wrists securely to the back of his jeans, hooking her to his belt, and his belt loop for good measure.

Face-to-face, chest to chest, hip to hip. It was close quarters. And incredibly humiliating.

And now he'd roped and duct-taped Tyler's hands around the back knot of her halter top! This was insane, even for someone like Sluggo. Should she check for video equipment? Was this *Candid Erotic Camera?*

"Couldn't you just tie us up the regular way? You know, get some chairs, back to back?"

Sluggo shook his head. "Your girlfriend's got a big mouth. You want I should gag her before I stick you in the closet?"

"I'm thinking about it." Tyler smiled tightly as Emily kicked him in the ankle. She would have made more of an impression if she'd still had her wooden sandals. "No, I guess not," he said finally.

"It's your funeral."

"That's what I'm trying to avoid," Tyler remarked lightly.

He was taking this awfully well. Emily tipped back her head far enough to send him a suspicious glance. He was probably enjoying it. She narrowed her gaze. Maybe he'd been dreaming about tying her to The Wild One bed just like she'd been dreaming of him, handcuffed and helpless, fastened to that sexy chrome motorcycle footboard.

Okay, so she had wicked fantasies in the privacy of her own mind. But unlike Tyler, she had no desire to act out her fantasies in front of the likes of Sluggo.

Besides, in her fantasy *she* wasn't tied up, he was.

"Come on," the hoodlum said, knocking them sideways so that they had no choice but to shuffle back to that damned minicloset. "I'll bet you can get up to all kinds of trouble in there. Like little bunnies, huh?" His piggy eyes all but disappeared as he surveyed his handiwork. "Always wanted to do that. Look, ma, no hands!"

Very funny.

Emily had the bizarre impulse to stamp her foot and use all those new swear words she'd just learned. This whole thing was infuriating!

"Don't tell me," Tyler said dryly. "You're fit to be tied."

"Fit to be...? This is no times for jokes!"

"Sure it is."

But Sluggo had them wedged back into the closet, and he swung the door closed. "Have fun!" he called, thumping the door behind him.

Fun? Tied up like a sausage, lashed to Tyler as if they were playing some strange bondage sex game, and dumped in a closet?

Emily stopped. She found Tyler's eyes, afraid of what she would see there. But it was too late. They had both come to the same conclusion.

God help her, it actually *was* kind of fun.

9

"WELL," SHE TRIED, "it could be worse."

"Yeah." Shifting a bit, he flexed his hands, testing the bond at the back of her halter. "I suppose they could've thrown us overboard."

"At least we're together," she offered.

No answer. Tyler continued to fiddle with his bonds, but he couldn't get them to budge. While he worked at it, Emily tried not to moan or groan. But she couldn't take much more of this nerve-racking friction, as the fabric in the front tightened and chafed her breasts every time he jiggled the back.

"Maybe you should leave that alone for a minute," she requested, breathless and flushed. "It's a bit, um, uncomfortable."

"Uncomfortable?" He glanced down. "Oh. I see."

That was an understatement. The rubbing had made her nipples stiffen into hard little peaks, pressing through the thin tie-dyed cotton of her top. Plus her modest breasts were being pushed up by the hard wall of his chest. Was it her fault if this configuration worked better to boost her bust than any Wonderbra? All in all, she was making a real spectacle of herself.

A tense silence hung between them.

She felt sure it didn't really last that long in terms of minutes ticking off on the clock. But it certainly felt drawn out and uncomfortable, especially with Tyler pretty much staring right down her cleavage and her afraid to breathe for fear things would spill out even more.

"Aw, the hell with it." His hard, hot mouth swooped down over hers without warning. His lips and his tongue stoked her, filled her, enflamed her, all in that one first rush of heat and desire.

Now she did moan. She couldn't hold it back.

Pressing herself into his kiss, she wanted badly to hold him more fully, to wrap her arms around his broad shoulders. But her hands were stuck down there at the small of his back, roped to his belt. She tugged up on the tangle of cord and leather, feeling no give but willing to try.

"If you keep doing that," he managed to rasp into her ear, "I'll be singing soprano inside this closet in about five minutes."

"Oh." She got it. She relaxed her hold on his pants. "Sorry."

"Oh, God." He broke off, sliding his jaw over her hair. "We can't do this."

"We can't." But she lifted up enough to nip at his chin, hungry for his mouth again.

"There's no way this can work," he whispered darkly. But his lips brushed kisses over her neck, her cheeks, her mouth, just the same.

She tipped her head back, more than willing to take anything he was offering. No way it could work? Her mind refused to process that. Physically, because they were tied up? Or emotionally, because they were in such a mess?

She had no idea, and she didn't want to stop to ask. But he was right about one thing. "We shouldn't be doing this," she murmured, loving the feel of his mouth on her bare shoulder. "They could hear us."

"They can't hear us. They're up on deck. Didn't you catch all the bashing around and swearing?"

"Yes, but..." She hadn't paid any attention. All she'd heard was the rapid, uneven beating of her own heart. "But that could just be two of them. What if Sluggo...? What if he's sitting outside with his ear pressed up against the door, waiting for us to do this?" She shuddered, holding back. "I got the idea this was just what he wanted."

"Okay, okay. You're right." She could see that Tyler was working hard to pull together the shreds of his self-control.

She had the same problem. All she wanted to do was get out of the few clothes she had remaining, drag him out of his, too, and have her wicked way with him. Luckily for her, there was no way to get anyone out of anything at the moment. Undressing was awfully hard with no hands, especially with her hands rather stubbornly attached to the back of his pants.

But that didn't stop her mind from sensory overload. She bit her lip, hard, hoping pain would bring clarity.

Expelling air in a restless rush, Tyler focused on a point over her shoulder, and she could see his lips forming numbers as he counted to ten, then twenty.

Finally he asked, "So, if we can't do what we really want to do, what else would you like to try? Cards? Bingo?"

The wry comment caught her by surprise and she laughed. "Cards?"

A crooked smile lifted the corner of Tyler's narrow lips. "Don't have any on me. You?"

"Sorry."

"Well..." Wincing, he edged back far enough to rest his bottom on a life preserver stuck at the back of the closet, putting him in more of a sitting position where he could balance her on his lap. The only way this was going to work was if she bent over precipitously or just gave in and straddled him. She gave in. "There. That's better," he murmured.

After that maneuver, their relative positions were less strained. Not exactly safe, but comfy.

"We could play a game," she told him, hitching up her knees, bracing her feet against the same life preserver he sat on. "This isn't so different from being stuck in the back seat of your parents' car when you go on vacation, is it?"

His expression was deadpan when he said, "I certainly hope so." But then he shook his head, and his tone lightened. "I can't believe your parents took vacations in a car. Now my family, sure. Loaded up the rusty station wagon and set off for Wisconsin. But the Chaplin family? Jets and yachts only."

She smiled, willing to accept the diversionary tactic. "We drove on lots of trips. It was just a better class of car."

"I can see it now. Baby Emily with all those bratty brothers beating up on her in the back seat of the Caddy. Now if *we* were in a Cadillac, you and me, we'd be a lot more comfortable." Leaning in, he kissed her quick and fast, pulling back before it had a chance to get out of hand. "There are a lot of things you can do in a back seat that a closet just doesn't let you."

There was that thrum of tension between them again. "And I'll bet you've tried every one of them," she whispered.

"Uh-huh." He paused, staring down into her eyes. She knew what he was thinking. *You, me, back seat of a car, any car, as soon as we get out of here.*

She licked her bottom lip, sending back her own telepathic message. *I want it just as much as you do.*

"Okay, you got me," he said finally, very clearly changing the subject. "What's your game? Keep in mind we're not likely to see many license plates in here."

"Duly noted." She pondered, running her mind over every childhood time-waster game she could think of. It wasn't brain surgery, but it was enough to keep her there, on that safe turf, rather than worrying about how they were going to get out of this idiotic predicament or if her bodily impulses ever planned to calm down and behave themselves. "Okay, I've got it. The 'who, which and where' game."

"Never heard of it."

"It's a good one. It's not a game that you win or lose, just an imagination game."

"No wonder you like it."

Ignoring that last gibe, she angled her head so she could look up at him. "For round one, I'll start with an easy question. If you were one of the Seven Dwarfs, which one would you be?"

"Hmm…" He gave it more serious consideration than she would have imagined. "That's a toughie. I'm not sure I know my dwarfs that well."

"Oh, come on. You are so Grumpy."

"Grumpy? Me?" His face was a study in mock outrage. "I don't think so. Meanwhile, who are you?"

"I have an advantage," she admitted. "I'm an expert at this game, so I've already thought of my answers. I *am* Sleepy. I can sleep anywhere, anytime, upside down, on the floor, in a tree, whatever. I know, I know. You probably think Dopey and I are two peas in a pod, but it's just not so. Definitely Sleepy."

"I wasn't going to say Dopey."

She rolled her eyes. "Yes, you were."

"No, I wasn't." Very carefully, he dropped a kiss on the tip of her nose. "No, I was just thinking that, at the moment, you and *I* are much more like peas in a pod than you and Dopey."

Flush up against him, how could she disagree? "You have a point there," she allowed.

He might be too sexy for his own good, and definitely too sexy for hers, but he could be really sweet, too. Who could ever have guessed he would be good company in this impossible situation? Not irritating, not panicking or blaming, just good company. Her heart seemed to constrict a little. *Uh-oh.* Way past mere physical attraction, she was starting to feel, well, smitten, just like Kate had contended all along.

"What are you thinking?" he asked.

"Not telling. Okay, round two." In need of a stronger distraction, she moved to her favorite question. She'd been able to spin stories in the back seat for hours with this one. If this wouldn't get her off the Tyler fixation, nothing would. "If you could live anywhere in the world, where would you live? The Riviera, Tahiti, the moon—it's all up for grabs. But you have to say why."

But Tyler said nothing. Once again, there was a spark of something in his eyes, a warmth and tenderness, even a vulnerability, that she could read like a book.

If I could live anywhere, it would be with you.

She knew that's what he was thinking, just as surely as if he'd said it aloud. It took her breath away.

"You really mean that?" she asked in a soft, unsteady voice.

"I didn't say anything."

"I heard you, anyway."

"Oh, Emily..." With a regretful sigh, he gathered her as close as he could inside their shackled embrace. "What am I going to do with you?"

"Well, that is the million-dollar question, isn't it?

There was no chance for him to make any kind of response. They were interrupted by a particularly nasty outbreak of shouts and curses from above them.

Emily cringed, even as she welcomed the intrusion. "You think they found Slab's treasure trove?"

"Nah. That didn't sound like they were celebrating."

"But what if...?" She hesitated. They were safe in their tiny cupboard for the moment, but what would happen when Sluggo and his pals found what they were looking for? Or didn't find it?

"We'll be fine, Emily."

"I know." Tipping back as far as she could, she found a smile for him. "Maybe you should tell me how this all started, with Slab and all, I mean. I still don't know."

"Story time, huh?" He frowned. "Okay, I suppose. If you really want it. Let's see. How do I start?"

"Once upon a time..."

"Works for me." There was a sardonic light in his eyes, but he began just the same. "Once upon a time there was a very bad man named Fat Mike."

"Uh-huh," she whispered. But she was struck with an ache, a painful cramp, in her back. Stretching, she rolled her shoulders as much as she could to ease her muscles.

As she moved, Tyler's gaze seemed to get stuck on the curve of flesh down the front of her top again. She caught herself. "Fat Mike," she prompted, feeling the cramp ease. "A very bad man named Fat Mike."

"Right. Fat Mike."

"And why is Fat Mike so bad, anyway?" Emily inquired, trying to pull him back to the story. "What did he do?"

Tyler shrugged inside his bonds. "Extortion, protection rackets...but mostly he loans people money. And then he has guys who break their kneecaps if they don't pay him back fast enough." He slid the inside of his arm back and forth against her knee where it brushed him. "And speaking of kneecaps, I would just like to point out that you have some very fine specimens right here."

"Thank you," she said with a knowing smile, hugging him closer with those knees. "But back to Fat Mike..."

"Right. Loans money, breaks kneecaps," he repeated. He shifted restlessly against her. "So Slab has worked for Fat Mike and his organization in a variety of odd jobs over the years. Now, since the Feds are very interested in putting Fat Mike away, they are also very interested in what Slab might be able to tell them."

"Like testifying, you mean?"

"Uh-huh. Only that would be very bad for Slab's health, so he isn't inclined to do it." Tyler pressed his lips into a thin line. "So the Feds have been watching Slab, waiting for him to screw up. Not being the sharpest tool in the shed, he did."

As if it were yesterday—with shock, she realized it *was* yesterday—she remembered the conversation at the Rainbow Rest-O-Rant. "Robbed another bank, did he?"

"So you know that, too." Tyler's voice picked up more of an edge when he confirmed, "Yeah, he robbed another bank and got himself arrested. And Fat Mike put up the bail money, which Slab can't pay back. And which," he added darkly, "is now probably forfeited since he's in jail here in California. I can't imagine they're going to count it as showing up for trial if he's in the middle of getting extradited.''

''Oops.'' Emily tucked her knees under Tyler's arms. ''So Slab can kiss his kneecaps goodbye, huh?''

''Who knows?'' But Tyler's green eyes were cloudy, gloomy. ''Unless he wants to play ball with the Feds, I suppose. Roll on Fat Mike, take witness protection, something like that.''

''See?'' This time it was Emily who reached up to dab a small kiss on his lips. But she lingered longer than she should have, and her brain started to swim. *Back up. Back off.* Yeah, right. Where to? Out loud, she said shakily, ''It's not so bad. But where do you come in?''

''Me?''

''Why did you have to help Slab?'' she tried again. ''Dragging yourself out here to chase him down and bring him back. What's it got to do with you?''

Tyler took his time, and when he responded, his expression was even more oblique. ''Remember Jozette at the coffee shop?''

''The waitress? Sure.''

''She's not just a waitress. She owns the place. And let's just say that she and I go back a long way. I owe her,'' he mumbled.

Emily figured what he owed her was rent. Didn't he live over her restaurant? Didn't he have money troubles? She could add two and two.

''She happens to be Slab's sister,'' he continued. He

glanced away, studying the nearest knot in the pine wall confining them. "I took him on for her sake."

"Oh, Tyler, you and your underdogs." She couldn't help herself—he was just too wonderful and giving and kind.... Tilting up, she brushed her mouth over his, softly at first, but then closing her eyes, pressing harder, making the kiss everything she really wanted to say.

A few little kisses wouldn't hurt anything, would they?

"Emily," he tried to say. "Emily?"

"I know, I know." Frustrated beyond belief, she snapped, "We shouldn't do this. I know!"

"It's not that." He held himself very still. "Do you hear anything?"

"Not really." But she listened as intently as she could. "Maybe...is that waves lapping against the boat?"

Funny, she hadn't noticed the sound of waves before.

Tyler shook his head grimly. "Hell," he swore. "That's waves all right. But no more noise from upstairs. Emily, I don't want to scare you, but I think the boys took a powder. I think they're gone. And we're adrift."

"A-adrift? As in, floating in San Francisco Bay?"

He muttered, "We have to get out of this closet."

"Well, duh!" she exclaimed. "But how? If there was a way out of this closet, I figured you would've made it happen a long time ago."

"I don't know any better way than you do."

"So we're stuck? Floating in San Francisco Bay,

trapped inside a closet on a leaky old boat with holes all over it?'' she cried. Who knew what major crevices and chasms had been smashed in *Sweet Shanda* by now, with Mack and Sluggo and dim-bulb Jimmy going at it with sledgehammers? Those three wouldn't know a hull from a handbasket if it hit them in the face. Who knew whether there was seawater seeping into the boat right now? ''Tyler! Get me out of here!''

''This is no time to panic.''

Who made him arbiter of all that was calm and reasonable? ''I'm not panicking!''

''Hold on.''

''To what? My hands are tied behind your back!''

He swore under his breath, and then he kissed her again. ''Hold on to me as best you can. On the count of three, we're going to throw all our weight against the door. Okay? One, two...'' He paused long enough to press his lips to hers one more time. ''Three!''

Squeezing her eyes closed, Emily turned her head into the safety of his chest and launched the rest of her at the closet door. She heard a crash, she felt the impact, and her whole body vibrated, but the door didn't give.

''One more time. Harder,'' he commanded.

With adrenaline and fear and pent-up emotion pulsing through her veins, Emily put everything she had into this lunge. Tyler's arms felt like steel bands around her, and his hands yanked on the back of her shirt, cutting into her ribs, but she blocked it out. She tensed, he yelled, ''Three!'' and together, they smashed through the barrier.

The next thing she knew they were tumbling helter-skelter out onto the floor of the cabin. As Tyler swung underneath her to bear the brunt of their fall, she heard a huge *rip* and his hands sprang free, taking her entire top with them.

Cool air lashed her naked skin. She gasped.

But she had no time to react before Tyler rolled her into the bottom half of their sensual somersault. On top of her, he impatiently shook the torn strips of fabric from his wrists, fiercely covering her mouth with his, filling his hands with her hair, slashing her harder with his kiss. He slid his fingers over her shoulders, down to her tingling, aching breasts, stroking her to immediate, irresistible passion.

She couldn't breathe, couldn't think. Wasn't this what she'd wanted every single second they were squashed in that closet?

"Yes," she breathed. "Oh, yes…"

At some point in their struggle, her skirt had gotten scrunched up into a thin line at her hips. Now she took advantage of that, angling a bare leg around his jeans, arching up into him. Murmuring her name in a rough, throaty whisper, he slipped a hand underneath her, finding the round mound of her bottom. His hasty, hungry fingers closed on the ribbon-thin strip at the side of her panties, ripping the fragile silk with one swift, insistent yank. He tossed them aside as if they were merely an annoyance, resuming his ruthless assault, touching her so intimately she moaned under him.

But as his mouth slid over the slope of her neck and she tugged him nearer, she was hampered by the bonds at her wrists. And she realized suddenly that she was still tied.

"Tyler, aren't you going to untie me?"

"I'm thinking about it."

If she'd had a free hand, she would have smacked him. But he continued to nip at her, kiss her, move above her, pinning her to the hardwood floor with the relentless pressure of his long, hard body.

She wiggled against him. "I want you," she whispered. "All of you. Let me touch you. Please?"

His lips brushed hers with a tantalizingly fast caress. "Let's do this. All the way." His hands moved to the top of his pants, and she could feel his fingers unbuckling his belt between them, hear the rasp of his zipper slipping down.

All it took was that tiny chink of metal meeting metal. She held her breath, trembling, shockingly turned on by the sounds and sensations rippling over her. She wanted him so much it was like madness, and she couldn't think of anything else but this shimmering, crazy, sublime desire.

"I still can't reach the back," he muttered. "Damn it, Emily, how are we going to get you untied?"

"I don't know, but if we don't do it soon, I'm going to die, right here, right now," she promised. "Isn't there something sharp around here?" Out of nowhere, she remembered Mack's knife. Salvation. "Wait. In my purse. I have a knife."

He reached over her head, snagging her purse where it still lay on the floor near the bed. His T-shirt rode up over his slick, muscled torso, stretching past her.

Frustration swamped her. She could barely lick him as he hovered there, out of reach, but couldn't touch him. Biting her lip, she burned with the need to get her hands on him. Now.

Quickly, carelessly, he tossed out cosmetics and a hairbrush, pens, a pocket calendar...

"How hard can it be to find a big honker of a knife?" she demanded. She shivered with unspent passion, needing him this instant, not in five minutes. *Now.*

But his fingers finally closed on the tapering handle of Mack's knife. "You brought this with you?"

"I thought I might need it," she returned. "And I was right! Get to it, will you?"

"Careful, careful," he warned, easing the blade behind his back, slicing through his belt loop, ever so gently shredding the cord around her wrists, finally, blessedly freeing her hands.

"You drive me insane," she muttered into his lips, bracketing his face with her fingers.

"Ditto," he retorted.

But he was already discarding his T-shirt and his jeans, meeting skin with skin. Emily wrapped herself around him every way she knew how, her hands roaming wild. It was furious, reckless, a clash of passion and longing. It was the best she'd ever felt in her life.

And right there, on the knotty pine floor, he plunged into her, grasping her to him, calling out her name. Emily splayed her hands on his back, wanting, *needing* him closer, harder, faster, rocking with the sheer pleasure of it.

Madness. Euphoria. Tyler.

He was inside her, outside her, and she stayed right with him. A shivering, shuddering climax tripped over her, and he spent himself inside her, just as she reached the highest peak.

"Unbelievable," she managed, gasping for air. As she drifted back to earth, she murmured, "Who'd have thought it could be like that?"

"With you? I did." Under a sheen of perspiration, he looked exhausted. But he smiled.

It was a beautiful, shy, beaming smile, and her heart turned over.

"Tyler," she whispered in awe. "You love me."

"How could I help myself?"

His arms closed around her, as sweet and gentle as they'd been harsh and unyielding seconds before. He leaned back into the floor, settling her against him.

"I can't believe how amazing this was. How amazing you are." She propped herself up far enough to look at him, to drink him in. "But there's one more thing." She licked her lip. "I didn't tell you—that I love you, I mean. You know, don't you, that you are everything I ever wanted? Tyler, I do love you."

"You said that already," he teased.

Now it was her time to smile. "I like the sound of it," she confessed. "We are just so right, you and me."

"Yeah. The perfect couple." *Uh-oh.* The cynicism had crept back into his voice. Mockingly he continued, "What will we be? I can see it now—Emily Chaplin and her low-rent boyfriend. Or if things go really badly, we can be the judge's daughter and the defendant."

She skewered him with a quelling stare. "Don't be so negative. I'm telling you, we can do this."

"Emily, I—"

"No, no," she interrupted. "I'm serious. When we get back to Chicago, I will do my best to sort out your legal troubles, however you're involved in this whole Slab thing. What is it, aiding and abetting or something?" She shook her head. "I don't believe it for a minute. Listen, I know I've never practiced criminal law, but this seems like a great time to start."

"Emily," he said gently, "thank you for the offer, but I don't need your legal help."

"Then why did you call yourself a defendant?" she argued.

"That's not what I mean." He sat up, pulling her with him. "Emily, how could you not have noticed? What kind of help did you think I was giving Slab and Jozette and even Kate, way back when?"

It was her turn to be utterly confused. What was he getting at? "I—I don't know. I guess I thought you were an investigator. Like a P.I.?"

"I'm a lawyer," he announced flatly. "I realize I am not the world's best. I mean, granted, my clients are mostly a bunch of lowlifes and I may lose my office because I can't pay the rent, but—"

"You're a *what?*" Emily's jaw dropped. "But you can't be!"

"I am."

She was filled with dread, outrage, incredulity. Her head was spinning. Her whole body was spinning.

"There is no way this is possible. The love of my life absolutely, positively cannot be a..." She gulped for breath. "A lawyer!"

10

_____

"EMILY, I WOULD HAVE TOLD YOU," he tried, "but at first it was none of your business, and then I thought you might be from the ethics committee or something."

"You could've saved both of us a lot of trouble if you'd told me," she said angrily. "I hate lawyers! I never would've come near you."

"Come on, Emily. Give me a break."

Bolting to her feet, she jerked her skirt back down to a somewhat respectable place and crossed her arms over her bare chest. It was the best she could do at the moment. Wordless, he tossed her his shirt.

"Thank you," she said stiffly, tugging it on.

Shaking his head, muttering to himself, Tyler jammed his pants back on. "I told you this was never going to work."

She wanted to throw something at him. Or at least bash him over the head with one of her monkey-and-palm-tree sandals, the ones that had been pitched down a hole in the floor, sort of like her heart.

Get over it, she told herself crossly. _You knew what you were getting into, you were the one who pushed this, and you have no right to whine now._

But her brain was riddled with conflicting emotions—hurt and disappointment and foolishness—and she didn't know what to do, what to feel, where to look. She found herself staring at the knotty pine floor.

I just made love on the floor of a boat with a man I barely know, her mind cried. *I know him so little that I didn't even know he was a lawyer. How stupid could I be?*

It was a matter of wounded pride and exposed nerves. She knew that. What difference should it make if he was an attorney? She'd been willing to accept that he might be a private investigator or a bounty hunter or even a crook. But a lawyer...it was just so humiliating!

She'd wanted to be the high-and-mighty lawyer who stepped in and helped the poor bad boy. Instead, she felt like an interfering fool, as if he'd been laughing at her since day one.

It wasn't her heart down in that hole with her poor sandals—it was her pride.

Suddenly, for no real reason, she was seized with the idea of getting back her shoes. So she turned away, kneeling to peer into the big hole Mack and his cronies had hacked in the middle of the floor. She leaned over far enough to lasso one by the ankle strap, but the other eluded her.

"What the hell are you doing?"

"My shoes," she replied as calmly as she could manage. "I got one of them, but the other one is too far down for me to reach. I really want my shoes back."

"All right, all right." He lowered himself far enough into the hole to retrieve her shoe, tossing it into her lap. "I could ask why you want it back, but I won't. You and I both know you are never going to wear those shoes again once you go back to Chicago. This was it, Emily. Your walk on the wild side. I hope it was worth it."

"How many times do I have to tell you that this wasn't any walk on any wild side? Not a walk, not a ride, not even a—"

But her words were drowned out by a long blast from a ship's horn.

Tyler wheeled. "What is that?"

"Ahoy there," an amplified voice boomed. "This is the police. Prepare to be boarded."

There was a sudden and quite overpowering whirl of activity, as the seagoing version of the San Francisco P.D. came crashing down to the cabin. The two of them tried to explain, but Tyler barely had time to grab his leather jacket and Emily her purse before they were carted out of there. Although she again tried to clarify the situation once they were safely on the police boat, nobody seemed to be listening. And Tyler had clammed up big-time. All he did was glower at her. She wanted to say, *Give me a minute to process all this. Okay, so I didn't know you were a lawyer. But I still love you!*

But she didn't utter a word.

Finally the two of them were shoved inside the station and into separate interrogation rooms.

"We didn't steal the boat!" she insisted, as soon as

they sat her down. "We were kidnapped and thrown in a closet by Sluggo and Mack and this guy, Jimmy. Gangsters! You should go catch them and give us a medal."

"Ma'am," the younger of the two cops interjected politely. His name tag told her he was Detective Hogan. "We don't think you stole the boat."

"No?" She blinked. "Then why are you arresting us?"

His partner, an older, crustier type, with Bellini on his nameplate, stepped forward. "Actually, we're not arresting you. But we *were* looking for you," he said acidly. "First, there's the matter of a missing persons report."

Jeez. Gone for less than thirty-six hours and her mother was already calling in the bloodhounds. Meanwhile, with her world topsy-turvy, her heart in turmoil, the last thing she needed was a visit from her fussbudget family.

"Missing person?" she echoed innocently. "You don't mean me."

Bellini responded first. "Uh-huh. Your mom, your dad, a bunch of brothers…they're all here in San Francisco looking for you. Seems they tracked you down with credit card receipts and airline tickets." He shook his graying head. "They're a tough bunch. Glad they're not my family. Anyway, they were pretty anxious to locate you."

"So, here I am. And I do thank you for the rescue from the boat. But why am I still here?" she inquired. "In here, I mean. With you."

"Well, you see..." The conversational ball had bounced back to Hogan, who pulled up a chair, as if he expected to stay a while. "We have some questions for you, Miss Chaplin."

"About what?"

"The usual. What you were doing on the boat, who threw you and your boyfriend—if he is your boyfriend and not your kidnapper—in the closet, what this all has to do with Joseph Slabicki and Michael Delanty, and whether you're interested in filing charges or supplying information that might help us prosecute any or all of these personages." He opened a thick file in front of him. "So, what do you think?"

I think I'm in over my head. "Okay, well, you should know right off that Mr. O'Toole is not a kidnapper," she said quickly. "If anything, it's vice versa. As for the rest...well, who are Joseph Slabicki and Michael Delanty?" she asked, stalling for time.

The older detective glared at her, while the younger one flipped pages in his notebook. It was Hogan who finally spoke. "The boat you were on belongs to Joseph, a.k.a. Slab, Slabicki, a small-time hood who we picked up yesterday on a bail violation. Mr. Slabicki is someone we've wanted to talk to for a long time, seeing as how he and some pals robbed a Brink's truck back in '87 and the money was never recovered."

"Oh. How interesting."

"Yeah. And there are holes all over the boat, as if someone were, oh, I don't know, digging for buried treasure?" Hogan gave her a superior smile. "Kinda makes us wonder if somebody didn't find Mr. Slabicki's buried treasure.''

"I..." Emily faltered. But she knew what to do. "I'm not saying anything until I speak to my attorney."

"Right." The grumpy one went to the door. "We were expecting that. So which one do you want, Mom, Dad, Bro One, Two, Three or Four?"

Emily swallowed. "None of them. My attorney is..." She lifted her chin. "My attorney is Tyler O'Toole."

In the next interrogation room over, a different set of detectives was giving Tyler a hard time. And he was very rapidly losing patience with them.

"Look, we know you've been investigated back in Chicago, we know you're in bed with Fat Mike Delanty and Slab Slabicki, and we know you were out here looking for the Brink's take from '87. So just tell us what you found and where it is, and we'll think about making a deal."

"I'm sorry, guys, but I don't know anything about any of this." He shrugged, much more concerned about where Emily was and how she was faring. He was used to this kind of crap, but she was a babe in the woods. *Damn it.* The best day of his life, shot to smithereens. Emily, taking a chance on him, handing him her heart. Emily, trusting him. How could he have let this happen?

There was no way she was ever going to speak to him again. Sure, she'd wanted a little fun, a little dance with danger, but now that she'd been tossed in the pokey and treated like a criminal, the game would lose its appeal pretty damn quick.

"Come on, O'Toole. Give us what we want, and you can take the cutie pie home."

"I don't think the cutie pie is going anywhere with me." But he changed tactics. He didn't even want to mention Emily here. "Listen, here's the deal. I don't know Mr. Delanty, I don't know anything about a Brink's take, but I am acquainted with Mr. Slabicki. I am not at liberty to discuss him with you, however. Attorney-client privilege."

"Okay, so you want to play hardball." The larger of the two cops leaned in over him. "We can do that."

"No, I don't want to play anything," Tyler said curtly. "As far as I'm concerned, this interview is over."

The cop laughed. "Yeah, we got it. You want to see a lawyer."

"Yes, I do." He wanted to see her so badly he could barely breathe. "Emily Chaplin. She's my lawyer."

HER DETECTIVES WERE GONE a long time. Emily had never chewed her nails before, but she was willing to take up the habit just to pass the time.

Finally Hogan came back alone.

"Where's Tyler?" she asked immediately. "I said I wanted to speak to him."

"You both asked for each other and we don't know if we can do that," he said reluctantly. "Possible co-

conspirators who request each other as counsel. Well, that's a new one on us.''

"He asked for me?" That was a surprise. A nice surprise. *He asked for me.*

"But, hey, it's your lucky day."

"I get to see Tyler?" she asked hopefully.

"Nope. You're free to go. A patrolman just picked up three guys with burglary tools down by the marina. We know them." He frowned. "In association with Mr. Slabicki on that Brink's job. Slabicki says they're the ones who beat him up last night, and Miss Leer says they burglarized her premises as well. I'm guessing they're also the ones who attempted to destroy the *Sweet Shanda.*"

He shook his head. "Stupid mopes. Turns out Miss Leer found the money years ago and spent every dime to buy The Flesh Pit. So there was no treasure after all."

"Poor Slab. But this lets us off the hook?" She wasn't quite convinced, but she was willing to let it ride. "You're releasing both of us?"

"Yeah. We think you and your boyfriend just stumbled over something stupid and didn't have the sense to get out of the way." As she rose from the table, he added, "Besides, your mother has been throwing a fit and threatening to get F. Lee Bailey and Johnnie Cochrane and Clarence Darrow in here to sue the P.D. and the city and anyone else she can think of."

"Clarence Darrow has been dead for thirty years," she told him.

"Yeah, well, tell that to your mother." Hogan

opened the door for her. "Don't take any more sudden vacations, will you? We know where to find you, and we'll be in touch if we need you or the boyfriend." With a smirk, he added, "Have fun out there. The whole family is waiting."

Don't remind me. Emily straightened the too-long T-shirt she'd borrowed from Tyler, pulled down her too-short skirt as much as she could, and tried to walk tall and proud in her wooden wedgies. Still she knew in her heart that any police interrogation had to be preferable to facing her parents.

Hogan escorted her down a corridor. No sign of Tyler. He'd probably already been released and taken a powder.

"He can't be gone," she whispered with a tiny seed of anxiety starting to take root. "He would wait for me. I know it."

But his face was not among those who greeted her.

"Emily?" Her mother's cool voice brought her up short. Judge Patience Burr-Chaplin looked immaculate and self-possessed, as always, even if her forehead was creased with worry. "Are you all right, darling? We were frantic."

"I'm fine. Absolutely fine."

But they were all crowding around, poking at her, demanding to know what she was wearing and where she'd gotten those dreadful clothes and what she was doing in San Francisco in the first place. Trust Dad to give her a gruff hug and then ask if she still had the Bentley file.

Meanwhile, where was Tyler?

"I said I was fine—I will explain everything later— but right now—"

"I understand, Lambie," her mother said soothingly. "First you want to shower and change out of those awful clothes, and then have a nice meal. We've reserved suites at the Fairmont for tonight, and then we'll pop you home safe and sound tomorrow."

Her panic grew. If she didn't stop this right now, they would all be steamrolling her just the same as always. "Mother, listen, I..."

But then she saw him, coming through the same door she had, led by a different cop. Her voice died. Behind her, her parents and her brothers continued to make plans and formulate strategy. She didn't even hear them.

He strolled through the door and paused, gazing at her. Since she had his T-shirt, he was wearing his leather jacket zipped up over a bare chest. She smiled.

"Emily?" he murmured, with the hint of a question at the end of it.

She didn't waste a minute. She threw herself headlong into his arms. And Tyler caught her and held her tight, just as she knew he would.

"Tyler," she said breathlessly, "you asked for me! You told them I was your lawyer. That is so sweet. I can't believe you did that."

"And you asked for me." He laughed and kissed her quick. "Good job, Em."

"I love you," she told him, kissing him back, pressing herself into the worn, familiar leather of his jacket.

"Emily!" her mother shouted. "What are you doing? Get away from that man immediately!"

"Who the hell is that?" demanded Rick, her oldest brother, while David and Rob, the next two in line, each took a step in her direction, bristling with indignation.

Emily slid out of Tyler's embrace. "Mother, Father, boys, this is Tyler O'Toole. Tyler, this is my family."

But instead of acknowledging the introduction, the Chaplins sort of growled at him. David and Rob took another step. One of them snarled, "Take your hands off my sister."

This wasn't going well, was it?

Tyler seemed to weigh their responses, glancing at her to see what she wanted him to do. "Maybe it would be better if I left you—"

"No," she said firmly. She clasped his hand and turned to face the music. "No. They're not staying."

"That's right," the judge put in. "None of us is staying. We're taking our daughter to a decent hotel where she can recuperate from this trauma you've put her through."

"Mother, you need to be quiet."

Emily Patience Chaplin was at the end of her rope. No more sweetest little Emily. No more "Lambie." It was as if the lion she'd always had hiding inside her roared to the forefront—with a vengeance.

"Mom, Dad, boys—you're all taking the next plane back to Chicago where you belong," she announced with steely resolve. She had never spoken to them this sternly, and all six mouths dropped open in surprise.

"You can see that I'm fine, that there was no need for you to fly out here or make fools of all of us with your missing persons report."

"What?" Her mother faltered. "I can't believe you're saying these things."

"Mom, listen. Everyone has to grow up sooner or later, even the youngest and only female Chaplin. I'm sorry you went to all this trouble, but it really wasn't necessary. I'm fine." As Tyler lifted their combined hands to his lips, brushing a kiss on the back of hers, she found her smile again. "And I'm going to stay that way."

"I can't believe this," her father echoed.

"Em, are you sure?" said her youngest and nicest brother, Mike. "It is kind of hard to believe, that you ditched work and flew out here and hooked up with this guy. And the way you're dressed…it's very unlike you."

"I don't know why it's so hard to believe." Emily shook her perfect pageboy, making a mental note to get a more interesting haircut soon. "I'm every bit as headstrong and pushy and impossible as the rest of you. What you see before you is practically my birthright."

"Oh." The light finally dawned in her mother's eyes. "You're serious about this, aren't you? And about him?"

"Yes. And his name is Tyler. You'd better get used to it." Emily's smile widened. "I haven't told you the best part yet. As of Monday morning, Tyler and I are going to be working together in criminal defense." He made a small choking noise next to her, but she went on. "I don't know if any of you remember, but criminal law was always my favorite in law school."

"Where does that leave Chaplin, Chaplin & Chaplin?" her father blustered.

"Sorry, Dad, but I've always hated tax law. But you know, you'll be fine with the boys at the firm." She shook her head. "It's just not right for me."

He grumbled something she couldn't understand.

"Don't worry," she added, "the Bentley file and my resignation will both be on your desk Monday. And then—" she grinned "—Chaplin & O'Toole, for the defense. I can't wait!"

"Emily, can I speak to you?" Tyler narrowed his eyes at her, pulling her aside. "You haven't even asked me, and besides, who says you get top billing in the name of this mythical law firm?"

"Oh, Tyler, come on! It's alphabetical. It just stands to reason—"

"Stands to reason? I think I deserve a say in this, don't you? O'Toole & Chaplin. And maybe I'm sick of criminal law."

"Well, then you can handle everything else and I'll take the criminal cases."

"And how are we supposed to financially support the launch of this new practice? Did you think about that?"

"Actually, I did. I had a lot of time in there in the interrogation room." She shrugged. "It's really very easy. Grandmother Burr's trust fund was intended for something exactly like this."

"Oh, no! Not your trust fund. To support me? I

don't think so. I can support myself, thank you very much.''

"I have to admit," she heard her mother comment behind her, "they do seem perfect for each other. Nobody bickers like that unless they belong together."

But her family faded into the background as Tyler led her out onto the street and hailed a taxi, arguing all the way.

"This isn't over," he told her, ushering her into the cab. "Not by a long shot. We have a lot of details to work out."

Emily's lips curved into a bright smile. "I know. I'm counting on it."

"Oh, you are, are you?" There was an odd light in Tyler's gorgeous green eyes as he suddenly pulled her over into his lap. "You know, this isn't going to be easy."

"Would it be any fun if it were?"

"No." He framed her cheeks with his hands, closing his eyes as he pressed his lips into hers fiercely, with a sense of belonging and joy. "I love you like crazy. Did you know that?"

"I was counting on that, too." But her heart seemed to swell just to hear him say it. "Tyler?" she ventured, afraid to break the spell.

"Uh-huh." Distracted, he continued to kiss her as the taxi sped along.

"Where are we going?" she gasped. "Right now, I mean."

"Where do you think? Beau's B and B."

"Oh, good!" She gave herself up to his caresses,

laughing into his mouth, sliding down into the seat. "I really didn't want to leave San Francisco until I got to make love with you on that amazing Wild One bed. Leather and chrome…handlebars…" She shivered. "I don't know. It just does something to me."

"You do something to me," he said huskily. His voice rose as he leaned forward slightly. "Driver, pick up the pace, will you? We haven't got all day."

"I love a man in a hurry," she whispered in his ear.

"You're going to love one who takes his time as well." His tone was so dark and dangerous she trembled at the very sound of it. "This time, Emily, just you and me and The Wild One room, we're going to take it slow. After all, we've got until Monday…"

"Driver?" Emily grabbed the back of the front seat. "Could you please hurry? There's somewhere we really need to be. *Now.*"

The Wild One room. Tyler. A whole day with nothing to do but fool around, plot their future, and make each other crazy.

Her mind filled with pictures of love and desire and the best kind of adventure. Life. She loved every bit of it.

COLLEEN COLLINS

In Bed with the Pirate

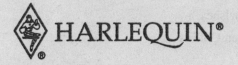

HARLEQUIN®

TORONTO • NEW YORK • LONDON
AMSTERDAM • PARIS • SYDNEY • HAMBURG
STOCKHOLM • ATHENS • TOKYO • MILAN • MADRID
PRAGUE • WARSAW • BUDAPEST • AUCKLAND

Dear Reader,

Julie Kistler and I love old movies, so we had great fun creating the rollicking, romantic Beau's Bed & Breakfast (the San Francisco setting for both of these Duets) that has rooms named after such film classics as *Kismet, The Pirate, The Wild One* and *Pollyanna*. Inspired by these films, we got even more inspired to create sexy, romantic heroes who feel at home in these rooms (all but Pollyanna, that is!).

In my story, *In Bed with the Pirate,* corporate raider Toby Mancini discovers his inner swashbuckler—a plundering, sexy alter ego who ignites Kate Corrigan's secret dreams and passions as he sweeps her off her feet and into the magical realm of her pirate fantasies.

A realm in which I, too, love to escape! Just like Kate, I delved into my own pirate fantasies...and fell head over heels for Toby's sultry swagger and passionate heart. But best of all, he's a man of integrity. Sex appeal, intelligence, integrity—plus a sense of humor—and you have my ingredients for one hot hero!

I hope you enjoy reading this book as much as I enjoyed writing it. I'd love to hear what you think. Write to me at: P.O. Box 12159, Denver, CO 80211.

Best wishes,

Colleen Collins

To my dear friend, Cheryl McGonigle, for her patience, sense of humor and willingness to share her incredible writing talents and insights. We started out ten years ago as critique partners and, over the years, developed a friendship that will last a lifetime.

"Think where man's (woman's) glory most begins and ends, and say my glory was I had such friends."
—William Butler Yeats

1

ROLLING HER SHOULDERS in time to the throbbing beat of a Motown tune, Kate Corrigan threw back her head. Then meeting her own blue-eyed gaze in the mirror, she performed a smooth dance step while silently mouthing the words to the song.

A fat yellow tabby cat, perched on the edge of her maple dresser, stared at her with a glazed here-we-go-again look.

Kate stopped singing as the Supremes continued in the background. "Beau, would it kill you, for once, to act *mildly* excited while an extremely talented unknown lip-synchs her heart out?" Running her hands through her short hair, Kate glanced at the antique cherry wood clock on top of her bookcase. "Okay, you have a point. It's midnight. Time to turn off the music—we don't want to disturb our guests."

Kate danced her best soulful strut over to her CD player, lodged on a bookcase shelf between *How to Fix Anything* and *The Three Musketeers*. After swiveling her hips to the last few notes, she tapped the power button off. The brief silence was suddenly broken by raucous barking.

In two steps, Kate was at her window, peering past the flower garden to her neighbor's stately Edwardian home. Beau, on instant dog-alert, hopped onto the sill next to her. "Weird," Kate confided to her cat, "I never knew they had dogs." But the barking stopped as abruptly as it had started. "Maybe they had their TV volume up too high?" she mused. After one last glance at her neighbor's house, Kate yawned, then shuffled across the hardwood floor and dropped into her rocking chair.

Running an inn could be tiring, but add a surprise visit from your mother, the homemaker of the century, and the day suddenly felt heavier than a batch of her mother's award-winning brownies. Kate sank into the rocking chair and stared out her bedroom window at the inky San Francisco night sky. Even though it was summer, a low fog blanketed the distant hills. What had Mark Twain said? The coldest winter he'd ever spent was August in San Francisco?

"Not like your namesake city," Kate confided to Beau as she reached over and scratched him behind one nicked ear. "Beaufort must be sweltering right now." Kate recalled the many long, hot summers she'd spent growing up in Beaufort, South Carolina, the air so warm and thick, you didn't just breathe it, you wore it.

She stared at the full moon. Round and golden, it looked more like the sun's cousin than its sister. "Granny would have called this a 'Captain Blood night,'" she whispered to Beau, who continued to stand guard on the sill. "She always said that on a night like this, the air was charged for adventure and passion—all you had to do was close your eyes and dream."

As a little kid, how many times had Kate done just that, closed her eyes and escaped into a rollicking swashbuckler fantasy? A habit she found hard to break, even at thirty-three. Closing her eyes, she resurrected an image of a youthful, swarthy Errol Flynn, sword in hand, sea winds tousling his hair as he rousted his fellow pirates to charge into battle. Sometimes Kate imagined herself standing nearby, the object of the pirate's fiery love.

That was the ultimate fantasy. A man who not only captured ships and treasures, but also a woman's heart.

Dingdong.

Her eyes popped open. Two couples were staying at the inn tonight, and Kate had heard both of them retire over an hour ago. She arched an eyebrow at Beau. "It's either one of your lady friends paying you a visit...or it's—" she dropped her voice to an ominous level "—Melanie."

Kate stood and slipped her feet into a pair of well-worn purple velvet slippers. "Now I remember, she wanted to check if the tassels on the sitting room curtains hung evenly at night." Shuffling across the hardwood floor, Kate gave her head a weary shake. "Who besides my mother would ever feel the overwhelming need to check hanging tassels at midnight?"

Kate opened the door and entered a small alcove, in which sat her pine desk where she checked in guests to Beau's Bed-and-Breakfast. Pine didn't fit with the inn's downstairs Victorian motif, but she'd lovingly refinished this piece by hand, so it stayed.

"I gave you the code to the outside security box so you could come and go as you please," Kate muttered, saying what she couldn't to her mother's face. After all, she'd only arrived this afternoon from Beaufort, her first visit—unexpected, but nevertheless, a visit—in two years. A daughter shouldn't be irritated that her Southern-as-pecan-pie mother had accidentally locked herself out...except if that mother arranged each pecan in an intricate, perfectly aligned pattern that made Kate feel guilty for sticking a fork into it.

She lay her hand on the cold brass doorknob. Did other mothers suffer from midnight tassel fever?

With a bit too much strength, Kate swung open the door. "How're they hanging?"

She gasped.

A naked man stared back at her.

Kate meant to take a breath, but instead sucked in so much air, she felt light-headed. In her mildly dizzy state, she tried to get a handle on the situation.

The man wasn't totally naked. He wore thick, black horn-rimmed glasses. Her gaze dropped. And a pair of red Calvin Klein underwear. "Red?" she croaked.

"I'm your neighbor, Toby," said a deep voice somewhere above the red stretchy material that didn't leave a whole lot to the imagination. "Toby Mancini."

"Right," she breathed, forcing her gaze up to meet dark eyes that looked oddly large through the lenses. Like two dark, full moons. "Toby," she repeated. "Mancini. I didn't recognize you…" *Naked.*

Jeez, was this Toby Mancini, the nerd who lived next door? The guy she'd asked Verna, her friend and chef at the inn, to call twice to complain that if he blasted Beethoven any louder, her windows would shatter. The guy who'd responded that it was far better to be shattered by Beethoven than pulverized by Motown?

"May I come in?" he asked in a deep tone.

With that mix of rough velvet voice and nearly naked body, Kate wasn't sure if her insides were shattering or pulverizing. She meant to say yes, but she only got as far as dropping her jaw. Six years ago, when he'd moved in next door, she'd been glued to her windows, watching his sinewy, compact body carrying furniture and boxes into his house. She'd imagined him to be a pirate, carrying away plundered treasures. And even after he'd moved in, she'd still envisioned him as a pirate…until she accidentally blew up his car.

Kate snapped shut her mouth.

At the time, he'd been so furious, all her fantasies about him had blown up, too. And in her mind, she'd purposefully replaced the plundering pirate with a geeky nerd so she'd stop gluing herself to windows like some kind of human decal whenever he appeared outside. But in this speechless moment, she had to admit to herself that Toby Mancini had *never* been a nerd except in her mind.

"May I come in?" he repeated, an edge to his voice. "I...accidentally locked myself out of my house."

"Dressed like that?" she blurted.

"Yes," he answered curtly, "dressed like this." He breathed in and out deeply, as though suppressing a vat of anger. Kate couldn't help but notice how his pectorals bulged when he breathed like that. Or how much hair covered those pecs. Those swirling wisps were dark turbulent seas to her fanciful mind.

"I hate to intrude," he said gruffly, interrupting her thoughts, "but if I stand out here much longer, someone might call the police." He gestured emphatically, giving Kate a wide-open view of those red stretchy undies.

She jerked open the door. Too hard. It accidentally slammed against the wall. "Sorry," she mumbled, stilling a picture frame that rattled. As he stepped inside, she caught a whiff of cologne, woodsy, fresh. Strange that a business kind of guy would wear an outdoorsy smelling scent. But then who would have thought he wore bright red undies?

She shut the door, carefully this time. "Would you like to use the ph—" Turning around, she halted midsentence. For an instant, she forgot where she was. If asked her name, she'd be hard put to remember that, either.

Light from the fake Tiffany lamp on the carved elm wood table splattered over him in a kaleidoscope of color—the red, blue and gold hues tinting his body in a glowing patchwork. She wouldn't have imagined that a guy who wore business suits would have a body made for Speedos. Red light spilled over the hard curve of his shoulder. Blue played along the corded muscles of his arms. A touch of gold highlighted the ridged slope of his stomach and glinted along those thick, curling chest hairs.

And for a fleeting moment, the dark line of his glasses almost resembled an eye patch.

He looked like a living, breathing figment of her imagination. A swarthy, mystical male who'd stepped out of her swashbuckler fantasies.

She cleared her throat. "Th-there's a sword behind the desk."

"Sword?"

"Phone." She pointed limply toward her pine desk. "I meant phone." Sword. Jeez, she was losing it.

Toby didn't move.

"Isn't Acorn home?" Kate finally asked.

"Her name's...Free."

"Right. Free. I forgot." His girlfriend—who changed her name more often than most people changed their minds—had been a variety of names. At one point she'd called herself Acorn. At another, it had been something like Deer or Dove. No, his girlfriend was a vegetarian so it must have been Daisy. Even if her names weren't logical, they methodically followed the alphabet like a Sue Grafton book title. *A* is for Acorn. *B* is for Butterfly. *C* is for Calla Lilly. And so on up to F—so far.

"You can phone Free," Kate said. "I mean Free as in your girlfriend's name, not that I'd charge you—"

"No thanks," he said brusquely. He looked around, shuffling from one foot to another. Poor guy was barefoot. Kate wondered how long he'd stood outside on the cold concrete, debating whether to ask the car-bombing neighbor for shelter. It wasn't her fault about the kid's sparkler that Fourth of July.

"Look," Toby finally said, squaring off to face her. He'd obviously again forgotten the importance of covering his privates because he gestured as he talked.

"This is how it is. I can't go back because—" he stopped gesturing and raked a hand through his fabulously unkempt hair "—there's a couple of strange Dobermans in my house. That's why I need a place to stay tonight, maybe a little longer." Even in the splatter of multicolored light, she caught a look of pain—or was it rage?—on his face.

"Dobermans? You're kidding."

"I wish."

So that had been the barking she'd heard earlier. "I have one room available."

"I don't have any money on me."

She'd have been extremely surprised if he'd been able to slide even one thin dime into those skimpy, skin-hugging Calvins.

"I'll pay you when I get...some of my things."

Get some of his things? Now that she knew about the Dobermans, he obviously hadn't accidentally locked himself out. But it didn't explain why Acorn-Butterfly-Calla Lilly-Daisy-Everglade-Free had let him leave dressed only in his underwear? How coldhearted could a woman be? Pondering if vegetarianism might have something to do with it, Kate said, "No problem. I'll put you up in Kismet."

Leaning over her desk, Kate opened a drawer and retrieved a string of keys. "Follow me," she said, heading toward the staircase. Tiny lights ran along one side of the stairs, illuminating the richly colored carpet that rippled down the wooden steps. How many times had she imagined a pirate carrying her up this staircase? She never dreamed she'd have one following her instead.

"Kismet?" Toby asked, following her.

"The rooms are named after some of my favorite old movies." Except for Pollyanna, but *that* name was a peace offering to Melanie. "Kismet is lush, exotic, sultry." *Try not to think that a naked man is following you.*

Kate cleared her suddenly dry throat. "So, she's been Free for about a month now, right?"

"You can say that again," Toby muttered, a sarcastic edge to his words.

Kate made a mental note not to say the name or word *free* again. It was too easily misunderstood. Or was it? Most of the neighborhood thought Free was too free when Toby was out of town, which seemed to be often. But no one knew him well enough, or felt it was their business, to tell him his girlfriend with the revolving names appeared to enjoy a revolving-door dating life when he wasn't home.

"Sorry," Kate murmured, feeling bad about whatever had happened to have him end up in his skivvies, homeless.

They reached the landing at the top of the stairs. Above, moonlight gleamed through a circular skylight. Toby stood on the edge of the spill of light, the moon's glow illuminating the contours of his body. Kate thought back to the last time she'd seen a man in his underwear. Had it been two years ago? Three?

She really should get out more often. Maybe take in a few museums and check out the naked marble statues. That way, if another undressed male ever landed on her doorstep in the middle of the night, she might act a bit more sophisticated about the whole thing.

A door creaked. Bright yellow light backlighted a middle-aged woman's form. "Heavens!" she drawled. "There's a naked man out here!"

Toby again folded his hands in front of his privates.

Kate released a weighty sigh. "Melanie, this is Toby. Toby, my mother, Melanie."

"Nice to meet you, ma'am," Toby said.

Melanie stood ramrod straight in a flower-printed housedress, her pinched expression wrinkling a green mint face mask. "Do you always traipse around your home—your *business*—with naked men, Katherine?"

Kate swore the multitude of pink rollers, more neatly arranged on her mother's head then pecans on a pie, quivered as Melanie stared accusingly at her. The tang of mint mingling with her mother's White Shoulders perfume could have made a marble statue cringe.

Kate slouched against the handrail. "I don't always traipse," she said. "Sometimes I skip."

Melanie sucked in such a big breath, Kate swore she'd created a vacuum. "Kath-e-rine Corr-i-gan." Her mother crossed her arms under her breasts. "You're incorrigible."

"Ma'am, this isn't what it looks like." He started to gesture, but stopped when Melanie's wide-eyed gaze dropped to his underwear.

She quickly looked up, her eyes and mouth open so wide, some of the green face mask cracked. "I wasn't born yesterday, young man," she said hoarsely before shutting her door with a crisp click.

The landing was submerged in shadows again. In the following silence, Toby whispered irritably, "It's bad enough I flashed her, but did you have to tell her we were 'skipping'?"

"Sorry," Kate murmured, straightening. "Pushing my mother's buttons is a lifelong habit. My only defense against perfect tassels and award-winning brownies." And her only defense against feeling as though she'd never be competent or capable compared to Melanie. "Let me find the key to your room."

She felt along the cool metal ring, knowing each attached key by its feel. The Pollyanna key, for the room in which her mother was staying, had a smooth bump along the edge. The Wild One had a scratch along its base. The Pirate had a serrated edge that was unmistakable. That left Kismet, the key with the slight twist of metal on its top. Kate had always thought that twist was fitting because in Arabic, Kismet meant *fate*. And wasn't fate like that—twists and turns you didn't expect?

"Follow me," Kate said, heading to the left. They walked down a short passage, passing a door with a saber. At the end of the passage was a door with a gold-mesh veil tacked to its outside.

"This is Kismet," Kate whispered, keeping her voice low so as to not bother the inhabitants of The Pirate, the door with the miniature saber. Inside that room were a young couple from Milwaukee who had kept kissing the entire time they checked in. Kate had had to wait for them to break for air to ask for their credit card. Fortunately, she had a lot of experience timing her questions to lip-lockers. Honeymooners often returned to Beau's B and B—especially the ones where she'd played matchmaker—a talent for which she was almost famous.

She opened Kismet and flicked the light switch.

"You've got to be kidding," Toby murmured. He scanned the red rug, red curtains, red chair. "Does red have some esoteric connection to fate?"

Ohh! Her pulse throbbed at his perceptiveness. She typically had to explain that Kismet meant *fate* in Arabic—maybe elaborate that Kismet was evocative of the dance of the seven veils and all that—but Toby Mancini didn't need those definitions. One look at the room and he'd been in sync with her imagination.

He made the connection between passion and destiny.

Toby looked around. "Couldn't you find anything else red for this room?"

"I did," she murmured under her breath. "You in those undies." She slid him a glance.

"Is that a bed?" he asked incredulously.

The oversize round bed, covered in a plump red-and-gold-stitched satin comforter, sat smack in the center of the room. "Yes, that's the bed," she answered, feeling a smattering of gilt-edged joy at his reaction. Her yearning for romance and passion, which always seemed buried deep within her like a sunken treasure, was revealed by touches like this fabulous bed.

He looked around. "Where's the head?"

"To the bed?"

"No, I meant—"

"Oh, right." She had to get her mind off passion and beds and focus on life's practicalities. "In the conical tower—that rounded corner over there—is the toilet, behind the paneled divider."

"That wooden thing draped with red scarves?"

"Yes." She gestured toward an alcove on the other side of the room where a curtain, tied back with braided gold rope, offered a teasing view of a claw-footed bathtub big enough for two. Behind the tub was a faux marble sink, over which hung a gilded mirror. "There's soap and extra towels in the cabinet below the sink." She turned to Toby. "Breakfast is served from seven to nine every morning. We typically ask guests if they'd like to eat in the dining room or have the meal delivered to their room, but considering your circumstances—" it took tremendous willpower, but she kept her eyes focused on his "—I'll bring breakfast to your room. What time?"

"Seven's fine." He stared at the thick crimson carpet that lay on the hardwood floor. When he lifted his head, she again caught that look she'd seen earlier. Although he was more expressive than most guys, she couldn't decipher if those creases in his forehead and the slant of his mouth signaled pain or anger.

"I've never had to ask for..." He paused, as though debating how much to say. "Thanks for helping me out," he finished quickly.

She had the urge to hug him, assure him things would be okay. But hugging a nearly naked man in Kismet? A nearly naked man who, if the lighting was just right, looked like a swarthy, sexy, hunky pirate from one of her Captain Blood fantasies?

"Hungry?" she asked on a rush of breath. "Now? Something? Sandwich?" Jeez. She sounded like Kate, the one-word question girl. Not trusting herself to speak further, she nodded a bit too vigorously as though that adequately finished her question.

He stared at her for a long moment.

Realizing she hadn't stopping nodding, she jerked her head to a stop. "I'll make you a sandwich," she said quickly, "if you'd like." If he didn't like sandwiches, he was out of luck because, unlike Melanie, Kate's only culinary specialty was turkey and cheese on rye with mustard. Sometimes, if she was feeling a little wild, she'd add a splash of horseradish or a few jalapeños.

"Sure," he answered, watching her as though another part of her body might start gyrating any moment.

"Turkey and cheese?"

"Sure."

"Rye?"

He nodded.

"Horseradish? Jalapeños?"

He grimaced.

"I'll be right back." Kate scooted out of the room, shutting the door behind her.

Toby stared at the closed door. What was that bobbing thing she did with her head? Maybe it would help if she wore tamer colors. Yellow drawstring pants, a red blouse and purple slippers. Add those big blue eyes and you didn't have a person—you had a color wheel. The only thing that toned it all down was her dark brown hair.

No wonder she blew up my car. Any woman who wore such no-holds-barred colors obviously had zero self-control.

Toby looked around. He hadn't seen this much red since his kid brother Marco cut his head with the can opener and gushed blood all over their mother's white living-room carpet. To this day, no one in the family fully understood why Marco was using a can opener on his head in the first place. Or why he then proceeded to run in circles on the living-room rug when he could have run in circles on the kitchen linoleum floor.

Toby's main memory of that event—besides all the red—was his being the ever-responsible big brother as he rushed thirteen-year-old Marco to Emergency. Fortunately, the cut only required a few stitches. Afterward, Mrs. Mancini had smothered Marco with motherly concern before grounding him for a month.

Kate's mother, Mrs.—what was Kate's last name anyway?—seemed to have a different kind of motherly concern. A standoffish motherly concern. And why did Kate call her "Melanie" and not simply "Ma" or "Mom" like other people?

But then Kate didn't exactly fit the mold of other people. First of all, she could be the poster girl for Crayola. And second, she seemed more like a grown-up tomboy than a grown woman. He'd never seen her in anything but pants, or sometimes shorts. It surprised him that tomboyish Kate Corrigan, proprietor of Beau's Bed-and-Breakfast, had decorated rooms to look so... He scanned the gauzy red curtains and shiny red satin bedspread. What had she called this room? Exotic. Lush.

Obviously Kate had a wilder inner life than her outer life revealed and he was fairly intrigued. As a corporate raider, he'd learned to look for hidden assets, secret objectives...

From across the room, he caught his reflection in the large oval mirror behind the bathtub. There he stood, naked except for a pair of red underwear. With his rumpled hair and glasses, he could pass for an Austin Powers look-alike.

And he'd just imagined *Kate* to have a wilder inner life than her outer one?

He groaned, remembering how he'd ended up this way. His stomach twisted into angry knots with the rush of recent memory. *Free knew I was coming home tonight. Yet she let me find her in the kitchen....* His insides rocked and rolled—like the music Free loved to play.

He'd gone to his bedroom to change, then hearing noises, had found his girlfriend in the arms of another man. He'd hardly digested that image before a couple of snarling, hair-raising Dobermans had chased him down the hall and outside.

He had to figure out how to get back by Monday evening—two nights from tonight—when he was supposed to cook a dinner for his potential boss and his wife. If that dinner went smoothly, Toby knew he'd be offered the position of Director of Software Development. He needed this job, a regular job where he could flex his creative side. A chance to be the good guy, not the Darth Vadar of the business world.

Toby swiped his hand across his eyes, as though the action could wipe out the image of Free and some guy kissing and writhing against the antique stove that cost him more than several mortgage payments. "You knew I'd find you," he grumbled. "Why'd you do it, Free? Living up to your promise to get even for all the nights I left you alone?" He shook his head. "But even I heard the rumors. You were rarely alone."

Argh. Toby punched the air so hard, his wild swing threw him off balance. He stumbled toward a walnut dresser—vaguely aware it wasn't red—and slammed into it. As the heavy piece of furniture crashed against the wall, an oversize porcelain pitcher sitting inside a humongous porcelain bowl slid toward the edge of the dresser.

Toby lunged. His body twisted midair, and he caught the handle of the pitcher. *Thunk.* His body hit the hardwood floor. *Whomp!* Air gushed painfully from his lungs as the bottom of the pitcher wedged into his solar plexus. Wheezing for air, he watched the bowl hit the floor next to him, bounce, then twirl upward like some kind of rotund ceramic ballerina.

Clutching the pitcher with one hand, he reached for the airborne bowl with the other. Desperately sucking a thin stream of air into his lungs, he stretched...and reached...

Smash!

Ceramic splinters shot through the air.

In the numbing silence that followed, he realized why he'd never been the kind of guy who resorted to his fists. With one swing, he might demolish a city, start an avalanche. Break a china set.

Knock-knock.

Toby lay still and listened. Was Kate back already? How would he explain the mess on the floor? If only he was bleeding, he might evoke sympathy. Maybe she'd coddle him, then ground him for a month. That'd work for him. He'd have a place to stay.

"Are you all right?" asked an older female voice, her Southern accent elongating the word *right* so it sounded like a long, breathless vowel surrounded with consonants.

Kate's mother, who wasn't born yesterday. What was her name? Mel-something. "I'm fine, Melody," he croaked.

"Melanie."

"Melanie. Sorry if I was...loud." Loud? Hell, after all that thumping, smashing and crashing, they probably thought they'd let in a madman. His only hope was that people from the South deemed such behavior as normal. After all, his great-aunt from Mississippi often talked to her husband, who everyone in the family knew had been dead for over twenty years.

"I have a son," Melanie said from the other side of the door. "I know how boys are. You need some ice?"

How boys are? Toby was thirty. "Ice? Uh, no."

"How about your...friend?"

Friend? He frowned. Then it dawned on him. She thought he'd been duking it out with someone. If only he had earlier! A roaring indignation filled his veins as he wished he'd pummeled that oven-writhing scumbag when he'd had the chance. "He's no friend," Toby growled, fiercely clutching the pitcher. "He's a dirt-licking, scum-digging dog."

He heard a soft "Heavens!" from the other side of the door.

"But he's gone now," Toby lied, realizing Melanie might call the cops. With an important career change ahead, the last thing he needed was bad publicity. He imagined the newspaper photo—Toby in his underwear, his hands cuffed. Maybe they'd let him carry the pitcher in front of him as they carted him to the police car. The image flashed in his mind. If he held the pitcher length-wise, everyone would wonder why Free had ever fooled around on him.

"You're all right?" Melanie's voice sounded closer, as though she were pressed against the door. "Is there anything I can do?"

Maybe she was standoffish with her daughter, but right now he heard something different in Melanie's tone—a mother who needed to be needed. The macho pitcher image was replaced by one of Kate's mother's green-caked face, etched with concern. It reminded him of his own mom and how she'd fret over her six children. "I'm okay." *But I'll be better when I get Free out of my house.* Until this moment, he hadn't realized how much—or how long—he'd wanted that. He'd put up with her two-timing because he was always on the road, too busy to deal with the realities back home. Unfortunately, he'd already told his potential employer that he lived with his fiancé, Free. Toby frowned. He couldn't suddenly say his engagement was broken. Somehow, some way, he'd have to pretend his home life was stable, at least for the duration of dinner on Monday.

A rustling sound reminded him that Kate's mother was hovering on the other side of the door. "Good night, Mrs.—" What *was* their last name? Beau? Best to stick with what was certain. "Good night, Melanie."

"Good night, son," she said softly. Footsteps padded back down the hallway.

A wave of melancholy washed over him as he recalled the many nights his mother had systematically gone to each of her children's doors to bid them good-night. Despite working out of the home at a job and raising six kids single-handedly, she was never too tired to insure each day ended on a note of love.

He looked at the shattered pieces of ceramic. If the banging, clattering and crashing had been heard by Kate's mother all the way down the hallway, the people in the next room had to be wide-awake, fearful of their neighbor. This was a nice place. Kate's *business,* as her mother had indignantly said earlier. Even if Kate had a bizarre color sense and a head-bobbing problem, this inn was her bread and butter. And he, of all people, could appreciate a woman working hard to earn a living.

I have to get a grip.

He stared at the pitcher in his arms. "And not just on you." He looked around at the splintered mess on the floor. "After I clean up this mess, I'll figure out how to clean up my life."

With some effort, he stood, returned the pitcher to the dresser, then walked over to the window and sat on an overstuffed loungelike chair. Red, of course. He looked out the window at the moon. Was he getting paranoid or did the man in the moon look at him with a pitying expression?

Toby jabbed a finger at the moon. "Wipe that look off your face, ol' man, 'cause I'm going to turn this sorry state of affairs around. *Fast.*"

He suddenly felt tired, exhausted. He pulled off his glasses and set them aside. Rubbing his eyes, he let his anger subside as he pondered his options. Although another man—even one wearing only briefs—might storm over and confront Free and her boyfriend of the moment, Toby had never been one to resort to violence. Backed against a wall, he typically resorted to a burst of Italian emotion followed by a rush of logic, a side effect of being an engineer.

Plus, being the eldest son in a large Italian family, and with his dad gone most of the time, Toby had learned to set priorities rather than indulge his moods or innermost desires. Which meant rather than hang out with his pals after school, he'd helped his mom prepare dinner. Toby smiled to himself. Once he'd almost gotten into a brawl with another kid who'd tried to steal Toby's jacket, but there was no time to vent because Toby had had to race home to fix dinner. Thanks to those experiences, he knew more about cooking than fighting. Hell, the most he'd ever punched was the air in Kismet.

Knock-knock.

He got up, sidestepped pieces of former bowl and headed to the door. Pressing his forehead against the smooth wood, he said, "I'm okay. You can go to bed."

"Don't you want your food?"

Kate. Food. He'd almost forgotten. He toyed with saying he wasn't hungry, but she'd gone out of her way to fix him something. Damn. If his mother had taught him anything, it was not to be rude. Even if Kate had blown up his car five years ago on that fateful Fourth of July.

Although she never took full blame, claiming something about a kid's sparkler...

Still, he could use her guilt about that incident when he confessed he'd broken her big porcelain bowl.

He edged behind the door and opened it a crack. Kate, offering a small smile, held out a plate. It looked like his insides felt. A mishmash of feelings that he didn't know how to put back together again. Except the mishmash on the plate also had bits of lettuce sticking out.

"I have a confession," Toby said, keeping his voice low.

Kate's blue eyes widened. "You're not wearing your underwear?"

Was she blushing? Or maybe all the red in the room was reflecting off her face. "No," he said slowly, "I broke your bowl."

She craned her neck and peered past him. "Oh!"

"It fell off the dresser."

"How'd that happen?"

"I fell against the dresser first, then the bowl fell second." That was the problem with being trained as an engineer. He had to explain everything in sequence. Why couldn't he have cut his head like Marco? Then he'd be getting some sympathy over his wound instead of a strange look.

Kate handed him the plate. "There's a broom in the closet at the end of the hall. I'll go get it." She was gone before he could explain further. Which was a good thing. If asked why he'd fallen against the dresser, he didn't want to admit he was slugging the air.

Kate reemerged with a broom and dustpan. With more clattering and clanging than when he'd broken the bowl, she seemed to fight the broken pieces rather than sweep them up. After some muttered curses, a few of which he found quite inventive, she finally swept up the mess and scooped it into a small trash can.

Kate, her face flushed, walked back to the door with an air of triumph. "I swept it all up," she announced, her voice infused with pride.

Not only did she have a thing for blowing up things, she seemed to have a thing for sweeping up things, too. "Yes," he agreed, keeping his voice purposefully even. "Yes, you did, indeed."

Kate blinked. "I never learned to tat or whatever like Melanie, but when I put my mind to it, I can clean—" Kate gestured awkwardly toward the plate "—and cook."

Maybe Kate was saying she could do these things, but her hesitant tone told Toby otherwise. "Well, thanks... I'm going to call it a day. Hit the sack." He forced a smile and started to close the door.

"Aren't you going to eat first?" she asked, looking anxiously at the plate.

"Eat?" He looked down. "What is it?"

"It's a sandwich."

"Did you drop it?"

"No," she said tightly, "I didn't drop it. I *made* it." When he continued to stare at the plate's contents, Kate said defensively, "It's a turkey and cheese sandwich."

The description helped. "Thanks," he said, studying her downcast expression. He'd never seen someone take a mistaken sandwich so personally. "Sorry I disturbed your mother," he added, swerving the sandwich conversation to another topic. "She came down here to check on me. I think the, uh, bowl-breaking incident was a little loud."

An annoyed look flickered across Kate's face. "Did she check the room's tassels, as well?" Before Toby could assimilate whatever that was supposed to mean, Kate sighed heavily and said, "She's run away from home, too. Except she brought her entire wardrobe with her."

"Maybe I could borrow one of her housedresses," Toby said, almost meaning it.

One corner of Kate's mouth quirked upward, giving her an impish look. "The pink-flowered one or the yellow-flowered one?"

"Yellow. Pink isn't my color."

Kate laughed softly, a warm, bubbling sound that lightened the moment. And his perception of her. "Good choice," she said, her gaze darting down, then back up. "Yellow goes nicely with red."

Before he had the wherewithal to answer, Kate had disappeared down the shadowed hall, leaving Toby holding a plate of mishmashed feelings.

2

KATE STUMBLED INTO THE KITCHEN and squinted at the
wall clock, a Captain Hook clock with the captain as the
big hand being chased by the crocodile, the little hand.
Together the hands showed six forty-five. "Show me the
coffee," she mumbled groggily, rubbing her eyes.

"My daughter hasn't changed a bit," Melanie told
Verna, energetically stirring something in a bowl. "Rolls
outta bed at the last minute 'cause she's stayed up till
the wee hours, watching those old movies on video." In
a surprised undertone, she murmured, "Or *usually* she's
bleary-eyed from watching those videos." Raising her
voice, Melanie continued, "Verna, darlin', I hope you
make my child eat a decent breakfast. Otherwise, she'd
blast through the rest of the day, fueled only by large
quantities of caffeine."

Strands of Verna's ash-blond hair glinted in morning
light that streamed through the kitchen window. Busily
spooning strawberry preserves from a kitchen jar into
serving dishes, Verna started to respond when Kate interrupted.

"Child?" She swiped her finger along the edge of the
jar. "I'm thirty-three, Melanie. A grown woman." She
sucked the jam off her finger, leaving a smudge of it on
the corner of her mouth.

"Oh, I've noticed all right," Melanie said softly, stopping her bowl-beating duties long enough to dab at the
corner of Kate's mouth with her apron before returning

to her culinary task. "I also noticed you have a hankerin' for cavorting in the midnight hours with naked men."

Verna dropped her spoon. It clattered across the linoleum floor.

Ignoring the commotion, Kate ambled over to the coffeepot and sloshed some of the hot black liquid into her favorite mug—a ceramic cup decorated with fat, yellow cats. Verna, picking up the spoon, flashed Kate a what's-this-about-naked-men? look. Kate rolled her eyes, which in girlfriend sign language meant, *I'll spill later.*

At the tail end of the eye roll, Kate's gaze landed on her mother. "What're you making, Mel?"

"It's bad enough you call me Melanie," her mother answered peevishly. "But Mel? Please! You make me sound like a bartender at some seedy tavern." *Beat-beat-beat.* "I'm making my brownies for this evening's treats."

Beaufort's Best Brownies. A prize Melanie Corrigan had won three years in a row. As Kate stirred cream into her coffee, she took a moment to peruse Beaufort's Best Brownies' maker.

Melanie always looked as though she'd just stepped out of 1960, the year she married her high school sweetheart, Max. Kate often thought her mother had gotten trapped in a time warp back then, trapped in some kind of perfect homemaker time capsule.

Everything about her mother was perfect. Her makeup, her cooking, her cleaning, even the way she ironed her husband's handkerchiefs and folded them into perfect triangles. Kate tugged on a strand of her tousled hair. Even her mother's hair was perfect. A perennially curly, auburn bouffant with two matching curls at her temples that always reminded Kate of quotation marks, framing some unspoken thought in Melanie's mind.

It had been hard growing up, competing with perfection. At an early age, Kate stopped competing. Instead of baking cookies, she learned how to tune a carburetor. Instead of polishing furniture, she fixed the plumbing. Skills that came in handy running an inn. Combined with her summers working at hotel resorts, she also knew how to hire a competent staff, manage the books, arrange tours. Her bed-and-breakfast had grown so successful, she was now toying with the idea of expanding by opening a restaurant.

Feeling better about her own successes, Kate grabbed her coffee cup and shuffled to the butcher-block table in the middle of the kitchen. Perching on a wooden stool, Kate asked, ''What're we serving this morning, Verna?''

''Eggs olé. Scrambled eggs with onion and avocado. Salsa on the side. And your mother made whipping-cream biscuits. From scratch!'' The admiration in Verna's voice was unmistakable.

The two of them were kitchen-bonding again. Just as they had during Melanie's visit two years ago. Whereas Verna was experimental with her cooking, throwing in a sprig of this or a dollop of that, Melanie was steadfastly traditional, adhering to recipes with a ritualistic fervor. Yet despite their different approaches, Verna and Melanie were like a culinary yin and yang. They inspired and balanced each other, oohing and aahing over their cooking coups.

Kate had always wished she could kitchen-bond with her mother. Heck, just bond. ''Who's getting room service?'' She always delivered the breakfasts upstairs while Verna served guests who preferred the dining room. In between, they'd eat their own breakfasts at the butcher-block table while swapping stories and gossip.

Verna checked the list tacked on the corkboard next to the fridge. ''Let's see, The Pirate wants to eat in the dining room, nine o'clock. The Wild One wants room service at seven.''

''I bet he does after that wild brawl in his room last

night!'' Melanie exclaimed, her batter-beating tempo increasing until it sounded like the rapid *fwap-fwap-fwap* of helicopter blades.

Fearful her mother might *fwap* out of control, Kate explained calmly, ''The Wild One is the room next to Pollyanna, remember?'' *The room filled with the many dolls Melanie bought me but I never played with.* She looked back at Verna. ''We had a late check-in last night. He's in Kismet, and he also wants room service at seven.'' Ignoring her mother's cough, Kate slugged down another sip of coffee. ''I'll get The Wild One's up to him and then—''

''Dressed like that?'' Melanie said, one penciled-in eyebrow arching in a perfect loop. At least she'd stopped *fwapping.*

Kate looked down at her jeans, navy sandals, sapphire silk blouse, and macramé vest. ''What's wrong? Except for the vest, everything matches.''

''You look like a hippie.''

''Melanie,'' Kate said irritably, ''no one uses the word 'hippie' anymore. This is my very own, comfy Kate Corrigan style.''

Her mother's nostrils flared slightly. ''I told Max we should have waited.''

''Should have waited?'' Verna prodded, stacking squares of butter next to the preserves.

''Waited until '68,'' Kate explained, ''rather than having me in '67—'' she dropped her voice dramatically low ''—the *summer of love.*'' To Melanie, her child being born in that fateful summer made Kate a renegade, someone who ran off to San Francisco, the summer-of-love city, and did what no Corrigan woman had ever done before—opened her own business.

''Like I said,'' Melanie continued, ''I'd tell Max again, but I'm not talkin' to him right now.''

Which was the only explanation Melanie had yet

given on why she'd run away from home. Kate seriously doubted Max had been caught with another woman—almost forty years of marriage and he was still crazy about her mother. He'd probably committed the mortal sin of wearing plaid with checks, or a mismatched vest with one of his golf shirts.

Melanie pulled off her apron. "I'll deliver the breakfast to the wild room," she said in a tone that left nothing for discussion. "You finish your coffee."

Kate suppressed a sigh. She never contradicted her mother's dictums—directly, anyway. She'd learned long ago it was easier simply to let Melanie take control and do what she thought best. Unfortunately, Kate hadn't learned to confront anything or anybody else, either. That's where she had her own yin and yang relationship with Verna, who would call or talk to someone Kate didn't want to face.

Melanie set the prearranged plates—each adorned with a sprig of parsley, a wedge of orange, and two biscuits—on a tray. She added napkins and utensils and one of the dishes of butter and jam.

"Ready, Verna," Melanie said as though the two of them had been doing this for years. On cue, Verna spooned eggs olé into the center of the plates. With a satisfied smile, Melanie then sailed out of the room, carrying the tray as though it were an offering to the food goddess Betty Crocker herself.

As the kitchen door creaked shut, Kate murmured, "She's taking over my job."

Verna chuckled. "Don't be silly."

"I know." Kate stared glumly at one of the fat cats on her coffee mug. It, unlike her, looked blissfully happy. "But around Melanie, carrying the trays upstairs feels like the one thing I can do well."

"You do that lip-synching act pretty well, too."

Verna had caught Kate on multiple occasions doing

her thing to one of The Supremes' Motown tunes. "Thanks. But I *excel* at carrying and serving breakfasts and now, thanks to Melanie's surprise visit, I've lost the opportunity to savor that singularly spectacular accomplishment."

"Now, now," Verna chided. "You do this every time your mother visits."

"Get dramatic?"

"You do that whether she's here or not."

"I regress," Kate admitted. "How old am I this time?"

"About thirteen."

Kate nodded. Thirteen felt about right. That was the year her mother not only sewed her cousin's wedding dress, but also hand-stitched hundreds of seed pearls on it. That same year Kate, for her Home Ec class, hand-sewed a pot holder, pricking herself more than the material. Her teacher commented the pot holder had more blood spots than a Civil War battlefield. "I don't know why I feel I have to compete with the homemaker of the universe," Kate said dejectedly.

"This isn't a competition," Verna said, decorating a plate with parsley and orange. "This is simply a friendly visit from your mother—"

"Who's mysteriously run away from home," Kate interrupted. "What if she never leaves? I'll be condemned to homemaker hell."

"Even in homemaker hell, I'll make sure you get to deliver some trays to the rooms," Verna said in the soothing voice she adopted whenever Kate veered toward the overly dramatic. Verna was only four years older, but she'd experienced things Kate hadn't—marriage, children and, sadly, widowhood. Verna had just lost her husband when she started working at the inn five years ago. Verna had immediately proved to be hard-working, but had been quiet at first. Eventually she eased out of her shell and the two women shared their love of North Beach, food and stories—the latter provided endlessly by the inn with its constantly changing guest list.

"Being a mother myself," Verna said, "I have a sixth sense that your mom's visit isn't just about leaving Max. I think it's also about being with you. Maybe, just as she needs to mend things with Max, she needs to do the same with you."

"She could start by letting me serve the breakfast trays," Kate said.

Verna smiled indulgently. "You can serve this next tray to Kismet."

"Better load more olé on that plate then, 'cause it's Kismet Melanie caught me cavorting naked with."

Verna, her spatula held midair, turned her gray eyes on Kate. "You?"

"What? You don't think I occasionally do a naked cavort or two around the inn?"

Verna blinked as though trying to see Kate clearly. "No. You're the type to maybe jog around the inn, or deliver breakfast around the inn, but cavort naked in the midnight hours with strange men?" She shook her head adamantly. "No way. Nada. Never. What's the real story?"

Kate pouted. "I feel a little hurt that you don't believe I have a seedy, tawdry other life."

"My dear, I hate to disappoint you, but you're about as seedy as Pollyanna."

Kate planted the back of her hand against her forehead. "Oh, dredge up the bitter past." Seven years ago, when Kate was in the midst of decorating the inn, her mother had visited and promptly had a full-blown Southern-mother fit. People would swear the inn was a brothel, she raved, with rooms named "Kismet," "Gone With the Wind," and "The Pirate." Well, one was formerly named Gone With the Wind—now it was The Wild One.

But at that time, when Melanie proceeded to faint in the all-red Kismet, Kate gave in and named the fourth room Pollyanna.

Her mother had instantly revived. She'd even made a pecan pie to celebrate.

"The real story," Kate continued, lowering her hand, "is that Toby Mancini showed up on the doorstep at midnight, wearing nothing but a pair of the sexiest red Calvin Kleins you ever laid your baby grays on."

"Toby Mancini? The next-door neighbor?" Verna stared out the kitchen window as though envisioning the meeting. "Boxers or briefs?"

"Briefs. Very, *very* brief."

Verna squinted, as though visualizing just how brief. In a rush of movement, she suddenly scooped a heaping mound of steaming eggs olé onto a plate. "Take this up there now, while your mother is busy telling biscuit stories to The Wild One. You know," Verna said, lowering her voice conspiratorially, "out the kitchen window this morning, I saw Free—dressed in one of her bead outfits—with a new man. Figured Toby was out of town again." Verna pointed the spatula at Kate's blouse, "Unbutton your top button."

Kate blinked. "Why?"

"Time to show a little flesh."

"Verna, I think the heat from the oven is getting to you."

"Take a flying leap. Go for the gold. Unbutton your button."

Kate gave her friend a double take. "I'm not sure what worries me more—you spouting clichés or your sudden button fetish."

Verna fisted her hands on her hips. "I've seen you go through several men, all wrong, wrong, wrong for you."

"Go through several men? You make me sound wanton and depraved."

"Okay, two men in four years. But both bad choices. It's time for you to go for the real thing. Make a pass at Toby."

Kate blinked again. "Pass? You seem conveniently to forget he lives with Free—"

"Whom we all know is *too* free. That man deserves someone trustworthy, frugal, good with tools."

"You make me sound like a cross between Scrooge and Ms. Tool Time."

"Did I forget to add that you're cute, too?" Verna added, tucking a strand of Kate's wayward hair behind her ear. "If Meg Ryan had dark hair, you could be her twin."

It was hard to force a frown while grinning, but Kate gave it her best shot. "Okay, I'm flattered. But since when have you been one to give such effusive compliments—" She stopped short. "Oh, I get it. You're playing matchmaker. I thought you'd decided to leave that to me after trying to set up the bakery guy with that woman."

"How was I to know he was gay?"

"Or after setting up that couple who had so much in common—came from the same city, had kids the same age."

"I didn't know they'd just gotten divorced," Verna murmured.

Kate paused. "You're my best friend, and a dynamite breakfast chef for Beau's Bed-and-Breakfast. But I don't think you're all that suited to be a matchmaker as well." Kate winked. "That is *my* role around here."

"Okay, so maybe I set up a gay man with a woman, and accidentally tried to reunite two recently divorced people. But as your best pal, I am well aware of your thing for pirates. And that Toby Mancini is a pirate in the rough if I ever saw one. Plus, Kate, it's time someone clued you in that brisk walks to Fisherman's Wharf and treks to Caffé Trieste for almond-flavored lattes do not constitute a *real* social life.'' Verna handed the breakfast tray to Kate. With both of Kate's hands clutching the tray, Verna leaned over and popped open the top button of Kate's blouse.

Kate, looking down at her exposed collarbone, gasped. "Now I look like a serving wench!''

Verna smiled mischievously. "Exactly.''

KNOCK-KNOCK.

Toby, lying in the lounge chair that had also served as his bed last night, flicked his wrist and stared at the hairs on his arm. *My watch is still on my dresser, back in my house.* He glanced toward the door. *Must be seven. Time for breakfast.*

He stood slowly, feeling every ache in his body. He'd fallen asleep on the chair in the wee hours while watching his house, contemplating how he could pull off the Monday dinner, but he hadn't concocted one damn idea. Analyzing mergers and acquisition deals was one thing. Analyzing how to get back into his home, pretend he was still engaged to Free, and at the same time outwit her new boyfriend's snarling Dobermans—had he heard the guy call them Mickey and Minnie?—was a different story.

Toby trudged across the room. *Mickey and Minnie?* The guy probably also had two German shepherds named Donald and Daisy. Reaching the door, Toby opened it.

"You look awful!'' Kate blurted.

"Good morning to you, too.''

She scrunched her face. With her eyes squeezed shut, she said, "Insert foot?''

"No offense taken.''

She opened her eyes and grinned. He liked the way her lips curved when she smiled, giving her an impish appearance. He'd never noticed before how her blue eyes sparkled, like sunlight glittering on the ocean.

"I brought breakfast." She held up the tray. "And I didn't drop it, either."

He looked down. Scrambled eggs, biscuit, jam, butter. Things he could easily recognize, even without his glasses. When his stomach rumbled loudly, Toby placed his hand on his midriff. "Guess I didn't realize how—" His hand froze on his bare stomach. He was standing in front of her in his underwear, *again.*

He quickly folded his hands over himself. "Sorry. Heard you knock. Forgot how I was dressed. Or not." He edged behind the door.

Kate laughed, although he detected a nervousness in it. "I have a brother a few years younger than me. I've seen him in underwear and plenty less, although you're nothing like my brother! Shall I put this tray on the table next to the window?"

Nothing like her brother? Did that make him less or more? "Sure."

As she passed, Toby inhaled the tantalizing aroma of buttery eggs and roasted coffee—and mingled in with those smells, the faint scent of soap and lilacs.

Kate's scent.

He was glad he was behind the door, because his body was reacting in ways that it shouldn't for a man whose world had supposedly been turned upside down.

"Shall I set the table for you?" Kate asked from across the room.

A hazy light outlined her form as she stood in front of the windows. Without his glasses, she had a slightly fuzzy quality that made her look almost ethereal. Her hair, short and unkempt, framed her oval face like a spiky, dark halo. He wondered if she purposefully wore her hair that way, or if she just couldn't be bothered with putting a lot of effort into a style. Funny how

Kismet—fate—had brought this Motown-playing, car-bombing woman so powerfully back into his life.

He realized Kate was waiting. "Sure," he said, having completely forgotten what she'd asked, reasonably certain it had something to do with breakfast.

As she pulled utensils from a rolled napkin and set them next to the plate, he checked out her color-wheel outfit of the day. Except for that stringlike vest, she'd kept to one color—blue. Even her sandals were blue. Compared to the blast of colors she wore last night, this morning she looked almost tame—like a piece of soothing sky had floated into this red, angst-ridden room.

She didn't seem to want to leave. "Shall I pour your coffee?"

He didn't seem to want her to leave. "Sure."

When she bent over, his gaze wandered down her soothing blue blouse to her curvaceous bottom. In the window, her silhouette was lushly defined. Round. Firm. He gulped. Suddenly the blue of those jeans wasn't so soothing after all.

Stop staring at her blue behind.

He quickly tried to look elsewhere. As though he couldn't aim his eyes properly, his gaze ricocheted wildly to a painting, bounced off a curtain rod and skidded over a lamp shade before it finally landed on the coffee she was pouring. Steam rose from the cup, hot and transparent like his thoughts.

"Milk?"

"Sure," he croaked. He never took milk in his coffee. But just as the liquid cooled the coffee's temperature, maybe it would also temper his hot thoughts.

"Sugar?"

He groaned. His hot and sweet thoughts.

Kate tilted her head and flashed him a perplexed look. "Was that a yes or a no?"

"Yes," he answered huskily. He stepped a bit more behind the door, wishing these damn stretchy undies were boxers.

She filled a heaping spoonful and stirred it into the cup. "Come and get it while it's hot!"

Great. I won't be able to leave this room for the rest of my life. "I'll...wait until you leave."

Kate stiffened and turned her back to him. "Oh! Right! You're—" holding her head at an odd angle, she began slowly walking backward toward the door "—you're naked. Nearly. I'll leave now...give you your privacy." She rapidly shuffled backward, her arms swinging as though she were doing a moon-walking dance. She had hit a pretty impressive pace when the back of her foot hit the edge of the gargantuan bed. Her arms flailed wildly as she teetered.

Toby lunged from his hiding place and caught her just as she toppled backward. The impact of her weight pushed him off balance. He staggered back a few feet, his arms grabbing Kate's middle, just as he had grasped the pitcher last night—

Whomp!

They fell sideways onto the bed, their sandwiched bodies bouncing in tandem on the plush red cover. Toby attempted to steady himself by grabbing a chunk of the slick satiny cover above Kate's head. *Whoosh.* It yanked loose. He flew back, pulling the cover and something heavy on top of him. Something smelling of lilacs.

He opened his eyes and stared into a pair of big blue ones. *Just what I need—more blue.* Kate lay on top of him, the red satin cover enveloping both of them like a plush, exotic cocoon. A plush, bouncing, throbbing cocoon.

"What's...wrong...with...this...bed?" Toby asked between surging motions.

"It's a...water bed."

He didn't dare nod his head in understanding. The motion might trigger a mini-tsunami. Trying to quell the up-and-down motions, he lay stiffly—or as stiffly as a water bed allowed one to lie—wondering how in only a few moments, Kate had gone from serving breakfast to lying on top of him. He tried to think how to extricate himself from the motion, the blue, the red cocoon, the lilacs, but they all conspired against him. He could only think about Kate's breasts, squished against his chest like two sweet...water balloons.

"Sorry about this," Kate said breathily.

"It's okay. I like water balloons." Water balloons. God, he was losing it.

"What?"

"Beds. I like water...beds."

Kate sighed, which made her breasts press harder again his chest. Toby thought feverishly of baseball. No go. He switched gears to a long-ago memory of a Monopoly game. Traveling fast, he had two hotels on Boardwalk when Kate whispered, "I never should have let Verna unbutton me."

"What?"

"Nothing. Your breakfast is getting cold."

It's the only thing that is. He tried to move from underneath Kate, but the wriggling and pushing only worsened his condition.

He didn't think her eyes could get any wider, but they did. Those big blue saucers blinked. Her hair, which before had looked stylishly unkempt, now looked positively wild. With those guileless eyes and heathen hair, she was like a mixture of innocence and sin. Blue and red. Water and balloons.

"Kath-e-rine Corr-i-gan," squealed a high-pitched woman's voice. "You're supposed to be servin' *breakfast!*"

After a beat, Toby offered, "This isn't what you think, ma'am."

"I wasn't born yesterday." With a self-righteous snort, Melanie walked briskly past the bed to the table. Peering through a gap in Kate's wild hairdo, Toby watched a fuzzy Mrs. Corrigan adjust what appeared to be the angle of the fork and knife. "Katherine forgot the salsa, so I brought some—although it doesn't appear you two really need it."

Melanie set a container neatly on the table, turned and walked past them, her gaze glued to the door as though she had on blinders.

"Thank you, ma'am," Toby mumbled. If he weren't pinned to the bed by Kath-e-rine Corr-i-gan, he'd have kicked himself. He was brought up always to respect women, but Mrs. Corrigan would never believe that after catching him nearly naked, *twice,* with her daughter. And this time, in bed.

Melanie halted. "You're welcome," she responded belatedly. "Katherine, I believe there are other guests who need your attention. *If* you have the strength."

"I don't know," Kate answered in that droll tone he recognized from last night when the three of them had met on the landing. "Toby's done plumb taken it out of me."

With a snort of shock, Melanie strode from the room.

3

KATE PUSHED HERSELF off Toby and jumped onto the floor. "That's the last time I serve breakfast unbuttoned," she said shakily, fumbling with her top.

She seemed more excited than flustered. Toby debated if their reactions to each other were because of this red room, or was there some red-hot chemistry between them? "The most I saw was your collarbone," Toby countered, mainly to calm Kate's reaction. He sat up and tugged the satin cover over his middle. "Why'd you tell your mother I took it gum out of you?"

"Plumb."

"Mothers don't like finding their children—especially their daughters—in compromising positions. After last night's bowl incident—and this morning's bed incident—she probably thinks I'm a marauding, sex-starved heathen."

A rush of pink stained Kate's cheeks. Blinking, she stammered, "I—I don't think you're a heathen."

"Just marauding and sex starved?"

The pink in her cheeks deepened to red. Kate cleared her throat. "Funny," she said, "Melanie didn't mention any of the bowl stuff this morning. She's usually the queen of the rumor mill."

So Kate wasn't going to answer his question. Which answered his question. "Maybe she's giving me the benefit of the doubt," he said gently. "Mothers are like that."

A light flashed in Kate's eyes. "My kid brother always got the benefit of the doubt. So I guess you do, too. But then, in my family, the men wore the pants."

He cocked one eyebrow at her outfit, opened his mouth, then closed it. Some things were best left unsaid. "Your mom's just being a mom. Have you ever thought it might shock—even upset her—when you say things like you 'skip' around with naked men or that I took it 'plum' out of you?" He gave his head a shake. "What is that—some kind of Southern fruit expression?"

"Yeah, we Southerners like to mix up fruit in our sayings," Kate answered in an exaggerated drawl. "Like 'peachy keen.' Or 'sassafras.'"

"We Italians have our sayings, too." He remembered a saying his mom often said. *"Questa casa non èstà un albergo. This house isn't a motel."* Ironic how, for Kate, it was both. "Sassafras isn't a fruit," he added teasingly.

"Too bad. It would have been a good one."

He suppressed a smile. Kate had spunk and fire—attributes that were refreshing compared to most of the women he'd known. "It's your business how you converse with your mother, but if you wouldn't mind a bit of friendly advice, instead of reacting to her, you might try to understand her."

"Reacting?" Kate ruffled her fingers through her hair, which caused several tufts to stick up higher.

"Yes, reacting. Those skipping and Southern-fruit expressions are reacting."

"It's like I told you last night. These comments are my only defense."

"Has anyone ever told you sarcasm is a form of indirect anger?"

"Thought you were a businessman, not a shrink."

"I subscribe to *Psychology Today.*"

"Oh." She leveled him a look. "Does that magazine

also tell you why you blast Beethoven? Maybe he was deaf, but the rest of us aren't.''

"No," he answered, sitting straighter. "But the magazine did have a fascinating article on women who blow up people's cars." The article was really about women who blow-dry their hair, but he had the urge to stretch the truth and one-up that little Beethoven dig.

Kate crossed her arms. "And why do they?"

"Would you believe...repressed stick-shift envy?"

Her mouth dropped open before it snapped shut. "I don't believe that!" Her eyes narrowed. "But I do believe you'll never forgive me for blowing up your car, which wasn't entirely my fault, by the way." She paced a few steps, as though burning off some excess energy.

If he didn't need to remain sitting on the bed, covering his underclad body, he'd pace, too. He'd *loved* that car, a tan Firebird with gold trim. Sleek. Powerful. He'd had it only one week, and then *bam*. It went from Firebird to fireball. "So if it wasn't entirely your fault, whose fault was it?"

She turned, her eyes wide, as though amazed he might finally be willing to hear an explanation. "The kid with the sparkler," she said simply.

"Thought your pickup had a gas leak. Was that also his fault?"

She skewered her mouth. "No," she finally said. "Of course not. But I didn't know it had a gas leak. For that matter, I didn't know that kid would throw the sparkler onto the stream of gasoline that led to..."

"My car. That string of events led to my car exploding in a ball of fire." He meant to be ticked. But instead, he was overly aware that *he* felt like exploding into a ball of fire. Exploding, burning and...consuming Kate?

They stared at each other for a long moment, the intensity of their gaze building until it was palpable, like a stream of gasoline waiting to be ignited. His gaze dropped from her eyes to her top button—she'd been so anxious trying to button it, she'd missed. The material fell open, offering a teasing glimpse of creamy skin. If he glanced farther down, he could detect the soft swell of the top of her breasts, which were rising and falling with her increased breaths.

A bolt of desire seared through him. He was tired of being the businessman, playing the game, abiding by the rules. He wanted to break loose, live, feel, experience. Again he thought there was a reason they were in Kismet: fate had brought them to this moment.

"Kate," he murmured huskily. "Come here."

Her blue eyes sparked fire as she took a step toward him, then stopped. "Free," she said softly.

He started to say it was over between him and Free. Hell, Free had some boyfriend with Disney Dobermans—there was hardly room for Toby. But he wasn't ready to explain all that right now. Tomorrow night, he needed to pretend to his future boss and his wife that Free was still his fiancé. And he'd learned in business that to cinch the deal, you didn't preview your game plan. Not to anyone. Because you never knew what small piece—what seemingly insignificant admission—might blow up the entire transaction.

But despite the justification, he felt guilty not telling Kate the truth.

When he didn't answer, Kate nodded as though understanding that Free stood between them. Looking away, she murmured, "Now your breakfast really *is* cold. I'll get you another plate of eggs."

"I'm not all that hungry, actually. The biscuits and coffee will be plenty." Now *he* felt like a dog, letting the conversation shift to something inconsequential, like eggs and biscuits. But he had no choice. "I'd rather you brought me some clothes," he added quickly.

"Okay!" Obviously eager to be of help—or maybe

eager to escape their heated moment—Kate walked toward the door, which with her long legs took two or three strides. "I'll go next door and ask for your—"

"No!" Toby had one foot on the floor, but stopped himself from following her. He really wasn't in the mood to run after her dressed only in his Calvins. When Kate turned back with a surprised look, he explained, "I don't want you going to my home."

"Why?"

"It's early."

"Not that early. Besides, Verna's already seen Free in her signature bead outfit. She was walking with—" Kate pursed her lips. "Anyway," she continued, "Free must know you're running around town naked, or nearly naked. It would make sense *someone* would show up requesting your clothes."

"But not you."

Kate smirked. "Why? Will she think I'll try to blow up your shirts?"

She'd probably welcome that. Because right now she's ripe to act out some of her misguided anger. "No, I don't want your going over there because I don't want Free to know I'm staying next door."

"Why?"

"She might try to get even." Might? She'd already shown her hand with the boyfriend and his Dobermans. Probably thought she'd successfully ruined Toby's dinner, his job opportunity. Toby knew it was best to let Free keep thinking that, rather than give her another opportunity to screw things up.

"Vengeance?" Kate looked perplexed. "What'll she do—throw beads at us?"

Chalk one up for Kate's humor. "No," he said, fighting a smile. "Let's just say I don't want her to think I'm fooling around."

"You?" Kate sputtered. "As though she's so innocent!"

Touché. "It'll only aggravate things if she thought I was getting back at her. You know, a tit for a tat." Now he felt his face go hot. "Although she'd probably never dream I'd be getting back at her with you."

He felt bad as soon as the words came out of his mouth. It sounded as though he were telling Kate she wasn't alluring. Because she *was* alluring—in her own spontaneous, high-energy, colorful way. Plus, she was pretty damn cute with that mind-of-its-own hairdo.

He gave his head a shake. This was insane, thinking about Kate when he had to get back on good footing with Free. One thing at a time. "She probably thinks I called my best friend from a phone booth, asked him to pick me up, and that I'm now staying at his place in Mill Valley," he continued. "Thinking I'm far away, her guard will be down. She won't feel the urgency to change locks, for example. Which means I have a good shot at getting back inside the house, which will give me a chance to retrieve my keys and clothes, get stuff ready for dinner—"

"Dinner?" Kate quirked one eyebrow. "You're thinking about cooking at a time like this? That's just like my mother. We could be in the middle of an earthquake, and she'd be fretting the soufflé might fall."

He smiled. Although Kate could sometimes irk him, she could also lift his mood with her quirky life views. It he were totally honest with himself, Free had never really affected his moods one way or the other.

Pushing that insight aside, Toby explained, "I have to throw a dinner party tomorrow night because I think— no, I *know*—my potential employer is ready to offer me a job, if I don't blow it. I need to do everything in my power to insure my home life is normal by then." He didn't want to ponder what "normal" meant. Or how he planned to reach this pretend normalcy in a little over twenty-four hours.

"Okay, if you don't want me to knock on your front door, and you don't want to saunter over in your red undies, what do you expect to wear for the time being?"

"Your mother's yellow-flowered housedress?"

"It does go nicely with red."

Kate stared at Toby. One corner of his mouth crooked upward, as though he couldn't decide whether to let go and laugh or just silently enjoy their moment of whimsy. He still looked tired, but a bit more relaxed than when she'd first seen him last night on her doorstep. Plus, she liked him without glasses. She could see the soft brown of his eyes better, which she'd *really* seen better when she'd lain on top of him. Up close, his eyes were a deep, rich caramel, which complemented his butterscotch-colored hair.

If this guy were food, he'd be yummy.

Her gaze dropped. The same yummy butterscotch also carpeted his chest. Swirls of thick hair ran rampant over his pecs and cascaded down his midriff. With that hairy, nicely molded chest rising above the red satin cover, he no longer looked like next-door neighbor Toby. Last night, she'd thought he looked vaguely like a swash-buckler in the glow of the lamp, but he still had that aura, even in daylight. She recalled his sultry invitation. *Come here.* In that heated moment, she'd almost gone. She, who'd *never* gone after a man, much less full speed ahead, yet she'd had the urge to shove her passion into overdrive and go for it.

"What are you thinking about?" Toby asked.

"Driving," she croaked. *Driving?* Time to get back to the planet Earth. "I have an idea," she said quickly, trying to sound grounded and together even though her insides were anything but. "You have no money, and you obviously can't go next door to get your wallet, so I'll use my credit card and purchase you some clothes.''

He frowned. ''What kind of clothes?''

''Guy stuff. Trust me, I have a younger brother so I know what guys wear. Plus, I have a keen dressing sense.''

His frown deepened as he gave her a once-over.

She decided to ignore his obvious disapproval of her dressing sense. She didn't dress for men, anyway. She dressed to please herself.

He gave her a dead-on look. ''I don't want to look like a walking color wheel.''

''What's that supposed to mean?''

He pointed a very determined index finger at her. ''No crayon box colors. Especially nothing red. I'll blend in with this room and no one will ever find me again.''

Jeez, he could get touchy. Must be his Italian nature coming to the forefront. ''No problem.''

He looked relieved. ''Hand me that notepad on the table.'' She did as told. He began jotting something down.

''Don't you need your glasses?''

He barely looked up. ''I'm nearsighted. It's the far-away stuff that gets blurry.'' He began scribbling. ''I must have a pocket on my shirt, left side preferably.''

''Front of your shirt—or back?''

He offered a small if-that-were-really-funny-I'd-laugh smile before continuing. ''And I abhor black pants.''

Abhor. That had to be worse than *hate.* ''What about purple ones?'' When his eyebrows shot up, she quickly mumbled, ''Just kidding.'' But she wasn't. After red, purple was her favorite color, but it didn't seem helpful to mention that right now.

''As I said, no black pants. My closet was filled with them growing up—black pants for school, for church, for weddings. I prefer—''

"Khaki. Beige."

His brows drew together. "How'd you know?"

Because I've observed you for the past five years wearing those boring colors. Buddy, if you walked in the Sahara Desert, no one would ever find you again. "Because that's what I've seen you wearing," she said sweetly.

He jotted something down on the paper. "So it's understood. No—"

"No black pants." She pressed her fingers to her temples and squeezed shut her eyes. "It's burned into my memory forever. I'll never again buy black pants for myself. Or my children. Or my children's children." She opened her eyes. "Anything else?"

He shot her a look. "Here're my sizes," he said, ripping off a piece of paper. "And I like, uh, extra breathing room in my pants."

She accepted the paper, holding her breath as she imagined what that meant. Maybe what they said about Italian men was true. Stallions. They were so hot, so passionate, they needed... "Extra breathing room," she repeated breathlessly, gripping the paper so tightly she heard it crinkle. She loosened her grip for fear her sweaty fingers would smudge the numbers. How much extra was extra?

Her mind was reeling.

"Is the room rocking?" She walked lock-kneed to the bedpost and grabbed its smooth knob. Holding on, she braced herself. Had to be a three on the Richter scale. Maybe a four.

"No. But you're swaying."

With horror, she realized he was right. It was that damn breathing-room comment. She dropped her hold on the knob and pretended to read the piece of paper, which she might have been able to do if she wasn't shaking. Staring at the jumping numbers, she said, "Extra.

Breathing. Pocket." Kate, the one-word girl, was at it again. She began backing up toward the door. "I'll leave." Good. Two words. "Now." *Damn.*

"I bet if you face the door it would be easier to walk out."

Bobbing her head in agreement, she swiveled in a half-turn and sped from the room.

AN HOUR LATER, Kate strode down Columbus Avenue, a woman on a serious clothes mission. Unfortunately, this serious mission had a serious hitch—few North Beach stores were open at eight o'clock on a Sunday morning. In fact, the only two businesses she'd found open so far were a tattoo parlor and a bakery. Needing fortification, she'd grabbed a latte at the bakery. They didn't "do flavors" as the surly guy behind the counter informed her, so she'd had to take hers straight up, no almond flavoring.

Sometimes a girl on a serious mission had to rough it.

At that moment, a woman with long, wavy black hair walked outside a storefront, lugging a flat rectangle of wood. She wore a flowing yellow dress embroidered with brightly colored flowers along her neckline and hem.

"Good sense of color," Kate thought. *She's probably a very interesting, with-it person.*

The flat rectangle the woman was lugging turned out to be one of those sandwich signs. As she propped it open, Kate saw that both sides were chalkboards. In orange, yellow and blue chalky script, Kate read the words Bab's Barbary Post.

Barbary Post. A cute play on Barbary Coast, the name of this part of San Francisco during the Gold Rush. Kate had always liked to imagine what the Barbary Coast had been like, filled with danger and sailors. She'd read stories about the saloons, miners, shoot-outs, and gambling, but all that faded in comparison to *her* fantasy of the Barbary Coast, which included swashbuckling, dangerous pirates.

Of course, her fantasies of anywhere in the world—even Fargo, North Dakota—included swashbuckling, dangerous pirates.

Approaching the plate-glass window of Bab's Barbary Post, Kate gasped. There, in the window, was a mannequin dressed in black leather pants and a flowing red shirt, its neckline revealing a lot of mannequin chest flesh. The poor guy had seen better days. He was missing one arm, and his painted-on hair was partially chipped off, but if Kate squinted just right, he had that hazy, dangerous image of a bad-boy pirate.

A sign, hung around his neck, read Come Inside, Matey. It was a call from the pirate gods. Katey the matey stepped inside.

"Good morning!" called the dark-haired woman.

"Mornin'," Kate answered, looking around. Bab's Barbary Post looked like a catchall for stuff from the sixties. Incense burned next to the cash register. A poster of Jimmie Hendrix decorated the back wall, his guitar pointing to an advertised "unisex" bathroom. An assortment of tie-dyed shirts hung on racks to her right. On a neighboring bookcase, a parrot perched on a shelf. Kate stared at it, wondering if it was moving slightly or if this was an extra strong latte.

"It's stuffed," Bab explained, following Kate's line of vision. "Loved that bird. Bought it because I wanted a pet that wouldn't be underfoot, you know, like a dog or cat. So I bought a parrot. Didn't know he liked to drink wine and walk everywhere."

Kate blinked. "It used to be your pet?"

"For nearly fifteen years. Francis—that was his name. Oh, and I'm Bab." After reaching over and shaking Kate's hand, Bab pointed a glittery red fingernail at the bird. "He and I had a better relationship than I had with any man." Bab's aqua-blue eyes—outlined in thick black eyeliner that matched her hair color—gazed lovingly at the parrot.

"Francis?"

"Named him after Francis Drake. You know, the explorer for Queen Elizabeth."

This was right up Kate's alley. "Francis Drake." One of the cooler pirates in history.

"Yeah. Had a wild side, though. Bet he stuck out in Queen Elizabeth's court."

"Bet she liked that," Kate noted, really speaking for herself now. She shifted her gaze to the mannequin, which had its back to her. For an inanimate object, it had an awfully cocky stance.

"That's Raymond."

For a mind-numbing moment, Kate wondered if that was one of Bab's former ex's, stuffed. But when she caught a gouge in the back of Raymond's neck, an indentation that revealed his plaster innards, Kate breathed a sigh of relief.

As she continued staring at Raymond, an image of Toby bounded into her mind. How last night he'd looked so wild, so daring in the splash of kaleidoscope colors. How the blues, reds, yellows spilled over the contours of his body. And how, at that moment, he'd looked like a swashbuckler par excellance.

And when he again put on his boring "khaki or beige" clothes, the pirate would be covered, hidden from the world. Could there be a greater sin than disguising a pirate?

Kate took a long sip of latte, the hot liquid warming her insides and firing her thoughts. "Great outfit," she repeated slowly, her gaze traveling over Raymond's clothes. She slugged down another sip of latte.

"Thanks," Bab said, rearranging some crystal figurines in a glass case. "Raymond—he was my boyfriend when I lived in Pacific Heights—had a fantastic dressing style, but underneath he was more boring than the mannequin. Just goes to show, you can't judge a book by its cover."

"I hear you," Kate agreed, thinking of the two "covers" she'd dated over the past four years. Cover number one, Davie, sported a devil-may-care style—it didn't take long to discover it was really a I-don't-care-about-anyone-but-myself style. And cover number two, Henry, swooped into her life, but failed to mention he was swooping into several other women's lives at the same time. Eventually Kate had to laugh at that one. Whereas most women got irked at some two-timing guy, Kate had landed a four-timing swooper.

Thinking about them now, Kate realized both were the opposite of Toby. He didn't dash, storm or swoop. Okay, he'd sort of dashed that night his car blew up, but otherwise he was a seemingly boring, businesslike guy...or so she had thought until last night. Kate was beginning to guess ol' Toby had more hidden plundering pirate in him than he showed the world.

Maybe she could help him show more of that hidden side. Not that it mattered one way or the other to her, of course. After all, he belonged to another woman. A two-timing, bead-loving, name-changing woman who had chased him, nearly naked, out of his own home—but who was Kate to judge?

She checked out Raymond's backside. From this angle, he looked to be about the same size as Toby. She pulled the piece of paper out of her pants pocket and reviewed the sizes Toby had jotted down. She hadn't looked at his handwriting before—each curl and stroke looked very exact. Was he that way in life, too? Overly cautious? Excessively careful?

This guy definitely needed help bringing out his wilder, more colorful side. "Do you have any clothes for sale?" Kate asked, trying to sound innocently interested.

"Sorry, no clothes." Bab continued adjusting what looked to be a Twiggy doll on a shelf.

"Oh." Kate glanced at the mannequin. "What about...those clothes on Raymond?"

"What about them?"

"What about my buying them?"

Bab propped Twiggy against a lava lamp and straightened. Looking Kate in the eye, Bab asked, "You want to buy the clothes off Raymond?"

Kate nodded.

Bab gave Kate a quick once-over. "Honey, I don't think they'd fit you."

"Oh, they're not for me." Kate waved the piece of paper as though that explained everything. "I have his— Toby's—measurements. We could check if his numbers fit Raymond's."

Bab waited a beat before responding. "Is Toby going to a costume party?"

Kate mulled that one over. "Yes," she lied. "It's a costume brunch. A literary event based on Robert Louis Stevenson's *Kidnapped*. It starts in an hour." Hey, this story sounded pretty good if she had to say so herself. Feeling a rush of dramatic flair, she continued exuberantly. "Everybody has to come as a character from the book—and Toby would look great as my swashbuckling fantasy. I mean, as a piratelike character. I'd seen Raymond—the mannequin, not your ex—in the window a few weeks ago and thought at the time how great Toby would look in that outfit at his pirate birthday party."

"I thought you said it was a literary event. And Raymond wasn't in the window a few weeks ago."

Kate raised her eyebrows, feigning surprise as she desperately backpedaled in her mind. "Yes, it's a literary event and a birthday party rolled into one. Toby's favorite book is *Kidnapped,* hence the literary angle, but we're also kidnapping him first, although I need to get him dressed before that, while he's still asleep, so we can roll him into the party looking festive.'' Kate swiped at her brow. This story was getting deep, and complicated. She wasn't sure anymore if she was rolling, dressing or kidnapping him. ''And I forget exactly when I saw Raymond,'' she said, plowing ahead. ''Maybe it was a few days, not a few weeks, ago. You know how time flies.''

Bab squinted, which made her kohl-lined eyes disappear into two thick, black slashes. ''How many lattes have you had this morning?'' When Kate started to answer, Bab cut her off with a wave of her hand. ''I wasn't particularly fond of Raymond the man, but I've gotten more attached to his clothes since they've been on Raymond the mannequin.''

Kate looked at the mannequin. ''Yes, yes, I can see what you mean.'' Actually, she didn't, but it felt good to be on Bab's side of the conversation instead of out there by herself in *Kidnapped*-literary-birthday-brunch land. ''But wouldn't it be nice to know they're on a living person again?'' She turned and smiled at Bab, trying to look sincere even though her top lip was quivering. Maybe that latte was extra strong.

''Hmm.'' Bab tilted her head and looked at the mannequin as though pondering the question. ''What kind of man?''

Kate clutched her latte, vaguely aware her fingertips were digging into the cup. ''A swashbuckler in the rough,'' she said huskily.

Knock-knock.

Lying on his lounge chair, the spot where he slept, rested and watched his home, Toby looked at the door to Kismet. Was it Melanie again, checking on him? Or worse, maybe she was ready to chastise him for lying on top of her daughter. He wondered if it would help his cause if he confessed that he hadn't lain on top of anyone except his two-timing girlfriend for the past six years. Wearing nothing but a pair of red underwear sorely undermined that argument. He looked like a professional layer if nothing else.

Knock-knock. "Toby?"

He recognized the trace of Southern drawl, which was softer than Mother Melanie's. He got up and headed toward the door, grabbing a towel and wrapping it around his midriff along the way. When he opened the door, there stood Kate, a grin on her flushed face.

"Hi!" she said, then waved awkwardly.

"Hi." His gaze dropped to a large white plastic bag with a Pudgie's Pizza logo on its side. "Pizza? I already ate the biscuits and coffee."

Kate frowned, then followed his gaze to the bag. "Oh, no. It's from Bab's Barbary Post. She recycles pizza bags for her merchandise. Very environment-friendly and economical."

For a fleeting moment, he felt as though he were carrying on a conversation with Free, who spoke in non sequiturs. And he'd put up with it, just as he put up with her other traits, because that was how he grew up—always being responsible and patient with his siblings, his mother, and anyone else who wandered into his life. "Okay." It seemed as good a response as any to Bab and her pizza bags.

Kate rocked back on her heels, like a kid waiting for something. "May I come in?"

Toby opened the door wide. Kate almost skipped past. With great fanfare, she set the bag on the bed. Gesturing toward it, she announced, "I brought you some clothes."

He hoped it wasn't something with pepperoni all over it. "Thank you."

Kate looked around. "So, what have you been doing since I left?"

"Took up kayaking. Tried my hand at parasailing." When she flashed him a puzzled look, he felt a stab of guilt. Maybe her hair looked as though she could pick up radio waves from Cleveland, but the real Kate obviously had a gullible streak. "Seriously," he said, "I wondered how I could woo Mickey and Minnie."

Kate paused. "You shouldn't be left alone too often."

"I'm serious."

"So am I."

He offered a small smile. "Mickey and Minnie are the Dobermans."

Her blue eyes widened. "You're kidding!"

"I'm serious. That's what I heard them called, anyway."

"Who'd name two ferocious beasts Mickey and Minnie?"

He pretended to ponder that for a moment. "Somebody who had a very bad childhood experience at Disneyland?"

Kate's impish grin returned. "Instead of pointy ears, do those Dobermans have big rounded ones?"

"Hard to tell when you're running for your life." He didn't want to pursue this line of conversation. It would lead to discussing things like Free, her boyfriend-of-the-moment, and Toby's needing to feign things were hunky-dory between him and Free tomorrow night.

He had better things to do, like get dressed. He headed toward the bag, but Kate beat him to it. She snatched Pudgie's Pizza away and held it behind her. "I'm afraid..."

"Of what? Leftover pizza?"

"I'm afraid you'll throttle me when you see what's in here."

4

"I DON'T THROTTLE. And even if I did, I'd do it in a car." *Car. Firebird. Fireball.* Whoever thought up word association had a cruel streak. He motioned toward the bag. "Give me Chubbie."

She looked stricken. "I don't call you 'Undie.'"

"I meant the bag."

"Oh. Pudgie's." She started to hand it over, then hesitated. "I—I should exchange them." Her eyes were so wide, he could see the white all the way around the blue.

"Why?" He gestured as though to say *What's the problem? I haven't tried them on yet.* He reached for the bag. She stepped back. "What have you purchased that's so horrible?"

"The shirt has no pocket."

"I'll live." He reached. She stepped back. He blew out an exasperated breath. "Kate, I don't care about the fricking pocket! I just want to put something on my body other than a red satin comforter or a fuzzy white towel!" He never blew up. But then he'd never been homeless and clothesless before, either. Holding his emotion in check, he said as calmly as possible, "I know you did your best and for that I'm eternally grateful."

"You won't be mad?"

"No." If he answered anything else, he'd be wearing a towel for the rest of his life.

"You sure?"

"Yes, I'm sure," he lied, stealing her head-bobbing

technique to make it seem surer. "Positive. Absolutely. Right now, I'd wear almost anything. I'd wear your mother's pink-flowered housedress even though we both know pink isn't my color."

Kate's lips curled into that impish grin that did funny things to his insides. "All right," she said slowly, drawing the bag out from behind her back. "Guess I'm just being oversensitive."

"Yes, I guess you are," he answered, taking the bag. He reached inside and felt something soft, buttery. He pulled it out. "Black…leather…?"

Kate fumbled with her hair. "They didn't have any other kind of pants. I know you said you hated black pants, but I figured black *leather* pants would be different."

"Different all right," he murmured. "I'll look like a dominatrix."

Was he kidding? No way would anyone confuse him for anything other than an all-male hunk. "North Beach is known for its leather."

"North Beach is also the heart of the Beat generation, but that doesn't mean I need to look like Jack Kerouac." *Kerouac. On The Road. Firebird.* Closing his eyes, he rubbed his fingertips in a small circular pattern against his temple. "I'm sorry. You did your best. Black pants aren't the end of the world." He needed to chill. Kate had given him shelter, fed him, dressed him. So what if she was a dangerous, car-bombing, Motown-blasting woman? Underneath that color wheel was a heart, a soft and generous woman who reminded him he had a heart, too.

As his mother would say, "When life throws tomatoes, make a great pasta sauce."

Opening his eyes, he donned his most valiant smile. "Just as long as you didn't get me a matching black-fringed leather vest, I'll be fine." He peered into the bag. "Good God Almighty."

"That was the only shirt they had, too," Kate whispered apologetically.

Toby pulled out the red silk shirt. "Where'd you buy this stuff? Was a flamenco dancer giving a garage sale?" He stared at the clothing clutched in his hands. "Black leather pants and a bloodred shirt. Forget the dominatrix. People will think I'm a gigolo." He leveled a look at Kate. "Your mother will faint."

"She already did. Seven years ago, in this very room."

"Another of your captive naked men episodes?"

Kate's eyes widened. "I beg your pardon! You're not my captive, you're my guest. My uninvited guest, might I add. And although Melanie seems to think I traipse around my inn in the midnight hours with naked—or nearly naked—men, I'll have you know that last night is the wildest episode I've ever had with a man!"

Toby swore her hair stood on end. Staring at those flashing eyes and spiky hair, he mentally reassured himself that his Audi was safely parked in his garage. "Sorry. I'm not captive, just naked. And you've been wonderful. Better than wonderful. You're magnificent. Generous. Skinny."

Her eyes sparkled with gratitude. "I'm not skinny." But the tone of her voice said, "Am I? Really?" She pointed at the Pudgie's Pizza bag.

"There's something else in there?" he asked.

She bobbed her head yes.

"Is it red or black?"

She shook her head no.

Then there's hope. "Let's skip the surprise part and you just tell me what it is."

"Well, you don't have any more...well, you know..." She motioned toward his crotch.

"Underwear?"

She bobbed her head again. "Right. Underwear. You only have that red stretchy, clingy pair." She gulped several breaths as though the room suddenly lacked enough oxygen. "So I got you some more. They're Raymond's, Bab's ex."

Toby stared at Kate for a long, solid moment. "Did I miss a U-turn in this conversation? Who's Bab? Who's Raymond?"

"Bab runs Bab's Barbary Post, the store where I got your clothes. Raymond is her ex-boyfriend. His clothes were on the mannequin, and Bab let me buy them."

Toby rubbed his temple again. If he stayed in this conversation too long, he'd wear a patch a skin off his forehead. "I can comprehend wearing hand-me-downs. My younger brothers got mine. But…" Toby eased in a stream of air, willing himself to sound calm. "But I draw the line at wearing this Raymond fellow's underwear."

"No! You got it all wrong. Well, part of it wrong. The pants and shirt are hand-me-downs, okay. But Bab remembered some unopened T-shirts and underwear she'd bought for Raymond before they broke up." A cloud passed over her face. "Kind of a sad story. Seems Raymond dressed wildly, but was really a boring guy underneath. Laid concrete during the day, watched TV nonstop at night. One evening, when she was talking to Raymond, he pointed the remote at her and pressed the off button. That's when she knew it was over."

Toby opened his eyes, wondering if he pointed a remote at his own home, could he turn off Mickey and Minnie. Maybe if he pressed again, he'd also turn off Free and her boyfriend-of-the-moment. Maybe that Raymond fellow was onto something.

"Anyway," Kate continued, "I mentioned you were only wearing a pair of skimpy, clingy…" She did that breath-gulping thing again. "So Bab offered Raymond's undies. Her apartment is behind the shop, and she went back and got them." Kate pointed at the bag. "They're new. Unused. Factory fresh."

Toby dug inside the bottom of the bag and extracted a plastic-wrapped package. "Tiger-striped underwear?"

"As I said, Raymond liked to dress wildly." Kate began backing up toward the door. "I should give you your privacy, let you get dressed. I guess after that you'll be leaving, right?"

"I'd like to, except I need some shoes."

Kate stopped and frowned. "Darn. Forgot to ask if Raymond had any leftover ones."

"That's okay. They'd probably be purple-tipped silver-gilded cowboy boots. Actually, I was thinking you could help me break into my house."

"Break in? Where are Free and...?" Kate clamped shut her mouth.

"I saw them—with the dogs—leave about an hour ago. Probably to her favorite breakfast spot, Columbus Café—which means they'll be gone for at least another hour. I figure we can sneak in the kitchen window, which is never locked, get my shoes and some more clothes, my keys, then plan our next move."

"*Our* next move? When did I become your accomplice?"

"When you robbed Raymond of his clothes." Okay, it was a far-flung reason, but Toby was accustomed to saying some outrageous things while negotiating a deal.

She paused, seemingly lost in thought. "No," she answered slowly, her eyes twinkling mischievously, "it must have been after you agreed to help me get Melanie back to South Carolina."

"I never agreed to that."

She arched one eyebrow. "Let's see...you need to pull off some dinner tomorrow night? Seems you'll be needing more than just a little breaking in. You need a matchmaker to help patch it up with Free so you can be back in your house and entertain your boss who's going to offer you a promotion—*if* your home life appears normal.''

She was good. ''Why do you want your mother to go back to South Carolina? You seem to miss the fact that she's here for you.''

''That's what Verna says,'' Kate murmured, looking perplexed. She gave her head a shake. ''I'll leave so you can get dressed.'' And with that, Kate strode out of the room, walking forward instead of backward.

''GOOD MORN—GOOD LORD!'' Melanie's cheeks stained to a perfect pastel pink.

Kate followed the line of her mother's vision to the staircase. She almost blurted ''Good Lord'' too, except she'd lost the power of speech.

Toby stood in the middle of the staircase, looking like the swashbuckler of her dreams. The tight black leather pants encased his legs closer than skin around a sausage. Kate's gaze roamed up his molded calves to his muscled thighs. She skimmed over the bulge, trying not to dwell on its tiger-striped secret, her gaze finally landing on the deep vee in the flowing red silk shirt. Within the confines of that vee was the carpet of butterscotch hair, swirls and whorls of it, a regular chest-hair mob scene.

Melanie snorted, or tried to. Maybe she was simply having trouble breathing. ''Young man,'' she said hoarsely, ''you seem to have forgotten somethin'.''

A knife between his teeth? A sword in his hand? Kate's mind went into overdrive, like a hormone-crazed hamster on a treadmill.

''Yes, ma'am,'' Toby answered, ''I don't have my shoes.''

Kate's gaze swept down to Toby's bare feet. From this

distance, it was difficult to tell if the masculine tufts of hair on his big toes were butterscotch-colored as well.

"Do they call these summer colors in San Francisco?" Melanie asked, obviously breathing better because the familiar you're-not-dressed-properly tone was back.

"It appears so," Toby answered, continuing down the staircase. Was it Kate's imagination or did Toby walk differently dressed in those clothes? He truly moved like a panther. It took the molded leather to reveal the stealthy, muscle-rippling steps of a hunter on the prowl.

Plundering.

He stopped at the bottom of the steps. "You look lovely this morning, Mrs. Corrigan."

Lord. Even his voice had a predator's warning growl. For the second time in her life, Kate watched her mother blush. "Why, thank you," she oozed, her Southern accent suddenly stronger than black-strap molasses.

Kate pursed her lips so as not to say something she'd regret like "suck-up."

"You look nice too, Kate," Toby said.

She tried to glare at him, but it was difficult when heat flooded her cheeks and her heart was racing. "Why, thank you," she said, hearing the same black-strap molasses in her own voice. *Impossible!* Things were getting out of control. Toby wasn't Toby any longer. Where before she'd caught glimpses of the pirate, she now saw the sinewy, plundering, sex-starved, marauding swashbuckler in the flesh.

And, in her imagination, she was his woman, the object of this pirate's fiery passion. And what would a pirate's woman say at this magical moment? "Want some coffee?" Kate squeaked, hitching her head toward the kitchen.

He obviously caught her head-hitch because he politely excused himself and headed toward the kitchen.

"Those pants look mighty tight," Melanie whispered

as he walked away. "And that shirt! What kind of man dresses for work looking like that?"

She didn't want her mother getting overly enthralled with Toby. After all, she wanted her mother to return home, not become a swashbuckler groupie.

"He's a gigolo," Kate answered crisply before following him into the kitchen.

Inside, she saw Verna over Toby's shoulder. Verna was holding a spatula straight up into the air as she stared wide-eyed at Toby. "Coffee's over there," she said hoarsely.

Toby looked around. "Where?"

"There." Verna pointed with the spatula toward the coffeepot, which was partially hidden behind a cookie jar. Her eyes, however, stayed glued on Toby. When he moved, her gaze remained frozen on the space where he'd been standing.

"Are you okay?" Kate whispered to her friend's glazed expression.

"Those pants," Verna whispered. "Mick Jagger, step aside."

"Anybody else want coffee?" Toby asked from across the kitchen, pouring himself a cup.

"No, I drank a superstrength latte earlier," Kate said. "Strong enough to put hair on my chest." She and Verna shifted their gazes to Toby's chest.

"He certainly doesn't need one of those," Verna said under her breath. She raised her voice. "So you're Toby, the man from Kismet."

He smiled. "And you're...?"

"Verna, the woman from the kitchen." The phone that hung on the kitchen wall rang. Verna gave Kate a pointed glance. "It's your father again. He's been calling Melanie every five minutes for the past twenty, but she always has me say she's not here, so I'm not going to answer this time and give the same lame excuse."

Kate flashed her friend a what-is-this-about? look, although she really couldn't concentrate on anything but Toby, who sparked her wildest fantasies just standing in the kitchen.

Verna shrugged. "She confided to me that she's claiming her independence. Wants to be a new woman. Seems after your kid brother left home, she felt like Betty Crocker in a vacuum. Those were her exact words. Said something about wanting to retrieve something she'd lost."

Betty Crocker in a vacuum? Melanie? This was a new twist for Beaufort's Best Brownies' maker. As the phone stopped ringing, it occurred to Kate that she really ought to ponder this new twist in her mother's character. But there was Toby, sucking up every single facet of her attention.

He was leaning casually against the counter. Kate tried not to stare at the curve of thigh muscle underneath the strained leather. "A while back," he said to Verna, filling up the awkward silence, "weren't you the one who called about my playing Beethoven too loud?"

She motioned with the spatula toward Kate. "She made me do it."

Kate started to sputter in her defense, but Toby continued talking to Verna. "So you're the cook?" When she nodded, he added, "Wonderful breakfast."

"Why, thank you," she said on an escape of breath. "Kate and I fantasize about one day expanding this inn so it includes a real restaurant." She dropped her head and stared at Toby with big, gray glassy eyes.

Suck-up. Had to be the outfit. Fighting a surge of wildly irrational jealousy that she pretended had to be heartburn, Kate took a giant step and placed herself squarely between Verna and Mr. Meltdown. "We can't stand around all day drinking coffee. We have less than an hour to plan our break-in," Kate said loudly. *Jeez.*

She never acted like this, all huffy and dictatorial. All right, maybe occasionally she did, but only when she was telling Verna who to call.

"Break-in?" Verna asked, back to her normal voice.

"I need to retrieve some shoes and other things," Toby said, and took another gulp of coffee.

"Lou had feet like yours," Verna said. "Big. But I didn't keep any of his shoes." A sad look flickered across her face. Aimlessly smoothing a pleat on her skirt, she said, "So, I guess you didn't bring keys to your place if you're needing to break in. How about outside? Any keys hidden in a flower pot or something?"

"No. But we always leave the back kitchen window open a notch for fresh air. I figure Kate and I can jimmy open the window."

Kate frowned. "Isn't your kitchen about the same level as our kitchen?"

Toby nodded.

"We'll need a ladder to get to that window. Unfortunately, I loaned mine to Mr. Nelson down the street."

Toby shook his head. "No problem. You'll stand on my shoulders."

KATE AND TOBY STOOD in the alley behind his house, looking up at his kitchen window. "You have plants on the ledge," Kate noted.

"Herbs. Mainly basil." He stepped onto a patch of dirt underneath the window and crouched. "Step on my shoulders."

"Can't you crouch down more?"

"If I had extra breathing room in my pants, yes. But I don't, so no."

Kate needed some extra breathing herself after that comment. "Melanie has some stretchy fuzzy slippers that would go great with your black leather pants and red silk shirt. You could wear those and we could forget this.''

Toby shot her a look. ''I'm not adding fuzzy women's slippers to this outfit. Because if I did, there are certain parts of San Francisco I could never walk through. Now, get on my—''

''Shoulders. I know.'' Kate gingerly set one sandaled foot on a shoulder.

Toby raised his hands over his head. ''Grab hold,'' he commanded.

Was it her imagination or was he acting more demanding, more...piratelike...since he'd put on these clothes? She put her hands in his, but her foot still on the ground hesitated. What was she doing crawling onto the shoulders of this man? Did she really believe his story, complete with Dobermans named Mickey and Minnie? Maybe this wasn't even Toby, but a Toby-look-alike who was breaking in to steal, say, money or beads.

''What are you doing?'' he asked gruffly.

''Thinking.''

''Care to share your thoughts? Quickly? I want to get this over with.''

''Maybe you're not really Toby Mancini,'' she said rapidly, ''maybe you're a bead thief.''

Hunched over, he was quiet for a moment. ''*That* was what you were thinking?''

''Yes.''

''This is *my* house. We're getting *my* shoes and *my* clothes. If I was a mastermind bead thief, I'd do this under the cover of night, with professional tools, not with my next-door neighbor on my shoulders. Issue settled?''

A convincing argument. ''Okay.'' In one swift movement, she hoisted her foot and planted it on his shoulder. Her weight was totally on him, every muscle quivering as though she were doing some overall body isometric. Growing up a tomboy, she was used to climbing trees, fences, you name it. But climbing on top of Toby Mancini was suddenly difficult, probably because he made her knees weak. Heck, he made her whole body weak.

"Hold on." Toby took a deep breath. She heard him exhale, slowly, like an athlete ready to perform. Or a pirate ready to plunder. "I'm going to stand. Ready?"

"Ready," she squeaked.

As he lifted, she death-gripped his hands while her mouth emitted a prolonged sound, like "Who-o-o-a!" or "Aeee!" or a mixture of both. It was like being in a fast-rising elevator minus the elevator. The next thing Kate knew, she was peering at a basil leaf that tickled her nose. "Now what?" she croaked.

"First, try and be quiet. Second, lift the window frame."

She felt like Teri Garr in that old Mel Brooks film, *Young Frankenstein. Put the candle back.* "What if the window revolves, takes me with it, and you can't retrieve me?"

There was a pause before he spoke. "I wish you had told me you had an overactive imagination *before* we did this. Trust me, the window doesn't revolve. Lift the frame before my knees buckle and we end up lying on top of each other again!"

Was he flirting or yelling? Talk about sending mixed signals.

"Grab it!"

"I will," she snapped. Releasing both his hands, she fell forward and grabbed the bottom of the window frame. With a primal yell, she shoved it upward.

Thwack! It slammed against the top of the frame. For several seconds, something shuddered. Kate finally realized it was her. Before Toby could yell another instruction, she hurled the top half of her body over the windowsill and its little green plastic containers of herbs.

She landed across a large porcelain double sink, one arm in each as though doing a mid air push-up.

"Are you okay?" she heard Toby yell from outside.

"Peachy keen," she croaked, staring at a crack in the bottom of the sink. Clumps of dirt darkened a corner of the right sink, remnants of toppled herbs from her lunge. Grabbing the far edge of the sink, she tried to pull inside the bottom half of her body. Nothing budged. "I think I'm stuck."

Strong hands grabbed her thighs. She squealed.

"I said be quiet!" Toby whispered harshly. "Someone will call the police."

"Somebody already did," said a gruff male voice from outside the window. "Mind telling me what's going on here?"

Kate stared at the far kitchen wall and the reflection of a flashing blue light on it.

"Officer, this is my home," Toby began.

Kate closed her eyes, wondering if there had ever been a more humiliating moment than this. Her rump hanging out a window like some kind of wall ornament while two men—both in uniform—carried on a discussion.

She heard Toby saying something about not having any identification on him.

Great. No ID might mean they'd cuff him and cart him down to the station. And even if she lay really, really still, pretending she was some kind of rump wall hanging, they'd probably want to cuff and book her, too. And how would they do that, considering she was stuck? Would they drag her back out the window? Cuff her feet instead? Despite the dire circumstances, only one thing could make this worse.

"Kath-e-rine Corr-i-gan, what is goin' on here?"

Worse just arrived. Kate dropped her forehead against the cool sink bottom, imagining Melanie, her hands on her mauve-flowered hips, conversing with Kate's blue-clad behind as though it might answer.

"I can explain, Mrs. Corrigan," Toby said. "I left my things inside, so Kate was helping me break in—I mean, get back in."

"Do you know these people, ma'am?" the policeman asked.

"I believe that caboose belongs to my daughter. And this man is a gigolo."

Kate groaned, the sound echoing somewhere deep inside the sink drain.

"I can vouch for him, officer. That's Toby Mancini, our neighbor," said a woman's familiar voice.

Verna to the rescue. They wouldn't go to jail. They could steal Toby's stuff and call it a day.

"Toby accidentally locked himself out," Verna continued. "So Kate—she's the proprietor of Beau's Bed-and-Breakfast next door—is helping him get back into his house so he can retrieve his keys. That bottom belongs to Kate."

There was a long silence. Kate closed her eyes, knowing deep in her heart they had all turned and were looking at her bottom. She hoped beyond hope that these weren't the pair of pants with the threadbare hole above the back pocket.

"Katherine," said Melanie, "you really should learn to sew. Then you can repair holes in your clothing."

So it was that pair. *God, take me now.*

"All right," said the voice Kate now recognized as the police officer. "Just had to check. You folks have a nice day."

Several long, humiliating moments later, Kate opened her eyes. There were no more flashing blue lights against the far wall. After Verna said something about smelling brownies burning, it grew abnormally quiet outside.

"Did everyone leave me?" Kate asked the silence.

When no one answered, she wailed, "Oh, fine! Everyone goes to save the brownies and leaves me behind! And not just *me* behind, but my behind behind, too!"

"I'm not saving brownies," Toby said. "I'm still here."

"And I'm still stuck," she said, trying to sound grown-up despite her previous wailing.

"So I see."

She didn't want to think of that hole. Or what color underwear she wore today. "Give me a push."

"Promise not to squeal again? We don't want someone else calling the police."

"Promise."

She'd hardly finished saying the word before his hands gripped her thighs. She hadn't realized how large his hands were. Or how hot. Big, hot hands. Her mind reeled with the possibilities.

"Ready?"

She gulped a breath of air. "Ready," she whispered. Toby pushed gently. With the momentum, she grabbed the edge of the sink and scooted her legs through the window. "I'm in!" she chirped, half-sitting on the edge of the sink. With a hop, she landed on the green-and-white-checkered linoleum floor.

"Open the front door," Toby called from outside.

She looked around the spacious kitchen. This house was old, probably built in the same era as her home after the 1906 earthquake, during the years when people rebuilt this area in a variety of Edwardian, Anne, and other styles. Hers was Queen Anne. His was Edwardian. And whereas her kitchen had one swinging door to the main hallway, his had two doors, both shut.

"Which door?"

"In front of you, to the left."

"And Mickey and Minnie are gone, right."

"Right."

She headed across the kitchen. A few minutes later, she swung open the heavy wooden front door. There stood Toby. That tumbling lock of hair over his brow was starting to give him a bad-boy edge she hadn't noticed before. Add that red shirt with the sweat-inducing glimpse of chest hair, plus those body-clinging, mind-numbing black leather pants, and Kate suddenly felt another earthquake coming on.

She sucked in a deep breath and clutched the doorjamb. Had to be a five on the Richter scale.

Oblivious to her earthshaking experience, Toby walked past her and into the foyer. "We've got to move fast. I don't know how much longer Free is out with…" He didn't finish the sentence but instead murmured a string of epithets suitable for a double-crossed, backstabbed pirate.

"Right," Kate murmured, closing the door.

"First, I'll get my shoes. You clean up the mess in the kitchen."

She froze. The earth stopped moving. He expected her to clean up the kitchen?

Toby reappeared in the foyer, a pair of black corduroy slippers on his feet. "You're still here?"

She glanced at his feet. "Slippers?"

"They're the only ones the Dobermans didn't use as chew toys. Found my keys, though, so all is not lost."

Okay, she felt bad he was reduced to wearing slippers, and not so bad he was wearing a drop-dead-gorgeous pirate outfit, but she still wasn't over the other comment.

"I don't do kitchens," she said tersely.

One butterscotch eyebrow quirked. "Well, I do. You can stay here or join me, because I've got to clean up the basil catastrophe—otherwise, Free will know I broke in through the kitchen window. Then she'll probably change the locks or destroy the place—or both—and I might as well kiss off tomorrow night's dinner.'' He strode purposefully down the hallway.

Okay, so the guy wasn't as traditional as her father. Maybe she had overreacted a bit. Walking sheepishly behind him, she noticed photos hung on the walls. In one, a large group of people sat around a table, everyone smiling at the camera. Standing in the back, holding a platter of food, was Toby, grinning.

She stopped and peered at the photo. He must have been the cook. And obviously he was serving everyone. This guy definitely did kitchens. And she could barely manage to put together a sandwich.

Shuffling her feet, she headed down the hall, ready to do her kitchen penance.

"It's in the bag,'' Toby said as she entered. He held up a plastic bag, filled with dirt and basil leaves. "All cleaned up.''

"You're fast.''

"I know kitchens, especially this one.'' He looked around, a sadness shadowing his features. "Funny, I used to dream of running a restaurant, but instead I ran this kitchen.'' He handed the bag to Kate. "Hold this. I'll close the window to where it was before.'' She watched as he closed it, carefully leaving it open an inch or so. He brushed his hands. "Let's go out the front door. We'll toss the baggie in the trash at your place.''

"Won't she notice several basil plants are missing?''

He chuckled, but it lacked humor. "She wouldn't know her way around this kitchen if I drew her a map. She doesn't even know what's in the refrigerator, much less what's on the window ledge. The only cooking she ever did in this kitchen was with that guy last night.''

"Cooking?''

Toby gave his head a shake. "Forget it. Let's go.''

He took the bag from her hands—a gentlemanly gesture that seemed second nature to him—and led the way back down the hallway. They were halfway there when Kate heard a jiggling sound on the other side of the front door. She nearly slammed into Toby, who'd abruptly halted.

"It's them!" he whispered hoarsely. "Damn."

For the first time in her life, Kate wished fervently she'd been born a bead.

5

TOBY GRABBED KATE'S HAND and bolted back toward the kitchen. Kate stumbled after him. "We don't have time to throw ourselves back out the window," she whispered frantically.

They hit the green-and-white-checkered linoleum floor. "No window," he muttered. He yanked Kate sharply to the left toward a door against the side kitchen wall.

Down the hall, the front door creaked open. A man's voice. A woman's giggle.

Toby pulled Kate to him, her body flush against his. His face was so close she could see flecks of gold in his brown eyes, could count the stubbled hairs along his jaw. He pressed one roughened cheek against hers and whispered huskily into her ear, "Pantry."

At that moment, she wouldn't have cared if he'd said, "Panty raid." Wouldn't have cared if it was an army marching down the hall toward them. Because she was caught in a bubble of Toby-the-Pirate sensations—the dangerous glint in his eyes, the rough velvet of his voice. The black leather straining over his thighs.

Another giggle drifted down from the hallway.

The bubble burst.

Toby opened the door, steered Kate inside and followed her. She saw shelves, filled with cans and packages, lining the walls before he shut the door with a soft click.

Kate stared into the darkness, broken only by a sliver of white along the bottom of the door. She eased in a slow breath, taking in the scent of oregano. And another scent, woodsy, outdoors. Toby's cologne. A little fainter today, but a trace of it still lingered.

A squeal!

Kate stiffened, hoping it hadn't been her again.

Footsteps hit the linoleum. Scurrying, scrabbling sounds. More giggling.

"Grrr, I'm going to get you!" A man's voice.

"Oh, Tiger! Don't eat me!"

Bark! Bark!

The Dobermans! Kate's insides did a triple gainer, landing somewhere at the bottom of her stomach in a big belly flop.

"Tiger, you animal!" That woman's voice again. Had to be Free. Free and Tiger? They sounded like an animal-activist group.

More scampering, scurrying.

Kate glanced at Toby. Even in the shadows she sensed his stiffened posture, straining forward, as though it took every ounce of his will not to blast through the door and stop the love play between his girl and another man.

"Grrr..."

"Tiger, stop!"

Creak. Clatter. Clank.

What were they doing? Moving furniture? But it sounded like something metal.

Toby began breathing in lungfuls of air and releasing them forcefully through clenched teeth, *whoosh* and *shh* sounds like steam escaping from her grandmother's old heater. An image not too far off the mark, considering Toby was steamed and he had every right to be! Kate swore she even smelled the sweat on his skin.

She hadn't fully realized the depths of Toby Mancini's passion. Free was messing around on a good man. He was smart, career driven, and maybe best of all, a man of integrity.

"Watch out for the burner!" Free shrieked. "You'll set me on fire!"

Burner? Could that be what Toby meant when he said he caught his girlfriend cooking on the stove? Kate didn't know much about psychology, but it didn't take a Freud to figure out that Free's "cooking" was meant to burn Toby.

"Baby," Tiger said, this time without growling, "I don't need no burner to set you on fire."

In a rush of movement, Toby's arm shot for the door. Miraculously Kate caught his hand with both her own. They wrestled a little as she strained to hold him back. If she didn't stop Toby, there'd be more thrashing, burning and screaming than when one of her guests accidentally set fire to her Gone With the Wind room. She had remodeled the room as The Wild One so no other "hot" couples would try to recreate the burning of Atlanta.

Mid-wrestling, Toby broke loose. His hand fell against a shelf with a *whomp.*

Instantly there was scratching and barking at the pantry door. Icy fright washed over Kate. *Mickey and Minnie smell us!*

"Something's in that room," said Free.

"What room?" Tiger asked.

"The one where Mickey and Something are growling, where Toby stores cans of stuff."

It's called a *pantry,* Kate thought. Toby was right. Free wouldn't miss any basil plants. It was amazing she knew the metal thing she was "cooking" on was called a stove.

"Could you check, Tiger?"

"Check what?"

"The can room."

"Baby, you're just imagining things. Mickey and

Minnie probably smell the food in there." He snapped his fingers. "Mick. Min. Get away from there."

Kate brushed a drop of sweat off her brow. That was a close call.

"Please," Free whined. "Check the can room."

A huge huff. "Okay, but after that I don't wanna play kitchen no more. We're going to the bedroom."

Just as Kate was wondering if she could scrunch up her body and fake being a sack of something, Toby snatched a can, set it on the floor, and gently rolled it toward the door.

As Tiger opened the door, the can rolled out.

Mickey—or was it Minnie?—barely nosed the can before joining the other Doberman in an eruption of barks and snarls.

I'm dog meat. Or Mickey meat. Fortunately, Tiger yelled something at the dogs, causing them to stand at attention, although they still growled menacingly.

Kate, holding her breath, shifted her gaze to Tiger, who watched the can. He was oversize with longish blond hair, hence the name "Tiger," she guessed. He was dressed in loose olive green pants and matching top, much like what hospital orderlies wore. Kate had the irrational urge to curl up and roll out in the hopes Tiger would think she was just another can, too.

"See, baby?" said Tiger, looking up at Free, "it was just a can from the can room." He turned to shut the door when his eyes widened. "There's a flamenco dancer in your can room!"

As though on cue, both dogs began barking again.

Toby moved in front of Kate, shielding her. She was immensely grateful because Kate, a cat person, had never owned a dog, much less faced two vicious Dobermans. And her mother thought Kate was incorrigible for traipsing around the inn with a naked man? What about being mauled by a Mickey, Minnie and Tiger in a pantry? Of course, her mother might find the pantry part somewhat redeeming.

As these thoughts, and a hundred more unrelated ones, ran amok through Kate's brain, Toby calmly stepped forward, his fists bunched. "Get control of your dogs, man," he said in a low, threatening tone.

Tiger, looking wide-eyed at Toby, grabbed both dogs by their collars. Kate followed Tiger's line of vision, her eyes growing wide, too.

It was as though Toby had become the pirate. He stood tall, his legs spread wide, his hands fisted, as though ready for battle. His eyes never wavered from Tiger's, daring him to make the wrong move.

"He's my guest!" Free squealed, hopping off the stove. Her golden-blond hair fell in shimmering waves to her waist. She wore a long, Indian-print dress decorated with beads. She looked more like a summer-of-love child than Kate ever could.

Free swerved her gaze to Kate. "Who's she?"

"She's *my* guest," Toby answered coolly, his eyes locked on Tiger.

Free put her hands on her hips. "She's no guest, she's that bed-and-something person from next door! The one who blows up cars." Free cocked an eyebrow at the pantry, then at Kate. "What were you doing in my can room?"

Kate attempted to smile, a difficult feat with a top lip that threatened to quiver out of control. "Canning?"

Free exhaled so hard, Kate heard beads clinking. "Get out!" Free pointed to the hallway door.

With the Dobermans securely collared by their owner, Kate started walking toward the door, then stopped. "Uh, Toby, are you coming with me, or...?" *Oh, be a grade A idiot, Katherine Corrigan.* Why should he go with you? Toby had taken refuge with Kate, not moved in with her. "I mean, uh, if you want to leave—which you don't have to, of course—I just thought, considering Tiger is already here, and Mickey and Minnie look a little hungry, you might not want to hang around...." Where had Kate the one-word wonder gone? She was babbling, big-time. She clamped shut her mouth.

"I'm not leaving until he does." Toby growled.

Tiger narrowed his eyes. "Make me."

"Tiger!" Free, her arms folded tightly, stamped her foot. "Stop it! Go home, I'll call you later."

Tiger turned into a pussycat. "But, baby, I thought we were gonna..."

Free tossed her head back and forth in a big, slow no motion. As her head rotated, her hair glinted and glistened as in a shampoo commercial. "I don't want a brawl on my hands," Free continued. "Go home."

Tiger, looking shattered, shuffled obediently out of the room, pulling Mickey and Minnie with him.

"I'll leave, too," Kate said. "You two need to be alone," she whispered, following Tiger—walking bowlegged like his dogs—at a safe distance down the hallway. Why had Free messed around with that green-clad orderly when she had a swashbuckling hero like Toby under her roof? Some women didn't know how good they had it.

Moments later, Kate was heading down the sidewalk toward her inn as Tiger and his canine entourage headed in the opposite direction. It was a lovely morning. Against the clear blue skies, her inn looked like a fairytale castle—pink with white trim, a mauve conical tower in one corner. To add to the ambiance was the scent of roses from her garden. A perfect day for two lovers to end their spat. Free was probably in Toby's arms, telling him it had all been a terrible mistake. Toby was probably stroking Free's shampoo-commercial hair, forgiving her, telling her how he needed her for tomorrow's dinner, needed her for the rest of his life.

"I should feel happy for them," Kate muttered to herself. "After all, I'm always happy when I matchmake people." Not that she'd exactly been a matchmaker for them, but she'd graciously left them alone to work out their problems.

Okay, maybe not so graciously deep inside, but it probably looked that way. The truth was, her heart ached, as though it had been kick-punted. "Get a grip, girl. You're feeling this way not because something life-altering happened between Toby and you, but because you got to dress him like a pirate. That's what you're going to miss—Raymond's clothes, not Toby." She tried to laugh at herself, but it came out more like a raspy sob.

She trudged up the steps to the front porch of Beau's Bed-and-Breakfast and stopped on the landing, not wanting to go inside. Melanie's mother antennae would pick up signals. Then she'd see the hurt on Kate's face, zero in on the truth, and try to force-feed her a brownie. Or Verna would see Kate's face, intuit what had happened, and feel badly that she'd tried to play matchmaker.

Kate paced a few steps, stopping to pluck a dead leaf off the ivy that curled over the white porch banister. "He was just a figment of your pirate fantasy," she told herself. "And you've had your share of figments. The next time you fall in love, really fall in love, it will be the genuine thing, not with some pseudo swashbuckler." This self-talking was supposed to help, but it didn't ring true. Toby was far from pseudo. She thought of him in the darkened pantry, breathing his anger, stepping forward to confront Tiger and the woman who'd cheated on him. A man of integrity. A man who was the real thing. *A pirate in the flesh.*

Kate tossed aside the leaf and headed toward the front door. Such thoughts were getting her nowhere. She had a life to lead. An inn to run. A cat to feed.

She started to turn the brass knob when the door

jerked open, pulling Kate inside. Catching her balance, she stood face-to-face with Melanie.

"It's about time you're back!" Melanie's hazel eyes flashed. "We're having a problem with The Wild One!"

"How did Free get in?"

Melanie rolled back her shoulders. "*Free*'s the word all right. The gentleman from The Wild One refuses to pay!"

In the background, a man's gruff voice was bellowing something about "like hell I'll pay" and "who's gonna make me?"

That wild one. The guy dressed in the dark polyester suit who'd checked in yesterday afternoon. As Kate had sat behind her desk, it'd been hard to avoid staring at his protruding stomach because it met her at eye level. Every time she looked up, it was like facing down the Pillsbury Dough Boy. She'd put him up in The Wild One, as she did with most men traveling alone, because of its masculine, motorcycle atmosphere. Although she'd had to smile to herself imagining the Dough Boy on a Harley.

Kate didn't feel like smiling now. "Where's Verna?" she whispered. The two of them had dealt with nonpaying customers before. Verna would threaten to call the police while Kate acted as though that action was a bit extreme. They'd play it back and forth, Verna getting tougher while Kate got sweeter. It was their personalized rendition of good cop, bad cop.

"Verna said she needed to arrange somethin'," Melanie explained in a strained voice. "Said she'd be right back."

For the first time in her life, Kate saw a side of her mother that was far from perfect. Her mother was obviously anxious, distraught. *Of course. Dad always handled the business side of the marriage. And now she's turning to me for advice?*

Kate looked over her mother's shoulder at the far end of the hall where the burly guy in the polyester suit stood, apparently taking a break from his ranting. From this distance, a good thirty-five feet, she could see he was scowling at her. Those had to be some deep grooves in his face, probably carved into his forehead from years of frowning. Kate had a tough enough time facing everyday stuff, like not getting enough almond flavoring in her latte or asking her neighbor to turn down Beethoven. How was she going to face this Pillsbury Dough Boy gone bad? She swallowed, hard, but it barely moistened the inside of her dry mouth. "I'll comp the room," she said in a cracked voice to Melanie. "I can't face this guy."

"But I can," said a male voice behind her.

Kate turned. Toby stood on the doorstep, the sun infusing his red silk shirt with so much light, it appeared the top half of him was on fire. "What's the problem?" he asked, stepping inside and setting down a computer case. His face looked different—more defiant—as though the world should step aside. And that lock of hair hung dangerously over his brow.

Melanie wrung her hands. "He won't pay his bill."

Toby didn't ask anything else. He simply strode down the hallway and halted when he reached the man.

"Is there a problem?" Toby asked, his tone civil but firm.

The guy smirked. "Yeah, your clothes. The slippers are a nice touch, too."

Toby didn't react to the insult. Calmly, he said, "The lady says you're refusing to pay your bill."

"It's none of your business, buddy."

"Yes, it is my business. And we can settle it as gentlemen—" Toby removed his glasses and set them on a walnut table nestled at the bottom of the stairs "—or we can settle it outside. Your choice."

"Heavens," Melanie whispered. "He's getting into another fight."

"Another—?" Kate looked at her mother.

"Whatever his name was, Toby creamed him. I offered ice, but he refused." Releasing a shaky breath, Melanie murmured, "He might be a woman's man, but he's a man's man, too."

"He creamed Tiger?" Kate murmured, amazed that she'd somehow missed this event. In between her leaving the can room and arriving here? "He's a dangerous, marauding pirate," Kate whispered in awe.

"Uh-huh," Melanie answered, drawling out the "huh" until it sounded like a groan. Both women turned and watched Toby.

The two men were deep into a staring match. "You got a bad attitude, buddy," the guy snarled.

"And you," said Toby, his voice edged with ice, "have bad manners. You don't stiff people, especially nice people. Pay your bill and let's call it a day."

Seeing Toby wasn't going to budge from his position, the guy finally huffed something under his breath and extracted a money clip from his pocket. "How much do I owe?"

Kate cleared her throat. "One hundred," she said loudly.

"Plus tax," Melanie added.

Kate cut her a glance. This was a first—she and her mother operating as a team.

The guy peeled off some bills, stomped down the hall and slapped the money on the pine desk. "Satisfied?"

Toby sauntered down the hallway, a smile creasing his handsome features. "Yes," he said pleasantly. "Have a nice day."

The guy stormed past Kate and Melanie. They watched him tramp across the porch, down the stairs and turn right onto the sidewalk.

Just as he'd disappeared from view, Verna walked up the sidewalk from the opposite direction, a bag in her hands. Heading along the walkway to the porch, she asked, "Wasn't that The Wild One?"

While Melanie began chattering the entire story to Verna, Kate slid a look at Toby, who had picked up his computer and was heading toward the staircase. He walked with the same sinewy, powerful grace she'd observed earlier. Small currents of electricity skittered crazily across her skin. *No, you're The Wild One,* she thought, not wanting to ponder what had happened with Free. Because all she cared about was that he was back. Her wild, dangerous pirate was back.

It dawned on her that, except for the computer, he'd brought nothing else with him. No clothes. No belongings. He was back, but for how long?

Knock-knock.

Toby, busily typing on the laptop computer, looked over at the door. "It's open," he called. He had nothing to hide, except his body, and that was finally covered. It hit him that, for the first time in his life, he had nothing to protect, to negotiate, even to fight over—except his own self. It didn't matter if he locked doors anymore. What could anyone take from him except his self-esteem? And that, he'd decided in the kitchen of his home a few minutes ago, wasn't negotiable.

Knock-knock.

Whoever it was probably hadn't heard him. He set the computer aside, got up and crossed the room to open the door.

There stood Kate holding a plate with one of those mishmash sandwiches. Next to it were some more biscuits and orange slices.

"Hi," she said. She did a little wave with her free hand.

He liked how the scent of lilacs trailed into the room, softening his harsh mood. Or maybe it was looking at Kate and her spiky, sexy hairdo that took the edge off. "Hi."

"You've been up here for a while. Figured you might like some lunch."

He accepted the plate. "Thanks."

"Turkey and cheese sandwich. On rye."

He fought the urge to grin. It was probably second nature for Kate to describe her sandwiches.

"Want someone to talk to?" She gestured toward herself. "Like me?"

Sweet. And to think he had ever viewed her as a dangerous, car-bombing woman. "I don't really have much to say." It was the truth. His insides felt gutted after his conversation with Free. But he wasn't ready to discuss that, yet. Maybe not ever. "Besides, I'm putting the finishing touches on a proposal for my potential employer."

"Well, if you want me—I mean, if you want to talk with me—I'll be in the garden with Beau. That's my cat."

So that was the Beau in Beau's Bed-and-Breakfast. From his home, he'd often seen a big, yellow tabby lounging in the inn's windows. Or curled up in some guest's lap outside on the porch. Or at night, prowling the neighborhood as though it were his personal kingdom. No wonder that feline had such an I've-seen-it-all-done-it-all attitude. The cat owned his own business!

"Thanks for the food," Toby said, "and the offer for company. I just have a lot on my mind right now—the job interview tomorrow night, stuff like that."

"Right! The job interview! For—?"

"Director of Software Development. Local company."

"I didn't know they had to travel all the time."

So she'd noticed how often he'd been gone. "Uh, they don't. I traveled before because I was analyzing companies."

"Analyzing?"

He'd cut to the chase, not try to whitewash it. "I was a corporate raider."

Her blue eyes widened. "Corporate raider?" "Raider" sounded more like a release of heated breath than a word. "Like a plundering pirate," she whispered hoarsely, her face flooding with color.

He started to deny the pirate charge, but Kate was too busy backing up and talking at the same time. "Well, just wanted to drop off a sandwich, which wasn't really dropped, by the way."

"Thanks."

"And I wanted to tell you that—" Kate stopped and fidgeted with a lock of her hair "—you were pretty darn wonderful the way you faced Tiger." She clutched her hands to her chest, as though holding back the emotions within. "And you were great handling that dough-boy guy. I was ready to comp him and then you showed up...looking so...so..." Her gaze roamed over him, and Kate gulped a few breaths as though the room suddenly lacked enough oxygen again.

"So...?"

She blinked rapidly, then waved her hand wildly through the air. "So like a pirate." The words tumbled out fast, and it took him a moment to realize what she'd said. He'd barely digested being called a pirate a second time when she began bobbing her head while walking backward. He wasn't sure what worried him more—the digesting, the bobbing, or the walking backward. Rather than tackle all three concerns, he opted first for her safety. "Please turn around. It makes me nervous when you walk backward."

"Oh." Without missing a beat, she pivoted and continued walking, her back now to him. "Better?"

He didn't mean to, but his gaze dropped to that blue behind. "Better," he whispered.

KNOCK-KNOCK.

Was Kate back already? Not with another sandwich, he hoped. It wasn't that the last one was bad. Actually, he'd been hungry and it had satisfied the rumblings in his stomach. It's just that he liked to be able to visually identify what he was eating.

Again he set aside the computer and crossed the room, grabbing the plate on the way. "It was great," he said, opening the door.

Melanie arched one of her penciled eyebrows. "I'm glad," she said. It hit Toby that Melanie was trying to act cheery but was actually nervous. She didn't bob her head like her daughter, but she kept pressing the tips of her manicured fingers together.

"Did you...need something?" Toby finally asked.

"Yes, it's about The Wild One."

"Free showed up?"

"What?" Melanie twiddled her fingers in the general direction of downstairs. "No, I wanted to thank you for helping us with that man, the one in that hideously dark suit." Under her breath, she added, "I'll never get used to summer colors in this part of the world."

"You don't need to thank me."

"Oh, yes, I do," Melanie said. She looked at him expectantly, as though waiting for something.

"Would you like to come inside?" he asked, taking his cue.

"Why, thank you," she said in that drawn-out Southern accent as she sashayed past him. Once inside, she stopped, looked at the room and shuddered. "The way my daughter loves red, she must have been a bull-fighter in another life." She sat on the edge of a red ottoman next to the tub and carefully adjusted her skirt over her knees. "I'm here to ask you a favor."

Toby waited. When she said nothing, he prompted, "Yes?"

Melanie stopped adjusting her skirt and met his eyes. "I know how you make your living."

He paused, waiting for her to say more. When she didn't, he asked, "Does that have anything to do with the favor you're about to ask?"

"Heavens, no!" She patted the back of her hair nervously. "I'm just worried for my daughter. I don't want her to get...well, she has this thing for pirates and I'm afraid she'll view you as someone romantic and dashing when, in reality, that's simply a skill you've acquired in order to earn a living."

He'd acquired romantic, dashing, swashbuckling skills to earn a living as a corporate raider? Hardly. He'd used his engineering background to help analyze high-tech companies for acquisitions and mergers. A career he might still be proud of if a single-mother's letter—painfully recounting how a merger he'd orchestrated cost her her job and forced her to parcel out her own children—hadn't dredged up the painful reality of his own upbringing. He'd quietly investigated other families' dilemmas, then systematically given away his own money to help the families whose lives he'd almost single-handedly turned upside down.

Which left him essentially with no money. Which meant he needed this new job tomorrow night.

But instead of voicing his thoughts, Toby smiled kindly at Mrs. Corrigan. The core issue was that she was worried about her daughter, just as he'd seen his own mother worry numerous times over her own children. "You needn't worry about your daughter," he said gently, "except when she walks backward."

A puzzled look flitted across Melanie's face before she again looked serious. "So you understand?"

"Yes." *I understand you love your daughter and want to protect her. Too bad Kate doesn't understand that.*

Melanie, looking visibly relieved, stood. "Good. I'm glad we understand each other." She walked primly to the door, but stopped before exiting. Looking back at Toby, she asked, "Do women really go for that get-up?"

Toby glanced down at his attire, then back at Melanie. "Except for the slippers, Bab liked the rest, it seems."

"Please!" Melanie held up her palm in a stopping motion. "Say no more. It's a world I want to know nothing about." And with that grand pronouncement, she strode out of the room.

KNOCK-KNOCK.

Toby, still befuddled as to why Mrs. Corrigan wanted to know nothing about some "world," also wanted to know what a man had to do to get a couple of uninterrupted hours. He had a dinner to produce, a proposal to finalize, a job to nail down.

He got up and opened the door.

Verna, dressed in a long black shift, smiled demurely. "Good morning."

"Good morning."

Verna tilted her head a little. "May I come in?"

Toby stepped back and ushered her inside, wondering if this conversation was going to be about dashing, romantic pirates or Toby's "getup."

Verna glided in as he shut the door. When he turned

around, she was at the window, looking outside. "Such a lovely, lovely, lovely day," she said.

For her, maybe. His could be labeled The Wild One, and it wasn't getting much better.

Verna met his gaze. She appeared to be in her mid-to-late thirties, but had the appearance of a grown-up Peter Pan. Maybe it was that short blond hair or the youthful twinkle in her eye.

"I want to ask you a favor."

He should have joined Kate in the garden when he had a chance. "If this has anything to do with how I earned my living, let's just say I did my undergraduate degree at San Luis Obispo, followed by graduate work at San Francisco State—computer science. That software engineering background I plan to use in my next job, which I plan to get tomorrow night no matter what dogs, men or women try to stand in my way."

Verna's eyebrows pressed together. "It's been a stressful day."

And to think it wasn't even noon yet. "Yes, it's been rather stressful." He'd been discovered in bed, lying on top of Kate, by her mother. He'd been caught by the police breaking into his home. He'd succeeded, only to overhear his girlfriend making love on his stove with some animal-trainer-wannabe. And then he'd forced some no-good, non-bill-paying bum into settling his debt with Kate. In between all of these things, he'd managed to squeeze in some bizarre conversations with different members of the opposite sex. "Yes, it's been stressful," he repeated, "but at least I'm dressed."

Verna's eyebrows shot up this time and her lips formed a small O. "Yes, indeed you are." She dabbed at her forehead with the sleeve of her shirt.

"You wanted to ask for a favor?"

"Yes." She stopped dabbing. "Would you like to go out to dinner?"

Now *his* lips were forming a little O. Verna was nice, but not really his type.

"With my friend?" Verna smiled sweetly. "I was supposed to have dinner with her, but I have to cancel. I figured you might go instead. It's already paid for. One of those prepaid dining-out things."

Prepaid dining-out things? "I—I don't have the right clothes…unless it's a restaurant with a flamenco theme."

Verna made a not-to-worry gesture. "You look perfect, perfect, perfect." Her voice cracked a little on the last "perfect."

He doubted he looked that perfect. Besides, it had been a rough day. He needed a quiet evening to himself. Time to reflect. Think about his conversation with Free. Decide what to do next. "I think I'll have to pass."

"Oh, no!" Verna shook her head vehemently. "There's no one else. If you don't go, we forfeit the dining experience. Lose all that money. And my friend will be…devastated. It's imperative you go." Verna tilted her head and looked at him imploringly. "Please?"

He had balked at "imperative," but that pleading "please" was almost more than he could stand. Good ol' responsible Toby felt himself giving in. He was needed. It was imperative. Well, after a questionable-looking sandwich, it would be nice to eat identifiable food. Besides, maybe this dining-out would be at an Italian restaurant. One with red walls so he'd blend in. "All right," he said, "I'll go."

Verna clapped her hands. She looked so happy he thought for a moment she might fly, just like Peter Pan.

"Wonderful! She'll pick you up at six."

So happy, he grew immediately suspicious. "Where?"

"Here. Your room."

"Who?"

"Why, Kate!"

6

_____

KNOCK-KNOCK.

Toby stopped his pacing and eyed the door. Had to be six o'clock. And it had to be Kate. An unexpected aching heated his insides at the thought of being close to her again.

From across the room, he checked his reflection in the large oval mirror over the bathtub. A stubble shadowed his jaw. He scratched the whiskers. He could have asked one of the ladies for a razor, but something inside him liked his new roughness. He perused the red shirt that fell open almost to his navel, the tight, black leather pants that hugged his muscles, toned from daily jogs.

Hell, he liked his new look. Responsible, businessman Toby Mancini liked finally ripping loose, being the man he usually kept a tight lid on. Being his secret self—wild, dangerous. What had Kate called him?

A pirate.

He turned toward the door. When had he crossed the line from engineer to exotic? He grinned to himself. When he first crossed the threshold of Beau's Bed-and-Breakfast.

The pirate opened the door. For a moment, he thought some of the room's color had seeped out and onto Kate. She wore a red T-shirt that matched her pants. A silky scarlet shawl—embroidered with miniature turquoise, yellow and blue flowers—draped her shoulders. Plus she'd glossed her mouth with a cherry-tinted lipstick that made her full lips look plumper, juicier.

"Do I look all right?" those plump, juicy lips asked.

All right? Does a goddess look "all right"? "You look okay." Okay? Had he lost his mind? That was like telling Céline Dion she sang okay. "Fine. Good. Great."

Kate smiled demurely, but her cheeks flamed. He wondered when a man had last complimented her. "Verna said you'd be ready by six, so here I am." She started to do a small wave but stopped herself.

"Well, I didn't exactly need to get ready, considering my entire wardrobe consists of a towel or this outfit. Both come with black corduroy slippers."

"I thought you were going to bring other clothes from home."

"Yeah. I thought so, too. But there wasn't time." He clenched his jaw, not wanting to explain further.

Kate paused, obviously aware she'd treaded on a sensitive topic. "You look great!" she finally blurted.

She'd skipped the "fine" and "good" and gone straight to the "great." Was she flirting with him? Kate? That hot ache filled him again as he stared at the cherry-red lips that moved in a delightful sequence of curves and puckers. Then they stopped.

"What?" he asked, realizing she'd been talking and he'd missed every single word.

"I said, if we're both ready, let's go. Reservations are at six-thirty. It'll take us that long to walk there." Kate tugged at a strand of her dark hair.

Good. Walking distance. Driving in North Beach could test one's sanity, something he and Kate didn't need after the events of the day. "Since we're walking, I'll wear my glasses." He retrieved them from a table and put them on. "And let me make sure..." Out of habit, he patted his back pocket and felt only flat, smooth no-bulging-of-a-wallet leather. It was difficult to remember he only owned the shirt on his back. Well, technically, off Raymond's back. But Verna had said this was some kind of prepaid dinner, so Toby didn't need to sweat being responsible and carrying money. "Let's go," he said.

As they headed down the stairs, the inn seemed abnormally quiet. "Where are the other guests?" Toby asked.

"The Pirate checked out around noon…after skipping breakfast."

"I can't imagine anyone wanting to miss Verna's meals."

"It happens sometimes, especially with the honeymooners. We're used to it."

Honeymooners. *Sex.* He glanced at Kate and caught a look in her eyes, something heated that matched his mood. She quickly looked away, suddenly immersed in watching her feet walk down the stairs.

As they ambled down the staircase, she pointed back toward the upper floor. "And it's quiet because the other rooms are empty. Melanie's staying in the Pollyanna room—the one with the teddy bear on the door—but she's busy baking brownies in the kitchen. And The Wild One—" Kate's finger swerved along the upper landing to a door with a small silver trophy attached to it "—is available, just no takers yet."

The Wild One. Walking behind her, Toby had the chance to let his gaze slip unnoticed down the back of Kate's formfitting red T-shirt to her red pants. They fit her comfortably, falling loosely over her rounded behind. But not too rounded. Just enough so the curved outline was discernible. His gaze traveled down those long, long legs to a pair of red sandals with rhinestone trim. Red, red and more red. He knew she meant The Wild One room, but tonight, it should be Kate.

Or he wished it would be Kate.

"Good evening," said a woman's familiar voice, followed by a small gasp.

Toby had just stepped off the bottom step and into the foyer when he looked up. Melanie stared at him with eyes so wide, her false eyelashes spread out like miniature fans.

"Good evening," Toby responded.

Melanie blinked those fans, then turned her gaze to her daughter. "What are you doing with…him?"

"Melanie," Kate said, shooting her a glance, "you're being impolite in front of company." Kate adjusted her shawl. "And you thought *I* was incorrigible," she said under her breath.

Melanie neatly folded a dish towel she'd been carrying. "Guess I momentarily forgot my manners." Her gaze shifted to Toby. "And I'll momentarily forget them again. What are you doing with my daughter?"

When had Kate's mother gone from being appalled at her daughter to being protective of her? "Walking down the stairs?" He felt like adding, "At least I'm not lying on top of Kate or traipsing around naked with her." Just the thought of doing either suddenly made him wish his pants had more breathing room.

"We're going out to dinner," Kate explained.

"Are you paying for him?" Melanie asked sharply.

"What does that have to do with anything?"

Br-r-ring-br-r-ring.

Kate looked over her mother's shoulder at the swinging door into the kitchen. "Melanie, the phone's ringing. Would you mind answering the one in the kitchen?"

Br-r-ring-br-r-ring.

"It's your father."

"How do you know?"

"He's been calling every ten minutes. So punctual, I can time when the brownies are done."

Br-r-ring-br-r-ring

"You're still not taking his calls?"

"I want him to think I'm busy. Kicking up my heels." Melanie pursed her peach-lipstick covered lips as though debating whether to continue. The incessant ringing seemed to encourage her to explain further. "It's about time I lived my own life, and not his. Not at his beck and call, so to speak."

Kate paused as the ringing stopped. That was the most definitive answer she had yet received as to why her mother decided to land in Kate's life with this surprise visit. Was this the mother who always had a box of Bisquick on hand in case Max had an urge for pancakes? The woman who dutifully sewed buttons on shirts and patched holes in socks?

This was too much to ponder on an empty stomach. Kate grabbed Toby's arm. "Well, we're off to do some heel-kicking of our own. See you later," she called, pulling him toward the front door.

Once outside, Toby said, "You know, I feel a little sorry for her."

"Why?" They had turned the corner and were walking down Stockton. Wisps of fog threaded the air. In the distance was the faint call of seagulls.

"For a moment," Toby explained, "she reminded me of my mother."

"She avoids her husband's phone calls, too?"

"Not her new husband. If anything, she runs to the phone whenever he calls. But there was a time, growing up, when my mother had a wistfulness about her, something I also saw on your mom's face tonight."

Kate waited for him to say more, but he didn't. As they walked in silence, she wondered if he felt any wistfulness, any regret over leaving Free. What had happened between them? At that time, Kate had been heading back to the inn, wondering if Toby was stroking Free's commercial-shampoo hair and forgiving her. But considering he'd come back to the inn so quickly, something entirely different must have occurred.

"So," Kate said, changing the conversation, "according to Verna, this restaurant opened just a few weeks ago. One of Verna's pals is the owner. She said to just give her name—everything's set up."

"Italian restaurant?"

"California Moroccan. It's a mixture of two cuisines, like Tex-Mex."

"California Moroccan," Toby mused. "Sounds like the waiters will be wearing swimsuits and fezzes." He blew out a gust of breath. "Maybe I'll blend in."

TOBY STARTED TO LOWER himself onto the portly tapestry pillow, then stopped in a bent-over position.

"Something wrong?" Kate asked, who'd easily sat cross-legged on her own floor pillow. She was playing with the brightly threaded mat that lay on the table in front of her.

Toby placed his hands on his knees and shot her a look. "How about if I eat standing?" he mumbled.

"Why don't you sit down?" Kate asked.

"Because I can't fold in two."

"Your pants...are too tight?" Kate whispered urgently, leaning forward. "I'm sorry. I failed you. You're the kind of man who needs extra breathing room."

Two matrons at the next table stopped talking and looked over, their gazes traveling along Toby's no-breathing-room black leather pants. One of the women winked. He quickly looked away. "Yes," he hissed, "I'm missing any extra breathing room, but we don't need to broadcast it.'' He could sit in Kismet because all he had to do was roll sideways onto the red lounge chair. But sitting on a Californian-Moroccan floor pillow required a bit more agility than rolling.

"Something the matter, sir?'' asked a genial male voice. A slender man in his thirties, dressed in what looked to be a flowing caftan, stood next to the table, a look of professional concern etching his face.

"My back's acting up,'' Toby said.

"His pants are too tight,'' Kate said at the same time.

Squeezing shut his eyes, Toby toyed with walking out of the place right now, except that would mean he'd be eating another questionable-looking sandwich for dinner. Not that that was a bad thing, it's just that he could use a change of taste.

"Leather stretches,'' Kate offered, looking hopeful. "Maybe if you just forced yourself to sit down.''

"Or I could get several of the chefs out here and we could lower you,'' the man offered, holding his hands together as though he were praying. "Or maybe they could spritz you with water and we could stretch the leather—''

"No!'' Toby barked. "No lowering or spritzing!'' Several heads turned, interested in the hubbub. "Rubberneckers,'' Tony mumbled. Levelheaded, responsible Toby was doing something he *never* did—cause a commotion.

Maybe that's because he wasn't his old levelheaded, responsible self anymore. He'd become an adventurous, dangerous pirate...who couldn't sit down because of his adventurous, dangerous leather pants. Who was going to be lowered or spritzed any moment if he didn't do something, fast. "I'll force myself down,'' he said between clenched teeth. He quickly sat, accompanied by a ripping sound.

The man's eyes widened. "Lowering or spritzing would have prevented that."

Kate's cheeks flushed. "Guess leather doesn't always stretch."

"Well, at least I'm sitting," Toby muttered, not adding that he was staying here forever because there was no way he was getting up and walking out of this place with his tiger-striped underwear peeking through the rip in the back of his pants. If one person—just *one*—called him "Tiger," levelheaded Toby would become hotheaded Toby. And world, watch out.

Kate touched her shawl. "We'll wrap this around you when we walk out," she offered.

"Great," Toby murmured. "The red shawl will match my shirt."

Mr. Caftan grew enthusiastic. With a twirl of his wrists, he said, "And hip-draped shawls are so *in* right now, especially when you let the silky ends hang ever-so-casually down your thigh."

Toby straightened. "I'm not hanging silky—"

"Now that you're seated," the man continued, ignoring Toby's testy aside, "I'll call your wait person." He lightly clapped his hands twice as he walked away.

A curly-haired woman approached, wrapped in a bright orange-and-yellow caftan that matched the red-and-orange walls the hostess had explained was a painting of the California sunset. She dropped off two tiles, upon which were written a list of items. At the top was scripted, "Rick's Place."

"'Rick's Place,'" Toby read out loud. "Considering the Moroccan atmosphere, this wouldn't be based on Rick in *Casablanca*, would it?"

The waitress smiled. "You got it! Would you two care for something to drink before ordering?"

"Does the California part of the theme mean you

have zinfandel?'' Toby asked. The waitress nodded, and he ordered a glass.

"Make that two," said Kate as she checked out the words on the tile. After the waitress left, she whispered, "Kefta Nasturtium? Chermoula Marjoram? These sound the way my sandwiches look." She laughed.

Toby laughed too, which he could do easily now that he had some extra breathing room in his pants. "Maybe after a glass of zin the names will make more sense." He looked around the room. "I had never heard of being able to arrange a prepaid dining experience, at a place like this before. It's an interesting idea."

"Yes, I'm glad I was free." She quickly looked up. "I meant 'free' as in available, not...well, you know." Kate held the tile so close to her face Toby could see her reflection in the white enamel.

"You already had these prepaid dining-out experience plans with Verna, right?"

Kate blinked. "No, she said you had some forgotten gift certificate for dinner for two—which just happened to be at her friend's new restaurant—and that you'd asked her, but she couldn't go, so she volunteered me."

"She said all that?"

Kate bobbed her head slowly. "Oh, now I know what my mother meant when she said Verna had told her she had to go out to 'arrange' something. She was playing matchmaker, arranging and paying for this dinner! We've been set up."

"Think you're right," Toby said, trying to sense if Kate thought being set up was a good or bad thing. Because to him it felt good. Kate was unlike any other woman he'd ever known. Spontaneous. Spunky. Fun. And underneath those color-wheel clothes beat the heart of a romantic. Who else would create rooms like

Kismet and The Wild One? Kate had a hidden self he wanted to explore, to plunder.

But Kate, obviously on a different wavelength, hunkered down a little as though trying to slip under the table and disappear. "This is mortifying. First you think I'm some kind of dangerous car-bombing Motown-blasting woman. Now you think my breakfast chef sets me up with any naked man who wanders into the inn."

"Actually, I think you lead a very interesting life. And I don't think Verna sets you up with any naked man, just any *nearly* naked man." He grinned mischievously. "A nearly naked man who'd like to see what's underneath your...facade."

Kate's cherry lips opened, but nothing came out. After gulping a breath, she said shakily, "You belong to someone else, right?"

Damn. He needed somehow to get on good terms with Free by tomorrow night's dinner. If he started romancing the next-door neighbor before that, it would be like throwing a sparkler on gasoline. He became engrossed with the words on the tile. "You're right. I'm involved with somebody else, so even if we have been set up, this isn't really a date." He didn't like how he felt—excited by Kate, but guilty for making her think a relationship still existed between him and Free.

"Right," Kate said softly.

"But I've been wanting to ask you something. It's rather sensitive, but I've been wanting to ask for a while."

Kate lowered her tile. "Yes," she said in a soft voice, "I'd go out with you if you weren't involved."

"No," Toby said slowly. "I wanted to ask why a tomboy like yourself—well, I heard your mother mention you had been a tomboy, anyway—opened such a romantic bed-and-breakfast.''

"Oh." Kate tugged hard at a strand of her hair, and Toby thought she might yank it out of her head. "Well, my granny left me a trust fund, which I used to escape Beaufort, because my father thought my career path should be marriage. And I moved to San Francisco where I bought this great fixer-upper in North Beach. I had stored all my pirate memorabilia in one room upstairs while I was remodeling the downstairs, wondering what kind of job I should get because my money would eventually run out. My only work experience—besides helping my dad fix cars, plumbing, stuff like that—was working as a concierge and bookkeeper in the resort industry back home. Then it dawned on me! One room already was decorated like *The Pirate,* an old movie I loved. Why not decorate the other rooms after other movies and, using my resort experience plus my handywoman skills, make the place a bed-and-breakfast?''

She smiled, but Toby could see it was forced. And despite her exuberance for her story, her eyes were moist with emotion.

"I'm so sorry—" she heaved a shaky breath "—for thinking you wanted to date me.''

Despite all her handywoman skills, she chose romantic films as a model for the rooms, which indicated a softhearted romantic was beneath that tomboy facade. "I'm flattered you'd want to go out with me," he said solemnly, "if I weren't involved—which, of course, I am." He hated this game.

The color of her face almost matched her top. "I think we've come full circle on that issue. Just for the record, I feel like an idiot.''

"So do I," he blurted. "Claiming to be involved when…" He didn't need to finish his sentence—they both knew what he was thinking. He looked like an idiot for remaining loyal to a woman who had been caught cooking with Tiger. But for right now, he couldn't explain his plan. In business, like cards, you didn't show your hand until you were ready to close the deal.

Kate skewed her mouth as though debating whether to speak. Finally she said, "May I ask you a question?"

He laid down his tile. "Yes, I'd go out with you if I weren't involved."

Her smile was so sweet, so grateful, he felt momentarily as though every decision he'd ever made in his life, right or wrong, had led him to this singularly perfect moment. Kate's blue eyes glistened, her cherry-glossed lips smiled, and he felt as though he could sit across from her forever, talking, sharing life stories.

"Okay, enough joking," she said, oblivious to his moment. "Why do you remain with a woman who's two-timed you?"

The singularly perfect moment popped. Maybe he couldn't tell the complete truth, but after his and Kate's flirtations, he owed her some answer. "I feel responsible." *Okay, that hit on an old truth.* "I know Free and I are very different. Some of my friends think we're not a very good mix, but I feel I should stay with her, work things out." Now he was lying, pretending he and Free were still an item, because of tomorrow night's dinner.

His mouth kept moving, but his mind went elsewhere. Back home to Pescadero, California, growing up in a household of six kids, no dad to speak of. Watching his mom try to keep the family together on her meager factory salary. Losing her job. The two youngest children, Frank and Angela, shipped off to live with relatives in New Jersey. His mother crying.

Yeah, he felt responsible growing up, trying to help his mom keep the household together. But the gut-wrenching loss of his siblings made him ever-after afraid to connect to others. Truly connect. Because connecting equaled family, and his darkest fear was that he might raise a family that would also be torn apart. So being on the road, traveling all the time, fit in perfectly with his inability to connect at home.

Until that woman's letter.

Then he realized he'd grown up only to tear apart other people's families, other people's lives. Big, hot-shot corporate raider. He experienced the trauma, the pain of his own family's separation all over again. But this time, he could do something. He'd given away almost every cent he'd ever earned to make it up to those families. Next, he wanted to put down roots. Shed the corporate-raider life altogether, use his engineering skills to get a normal job. Which he needed Free to get.

He hadn't voiced any of the thoughts going on in his head, but had let his mouth do some autopilot number about working it out with Free, blah-blah-blah. Kate was staring at him, blinking.

"I…I guess I understand that you feel responsible for Free after leaving her alone so much. But do you really blame yourself for her actions?"

Was that what he'd said?

"Any questions?" said their curly-haired waitress, a pencil and order pad in her hand. "The menu reflects a good mix of California and Moroccan cuisine, both of which complement each other with their blend of herbs, fish and chicken. I highly recommend the Chermoula Marjoram, which is bass marinated in a pungent sauce, whose main ingredient is marjoram…"

At the end of the waitress's spiel, he and Kate ordered several somethings the waitress recommended.

Mere moments later, a swarm of waiting staff in caftans arrived at their table with plates of food. Scents of marjoram, cilantro and oil swirled through the air. Their waitress held out a bowl filled with steaming white linens that smelled of lemon.

"What are these?" Kate asked, peering inside.

"Towels," the waitress answered. "To cleanse your hands."

Kate looked perplexed. "Before we eat?"

"Yes. And during. And after." The waitress set the bowl on the table. "If you need anything else, clap twice."

She turned to leave when Kate asked, "Could we get some silverware?"

"Oh, I'm sorry, I thought Marcus, the maître d', explained that at Rick's, you eat with your hands." And on that directive, she turned on her feet and left.

"Melanie would freak!" Kate said gleefully, wiping her hands before dipping her fingers into the chermoula and extracting a piece of fish. She nibbled at it, groaned, then stuffed the entire piece into her mouth.

With such an adventurous dining companion, Toby dug in.

"Melanie should see me now," Kate said, licking a dollop of chermoula off her finger. "Years of teaching me when to use which fork—" Kate grinned wide "—and suddenly, I'm finger-licking good!"

In between touching, fondling and licking their food, they laughed and talked like two silly, mischievous kids. "Mom—I mean, Melanie—tried for a solid year to make me a proper Southern young lady. She enrolled me in etiquette classes, some junior-culture group called Little Magnolias, modeling seminars, you name it. I was supposed to learn how to behave, talk and walk."

"Let me guess what you really did." Toby popped

an olive into his mouth. "You misbehaved, argued and walked backward."

Kate liked Toby's laugh, deep and rumbling. Unexpectedly she shivered as a zigzag of pleasure skittered up her spine. "I didn't walk backward then. That's a skill I seem to have perfected over the last day or so." She also liked how Toby looked at her, those eyes like caramel—that smile a little lopsided. His skin, darker than hers, took on a deeper hue with the rough growth of beard. But best of all, he looked so relaxed and happy, like a completely different man than she'd ushered in from her doorstep last night.

"Just over the last day or so? What prompted you to develop this new walking skill so recently?"

"You." She blurted it out without any forethought. Damn. And he'd just explained ad nauseam how he and Free were working it out. Kate looked away from those yummy eyes and stared at her half-empty wineglass. Maybe she could blame her admission on alcohol, but a few sips weren't much of an excuse.

"Me?" He cocked his head and slanted her a teasing look.

Beads of sweat broke out on her forehead. Maybe the chermoula was too hot.

Or maybe Toby is.

Clutching her water glass, Kate stammered, "You— your outfit. Makes me want to walk backward so I can keep looking at it." She threw back her head and downed the glass of chilled water. What she didn't say was that any schlump could dress like a pirate, but only a special man could actually look and behave like one.

A man who was, at heart, a swashbuckler.

Toby leaned back against a cushion and crossed his arms comfortably behind his head. The movement made his shirt fall open even more, exposing a wider view of his chest. All that hair. A woman could get lost in it, walking backward for days, years.

Kate slammed down the water glass and grabbed for another hunk of chermoula. It was almost to her mouth when Toby, quick as lightning, reached across the table and caught her wrist midair.

"I know you're one to thumb your nose at etiquette, but I think it's better to sprinkle salt on your food rather than shake it on your tongue, don't you agree?"

Kate shifted her gaze to her hand, which held a salt shaker, not a piece of chermoula something. "Thanks," she croaked, setting the shaker back onto the table. She pushed the half-filled wineglass away. "Half a glass is my limit. After that, I get too wild."

Toby's eyes twinkled. "So *you're* really The Wild One, aren't you?"

"Hardly." But Kate was so tongue-tied by this point, the only sound that came out was "har-har." She pretended to laugh to cover up.

"What would your mother say about your shaking salt on your tongue? And speaking of which, why don't you call her 'Mother' or 'Ma' or 'Mom'? What's with Melanie?"

"That's her name."

"My mother's name is Isabella, but I don't call her that."

This topic of conversation felt far safer than the last one. Kate eased in a slow, calming breath, grateful to be moving on. For safe measure, however, she pushed the salt shaker away a little farther. "I guess it was during that etiquette year that I started calling her Melanie. Probably because it irked her. Same reason I wore only red a few years later."

"Because it irked her."

Kate nodded.

"Is that why you decorated Kismet in all red? To irk her?"

"No. Because it really is my favorite color." She felt a bit embarrassed at her irking confessions. The truth was, she never felt she could compete with her mother's homemaking perfection. Her mother was always dressed in pastels, pretty dresses, her hair curly and intact like some magazine-cover hairdo. As a kid, Kate had secretly yearned to look so perfect, so soft, so...romantic.

Toby leaned forward on his elbows and leveled her a look. "Which room is most like you?" he asked huskily. "The Wild One? Kismet?"

"The Pirate."

One side of Toby's lips turned upward. "How did Miss Magnolia become a pirate?"

Kate helped herself to a lemon-scented moist napkin and wiped her shaking hands. Asking her how *she* was a pirate was like the kettle calling itself black. "Correction number one—I never made Miss Magnolia status. Correction number two—at heart, I'm not a pirate, but—" *the object of the pirate's passion* "—a romantic who dreams about her pirate," she said quickly. A bit of confession overload, but at least she'd skipped the pirate's passion part. "Melanie's mom, Granny Dot, kept a special room for me where I could let my imagination go wild. I filled it with ships and flags and just about anything else that seemed piratical."

"The things you put into The Pirate room, right?"

"Right."

"You're industrious, creative. But the best part is your wonderful romantic streak."

"How'd you know?" She bit her tongue, but it was too late.

He leaned forward, his eyes glistening with a look

that made her heart thump erratically. "Because I see it in you. In your eyes, your walk, your natural exuberance for life."

"My walk?" she croaked. She had strong legs, but they were romantic, too?

He cocked one eyebrow. "You have a long-legged, undulating stride that women would kill for. And that men admire." He rubbed his chin. "Let me correct that last statement. You have a walk that heats men's blood."

Was his heated right now? Hers sure was. And in her heated, romantic vision, Toby—the angles and shadows of his face casting him in a dangerous light— looked like her fantasy pirate. The man who would sweep her into his arms, carry her up the staircase and make love to her, the object of his pirate's passion, until dawn broke the night.

He belonged to Free.

That thought sobered her up more than shaking salt on her tongue. She cleared her throat. "So, uh, this job interview tomorrow—is this your fantasy job come true?"

"No. If I had my way, I'd be running a restaurant, not developing software. When I was a kid, my dad was...gone. So, being the oldest, I helped my mom as much as I could. I took over most of the cooking, among other tasks. Probably why I love cooking today."

Kate nodded, grateful they were on another subject. "I never had to cook, didn't even have to baby-sit. It was just me and my younger brother, the apple of my father's traditional eye. I made the better grades, but my father always made it clear a man goes to college, a woman gets married."

"He never asked you if that's what you wanted?"

"My father, ask a woman's opinion? He'd rather look into a crystal ball."

Toby grew contemplative. "I often asked Free what she wanted. She always said a trip or a piece of jewelry or dinner out. Do you know how many times I would love to have heard her say, 'You. You're what I want'?"

"Is that what you asked her?" Kate bit her bottom lip. It was none of her business what they talked about after she and Tiger left. But to her surprise, Toby responded.

"No. But Free said something else that haunts me. When I asked her why she'd done what she did, she said, 'What did you expect?' It killed me. I couldn't even go upstairs and get some damn clothes."

"I don't get it."

"Those were the exact words my mom said to me after my relatives took Frank and Angela, my kid brother and sister, away to live with them. Remember when I mentioned a sadder time of my mom's life? This was that time. My mom looked at me with that tired, beaten look I hated, and said, 'What did you expect?' I knew she was really talking to herself. Knew there was nothing I could have done. I still felt I'd let her down. Let the family down." Toby's eyes darkened, looking inward, back to those times.

Kate smiled, or tried to, but whatever camaraderie she and Toby had shared before felt muted, distant. He clearly felt he'd also let Free down. A barrier had been constructed between them, and her name was Free. Kate slid the scarf off her shoulders. "Shall we attempt the scarf-around-the-hips thing? Time for us to get home." But inside, she was saying to herself, *What did you expect, Kate? He belongs to another woman.*

7

THE EVENING SKY TURNED PURPLE, a dusky backdrop to swirls of gray fog. Kate and Toby headed north on Stockton, walking briskly down the sidewalk past Washington Square. As another blast of cold air whipped by, Kate tugged the shawl around her shoulders. "Summer in San Francisco," she said with a shiver, "is more like winter in some parts of the world. Are you okay with that rip? I mean, not too much cold air is getting in?"

"No," Toby said adamantly. He'd left the table at the restaurant with Kate walking closely behind. She'd giggled, saying they probably looked like Cary Grant and Katherine Hepburn in *Bringing Up Baby* when Cary had to walk closely behind Katherine to hide her missing skirt panel. Except in this case, Kate was "covering" Toby's behind. Later, in the men's room, he'd checked the damage. The rip was relatively insignificant. One would have to look really closely to catch a flash of his tiger-striped undies.

At the time he'd thought how cruel fate could be. Why couldn't he be wearing leopard-spotted undies? Or zebra-striped undies. No, he had to be wearing *tiger*-striped, like some kind of perverse reminder of Free's meanderings.

"Maybe tomorrow," he said, "you can pick me up something else to wear...." He let his voice trail off, hoping Kate hadn't heard his suggestion all that clearly.

Because if she bought him clothes again, he'd probably end up looking like Captain Hook.

In Washington Square, a group of Chinese tai chi practitioners slowly lifted their feet and swayed their arms in unison. Toby stopped in his tracks and stared at the group.

"What is it?" Kate asked, stopping with him.

"Let's jump one of those tai chi guys—someone my size—and steal his outfit." Maybe tomorrow night Toby could cook Chinese instead of Italian. He'd call his tai-chi getup part of the dinner theme.

"You're going over the edge."

"Actually, I went over a long time ago."

"You look great as a pirate," she blurted.

He glanced at her. Was Kate blushing? Maybe it was the angle of the streetlights that were starting to come on. "I look like what?" he asked, knowing he'd heard correctly but wanting to hear it again.

"Like a pirate," she whispered. She tilted her head and gave him a look that made his heart pound loudly, thunderously. "Because that's what you are," she added, her voice dropping to a husky register that made his blood surge. "A pirate."

Damn right. He'd spent his career as a corporate raider, the equivalent of piracy, but only at this moment, with this woman, could he grasp or embrace his own essential nature, his passion, his inner yearnings for adventure. He'd learned to despise plundering corporate America. But to plunder his own deepest nature, to call forth Kate Corrigan's fantasies, to invade and steal her admiration was to make his piracy something sacred. Meaningful.

He swallowed.

She was close, and he caught her scent again. Lilacs. The fragrance teased the cool evening air, and teased him. She was so near, all he had to do was take a step to close the distance between them. One step and he could embrace her, embrace a new life.

He opened his mouth to stammer something, anything, but a blast of chilly air rushed past. With an audible shiver, Kate began walking away, her long legs covering ground like a Thoroughbred. "Come on!" she called, her slim frame disappearing into the shadowy hues. "Let's get home, get warm."

Home. Warmth. Kate.

Take me to your home, Kate. Admit me to your heart. The thoughts sprang up from some dark internal well, just as his pirate persona had. The pirate—and the man— willingly followed her footsteps.

KATE AND TOBY LET THEMSELVES into the inn. The foyer was dark, except for the light from the faux Tiffany lamp that sat on the carved elm wood table. The reds, golds and blues spilled a patchwork of color onto the hardwood floor.

"That's funny," Kate said, switching on a light. "I thought Melanie would be up, baking a few extra thousand brownies." Something on the table caught her eye. "A note," Kate murmured, picking up a piece of paper. She read it out loud. "Katherine, dear, an elderly couple checked in, asked for The Wild Room. Verna will be in late tomorrow morning and I'll be in later this evening. P.S. I hope you didn't pay for dinner. P.P.S. Verna left some of her departed husband's clothes in Kismet for Toby. Love, Mother."

"She didn't say where she went?" Toby asked, peering over Kate's shoulder at the note.

"It's a little frightening imagining my mother kicking up her pastel heels somewhere in San Francisco. But who knows, maybe there's a Betty Crocker convention at the Moscone Center."

But despite Kate's flippant tone, Toby caught a look

of concern on her face. As she placed the note back on the table, he touched her arm reassuringly. "Your mother has common sense. She'll be safe."

Kate nodded slowly, obviously unsure. "San Francisco isn't Beaufort. But you're right, my mother is a big girl. Anyway, if Verna's going to be late, I'd better see what I can do to prep for tomorrow morning's breakfast. Usually Verna keeps some frozen rolls or something on hand that I can serve."

"How about sandwiches?" Toby chuckled to himself, but stopped abruptly when Kate flashed him a look.

"I *can* cook, you know," she said defensively, stopping in front of the swinging kitchen door. "Maybe not as well as Melanie, but it's not as though I don't know what an oven is."

"I, uh…didn't doubt it." Actually he had no doubt Kate could take apart an oven and put it back together in record time.

"You're just like my family, not trusting me in the kitchen." She fisted her hands on her hips, as though defying him to say anything.

He knew better than to respond to that. Growing up with two sisters and a mom had taught him a few things about how to deal with women, such as when to change the subject. "Forget the kitchen. What is the one thing at which you'd really like to excel?"

Kate blinked. "I've always wanted to perform a Motown medley to throngs of screaming fans."

Now he blinked. He also knew when to call it a day. "I think it's time for me to go to bed."

The look Kate gave him almost made him ask if she'd like to join him. After a moment of intense eye-locking, she murmured, "G'night. If you need anything, I'll be in the kitchen."

Back in Kismet, the land of fate, he checked out the clothes Verna had brought over: a pair of faded blue jeans and a black T-shirt, both washed and neatly folded. Toby unbuttoned his red silk shirt and hung it carefully over the back of a chair. Time to slip the pirate look and ponder his fate.

He stared out the window at his home, watching the shadows behind the living room drapes, wondering how to get back in there by tomorrow night. But his thoughts kept being interrupted by images of Kate. Kate in that killer red outfit, licking chermoula off her fingers. Kate in that killer red outfit, belting out "I Heard It Through the Grapevine." Kate in that killer red outfit doing anything.

Clank! Smash!

Was someone breaking in? Kate was downstairs, alone.

He tore out the door, down the stairs and raced through the swinging kitchen doors.

Catching his breath, at first he thought he saw a ghost. Then he realized it was Kate, coated with white flour. "What…happened?" he said between gasps.

She was breathing as hard as he was. "I had everything under control. A couple of electric beaters, humming like fine-tuned engines, were mixing batches of batter. I had lifted the flour bag, ready to pour some into another bowl, when I noticed one of the engines—I mean beaters—was overheating." She swiped at her brow as she looked around the white-dusted room. "I lunged for the mixer and dropped the flour."

He scanned the area. She'd obviously turned off both mixers. Despite her flour crisis, she'd kept her head. He glanced at her spiky hairdo, which now looked like a flocked Christmas tree. That fit in with the rest of the room's decor, which looked as if it had been sprinkled with snow.

"Are you okay?"

"Yes," she answered, sounding a bit unsure.

He wondered if she'd ever done anything in this kitchen besides pour herself a cup of coffee. Obviously there hadn't been any frozen rolls, so she'd resorted to cooking. Shaking his head at the mess, he gave her a look she took all wrong.

Kate's chin wobbled as a tear spilled over. It traced a wet path down a white-caked cheek. "Whatever this looks like, I'm not like Free."

"No, no, you're not," he quickly admitted. "I didn't mean..." Not only was she unlike Free, Kate was unlike any woman he'd ever met. But he kept that thought to himself. In her current vulnerable, Christmas-flocked state, she might misinterpret the compliment and feel worse than she already did. "What were you trying to do?" he asked, trying to sound upbeat as he surveyed the scene.

"I was trying—" her voice wobbled, her shoulders shook "—to make...biscuits." She began to wail.

She looked so fragile he felt a stab of remorse. "Let me help," Toby said, which was exactly how he would have handled such a crisis growing up, jumping in to save the day—or in this case, the biscuits.

He took a step toward Kate, meaning to wipe some flour off her cheek. When he raised his hand, however, she fell against him. Another sob broke loose. Just as he'd done on numerous occasions with his kid sisters, he put his arms around her, rocking her a little as she cried and sniffled on his shoulder.

Except she didn't feel like a kid sister, especially when she was pressed against his naked chest. Earlier, on the street, he'd wondered what it would be like if he stepped toward her and took her in his arms. Now he knew. Holding Kate felt warm, pleasurable. Her hair—soft, feathery—brushed underneath his chin. Her body molded against his as though they were two pieces that fit perfectly. A sizzling current shot through him and spun a few crazy laps around his stomach, igniting his insides with heat. If he kept holding her like this, he'd soon be hot enough to bake those biscuits himself.

He pulled back from her, holding her at arm's length. She looked up at him with big, blue teary eyes. "I'm not Free," she whispered shakily. "I know what a can room is."

He threw back his head and laughed. Kate had turned this heated, my-body-can-bake-biscuits moment into one of lighthearted whimsy. She had a knack for adding a delightful slant to life's darker moments. That was the kind of woman to spend a lifetime with. A woman who was not only your lover, but your friend. A woman who...was this woman.

Was he crazy? He had to get back on good footing with Free, at least for tomorrow night, not fantasize about Kate. Pulling away a little, he said solemnly, "Item one—you're not Free. Item two—what exactly are you making?"

"Southern biscuits."

"Sounds reasonable." Although he felt anything but as he looked into those liquid blue eyes. He quickly glanced away as though interested in whatever she'd been assembling for this Southern biscuit task. Without his glasses, the periphery of the room looked a little hazy, although he could clearly see the items on the counter: a bowl, what looked to be an assortment of forks and knives, a container of milk, a hammer—he opted to ignore why that tool was out—and several baking sheets, one of which lay on the floor.

She followed his gaze. "It was all going well until I picked up the bag of flour and got distracted. The bag was unwieldy, soft—I couldn't get a handle on it."

"You couldn't get a handle," he repeated absently. He definitely had a handle on her, though. His fingers gently kneaded her shoulders. She definitely felt unwieldy, soft…

"I lost my grip. It tipped."

He tightened his grip, not wanting to lose it yet.

"And the bag slipped." She jerked her gaze back to him. "Ka-boom."

He paused, still gripping the unwieldy soft package in front of him. "I've finally figured out how you blew up my car," he said mischievously, "but this is a new one—blowing up a bag of flour."

She put on the impish grin that did funny things to his insides. "No, it exploded when it hit the floor. For a moment, it was like a montage of *Mutiny on the Bounty* and *The Great Ziegfeld*—a whiteout swirl of sea foam and feathers." She gestured broadly. "Wild! Dramatic!"

Like Kate. That wild, spiky hair, that gamine face sprinkled with flour. She was unlike any woman, all right. She was the most unnerving, colorful, fascinating woman he'd ever known. Often a little, and sometimes a lot, dangerous. Dangerous Kate. Couldn't trust her around Firebirds or flour.

Or me.

He should back away…walk backward, like Kate, out through the swinging door and up to his room where he belonged. But he liked standing close to her, smelling that trace of lilac, staring into those blue eyes that sparkled like sunlight on the ocean. And he loved those lips, those full, still lightly cherry tinted lips. Did they also taste like cherries? Maybe. Plus a tad spicy from the chermoula. He trailed his tongue lightly along his bottom lip, curious to know, aching to taste. He hesitated, then leaned down, parting his lips.

"What's going on in here?" demanded a female voice.

Toby halted, catching a whiff of familiar White Shoulders perfume. Without turning his head, he said, "Good evening, Mrs. Corrigan.'' He released Kate, who stumbled back a step, a surprised look on her face.

''Hi, Melanie,'' Kate said weakly. ''We're baking.''

''I don't need to ask what,'' her mother responded under her breath, her critical gaze traveling from her white-dusted daughter to bare-chested Toby.

Br-r-ring-br-r-ring.

Melanie, ignoring the phone, stared at the back of Toby's pants. ''Do you want that rip fixed?''

Br-r-ring. Br-r-ring.

Duly impressed with her homemaker's eagle eye, Toby nodded as Kate headed for the phone.

''Beau's Bed-and-Breakfast,'' Kate said into the receiver. ''Oh, hi, Dad.'' Pause. ''She's...'' Kate looked at her mother, who stared back at her daughter with a beseeching look. ''She's not home, yet,'' Kate said, obviously picking up on her mother's unspoken wish. ''I think she's out, kicking up her heels.''

Melanie smiled, a smile so relieved and happy that Toby thought he was seeing the real woman for the first time.

''Oh, I'm fine,'' Kate continued into the receiver, brushing some flour off her top. ''Yes, the inn's fine, too. No, I'm not really dating Henry anymore.''

Now Toby cocked his head to hear better, but Kate didn't elaborate. What kind of man was this Henry? And if she wasn't really dating him anymore, why? Did he not treat her well? A spark of anger heated Toby's insides.

''Uh, thanks for calling, Dad.'' Pause. ''Yes, that's right, kicking up her heels. The pink pastel ones, I believe,'' she added, her eyes twinkling. ''She's become a new woman since her arrival.'' Pause. ''Nice talking to you, too.'' Pause. ''Sounds perfect. Love you, too.'' Kate hung up the phone.

Melanie's eyebrows arched so high they almost disappeared into her hairline. "I do believe I've befuddled your father for the first time in his life!"

"About time he discovered you're more than the perfect homemaker," Kate said.

"Maybe you've discovered that, too," Melanie said softly, her eyes misting over. She cleared her throat. "I've never heard you and your father converse for so long."

"He definitely seemed a bit befuddled about your kicking up your heels."

Melanie patted the back of her hair. "Actually, I took a taxi to the Saint Francis Hotel and enjoyed a cup of tea in their sumptuous lobby. Nothing wild, but Max will never know." Melanie's peach lips smiled like the Cheshire cat. "What was that 'sounds perfect' part?"

"He said he's sending me a set of new wrenches for Christmas."

"You were always his favorite apprentice," Melanie acknowledged. "Brad never got the hang of it."

"Yes, my brother excelled at partying and girls while I excelled at school and tools," Kate said edgily. Her face turned pensive. "He's still the one who got to go to college." Kate gave her head a toss as though to shake off the memory. "Hey," she said to Toby, "let's attack those biscuits."

"Biscuits?" Melanie looked over at the flour-dusted counter. "I can help—"

"No, no," Kate said, waving her away, "I'm determined to excel in the kitchen, for once. You can go, leave me to my business." Kate made a shooing motion with her hands.

Melanie's bouffant hairdo seemed to sag a little, like her spirits. "I'll—I'll go upstairs. You can drop off your pants later," she said quietly to Toby. She stopped and gave him a double take. "I guess your clients really go for the sprayed-on pants, no-shirt look."

Now Toby felt befuddled. "I'm only wearing these because Kate bought them for me."

Melanie blinked so hard one of her false eyelashes stuck. Peering at him with one eye, she exclaimed, "Bought them for you?" Her eye popped open. "Kath-e-rine Corr-i-gan, we must talk."

Kate, who'd been reading the recipe book, looked up. "Huh? About what?"

Melanie took such a deep breath, Toby swore some of the flour in the room shifted. "I realize you're a grown woman with your own business, making your own money, but we must talk about your paying for cer-tain…services." On that, Melanie pivoted on her pastel pink heels and strode out of the room.

Kate frowned. "What services? The cleaning staff comes in, but otherwise Verna and I run the rest of the errands around here." Kate turned back to her recipe book. "I've never understood Melanie, although I must confess I'm extremely impressed with that suppressed personality that's finally emerging."

"OKAY," TOBY SAID, dusting some flour off his jeans. After Melanie had left, he'd quickly gone upstairs and changed into the clothes Verna had brought. "Tell Verna she can be late for a week because we have enough bis-cuits for days!"

We? Kate liked the sound of that as she looked at the piles of half-inch-high dough rounds wrapped with waxed paper. *We. We have enough biscuits.* She pressed the wax paper around a bunch of biscuits. *We had fun baking together.* An unexpected sadness pooled in her stomach. *Be honest with yourself, Kate. A lifetime of "we" for you and Toby is about as realistic as one of your pirate fantasies.*

She set the mounds of biscuits in the refrigerator while Toby filled the dishwasher with the forks, spoons and other cooking utensils. "Tomorrow, we bake these at eight minutes, four-fifty degrees, right?" she asked. "Then we take them out, we put them on plates, and we take them up to The Wild One." She smiled to herself, thinking of that elderly couple. Had to be the Riddicks, that sweet husband and wife in their seventies, who liked to spend an occasional romantic night away in the city. Mrs. Riddick had once confessed to packing a few risqué nighties for these getaways. "The Wild Ones," Kate corrected under her breath. Raising her voice, she added, "Then we'll take more biscuits out onto the veranda where we'll eat breakfast together." Oh dear, she was back to "we." But wrong or right, she liked how it felt. "We" was slipping off her tongue as sweetly and easily as the butter they would put on their biscuits tomorrow morning.

"Sure, whatever you like."

So much for "we." Jolted back to reality, Kate straightened and looked around. In the past few hours, they'd sifted ingredients, rolled dough and cleaned the kitchen. It had been like tuning an engine with her dad— everything went smoothly, efficiently, like clockwork. She and Toby were like a well-oiled team. A we-team if there ever was one.

If there ever could be.

"Did you and Free cook together?" she asked, trying to sound innocently interested. "You know, cook as in food." She scrunched her face, wishing she hadn't said that last part. It was obvious they'd both witnessed Free's cooking with Tiger.

Toby cocked a knowing eyebrow. "The only cooking Free ever did was you-know-where and let's not go there." He wiped his hands roughly on a hand towel embroidered with frolicking cats. "Felt good to cook again," he said a bit too cheerfully. "Now I have to figure how to get back into my house to cook tomorrow's dinner.''

''Do you have to be in your house? What about here?''

Toby hung the dish towel on the oven handle. ''I met my potential employer at a business get-together at my place last summer. Free was out of town visiting family. Or so she said.'' Toby grew quiet for a moment. ''Anyway, I think he'd find it odd if I was suddenly cooking in the bed-and-breakfast next door.''

''Good point.'' As Kate finished wiping the counter, a thump was heard on the kitchen windowsill.

''Beau!'' Straightening, Kate headed toward her cat. He sat on the ledge, eyeing the kitchen, the king of this terrain. Kate scratched a spot behind his nicked ear. ''Your food bowl's on the back porch as usual, Beau. Are you checking the kitchen to see if you're missing anything tasty?'' When he craned his neck to look past her at Toby, she said, ''Beau, meet Toby.''

''Hello, Beau,'' Toby said, walking over. He chucked the cat under the chin. Beau emitted a raspy meow. ''Whoa, sounds like you've had quite a night.''

''He always sounds like that. Has that scratchy seen-it-all-done-it-all meow. Probably telling us about his most recent wild adventures in North Beach.''

''He's a pirate, too?''

''I like to think so.''

Beau stretched languidly, as though his swashbuckling status was pretty mundane stuff. After tossing a last green-eyed look at Toby, Beau hopped off the ledge and disappeared into the darkness.

''He does that,'' Kate confessed, watching his exit. ''Loves me then leaves me. But he always returns for breakfast in the morning.''

''Is that what Henry did?'' As soon as Toby asked, he wished he hadn't. First, it was an admission he'd been listening in on Kate's conversation with her dad. Second, it was none of his business. And third, well, he was jealous. He shouldn't be, had no right to be.

Kate watched the emotions play across Toby's face. What was going on in his mind? "Henry didn't jump off windowsills, if that's what you're asking."

"I meant, did he..."

"Love me and leave me?"

"Yes."

As she nodded yes, pink stained her cheeks. From embarrassment? Hurt?

Toby paused, pushing down the anger that flared to life within him. If this man Henry—hell, if any man— loved and left a woman like Kate, he didn't deserve to walk the planet Earth.

Kate flashed Toby an odd look. "Are you okay?"

It took every ounce of will to keep his voice steady. "What about Henry?"

She stared at Toby for a moment. "He loved and left me and three others from what I can figure out, but then I didn't keep a scoreboard."

"Four?"

"Yes." Kate brushed a stray hair off her forehead. "Some men—and women—two-time. But Henry was a four-timer."

"How did you know?"

"That there were four of us?" When Toby managed a surprised half nod, Kate continued, "Let's see... number one caught Henry with number two at that place on Grant Street, the Lost and Found Saloon—aptly named in this case. Seems numbers one and two dragged Henry out onto the sidewalk where they accidentally stumbled into number three, who was exiting the Grant and Green Blues Club with some guy, which adds an interesting twist to the story because it appears number three was two-timing the four-timer." Kate counted on her fingers as though to keep everyone straight. "Okay, then number three ditched her date and joined numbers one and two. All three then proceeded to rough up Henry a little. From what I heard, it was like a Charlie's Angels gone bad sort of scene."

"How did you find out about all this?"

"Well, in the midst of the Charlie's Angels thing, spineless Henry spilled that there was yet another woman. Me! Imagine my surprise when three women—looking a little scuffed up, but smugly happy—showed up on my doorstep late that night. They explained that we'd all been dating Henry, so I let them in. We stayed up until the wee hours, swapping tales, comparing Henry's lies, and that's how I discovered Henry had been one busy four-timing fellow. Last I heard, he settled down and married a librarian. I think his cheating days are long gone."

"He missed out on a good woman."

"You mean four good women."

"No, I mean you."

She cast her eyes downward. "Thanks, but I'm a better matchmaker than a matchmake-ee." She looked up. "I lack skills in both the homemaking and love departments, it seems."

Usually Toby had a keen sense of what to say. But facing Kate's innermost insecurities left him speechless, unable to conjure up the right words to boost her confidence. Instead, he opted to play it light. "Bet you were close to showing Henry the door anyway, even if he hadn't been—"

"Four-timing me?" Kate's eyes turned a deeper blue, as though a cloud had passed over her thoughts.

"He couldn't have been much of a pirate, Kate."

"No, he wasn't." Struck again by Toby's incredible insights, she admitted, "As silly as it might sound, I've always imagined a pirate swooping into my life and sweeping me away.'' Her smile was vague, distant. ''Just one of those childhood fantasies, I suppose.'' She looked sheepish. ''But for me, a childhood-turned-adult pirate fantasy. I guess other little girls dreamed of Christopher Atkins or Donny Osmond, but I wanted a pirate to go with my special room at Granny's. He didn't even have to look like a famous movie star, just be a swash-buckling, brawny, passionate, sword-in-his-teeth pirate. Crazy, I guess. I mean, who in this day and age imagines being swept away, especially in downtown San Francisco?''

''Marcus in his Moroccan-California caftan?'' Toby grinned, then turned serious. ''I have a problem.''

''Did Marcus ask for your phone number?''

Tony flashed her a black look. ''Hardly. I have to get back into my house by tomorrow night.''

''I've been thinking the same thing.''

''Meaning, I have to make amends with Free.'' Not that he wanted to but he couldn't admit his plan to Kate. He glanced up at the Captain Hook clock. ''Eleven o'clock. I heard barking a few minutes ago. Maybe I should go over, knock on the door and, when she answers, get on my knees and beg her forgiveness. That is, if the Dobermans don't get me first.''

Fury swirled through Kate. ''Over my dead body!'' When he looked surprised, she blurted, ''There's no way you're asking forgiveness after what she's done!''

''It's only for my job interview.''

''I don't care!'' Kate gestured wildly although she wasn't sure why. Clasping her hands together, she took in a deep breath and exhaled slowly. ''Okay,'' she said, trying to sound more grounded and together than she really felt, ''I care about your wanting that job, but there's no reason for you to ask forgiveness when you did nothing wrong.'' When Toby started to speak, Kate held up her hands in a stopping motion. ''I refuse to watch a wonderful, generous, kind, intelligent and extremely sexy man like yourself get down on his knees and ask that…that bead-strewn trumpet for forgiveness." She crossed her flailing arms and flashed him her best defiant look.

After a long pause, Toby breathed, "You think I'm sexy?"

Kate's cheeks burned. Hell, her entire body was burning. She had no doubt every inch of her skin matched her red outfit. Damn it. Trying to pretend she didn't care—okay, *lust*—for this man was like trying not to breathe in and out.

When in doubt, best to speak the truth.

"Yes," she whispered, "Way sexy." The last word sounded like more a release of steamy breath than actual speaking. She cleared her throat. And while she was on this truthful trip, best to clear the air on another topic. "I'm sorry I called Free a trumpet."

"Strumpet."

"That, too."

They both burst into grins. But Kate didn't stop there. She started giggling. Toby started laughing. The next thing she knew, they were doubled over, clutching their stomachs, laughing so hard she thought for sure she'd bust a gut.

"Trumpet," she managed to sputter between waves of laughter. "At least I didn't say horn."

"Or flute!"

"If I'd tried that," Kate said, trying to catch her breath, "I might've said 'fruit' by mistake!"

"A bead-strewn fruit!" Toby doubled over with laughter. Kate staggered toward him, holding her sides as she giggled loudly. "Or, in your vernacular," Toby said, barely managing to get the words out, "a bead-strewn sassafras."

"I told you sassafras was a fruit!"

They fell, laughing, into each other's arms. Every time one of them started to calm down, the other would say "sassafras," and they'd convulse with laughter all over again. After several minutes, they began to recover from their laugh-fest, their arms still draped around each other. They looked deeply into each other's eyes, reading the shift in emotions that had now silently taken place.

Reluctantly Toby pulled away, knowing if he didn't distance himself, he'd do something he'd regret, like kiss Kate.

He moved away from her to the butcher-block table and sat on one of the stools. "Okay," he said, keeping his voice level, calm, all the things he didn't feel inside. "I'm not going to beg forgiveness from Free, but I need to work things through with her, give it a second chance."

A twinge of hurt twisted Kate's insides. It was his life, his girlfriend, his choice. Kate was an outsider, always would be, no matter what had transpired these past twenty-four hours. Like falling head over heels for Toby. She tried to smile, to act as though this was still part of their good-natured exchange, but she felt gutted.

"Okay, you need to get back into Free's good graces and into your house by tomorrow night." She tried to sound upbeat even as her heart twisted itself into a small, tight, painful knot. "Come look at my postcards. Evidence of my matchmaking expertise." It would get them out of the kitchen, away from the bright overhead light where he might see the pain on her face, if he hadn't already heard it in her voice.

They walked through the foyer to Kate's pine desk nestled in an alcove next to the front door. She switched on a desk lamp that fanned a pale pool of light onto the desk, enough light to see the postcards mounted on a cork bulletin board on the back wall. Pictures of beaches, cathedrals, even one with a camel, on which two people waved at the camera.

"Different customers sent these to me...some from people I matched up while they were visiting the inn. Like this card—" She pulled the pushpin holding a picture of a metal piece of art. "This is a sculpture by Picasso."

"Looks like a horse. Or a guitar."

"Supposedly, it's the head of a woman. It's in downtown Chicago, the home of two people I matched but I pretended they did most of the work themselves. Two lawyers, Tyler and Emily, although I thought of them as The Wild One and Pollyanna while they were here. And talk about wild! Verna and I still chuckle about finding them rolling around on that leather bedspread minutes after they met!" Kate pinned the card back onto the board.

"What does the Picasso have to do with getting back into my house?"

Kate looked up at him. The reflection of the desk lamp imbued the air with a shadowy, sensual light. His eyes, normally brown, burnished with an inner flame, giving them an almost tawny glow. His heated gaze upset her, threw her off. "Just like I helped match up Emily and Tyler," she said haltingly, "I'll match up you and Free."

He didn't say anything. Instead, he turned and looked at the postcards, as though journeying to all those places in his mind. He reached out and touched one of the cards, a picture of a ship surrounded by pristine cobalt skies and lagoon-green seas.

Kate joined him, her gaze landing on the same picture. "I could plan a cruise for two," she said softly. "The tang of salt air, the warmth of the breezes. Miles and miles of bathwater-temperature water teeming with colorful, exotic fish."

She closed her eyes, imagining the beauty, the adventure. The Caribbean had always been one of her favorite pirate fantasy settings. Opening her eyes, she said matter-of-factly, "I'll plan this cruise for the winter, when the heat and allure of the Caribbean will be all the more welcome. I'll have my travel agent write it up as a romantic invitation that will be delivered to Free tomorrow. She'll be overwhelmed, thrilled, all that good stuff—and, whammo, you're back home in time to fix dinner." Playfully Kate clapped twice. Toby chuckled, sort of, but the moment didn't feel as fun and lighthearted as she'd hoped.

"Sounds like a plan," he agreed, although his tone was unduly somber.

"Trust my matchmaking instincts. It'll work great!"

"I've never been to the Caribbean."

"Neither have I. But I have some artifacts in The Pirate room that might give you a sense of that part of the world. No one's checked in there tonight. Come on, I'll show you." Kate bounded ahead, not wanting Toby to see the emotion in her eyes. Darn him, anyway. Why couldn't he have stayed the nerdy guy in her imagination? When exactly had he become a pirate, stealing into her home, and stealing her heart?

8

"WELCOME TO MY CHILDHOOD," Kate said, opening the
door with the miniature saber on it. She flicked a light
switch and a magical realm came to life. The fabric on
the walls shimmered green with metallic glints, as
though one were spying hidden treasures under the sea.
There were several pictures of ships, the most impressive
being a framed painting of a sloop, its sails billowing
against stormy skies. On the deck, several rough-looking
pirates raised a black flag with a skull and crossbones.
The ships tied in with the view from the window that
looked out on San Francisco Bay.

"I've always loved this room," Kate murmured.
"Some pieces, like the pictures, were from my room at
Granny's."

She followed Toby's gaze to the king-size four-poster
bed in the corner. Netting cascaded from the ceiling and
fell to envelope the bed, creating a private world to be
shared by lovers.

"That's some bed for a small-town Miss Magnolia,"
Toby said under his breath.

"I bought that bed especially for this room," she said,
shooting him a look. "At Granny's, I had a very normal
twin bed."

He cocked one eyebrow.

"Okay," she admitted, "with just a little netting."
She grinned. "And I had a saber on my door, the same
miniature that's on the door of this room. Granny said

she'd bought it from a suspicious-looking man with an eye patch, but I knew she'd really found it at a garage sale.'' Kate looked around with a dreamy gaze, pleased at the reality her fantasies had shaped.

Toby had seen Kate as dangerous, kitchen-challenged and tomboyish. But for the first time, he saw the dreamy, childlike Kate. The girl who'd grown up and still dreamed of pirates and romance. As she looked around, her eyes turned a soft blue, reminding him of the hazy morning skies over Mount Tamalpais. And her lips, which he'd often seen quirk into that impish grin, now curved sweetly in an almost ethereal smile.

''Sometimes,'' she said conspiratorially, ''when the room isn't rented, I'll come up here and sit by the window, watching the bay. I'll imagine that, far in the distance, I see marauding pirate ships, battling for treasures and loot.''

He didn't think it was his imagination that she looked at him as though he was one of those marauding pirates. He liked that look on Kate. Loved it, if he were truthful.

As though embarrassed by her own whimsy, she suddenly moved away to a far wall on which hung a poster. It showed a man with a ring in his ear, a devilish grin on his tanned, handsome face. She cleared her throat. ''Douglas Fairbanks, Senior,'' she explained, pointing at the man in the picture, ''in the title role of *The Black Pirate*. What do you think? This could be you, in the Caribbean.'' Kate pointed to the poster on the opposite wall. ''Or you could be Errol Flynn in *Captain Blood*.''

''You belong in the Caribbean.''

She held up her hand, stopping him from saying more. ''Don't,'' she said softly. She looked out the window. ''Remember last night when the moon was full? Granny and I called those Captain Blood nights because anything can happen. Granny said the air was charged for adventure and passion. All you had to do was close your eyes and dream." Kate closed her eyes. "I see you and Free on a big white ship, people playing shuffleboard and drinking Mai Tai's." Kate opened her eyes. "What do you think?"

"I think it sounds like a potentially sloppy shuffleboard game."

"Cruises offer other things, too. Gourmet meals. Exercise classes. Some even have spas on board."

"What happened to adventure and passion?"

"Well, that's up to you and Free, I suppose."

They stared at each other for a long, drawn-out moment. Finally Toby broke the silence. "All right. Plan a cruise with shuffleboard, and little drinks with umbrellas, and whatever else you think would be good. Because at this moment, I really don't care what Free and I do. All that matters..."

Is you, Kate, my sweet, passionate romantic. Blood pumped wildly through his veins, as though fighting for control of his intellect. Fighting for him to let go, to love.

"I'll be right back. " He quickly exited the room.

Feeling awkward at Toby's sudden departure, Kate decided not to second-guess his words, and to simply wait. Maybe, unlike the many promises Henry had made, Toby would really be right back. She bided her time by staring out the window. In the distance, the moon hovered over the vast, dark bay. It reminded her a little of Beaufort, and the many nights she and her granny sat and stared at the ocean, talking about life and pirates.

The door creaked open. She turned...and gasped.

There, in the opened doorway, stood the pirate of her dreams, his face submerged in shadows, his body encased in black leather pants and a red silk shirt that fell open with reckless abandon, exposing a chiseled, hairy chest. And between his teeth, a miniature saber.

Toby, a wicked gleam in his eye, stepped inside and shut the door behind him. He removed the saber and tossed it onto the bed. "Come here, Kate." He stood wide legged, his presence boldly intimidating. And wildly, forbiddingly sexual.

A shudder ripped through her as she released a slow, ragged breath. He was everything she'd ever fantasized about. And here he was in the flesh, asking for her, the object of his pirate's passion. "I want to," she whispered, "but..." One night of wild lust could only bring heartache in the long run.

She imagined the future. Looking out her window and seeing her neighbors, Toby and Free, who by then would probably be calling herself Goldenrod or Horsefly, stringing beads or whatever they did together in their spare time. Kate, still calling herself Kate, would wave hello as though she were just the matchmaking innkeeper next door while her heart shattered because of her one secret night of love with the man, the pirate, of her dreams.

But if she refrained, stopped it now, she could always remain the fun-loving, former-car-bombing neighbor who occasionally waved hello to Toby, the man with whom she'd always remained friends and never crossed the line to being lovers.

"Come here, Kate," he repeated in a low, throaty tone. He snapped off the light. The milky haze of moonlight filled the darkened room. "I want to make love with you."

She closed her eyes, trying to remember why she shouldn't go. But all she was aware of was the scent of his woodsy cologne swirling through the air like an invisible hook, drawing her senses toward him. Drawing her toward him.

She crossed the room, impelled involuntarily by her passion. She was a few feet away when he stepped forward and crushed her against him. "Be my lover," he whispered, his words thick with challenge and desire. "Be the woman I see inside, the romantic..."

Her heartbeat skyrocketed as she pressed her face into the warmth of his neck. "And the object of her pirate's passion," she said softly, giving into the moment, craving the experience, not caring about tomorrow.

He groaned as his mouth possessed hers, claiming her. Electricity tore through her as she returned his kiss. He tasted hot, salty. His lips alternately brushed, nibbled and devoured hers. She pulled away for a breath and his mouth seared a path of hot kisses down her throat.

"Oh Kate," he said roughly. And then he swept her into his arms and carried her to the far side of the bed. But instead of laying her on top of the burgundy satin cover, he set her down so she stood in front of him.

"I want to watch you," he murmured. "Savor all of you."

His hands encircled her waist, tightly, as though he never wanted to let her go. Then slowly, slowly, his hands slid upward, taking her T-shirt with them. Next, she felt the button on her pants pop, heard the rip of the zipper. He gently pulled down her pants, stopping at her feet. As though obeying his unspoken command, she kicked off her sandals, then stepped out of her pants.

She stood in front of him, feeling momentarily awkward in her white cotton bra and undies. A romantic woman would be wearing something skimpy, satin. But her insecurity diminished when she caught the look in Toby's eyes. Even in the moonlight, she saw his heated gaze, and how he looked at her as though she *was* wearing something skimpy, satin. She casually wiped at the sudden mist in her eyes. It didn't matter if she wasn't dressed perfectly, or did *anything* perfectly, because Toby saw her as romantic, desirable Kate just for being herself.

He picked up the knife off the bed.

Her heart lurched.

He held the blade up, the moonlight glinting softly off the blade's edge, which he moved toward her, slowly.

She thought she'd be afraid, but she trusted Toby. Knew he was playing out her fantasy of the plundering, passionate pirate. And knowing that made her skin prickle pleasurably at the anticipation of what was to come.

He eased the blunt side of the blade underneath the thin piece of cotton between the cups of the bra. Then he pulled the blade toward him, gently. And yanked. With a rip, the bra fell apart, exposing her breasts.

Her nipples puckered at the onslaught of cool air. "Beautiful breasts," he murmured. He tossed the knife onto a table and cupped her mounds, causing her nipples to harden. She moaned as his heated hands kneaded and stroked.

Then his mouth was nipping, sucking on her breasts while his hand slid down into her underwear, finding her delicate nub. He eased off her panties with one hand as, with his other, he continued to expertly massage her swollen cleft. She dropped her head against the wall and groaned with all the need, the hunger that had been pent up inside, yearning for release.

Then he withdrew his hand and stepped back. "Take my clothes off, Kate."

She'd never undressed a man before. But she felt eager, excited at the thought of unwrapping her fantasy pirate. She grasped the slick silk of his shirt and opened it wider. As she pulled off his shirt, she kissed and nuzzled the thick carpet of chest hair before tossing the shirt aside. She rubbed her cheek against the stubble of his beard, luxuriating in its roughness, before she kissed him again.

Then, slowly, she released the button of his pants and drew the zipper down.

He tugged the pants the rest of the way off and stood, hard and thick, in front of her. "Touch me," he murmured.

She curled her fingers around him. Liquid heat flooded her insides as she stroked, increasing the tempo with his escalating groans of pleasure. He was primed. She was ready. "Take me," she whispered urgently.

He again lifted her into his arms, and after pulling aside the netting, laid her on the bed. He stood next to her, but with his back to the window, she couldn't decipher the look on his shadowed face. Then the tone of his voice told her everything.

"You're my treasure, Kate," he whispered huskily.

Instinctively she drew him to her, taking the weight of his body on hers. Then, she took control, taking him inside of her, gasping at the intense pleasure.

His tongue plunged into her mouth as he entered her fully, plundering her, taking her. She matched the lunging of his hips, driven by the aching of their primitive need. And in a singularly euphoric moment when she felt his heartbeat against hers, heard his murmured words of desire, everything inside her exploded in a thrill of pleasure that propelled her beyond the edge of her fantasies.

Afterward, as they lay on the bed in silence, they watched the moon float across the inky San Francisco sky until it disappeared, like a pirate ship sailing over the edge of the world, leaving behind only the memory of its journey.

KATE YAWNED AND NESTLED against the pillow. She stretched a little, yawned again and flickered open her eyes.

When had she bought purple-and-gold-stripped pillows?

A deep groan, from somewhere near the pillow, dis-

tracted her. She glanced up at the hard line of a jaw
stubbled with beard. Toby! Kate reared back and
blinked. Toby, deep in sleep, lay on the far side of the
bed, a lock of his sandy hair falling over his broad forehead. Memories of their lovemaking flooded her. They
had consumed each other as though there would be no
tomorrow.

And yet, tomorrow was here.

But she still had these last few moments, precious moments, to soak in his essence, memorize his features.
These memories would have to last her a lifetime.

She eased out a pent up breath. No man had a right
to look so sexy first thing in the morning. Had she ever
noticed the slight flare to his nostrils? Or the tiny white
scar underneath his right eye? She'd never know the
story of that scar. Her insides caved in a little. Just as
they'd never fully know each other, know all the secrets
of their bodies, their desires, their dreams. And they'd
never again wake up together. Never sleep in each
other's arms. Never listen to the beating of each other's
hearts in the middle of the night.

Toby's eyes opened. He stared at her, those brown
eyes smoldering with inner fires as he obviously remembered their secrets of the night before. "Good morning,"
he said seductively.

He was sexier than a man had a right to be. She
pushed the bad-boy curl off his forehead, mostly for the
sheer pleasure of touching him again. "Good morning
to you, too."

One side of his mouth curled into a slow smile. "The
morning's good, but you were better." Then he winked.
A lazy, sexy wink that made her pulse beat faster than
if she'd consumed a supercharged latte. She started to
say something about his being even better than her better, but stopped short when she glanced at the clock on
the nightstand.

"Oh my God!" She bolted upright.

"What?"

"Time!" She started to scramble out of bed, but one of her feet got caught in the netting. She swung her foot this way, then that, muttering curses worthy of a pirate's woman.

"Kate, let me help," Toby said dryly. He reached over and plucked the errant netting from around her big toe.

She continued to hold her leg midair, watching him with a moony expression. "You have a way with your hands," she blurted, her skin flushing with heat as she remembered the night before.

"And you have a way that drives a pirate wild." Toby reached for her and tugged her close, murmuring things in her ear. Her suspended leg fell back onto the bed with a soft thud. He pulled away, his eyes burning with *that* look again. "What should we do right now?"

"Make biscuits."

He cocked an eyebrow. "Excuse me?"

"It's noon. We were supposed to get breakfast ready for The Wild One."

He laughed under his breath. "I appreciate a woman who appreciates business." He glanced at the clock. "But they'll have to accept lunch at this point, which, I suggest, isn't sandwiches."

"Verna always notes what time to serve breakfast on the corkboard," Kate said, playfully jabbing his arm for the sandwich comment, "unless Mom checked in The Wild Ones, but she wouldn't know to note it on the board, so I need to find her, and if she's not around, I need to get the biscuits in the oven."

"I'll help."

They both clambered to get off the bed, sliding every which way on the satin cover, and over each other, in the process. Toby grabbed Kate by the shoulders. "We need to coordinate who's moving in what direction," he said, "or we'll be here forever and no one will get biscuits."

Be in The Pirate forever? Not such a bad way to spend the rest of one's life. "Right," she said breathlessly. "I'll go first, you follow—" Kate stopped. "No, you stay here." She slipped off the bed and grabbed her clothes. "I'll drop your pants off with Mom, check the biscuit situation, then bring you your clothes from Kismet." She shimmied into her T-shirt. "That's where you left them, right?" She liked how they'd started out in Kismet, fate, and ended up in her fantasy world, The Pirate. Not a bad journey for a brief affair.

Brief affair. She didn't want to think about that now. She buttoned her pants.

"I feel bad that you're having to do all this running around while I sit and wait."

"You can run around, too, if you're in the mood to be an exhibitionist." She slipped her feet into her sandals.

"Okay." He thumped his heart with his fist. "You really know how to get to me with that quirky sense of humor."

Kate looked at where he'd playfully hit his chest, at that mass of butterscotch hair that curled provocatively over a set of nicely molded pecs. She'd miss his body.

She'd miss him.

But rather than insert even one millisecond of melancholia into their one and only morning—well, technically afternoon—waking up together, she said lightly, "I might take a few extra minutes in case I need to serve biscuits."

"Cook them first."

She grabbed his leather pants off the floor. "I'll try to remember," she said drolly before clicking the door shut behind her.

KATE NEARLY TRIPPED as she scampered down the stairs, tucking the T-shirt into her pants with one hand while clutching Toby's leather pants with the other. She hadn't even looked in a mirror. Her hair was undoubtedly sticking up, her eye makeup smeared, and who knew where bits of flour remained.

No, she doubted there was even one speck of flour left on her body after last night.

Scampering even faster with that thought, she hit the bottom step in record time. If breakfast still needed to be served, she'd run a comb through her hair, wash her face and heat up some biscuits. Heat up. What was that temperature? Four-fifty for eight minutes? Eight-fifty for four minutes? One of them would do.

Kate tore into the kitchen. Empty, except for the tantalizing scent of yeasty biscuits. Kate stopped and smiled. Someone had already baked them! A very good sign! She glanced at the stove, where a pan and spatula lay, bits of what looked like eggs stuck to the bottom of the pan. Another good sign! One of the kitchen queens had saved the day. Kate could forget about worrying if it was four-fifty or eight-fifty and get on to her next task.

She tossed the pants onto the butcher table—making a mental note to remind Melanie to please sew the rip—and bolted out the swinging door and down the hallway to her bedroom. She'd forgotten all about the cruise reservations! She needed to make those first, then she'd wash her face.

Damn.

She couldn't call her travel agent unless she knew exactly when Toby wanted to do this cruise trip. If she made the reservations, then changed the dates, there'd be a penalty fee. Cruises were expensive enough without tacking on penalty fees. Kate skidded to a stop next to the pine desk and glanced back down the hallway. No signs of life. The Riddicks were probably in their room, quaffing biscuits and eggs. Melanie was nowhere to be seen—maybe she was kicking up her heels at a Martha Stewart convention. And Verna was late—as her note had said—or she was out running an errand.

So no one would see an uncombed, smeared Kate if she dashed back up the stairs, asked when Toby wanted this cruise, then dashed back down to her room to call the travel agency.

Kate's long legs bounded up the stairs two at a time. She told herself her breathing was ragged and she was sweating because of all this running up and down stairs in record time, but her heart told her this whole damn cruise thing hurt, despite the fact she'd already—pre-lovemaking—accepted that Toby needed to work things out with Free. *Be a big girl, Kate. It's time to play matchmaker. You knew this time would come.* She glanced underneath the door to Pollyanna, wondering if she should have brought the leather pants to her mother's room.

Bam!

She smashed into something, hard. Reeling, she regained her balance and stared at a forest of familiar butterscotch. "What?" She paused, heaving a breath. "What are you doing out here?" *Dressed only in your tiger-striped briefs?*

"Thought you were serving breakfasts, I mean, lunch," Toby said, catching his breath. "What are *you* doing out here?"

"And what the hell are both of you doing out here?"

They looked over at Melanie, who stood in the doorway to Pollyanna, dressed in a crisply ironed lime-green and fuchsia-flowered dress with matching lime-green pumps. Her dark pink lips, which cannily matched the fuchsia of her dress, formed a thin line as she pursed them disapprovingly.

"Mother, I can't believe you're cussing in public."

Melanie's penciled-in eyebrows curved like two McDonald's arches. "And daughter, I can't believe you're calling me 'Mother' in public. But skipping that, I can't believe you look as though you've spent a night making wild whoopee with—"

"Tarzan!" squealed an elderly woman's voice. "Bernie, come out here and get a load of this!"

Toby, his hands folded over his privates, looked upward as though divine intervention might occur any moment.

"You're causing a spectacle!" Kate whispered irritably to Toby. "Get back to our—I mean, your—room!"

Toby, not budging, continued staring skyward. "Which one might that be?" he asked casually. "I'm locked out of both." He lowered his gaze to Melanie. "Unless your mother wants to take me in."

"I'm not that kind of woman!" Melanie snapped, stepping back as though she might be forced to do something against her will. "Katherine, what kind of place are you running?"

"I figured you might be a while," Toby explained, ignoring her mother's question, "so I thought I'd slip down to Kismet and retrieve Verna's clothes. But the door was locked. So I about-faced and raced back to The Pirate, which, unfortunately—"

"Was locked." Kate groaned. "The doors automatically lock when you close them."

"Thanks for the warning."

"See Bernie," said Mrs. Riddick, oblivious to the discussion in progress. "Other guys dress like Tarzan."

Bernie, dressed in faded gray-and-white-checkered flannel pajamas, gave Toby a bored once-over. "Janie, I love you, baby, but I just don't want to go the Tarzan route, okay? Let's eat our biscuit lunch and visit Fisherman's Wharf." On that pronouncement, Bernie lumbered back into The Wild One, taking Janie with him, and shut the door soundly behind them.

"I like that guy," said Toby. "If I run out of more clothes, maybe he'll let me borrow his pajamas."

More clothes. Kate looked at her mother. "Can you fix that rip in Toby's leather pants?"

"The ones you bought him?"

Kate gave her a perplexed look. "Yes, those."

"Did you also buy him those—" Melanie pointed at Toby's briefs "—leopard underwear?"

"They're tiger-striped," Kate corrected. "And yes, I bought those, too. But back to the pants."

"I must ask," continued Melanie, folding her hands primly in front of her. "Did you also pay him for last night?"

"Pay him for what?"

Melanie rolled back her shoulders. "For his services."

Kate felt her skin go hot. What was her mother talking about? It had to be about cooking. "For helping me bake?" Kate asked incredulously. "I mean, I know I'm not the best in the world, and I tend to get a little out of hand, but I don't need to pay for that kind of help! Well, except Verna, of course. I pay her. But I didn't pay him!"

Melanie blinked so rapidly, Kate wondered if one of those false eyelashes would break loose and fly away. "I told Max we never should have had a child in the summer of love." She glanced from Toby's underwear to her daughter. "As for the pants, I'll get to those as soon as I can. After all, when no one prepared breakfast this morning, I had to scurry and pull that together, although The Wild Ones didn't receive theirs until almost noon. And then I spent thirty minutes on the phone with your father."

Kate's mouth dropped open. "You did?"

"Yes. We're discussing my independence. My future role as a woman. A *new* woman."

Kate, speechless, just stared at her mother. "Mom, don't tell me you've discovered the feminist movement."

"Heavens, no!" Melanie patted the back of her bouffant hairdo. "What's there to discover? We've always been the stronger ones. It's just time your father figured that out."

"But Brad..." Kate said under her breath. "College..."

"This is all fascinating," Toby said edgily, tapping Kate on the shoulder, "but I'd really like to get into a room."

"Good morning!" called a female voice from the bottom of the stairs.

"I really don't want anyone else seeing me dressed in these tiger things," Toby nearly yelled. "Can you get me into a room, now, *please?*"

"Oh, right. I'll get the keys, put you back into Kismet." But just as Kate turned to head back down the stairs, Verna appeared on the landing.

"Oh, my goodness," Verna said shakily.

"Mine, too," added Melanie.

Verna seemed to have trouble breathing. Patting her chest as though that might force more air into her lungs, she stammered a string of incoherent words, "I-I...me go...back...biscuits...hot-hot-hot..." Her gray eyes zeroed in on Toby's undies.

"Let's go downstairs and talk," Kate suggested, taking Verna by the elbow and turning her away from the tiger stripes. "Mom, please go back into your room so Toby can have some privacy until I can get him into a room again."

"Again!" Melanie's voice rose several octaves.

"Look at you! Barefoot! Disheveled! Wasn't last night enough!"

Verna shot Kate a pleased look. "Was my matchmaking finally successful?"

Kate, taken aback, stared at Verna before shifting her attention to her mother. "Please go to your room!" Kate, flustered, steered a triumphant Verna down the stairs.

Melanie started to turn, then stopped. Looking Toby in the eye, she said authoritatively, "Young man—"

Toby held up one hand, palm out. "I know, I know, you think I'm a disgusting, degenerate, debased—"

"Oh, no!" Melanie glanced down the stairs. Lowering her voice, she looked back at Toby and said in a stage whisper, "Now that I'm a new woman, I was wondering if you'd give me a few pointers. You know, some things I might suggest to my husband." Melanie gestured toward Toby's underwear. "I'm not sure if Max is willing to play Tarzan, but maybe, if I got him a pair of those red stretchy ones, do you think he'll play Santa Claus Has a Special Treat?"

9

"I DON'T WANT TO BE ALONE with your mother anymore." Toby, dressed in Verna's husband's jeans and a black T-shirt, sat at the butcher-block table in the kitchen and started scribbling his grocery list for lasagna.

"Why?" Kate leaned against the wall. "Because she thinks you're a gigolo?" Kate giggled at the look of shock on Toby's face. "I confess, it was one of my defensive mother comments from yesterday." She skewed her mouth as though mulling something over. "You know, I don't feel the need to be doing that anymore."

"About time." He shot her a look. "So if I'm a gigolo, how much was I worth?"

Her eyes grazed over him. "More than you'll ever know," she blurted. As pink flooded her cheeks, she looked away. "I need to plan your cruise," she mumbled.

The cruise. He felt like a cad, not explaining the reasons behind this bogus cruise. But if he started to make such confessions now, everything—his job, his future—might blow up in his face. He tapped the pencil against the table several times, unable to decide what to say or do next. Angry at himself, and feeling worse than ever over deceiving Kate, he bent over and started scribbling furiously. "I need to wear something decent for dinner tonight," he muttered, changing the subject.

Kate fiddled with the phone cord, wrapping it around

her finger. "I could shop for some more clothes for you."

He looked up. "No!" He tried to laugh but it came out like a bark. Beau, resting on the edge of the counter, jumped and looked around. "I mean, no thank you. I don't want to end up looking like Captain Hook or Captain Marvel or some other Captain."

The way she looked at him with that dewy expression, he knew what she was thinking. In her mind, he was her pirate. And in his heart, he felt the same.

"I should call my travel agent," she whispered, turning away.

Kate had wanted to call her agent earlier, but things became a bit chaotic after Verna, Melanie, and Mr. and Mrs. Wild One had gotten an eyeful of Toby the Tiger. It had taken a solid thirty minutes to calm Verna down, who kept pressing for facts, asking if she'd finally achieved matchmaker status. Although Kate normally spilled all to her friend, this time she denied anything had happened. After all, what had occurred between her and Toby was precious, a treasure, not to be shared with others.

Meanwhile, Toby and Melanie had had some kind of heart-to-heart upstairs after which Melanie had sequestered herself in her room to call her husband. The two of them must have stayed glued to the phone like a couple of teenagers for nearly an hour.

"It's almost one-thirty," Kate said, picking up the receiver in the kitchen. "If they're still on the phone, I'm going to ask them to clear the line because we have a cruise emergency." Kate listened to the receiver. "Well, get a load of this," she said to Toby as she punched in numbers. "Melanie and Max have finally ended their phone-a-thon. Wonder what they were talking about?"

"Santa Claus," Toby mumbled as he continued writing.

"Santa Claus?" Kate tapped in the last number. "In August? I know my mother likes to be prepared for the holidays, but isn't discussing Christmas in August pushing it just a little—oh, hello, Gwen!" Gwen Gossett was her travel agent. Although Kate often called her Gwen, she sometimes called her "my other mother" because Gwen had often lent an ear when Kate needed someone to confide in. "Gwen, I need to plan a very special cruise."

Toby tried not to listen. After all, he needed to make up with Free, get past the Dobermans—who'd been yapping off and on this morning—get the promotion. Plus he needed ingredients for dinner. He quickly scribbled parsley flakes, tomato paste, Kate. *I need Kate.*

"To the Caribbean," she continued. "Next December, right?"

Toby looked up. Kate's eyes were focused on him, waiting for confirmation. Those big blue eyes that sparkled like sunlight on the ocean. That's probably how the light would play on the waters of the Caribbean. "December, right," he mumbled, although he didn't give a damn what month—he'd probably agreed to December because of all those Santa Claus questions Mrs. Corrigan had grilled him with earlier.

"Yes, a spacious room, not one of those below-the-deck numbers. How about one of those cruise liners with a spa onboard?" Kate cupped the receiver and whispered loudly to Toby. "You like mud baths?"

He cocked one eyebrow.

"Forget the mud bath, but do they have some kind of herbal spritzer?"

Toby couldn't stop himself from smiling. That was Kate, stirring a little humor, a little mischief into life. Even the fact that she'd blown up his car started to seem a little funny, and that was something he never thought he'd laugh about.

"Yes, yes, gourmet meals, dancing, the works. One or two weeks? Let me check." Kate cupped the receiver again. "Do you want to be gone for one or two weeks?"

"One." Because he was never going on this cruise, anyway. He wished he could say that to Kate now.

"One," Kate repeated into the receiver.

Only one more day and he could explain this entire scam to Kate. One day. Toby tapped the end of the pencil against the butcher-block table, beating out time. Tap-tap-tap. Seconds, minutes, hours. And then he'd explain, and everything would be different. Better. He hoped.

"Sounds good," Kate said into the receiver, sounding a little too upbeat, a bit too forced.

He pretended to write as he sneaked a glance at her slim frame, today encased in another wild color combo—pink pants, pink-and-white-striped blouse and a pair of white sandals. Last night, in the dark, he hadn't noticed that her toenails were a bright red. Red. Of course. Her favorite color.

"Bye, my other mother," Kate said, just as Melanie sauntered into the room. As Kate hung up the receiver, Melanie looked a bit taken aback.

"Other mother?" she asked.

"Oh, that was Gwen, my travel agent." Kate joined Toby at the table.

"Have you always called her your 'other mother'?" Melanie asked, her voice rising higher.

If Toby wasn't mistaken, Melanie looked crushed, like a fuchsia flower that had been stepped on or pushed aside. Toby already felt uncomfortable playing this cruise-planning game. Now he was in the middle of some mother-and-other-mother-a-thon. "Maybe I should finish my grocery list in the other room," he said, starting to get up.

"No!" Melanie and Kate said at the same time.

He sat back down. Great. He was stuck. He hunched

over his list, adding more ingredients than any lasagna had had since the beginning of time.

Kate sighed, then said sweetly, "I call her my 'other mother' because that's what she's been to me."

"But you already have a mother," Melanie said tightly. "Me." Peering over the edge of his glasses, Toby watched Melanie point one peach-polished fingernail at herself in case "me" might not be obvious.

Kate rolled her eyes. "But you're three thousand miles away! And Gwen is here! What did you expect?"

Toby winced. Powerful words, but he knew better than to intervene. This was between Kate and her mother, just as it had been between him and his mother when she'd tossed those same words at him, "What do you expect?" The same words Free had used with him, knowing the impact they'd have.

Melanie pretended to swipe something from the corner of her eye, which Toby well knew was a tear. He thought about making another exit attempt, but had a feeling these two wanted him here. Maybe it was because he was an impartial observer. Or maybe it was because they knew he cared about them. Odd. A little over a day ago, he'd been almost a total stranger. Now he was like part of this family.

Hell, he was wearing Verna's husband's clothes. He was living here. He'd counseled Mrs. Corrigan on some rather intimate details about her and her husband. If that didn't make him family, what did?

In a shaky voice, Melanie continued, "It wouldn't matter if I was halfway around the world, you'll always be my baby, and I'll always be your mother. It's like an invisible string that has always connected us, will always connect us. Maybe even beyond life."

Now Toby had to swipe at the corner of his eye. That summed up family right there. An invisible connection, unbroken by fights, distances, even death. This family could get emotional. If he didn't know better, he'd swear there was some Italian blood in this Irish clan.

Kate suddenly stood and began pacing. "But I can't sew. And I can't cook. Last night I pretended I could do biscuits, but actually Toby saved me there. I can't clean. I don't even know how to fix myself a hairdo—it's just a stroke of luck that this unkempt, sporty look is in these days."

There was a long, drawn-out pause broken only by the scratching of Toby's pencil on the paper. What they didn't know was that he'd run out of ingredients and was now playing ticktacktoe with himself. So far, he was winning.

"But you have the loveliest sense of color," Melanie finally said, "always have."

Kate stopped. "You hate red."

Melanie glanced at Toby. "Not anymore."

He nearly broke his pencil on an *x*. Some of those Santa Claus questions she'd asked earlier had seriously unnerved him.

Kate crossed her arms under her breasts. "I've always felt like a failure around you."

Melanie drew in such a long breath, Toby held on to his paper, just in case it blew away. "And I have always felt like a failure around you."

The two women stared at each other for so long, Toby won two more games of tick tack toe.

Kate uncrossed her arms, obviously taken aback by her mother's confession. "You're so perfect. How could you possibly feel like a failure around me?"

"Perfect? Me?" Melanie blinked with surprise. "*You're* the one I always admired. You were always so…adventurous, so unafraid of the world. I cleaned and cooked and sewed, but that's because I only knew how to control the world within my four walls. But you…" Melanie's hazel eyes glistened with pride. "You knew how to go out into the world and get a job. You worked at resorts, doing all kinds of interesting things. I still don't know what a concerta is."

"Concierge," Kate corrected.

"See? You even know a foreign language." Melanie was trying to smile, but her quivering fuchsia lips gave her away. "And then you got your trust fund and you moved away. Far, far away."

"I only moved to San Francisco."

Melanie gave a small shrug. "But in my entire life, I never left Beaufort. To me, my adventurous, free-spirited daughter picked up her life and traveled to a new world. Something I'd never have the guts to do."

Now Kate's eyes watered. "But you had the guts to run away from home."

"Yes, I ran away. But I was also runnin' to you."

"To me?" Now Kate blinked with surprise.

"I wanted us to have a second chance to be a mother and daughter. As you grow older, you realize more and more how precious life is. And the people in it. I love you."

"I love you, too." Kate, sniffling back a tear, stepped forward. Melanie, swiping again at her eye, stepped forward too. The next thing Toby knew, they were clutching each other and crying, blubbering things like, "I've always wished I could be more like you!" and "There's no other mother, just you."

Toby, tired of ticktacktoe, moved onto hangman. He was well into winning his first game when Verna suddenly entered the room. Now, if a man entered this room, saw a couple of women crying and clutching each other, his first thought would be that someone had died and he'd pray to God it wasn't the Forty-Niners' quarterback. But women were different. They're born with built-in radar that instantly deciphers an emotional situation with the precision of a laser beam.

Verna, in serious radar mode, pressed her palms against the sides of her face, grew misty-eyed and announced shakily, "Mother and daughter have finally bonded!"

Toby kept his head down and started another game of hangman.

Verna, meanwhile, gravitated toward the huddle of crying, sobbing women and attached herself to it. So now there were three sniffling, blubbering women saying things like, "I love you!" "Thank you for helping my daughter," and "Your biscuits were great."

It took another twenty minutes for the sniffling and snuffling to die down. Then another ten minutes for reminiscences, apologies and a few recipe exchanges. Hearing the latter, Toby decided the time was ripe to speak up. Finishing his sixth game of hangman, he said loudly, "According to Captain Hook—" he gestured toward the clock "—it's almost two o'clock. I'm locked out of my house. I have no ingredients for lasagna. And my potential boss is showing up for dinner in three hours, sharp."

The Three Muses, their radar on high, began babbling all at once.

Toby raised a hand. They stopped. "And," he added, "I need to figure out how to outwit Mickey and Minnie."

"The mice?" Melanie asked incredulously.

"No," answered Kate, "two vicious Dobermans that belong to Free's, uh, friend."

"Who are also unwanted houseguests at my home," added Toby. "If my mother were here, she'd be saying *Questa casa non è un albergo.*"

"*This house*—meaning Toby's—*isn't a motel*," translated Kate.

Melanie looked at her daughter in awe. "How many languages are you fluent in?"

"Mom, knowing one sentence in Italian doesn't make

me fluent." Fighting a smile, she turned to Verna. "Remember the guy who lost his Chihuahua?"

Verna nodded. "The poor little thing was hiding out in that armoire in The Wild One."

"Remember how we lured the puppy out?" Kate asked.

Verna slowly smiled. "We didn't have puppy treats, so we browned some meat and cheese. That dog reappeared in our kitchen like magic!"

"We could do the same thing to Mickey and Minnie. There's leftover ground beef from your breakfast burritos the other morning, plus my ever-present supply of sliced cheese for my sandwiches."

Verna pulled a pan out of a cupboard. "Let's start browning!"

"I can serve the dogs," Melanie offered.

"Mom," Kate said, pulling a paper-wrapped package out of the fridge. "These are Dobermans, not dinner guests."

Melanie straightened. "I'll have you know, when it comes to snarling and growling, I'm fearless. Ask your father." Holding her head high, she sashayed out of the kitchen, picking up Toby's pants on the way. "Call me when you're ready. I'll be upstairs fixing these pants."

After she left, Verna said, "That's some woman!"

Kate smiled with pride. "That's my mom!"

While Kate rummaged in the refrigerator for the meat and cheese, Verna crossed to Toby. "Grocery list?" she asked softly.

He nodded.

"I can run to the store for you. I know where everything is."

"Thanks." When Verna remained close, not budging, Toby looked up. Tears welled within her gray eyes.

"Sorry," she whispered, swiping at a tear that spilled over. "It's just...you're wearing Lou's clothes." She smiled tremulously. "It's been a long time since I've seen them worn. It brings back memories." She smoothed a spot on the T-shirt and Toby gave her a brief, warm hug before she headed to the stove. "I'll brown the meat, Kate," Verna said, assuming her kitchen privilege.

"Okay." Kate looked around. "You're browning. Mom's sewing. Where am I needed?"

"I need you," Toby answered. In more ways than she knew. "I need you to ensure Gwen delivers the cruise invitation to Free, get me back in her good graces."

"Cruise invitation?" Verna repeated, shooting a disapproving look at Toby over her shoulder. "Didn't know you two were—"

"Verna," Kate interrupted. "I'm helping Toby do this."

"You're matchmaking the two of them?" Verna stirred the meat with big, scraping strokes. "Isn't that a little off-kilter, like me setting up that bakery guy with—"

"This is different," Kate said firmly.

"Bad matches are bad matches, no matter what the circumstances," Verna mumbled.

"This is important," Kate said with great bravado. "Free will be ecstatic, she and Toby will make up, then Toby can go home and get his promotion and live the rest of his life happily ever after."

Toby's insides ached when he looked at Kate, whose false smile looked anything but happy-ever-after.

Verna coughed, diverting everyone's attention. "Free won't be home to receive that invitation."

"How do you know?" Toby asked.

"Because she's already received a special invitation," she said quickly, "hand-delivered by my son. I knew Toby needed to get back into his home by tonight, so I made a special invitation to an international bead convention being held today only in Calistoga. If she shows up by five o'clock this afternoon, she'll win a thousand beautiful beads of her choice. Of course, I made the instructions difficult to follow. I figured by the time she arrives in Calistoga, which should be close to five, then drives around looking for this place, she'll finally discover it doesn't exist. And nobody in their right mind drives in rush-hour traffic from Calistoga to San Francisco, so she'll probably wait until seven or eight to drive back, which means she'll return to North Beach by nine tonight at the earliest. Plenty of time for Toby to cook dinner and get his promotion." Verna looked apologetic. "I'm sorry. I didn't know other invitations were in the making. I thought I was being helpful."

If Beau hadn't jumped onto the sill and meowed raspily, the silence that followed Verna's statement would have been deafening.

"That's why I was late this morning," she confessed. "I was gluing little beads all over that special invitation." She took a deep, unsteady breath. "Please tell me you're not mad because I just saw Free drive away with that guy, minus the dogs, so they must be on their way to Calistoga."

Beau emitted a long, gravelly meow.

"I hear you, brother," Toby said. He dragged a hand through his hair. "Unfortunately, when the cruise invitation is delivered, Free won't be there to receive it. But I'm not complaining about your plan, Verna, because it means I'll be able to cook dinner tonight as though nothing unusual has gone on these past few days."

Nothing unusual? Just being chased by vicious dogs, running around nearly naked, and…falling in love with Kate.

TOBY INSERTED THE KEY into the lock of his front door and turned the latch.

Click.

This was followed by vicious snarling, barking and scratching on the other side of the door.

"Mickey and Minnie should be personal greeters," Toby said drolly, his hand on the knob. "Maybe we should call the pound, or a vet. Offering a bowl of meager hamburger to two vicious beasts seems a little like underkill." He cringed. "No pun intended."

Melanie, standing several feet down the walkway, looked unruffled in one of her signature dresses with matching pumps. She held the bowl of browned meat with cheese as though she were serving the main course to guests. "No need to get strangers involved," she said, "when it can be handled by family."

She sounded like his own mom for a second.

Kate, standing next to her mom, said, "Let me serve the meat."

"For the hundredth time," Melanie said authoritatively, "I want to do something adventurous outside of the home for a change, so please step aside, darling daughter."

Kate hesitated, then did as requested.

"Open the door just a notch," Melanie said, obviously proud to be involved in this expedition. "Just enough for Mikey and Mary to sniff a little."

"Mickey and Minnie," Toby corrected. As though he cared. He opened the door an inch. Instantly, two barking mouths, teeth bared, filled the small opening.

"They don't look too interested in sniffing," Kate said.

Melanie took several steps up the walk, talking softly as though approaching two misbehaving children. "Now, now, you two. What's all the commotion? I have a treat for you, you sweet little things."

One of the sweet little things had his lips pulled back,

growling ominously through bared teeth. The other kept barking.

Toby felt a drop of sweat roll down the side of his face. "Take it easy, guys," he said, speaking as much to himself as to the dogs.

"That's right," Melanie said, her words oozing that Southern accent. "Take it easy, Mickey and Minnie." She kept talking softly, holding the bowl in front of her.

The dogs started quieting down. One had his nose wedged in the door opening, his nostrils flaring as he sniffed the air.

Melanie was at the door. She held the bowl up to the closest pair of nostrils. "What does Mama have for you?" she asked sweetly.

One of the dogs smacked its lips and whined.

Toby almost felt like doing the same, he was so relieved.

"Open the door a little more," Melanie whispered.

"I don't know."

"It's all right," Melanie insisted softly. "These mean ol' beasts are becoming pussycats." Before Toby could stop her, she held one manicured hand over the bowl, palm down, for one of the nuzzles to sniff.

Next thing Toby knew, she was scratching Mickey— or was it Minnie?—under its chin. In the midst of her cooing and baby talk, she said to Toby, "Open the door farther."

"I don't know."

"It's okay," she said sweetly. "They're under my power."

Toby smiled. Like mother, like daughter. They both had a knack for quirky comments. He opened the door wider. At the same time, Melanie held the bowl in the opening. Mickey and Minnie began eagerly sampling the meat.

"That's good," sweet-talked Melanie, taking a step

back. "Follow me, you little mouseketeers." Melanie began to back away, holding the bowl in front of her. "Open the door wider, son."

He knew better than to argue. Toby opened the door, stepping away. Kate, meanwhile, was across the yard, her eyes wide.

Next thing Toby knew, Melanie had Mickey and Minnie outside, slurping and chomping their surprise treat while Melanie slipped sturdy ribbons through each of their collars. After they'd finished eating most of the food, she led them by their makeshift leashes back to the inn.

Toby, awestruck, watched as the three of them disappeared into Beau's Bed-and-Breakfast. "Your mother," he said to Kate, "has a knack for taming wild beasts."

"I have a feeling that's what she's been doing with Dad, too," Kate said with a wink as they headed inside the house.

"It's almost two-thirty," Toby said, checking a wall clock. "Phone your mom, leave this number. Ask her to call us when Verna gets in. We'll go over and pick up the groceries."

"Good idea. Where's your phone?"

"In the bedroom." He pointed over his shoulder. "On the right, next to the front door."

Kate headed back down the hallway, past the wall pictures she remembered from before. As she turned into the bedroom, she slowed down. Toby and Free's bedroom. Kate looked around. It was different than she'd imagined. For one thing, there weren't beads everywhere. But there was plenty of dark, masculine wood. Perhaps most impressive was the burl-and-walnut-paneled headboard. Definitely Toby's taste, which thrilled her with its sheer masculine power. It dominated the room, stamped it as his own. If Kate were his woman, she'd be his partner and mate—loyal in both. Such a man deserved no less.

But she didn't want to think about that anymore, or second-guess why he felt he needed to work things out with Bead Woman. Kate looked around and spied a beige phone on the walnut nightstand.

She also spied a staggering pile of clothes in the corner. A man's ripped clothes. More doggie toys, just like his shoes? Oh, this guy was having a bad-clothes day or two.

Sitting on the mattress, she dialed her number, listened to her voice on the recording. "You've reached Beau's Bed-and-Breakfast. We're either on another line or catering to our guests. Please leave a detailed message after the beep and we'll return your call as soon as possible!" Sheesh, she sounded chipper. The opposite of how she felt right now. "Hi, Mom and Verna. When you get in, call this number—" she read it off the label on the phone "—and we'll come over and get the groceries. Thanks!"

She hung up and stood, but didn't want to leave the room quite yet. She wasn't a snoop, but damn, this was the bedroom Toby slept in...with Free! "Bet he was never her pirate," she murmured, looking around. More photos hung on the far wall—antique photos. Kate moved over for a closer look. A couple stood stiffly, staring at the camera. The woman had dark hair and a pinched expression on her face. The man had blondish hair and deep brown eyes and, if Kate wasn't mistaken, a hint of that lopsided smile she sometimes saw in Toby. She looked back at the woman, whose lacy bridal gown was reminiscent of the straight line of the flappers' dresses. If that was right, the photo had to be from the 1920s. Toby's grandparents? Maybe they were newly arrived from Italy, wanting to start a family in the United States. Maybe they arrived alone, just the two of them, starting with very little except their love and responsibility to each other and to their dreams.

"Did you make the call?"

Kate turned. Toby stood in the doorway, an anxious look creasing his features.

"Yes. What's wrong?"

He released an angry breath. Between clenched teeth, he said, "The oven is broken!"

She tugged at a strand of her hair, sick about his wardrobe. "Wait till you get a load of your clothes."

TEN MINUTES LATER, Kate returned with her toolbox and set it next to Toby's stove.

"Why did she have to do *that* on the stove?" Toby said for the umpteenth time.

Kate didn't have to ask what "that" was. She'd already witnessed some of "that" when she and Toby had been stuck in the can room. "Maybe it was the only warm place in the house?"

"It's August! She knows the stove is my pride and joy. And she purposely—" He clenched his jaw, unwilling to say more.

"It can be repaired," Kate said matter-of-factly, taking a pair of needle-nose pliers out of her tool box. "Looks like it's just a collapsed gas injector. Piece of cake." Using the pliers to hold the tube in place, she held out her other hand, "Screwdriver, please."

Toby rummaged in the toolbox and extracted one. "This one?" he asked, handing it to her.

"Perfect." She began reaming out the collapsed tube. "This will take just a few minutes, then the gas can flow again and your stove will be good as new."

"You and your mother are quite a team."

"Dogs and stoves, our specialties."

"And cars," he teased.

Kate, working on the stove, smiled. "You never gave

me the chance to play mechanic on the car after the Firebird.''

''I should have given you a chance.''

Kate continued working, thinking how she deserved that chance and more. The chance to be his partner in life. His lover. But it was time to stop being foolishly romantic and grow up. He was working it out with Free. Kate couldn't look back. Had to look forward.

''Voilà!'' she said, holding the screwdriver up triumphantly. ''Give the knob a twirl and let's see those burners burn!''

Toby did. They all worked perfectly. ''You're amazing, Kate.'' As she stood, he pulled her close, giving her a hug. ''Thank you,'' he murmured, his breath hot against her cheek.

Reluctantly she pulled away. ''You're welcome,'' she said, avoiding his eyes. ''Let's go next door, get the groceries.''

She turned and left, not wanting to look back. After all, she had to keep looking forward.

10

DING-A-DING-A-DING-A-DING.

Toby had always hated the sound of his doorbell, but Free wanted a doorbell that sounded like the jangling of beads. He checked his wristwatch. Five-thirty. His boss was thirty minutes late, but that was a small bump in the road compared to the wild ride of the past forty-eight hours.

Toby took a deep breath before opening the door. "Good evening, Dennis!"

His potential boss, Dennis Doyle, a tall, lanky man with more smile lines than ripples in the sea, started to grin. It froze halfway, as though he was unsure whether to grin or grimace. His green eyes traveled slowly down Toby, then back up. "Good...evening."

The outfit. "Oh," Toby said, trying to sound breezy, "you're wondering about my clothes!" He'd made a mess of the jeans and T-shirt while cooking, and after discovering what the Dobermans had done to his clothes, he'd been once again clothesless. With time running out, Melanie, Verna and Kate had agreed that the black leather pants and red silk shirt were all right to wear for dinner. After repairing the rip in the pants, Melanie had taken the outfit to the dry cleaners for one-hour service, so at least it was clean.

Although, secretly, Toby wondered if all three of them just wanted to see him decked out as a pirate again. And when he'd put the outfit back on, he wondered the same thing about himself.

Clearing his throat, Toby offered the explanation the women had concocted, "I, uh, just got back from…my flamenco dancing lessons. Didn't have time to change. Plus, my feet hurt so much after those classes, I always put on these slippers. Hope you don't mind." He laughed awkwardly, acting as though wearing skintight leather pants and an open-neck red silk shirt was just a fun, postdancing sort of thing.

"No, I don't mind," Dennis said, shaking his head, although it seemed more to clear the image standing before him. He put his arm around the petite woman at his side. "This is my better half, Suzanne. Suzanne, this is Toby Mancini, the hotshot engineer I told you about."

Suzanne's wide-eyed gaze didn't budge from his chest. "Hello, Harry."

"Toby," Toby corrected.

She looked up, blinked. "Toby."

Dennis grinned. "We're watching our grandchild— told the baby-sitter we'd be home by nine. Hope that's not a problem."

Toby almost burst into maniacal laughter at the wonderfulness that they'd have to leave by nine. The coast would be clear by the time Free returned. "No, no problem! Come in, come in." He stepped back, holding open the door. "Welcome to my home." *The place I never thought I'd set foot in again.*

Dennis and Suzanne stepped carefully inside, looking around as though more flamenco dancers might come flying down the hallway. But when they saw the normal floor with the normal rug that ran down the hallway to a normal door, they visibly relaxed. As they walked along the hallway, Toby gestured toward the pictures on the wall. "These are my family."

Dennis peered at the one with the family gathered around a dinner table. Toby stood in the back, holding a platter of food. "So I see you're the family cook."

"Yes," Toby said, joining him in looking at the picture. "That's me. Family cook. I've always had a secret yearning to run my own restaurant."

Dennis leaned closer, peering into the photo. "Which one is Free?"

Suzanne joined her husband to look at the picture. "They're all married?" she asked, misunderstanding.

"No, Free is my girlfriend's name," Toby clarified. Girlfriend? The word felt odd as he said it. "This picture was taken before we met."

Suzanne looked around. "And where is the lady of the house?"

Damn. In the chaos of the past few hours, Toby hadn't thought this one through yet. "Her...great-aunt died. She's in Morocco at the funeral."

"Morocco?" Suzanne asked, looking confused.

"Uh, part of her family comes from California, the other part from Morocco. A Tex-Mex sort of thing." Dennis and Suzanne just stared at him.

"How nice," Suzanne said, tugging on her ear. Toby wondered if it was a sign to her husband to make this evening short.

"And in honor of *my* heritage," Toby continued, trying not to think more about the ear-tugging, "I fixed lasagna." Okay, he was relaxing. Italian. Lasagna. This conversation was proceeding, logically, from one topic to another. He pointed toward a door to the right. "Please, go into the dining room and make yourselves comfortable."

Toby led the way into the dining room. He pulled out a chair for Suzanne at the walnut dining room set. "Care for a glass of Chianti?"

Dennis grinned, the smile genuine this time. "Sounds delightful."

"I'll be right back with the wine." Toby sauntered nonchalantly out of the dining room, feeling in control for the first time in what seemed forever. After retrieving a bottle of Chianti from a wooden rack inside the pantry, the corkscrew from a drawer and three glasses from a cabinet, he strolled back to the dining room, a man in control. A man who would be offered a job.

He uncorked the lush red wine and poured it into the three glasses. Raising his, he began a toast. "To—"

Ding-a-ding-a-ding-a-ding.

Free? Without finishing his toast, Toby downed the glass of wine. "Be right back."

A moment later, he opened the front door, prepared for the worst. "Kate?" he asked, shocked. And relieved. "What are you doing here?"

She smiled apologetically. "Another pan of lasagna!" she explained, holding out a foil-wrapped pan. "Mom insisted. I told her you had things under control, but she didn't listen. Said you might need it just in case you run out...or whatever. She's like that—preparing too much food in case of a dining emergency. I have enough brownies to feed my guests until the year two thousand and four."

He looked into Kate's big blue eyes and realized how much he missed her. Hell, how much he missed her mother, too. "Tell her thank-you."

Kate's blue eyes got bigger and she seemed to be staring past him. "Oh, no."

"Oh, yes! Tell her!" He felt humbled at the lady's generosity, including the amazing feat of wooing Mickey and Minnie outside. Suddenly he felt bad at how he'd reacted to some of Melanie's earlier questions. "And also tell her," he said, lowering his voice, "I'm sorry I got shocked at some of those Santa Claus questions. Tell her the old guy definitely wears stretchy red underwear.''

''What old guy wears stretchy red underwear?'' asked a woman.

Toby turned. There stood Suzanne, holding a glass of wine.

''Uh,'' Kate said, ''my father?''

Suzanne blinked. ''And who are you?''

Now Kate blinked. After an awkward pause, she said meekly, ''Free?''

Suzanne turned misty-eyed. ''Oh, you poor dear!'' she said. ''Toby, don't make your girlfriend stand outside, her arms full.'' He took the pan from Kate's hands while Suzanne pulled her inside. ''You flew all the way back from Morocco after such a devastating ordeal.'' She glanced at the pan. ''You certainly travel light.''

Kate stumbled in alongside Suzanne, who kept murmuring things about death and life and moving on. Kate shot Toby a look. He shrugged and followed the two of them with Kate's carry-on luggage.

''Dennis, darling, this is Free,'' Suzanne said, still clutching Kate as though she might keel over from grief any moment. ''She just flew in from Morocco, the poor dear.''

Dennis stood and pulled out a chair. ''Sit down, Free. Can I get you a glass of wine?''

Kate looked out the dining room door. Toby sailed by, the pan in his hands. ''Just half a glass, thanks.''

Dennis poured her wine while Suzanne pushed her chair closer to Kate. ''Dennis talks about Toby all the time. What a great engineer he is, what a tremendous team leader. You must be awfully proud of your fiancé.''

Fiancé? Toby had never mentioned he and Free were engaged. ''Yes,'' Kate croaked. ''I'm, uh, proud of my fiancé.'' She took a quick sip of wine. *Fiancé?* They were getting married? Why hadn't he ever mentioned that? Jeez, she'd said she'd go out with him if he wasn't involved. She'd never have said such a dumb thing if she'd known the guy was headed to the altar. He wasn't as bad as four-timing Henry, but this little unknown fact didn't exactly earn him any Best Beaufort Brownie points. She took another sip, starting to feel a serious surge of self-pity coming on.

Toby reentered the room and put a plate, napkin and utensils in front of Kate. "If I'd known you'd be back so soon from your great-grandfather's funeral, I'd have set you a place."

"Great-aunt," corrected Suzanne.

"And if I had known you were getting married soon," Kate said, glaring at him, "I would never have left for Morocco in the first place!"

"We're not getting married!" he said edgily.

Suzanne tugged at her ear. "Oh dear. Grief does that, gets everyone's emotions all upside down. You two love each other, that's easy to see. This is just a grief-driven misunderstanding."

Kate took another sip of wine. "Yes, it's the grief. My late second cousin was a great lady." Dennis and Suzanne looked at her oddly. Toby seemed to be mouthing something like "and" but Kate couldn't quite decipher it. She turned to Toby, "I'm sorry about the misunderstanding about your—I mean, our—engagement. Of course, I'll marry you." Feeling happy, fuzzy and self-satisfied, Kate toasted the room.

Toby, looking a bit stunned, came to when Dennis got up and slapped him on the back. "Wonderful moment of a man's life—that moment when he commits to the woman of his dreams. Congratulations to a long, happy life together."

Kate almost burst into one of her Motown favorites,

"Baby Love", but figured she'd save that for the wedding rehearsal.

Everyone drank to the newly engaged couple, then Toby excused himself to get the dinner. He returned within moments with a pan of savory-smelling lasagna, which he set on the center of the table on a mat. He served Suzanne, Kate, then Dennis. After cutting a wedge of lasagna for himself, Toby opened another bottle and poured more wine into everyone's glasses.

"To friends," Toby said, holding his glass high.

"To 'Baby Love,'" Kate added, ignoring Toby's shocked expression.

"But *before* babies," Suzanne smiled endearingly at the couple, "to yours and Free's marriage."

Free. That sobered Kate up, fast. She was Free, all right. Free in every way, except free to really love Toby. With a small smile, Kate took a gulp of wine.

"So, Free, what do you do for a living?" Dennis asked pleasantly.

"I...collect beads," she said glumly.

Toby shoveled in a mouthful of food. Obviously not realizing how hot it was, he made a series of woofing noises as he attempted to breathe and suck in air simultaneously.

"Have some more wine, hon," Kate said, smiling sweetly at Dennis and Suzanne. "Maybe I overreamed that burner. Did my oven get too hot?"

Toby coughed so hard, Kate thought she'd have to do the Heimlich maneuver, but after several gasps and a hoarse "I'm okay, really," he seemed to recover.

Suzanne looked from Kate to Toby. "So when's the big date?"

Ding-a-ding-a-ding-a-ding.

For a long, horrifying moment Kate and Toby stared at each other, terror etched on their faces. As though psychically connected, they both suddenly jumped and yelled, "I'll get it!" But they'd barely scooted their chairs away from the table when a somber apparition— a woman dressed in a long black dress covered with a black cape—appeared in the doorway.

"Door was open. Hope you don't mind that I came in," said Verna. She held a basket that emitted aromas of garlic and butter. "I just happened to have this batch of homemade garlic bread on hand, so I thought I'd drop it by."

Kate's heart plunged. "Are you crazy?" she mouthed, knowing full well her friend couldn't resist this opportunity to play matchmaker.

Suzanne, finishing another sip of wine, blinked at the newcomer. "And you're—"

Verna, looking unsure how to explain why she'd walked into a home she didn't live in, ad-libbed, "I'm…the aunt."

Suzanne clutched her chest. "Oh, my God," she muttered, looking at Verna's black outfit. "Returned from the dead. And with garlic bread!"

"No!" Kate said, still standing. "She's just my aunt, not the great one."

Suzanne, looking pale but relieved, leaned back in her chair. Smiling feebly, she said to Verna, "So, you're part of the family?"

"Yes," Verna said, searching Kate and Toby's eyes, "that's right. I'm just the aunt. Aunt Verna. Not great, but a pretty good aunt."

Toby, still standing too, said very carefully as though Verna had just learned the English language, "Free and I were just entertaining my boss, Dennis Doyle, and his lovely wife Suzanne."

Verna looked aghast. "You and Free? But I thought she was still in Calistoga!"

"No, she was in Morocco," Suzanne said sadly, reaching across the table to pat Kate's hand. "Poor dear. Such a long, sad journey.'' After smiling benevolently at Kate, Suzanne turned her attention back to Verna. ''Sit, Aunt Verna, and tell us all about Free.''

''Meaning, me!'' Kate said, thumping her chest. ''Me, Free. Free's me.''

Verna sat down, a dazed expression on her face. ''I don't suppose I could have a glass of wine, too? I think I have some catching up to do.'' She gave a girlfriend sign language look at Kate that said, *Help! What's going on here?*

But Kate barely had time to signal back when Toby coughed, giving Kate a knowing look…except this one she didn't know how to decipher because she and Toby had never practiced the fine art of girlfriend sign language.

''I'm going to get a wineglass and a plate of lasagna for Aunt Verna,'' Toby said evenly. ''Care to help me, Free?''

''Right. Me. Free. Help.'' She was back to Kate, the one-word girl, but at this moment, it was the very best she could do. As she passed Verna, who had a look of concern and confusion on her face, Kate said, ''Here I got to help my fiancé Toby in the kitchen.'' She backed out the door, smiling at everyone as she left.

In the kitchen, Toby leaned against the refrigerator, his arms folded tightly across his chest. ''This is a mess,'' he mumbled. ''They think you're Free, they think Verna's a good aunt, and they think we're getting married.''

''You and Verna?''

Toby gave Kate a get-with-it look. ''No, you and me!''

''Oh, yeah.'' Was he angry because she'd misunderstood the Verna part? Or was he angry at the thought of marrying Kate? That it might be the latter hurt, like a barb pulled tightly around her heart.

"Things aren't so bad," she said in a strained voice. "At least we're not serving sandwiches for dinner."

The hard look in his eyes turned gentle. Shaking his head, he offered her a smile that thawed any lingering chilliness in the air. "What is it about you, Kate? I can be down in the dumps, hitting bottom, and then you turn my world upside down. And instead of staring at the gutter, I'm suddenly looking at the stars. You make me see the humor, the lightness in life. You're frustrating and fascinating and fun."

His brown eyes glinted with heat. Add the shadow of his beard, the confident set of his shoulders, and he was again her pirate. She suddenly felt giddy, as though she were free-falling through the stratosphere, riding a rush of elation.

"What are you thinking about?" Toby asked.

"Free-falling." *Free.* Kate closed her eyes, painfully aware of the word she'd used. *I'm pretending to be bead-loving, Tiger-taming, oven-breaking Free.* Kate's euphoria crash-landed with a painful thud back to planet Earth. She opened her eyes. "Those people— your boss and his wife—think I'm Free. And poor Suzanne, she almost had a coronary when she thought Verna was my dead great-cousin or second aunt or both." Suddenly Kate felt totally, utterly miserable. Planting the back of her hand against her forehead, she said in a tormented voice, "You're right. We've created a mess."

"Could be worse," Toby answered playfully. "We could be serving sandwiches."

She dropped her hand. There he stood, one hip cocked against the fridge, a mischievous twinkle in those caramel eyes. And that lock of sandy hair falling dangerously across his forehead only heightened his bad-boy-pirate look.

Kate had sworn she wouldn't succumb to her desires

again. How many times today had she sworn to adopt a will of iron, to move on, forget about her night of plundering, passionate lovemaking?

Will of iron? Right now Toby was the biggest, baddest magnet and she couldn't resist him if her life depended on it. Aching with a raw, primitive need, she moved toward him. She would have stopped, if she could, but his galvanizing look of desire only encouraged her, pulled her closer. Damn it, this man wanted her every bit as bad as she wanted him. Her heart thundered in her chest. Her blood roared in her ears.

Toby had seen Kate's passion in the moonlight. But here, in the blaze of light, he could see every nuance. Her blue eyes sparked and smoldered with longing. Her skin was flushed. She was heaving breaths, as though she couldn't consume enough air. It was startling, and intoxicating, to see this side of Kate. This sensual, demanding woman intent on indulging her passions.

And he wanted it, too, wanted it so bad, he thought his pounding heart would burst through his chest like a skyrocket. Desire burned within him, surged through his blood. And his pants were so damn tight he was tempted to grab a knife…but this time, rip his pants off.

She was too close, and he couldn't wait any longer. Stepping forward, he pulled her roughly to him, molding her against him. With a groan of need, he lifted her off her feet.

"Toby," she groaned, her breaths hot against his face. "I want to be with you."

And he'd never wanted anything, anyone, the way he wanted Kate at this very moment. It was as though his soul had found its missing counterpart. As though his body had found its perfect mate. He lowered her to the ground, luxuriating in how her soft curves filled the hollows of his body. Dragging his hand through her hair, he pulled back her head and looked into those glistening, half-shut eyes. "Kate," he murmured, lowering his face to hers. "Oh Kate."

He bent his head and tasted her. He felt like a dying man who'd been denied water, and now he was tasting, licking, consuming her lips and mouth as though his life depended on it. She tasted sweet from the wine. Sweet, hot, spicy.

She pulled back. Her arms locked around his waist, she looked into the depths of his eyes and murmured, "Toby, I love you."

He'd hardly digested the words before she kissed him with a hunger that wiped out everything else in the world but this cocoon of passion, of desire only the two of them shared.

"What's goin' on?" said a female voice from somewhere outside the cocoon.

With great effort, Toby pulled away and looked over the wild mane of Kate's hair at her mother, who was holding a pecan pie. "I'm making love to your daughter," he said breathlessly. "What does it look like?"

Melanie's false eyelashes barely batted. "No, what's goin' on outside? It looks like two hippies are headed to your front door. They were getting out of their van just as I reached your doorstep. The front door was unlocked, so I quickly stepped inside and locked it, but these hippies might be dangerous." The pecan pie was visibly shaking. "Remember the Manson murders? That happened right around the summer of love."

There were sounds of voices down the hall, giggling interspersed with "Tiger, stop it!"

Toby glanced at his watch. "It's hardly seven! Why are they back already?"

Kate looked frantically into Toby's eyes. "Should I get in the can room?" She paused. "Or maybe I should just get out of your life? Let you go back to Free? I told you I loved you…even if I have to let you go.''

He looked into those blue eyes, so sweet, so strong. "We're not hiding anymore—from Free, from my boss, from each other.'' And with that pronouncement, he grabbed Kate's hand and led her toward the hall.

Kate, who loved old movies, didn't exactly like this rendition of *High Noon* in the hallway. At the far end stood Free and Tiger, both of them looking shocked when they saw Toby and Kate. Kate glanced at Toby. His steely eyes shot rage at the people who stood at the end of the hall. She'd never understood the saying "if looks could kill,'' but she did now! Add that outfit—the red shirt, the leather pants—it was as though Errol Flynn, a movie-star hero, had stepped out of the film *Captain Blood*.

Only this was no movie-star hero. This was Toby Mancini, a real-life hero. *Her* Captain Blood. He gripped her hand defiantly, possessively, showing the world that she was his. He was so fierce, so dangerous and so knee-knocking good-looking, she had to squeeze her toes to stay grounded.

"What the hell are you doing with that bed-and-something woman?'' Free shrieked.

Suzanne, Dennis and Verna—all holding wineglasses—ran out of the dining room and into the hallway. Stunned, the three of them skidded to a stop, looking first at Free and Tiger, then at Kate, Toby and Melanie. They kept swiveling their heads like spectators at a bizarre hallway tennis match.

A bizarre hallway tennis *love* match.

"She's no bed-and-something woman,'' Toby thundered, "she's *my* woman.''

"His bed-and-*breakfast* woman,'' Kate corrected, unsqueezing her toes so she could stand a little taller.

"And, for the record, we were just making out against the refrigerator and we didn't break it!"

There was a long pause, during which Suzanne asked Dennis if he'd mind refilling her and Aunt Verna's glasses.

"And I love her!" Toby continued, pulling Kate close to his side. His arm wrapped around her, he stood spread-eagled, just like Errol Flynn in *Captain Blood*, defying the world to take him on.

Free swung her hair back as though she were starring in a shampoo commercial. "You love her?" she said sarcastically. She held up an envelope. "Then why did I just find this invitation to a romantic cruise—for you and I—in the mailbox?"

The spectators—Verna, Suzanne and Dennis—made an ominous "aah" sound. Like a group of dismayed Gregorion chanters.

Reinforced by their response, Free opened the invitation and began reading out loud. "One week in the Caribbean...for Free and Toby...from..." She glanced up, a look of feigned dramatic surprise on her face. "From Toby? That's you, right?" She slipped the invitation back into the envelope, which she continued to hold high in the air. "And the answer is yes. I'll go on the cruise with you. I'll take you back."

"After I just said I love Kate? And what about Tiger?"

The spectators murmured, "Ohh..."

Free swung her hair again and looked at Toby. "What did you expect," she asked, "being gone all the time?" She suddenly went into high-drama gear. The sparkle of tears was evident twenty feet away. "I was left alone, day after day, night after night, yearning for you, crying for you. Then one day Tiger followed me into church and said he'd like to light my candles—"

"Baby," Tiger interrupted, "you followed me into the Columbus Café and said you liked your eggs over hard, just like your men."

"How dare you make up such a lie!" Free said, glaring at Tiger. "You took advantage of me, knowing I was lonely, missing my Toby." She covered her face with trembling hands and sniffled loudly. "I love you, Toby. I want you back!" By now, she was crying so hard, the word "back" sounded like "ba-a-a!"

Kate watched Toby watch Free.

Verna, Suzanne and Dennis watched Free and Tiger, then turned to watch Kate and Toby.

Kate eased away, wishing she'd never gotten caught up in that kitchen moment where she'd admitted she loved him. Wishing she'd never opened her door the other night. Because there was no hope for Kate and Toby. He needed to work things out with Free. In a painful way, it reminded her of growing up, knowing her father's first loyalty was always to her brother, never to Kate.

What did I expect? Kate Corrigan, the world's greatest matchmaker, had set them back up. And she'd succeeded! Who was Kate to think she played a romantic role in all this? Free had the invitation...her arms were open...asking for Toby back.

She glanced at Toby, unable to decipher the look on his face. Was it pity for Free? Or was Free really getting to his misplaced sense of responsibility?

Folding her arms tightly around herself, Kate stepped back, wondering how she could make a graceful exit considering a crying Free and a confused-looking Tiger blocked the front door. Maybe Kate could bolt for the kitchen and hurl herself over the sink and out the window.

She was edging toward the kitchen, when someone grabbed her arm. "Don't go," Toby commanded. Kate tugged, but his grip was firm, rough. Like a pirate holding the object of his passion.

"I finished what I came to do," she said, fighting to sound neutral. "You and Free are reunited."

Suzanne swirled the wine in her glass. "I'm getting very confused as to who's Free and who's not." She looked up at her husband and winked. "But when we get home tonight, I think I'm in the mood to be a little free myself."

But Toby ignored her, and everyone else. Holding Kate's arm, he said sharply, "It's finally dawned on me. I've been afraid to connect in a relationship because my family was torn apart. I thought I'd lose it all again." He looked at Free and knew she would never, never understand—had never understood. He looked again at Kate. "But families can come together. I've learned that from you and your mom, Kate. Love can heal, families can grow stronger!"

Verna yelped a small "bravo!" She and Suzanne clinked glasses.

Toby looked down the hall. "Free, that cruise invitation…"

Free started hopping up and down, obviously thinking she'd won.

"…is canceled," continued Toby. "Just like our relationship. I wanted to patch things up so I could get this job promotion, but I'm tired of playing games, tired of relying on cunning tactics to seal the deal."

"But don't fret," Verna interrupted with a smirk. "Maybe Tiger can take you on a road trip—to a bead convention or something."

Toby looked back at Kate. "Right now, there's nothing more important to me than to follow my heart." His voice dropped to a husky urgency. "And to love this precious woman for the rest of my life." He pulled her closer. "Kate Corrigan, will you marry me?"

Only a moment ago, she was ready to do a backward hurl. Now her heart was doing a forward flip. Kate Corrigan was playing the romantic lead? "But I'm the matchmaker," she whispered haltingly.

Verna giggled as Free stomped out the front door with Tiger in tow. "I think I get the honor of being the matchmaker. This one, Kate, is my success!"

Kate's concerns settled into the dark recesses of her mind as a hazy, sensuous aura surrounded her and Toby. No, not an aura. A feeling. Love? Toby's expression stilled as he waited for her response.

"My beautiful, romantic Kate, the object of my heart's passion..."

Kate let his words flow over her, smother her, warm her right through to the innermost corners of her soul. She reached up and touched his lips with her own. When they kissed, it was as though their souls, like two precious metals, soldered together, never to be apart. She pulled back and looked into his brown eyes, which glinted with promise. A lifetime of promise. She'd once told him she wasn't good at facing things. Well, she was facing the rest of her life at this very moment and nothing, nothing in her life had ever felt more perfect.

"Yes," she whispered.

Melanie, holding the pie as though it were soldered to her fingers, stepped forward. "And before anyone gets the wrong idea," she announced matter-of-factly, "my daughter does *not* pay Toby for sex."

Verna, always the one to keep her head together no matter what the circumstances, laughed full-heartedly. "Now that we have *that* settled," she said joyfully, "let's eat dessert and celebrate, celebrate, celebrate!"

BR-R-RING-BR-R-RING.

Kate, sitting at the butcher-block table in her kitchen,

looked at Toby and her mother. "According to the Captain Hook clock, it's nearly ten o'clock. Customers rarely call this late. Must be Dad calling Mom."

But Melanie, putting an empty pie tin into the dishwasher, didn't head for the phone. "I think he's calling you this time."

Br-r-ring-br-r-ring.

"Me?" Kate asked, getting up. Crossing to the phone, she tossed a questioning look at Toby. "I think my dad has made more phone calls in the past few days than in his entire life!"

Melanie chuckled. "And he's asked me my opinion on things *twice*."

"Better watch out—next he'll start doing laundry." Kate picked up the receiver. "Beau's Bed-and-Breakfast." Pause. "Hi, Dad. Want to talk to Mom?" Pause. "To me? Okay."

Toby, sitting on a stool next to the table, leaned back and watched the gamut of emotions that crossed Kate's face over the next few minutes. Surprise, confusion and, finally, bewilderment. When she eventually spoke, her voice sounded soft, fragile. "I'd love to go to college. Thank you for that Christmas gift. No, you don't need to send me a set of wrenches as well. Well, okay, if you insist."

Even without his glasses, Toby saw the tears welling in Kate's eyes. Tears of happiness and gratitude. She cleared her throat. "Maybe I'll go to San Francisco State. I need to think this through, decide what degree will enhance my fledging restaurant career. You know how I've been wanting to expand my bed-and-breakfast business. Since Toby just got a great job offer tonight, we're talking about adding a restaurant next door in a year or so." Pause. "Yes, Toby. He owns the house next door. Yes, he got a *fantastic* job offer, which didn't surprise anybody except Mom who thought he was really a...oh, never mind. Anyway, Dennis, Toby's manager, said he'd never seen a man handle multiple crises as well as Toby did tonight. Who's Toby? My fiancé, Daddy! After working a few more years in the software industry, he'll quit and run the restaurant full-time."

Whoa! Toby sat up. Not only did her father now know Toby's history and dreams, he was also finding out this was his future son-in-law. Her father might be becoming new-age, but the man probably had some old-fashioned notions about a suitor asking for his daughter's hand.

"Yes, I said 'fiancé'," Kate continued, a lilt in her voice. "I know, lately I'm just like Mom—full of surprises. Guess you'll have to make a special trip here to meet him."

Toby eased out a breath. He needed to relax. So what if he didn't get to ask Kate's dad for his daughter's hand—at least her father found out about the engagement on the same night as everyone else, including Free and Tiger. Toby chuckled to himself. After Melanie had retrieved Mickey and Minnie for them, they'd taken off in the van. Perhaps the four of them were heading out on that road trip right now.

"So," Kate continued, "want me to put Melanie—I mean, Mom—on the phone? Love you, too." Kate handed the receiver to her mother, who acted as though she didn't see it.

"Mom," Kate whispered urgently, "it's Dad."

"But he asked for the wrong woman," her mother answered.

"He asked for you!"

"No," her mother said quietly, preoccupied with wiping a spot on the counter. "My new name is Scarlett, not Melanie." She gave her daughter a conspiratorial wink. "Tomorrow I fly home and your father had better be ready to say goodbye to Melanie and hello to Scarlett O'Hara because I plan to take the South, and your father, by storm." She accepted the receiver.

As her mother whispered and giggled on the phone in the background, Kate sat down next to Toby. "Scarlett! Can you believe the change in her? She's grown incorrigible!"

Toby grinned. "Uh, I think your mother discovered her true inner nature—just as you did."

"Look who's talking, my wild, plundering pirate." Kate grinned. "*Questa casa non è un albergo.* Right? This house isn't a motel. But you got both, rolled into one!"

Toby looked into Kate's eyes, wondering if the Caribbean was that blue, that sparkling. He guessed he'd discover the answer when they were on their cruise. "So," he said teasingly, "is Kismet where I sleep tonight?" He looked at her with such desire, such intensity. "What do you want?"

"Kismet? I think fate has played its hand. Our room from now on is The Pirate." Kate flashed him that impish grin. "And for the record, I want you."

Toby smiled warmly. "You just said the magic words." He stood and swept Kate into his arms, crushing her to him like a long-lost treasure. He carried her out the swinging kitchen doors and up the stairs, the pirate laying claim to the object of his passion, his love, for the rest of his life.

Three heart-stirring tales are coming down the
aisle toward you in one fabulous collection!

LOVE, HONOR & CHERISH by
SHERRYL WOODS

These were the words that three generations of
Halloran men promised their women. But these vows
made in love are each challenged by the test of time....

LOVE
Jason meets his match when a sassy spitfire turns his
perfectly predictable life upside down!

HONOR
Despite their times of trouble, there still wasn't a dragon
Kevin wouldn't slay to honor and protect his beloved bride!

CHERISH
They'd spent decades apart, but now Brandon had every
intention of rekindling a long-lost love!

"Sherryl Woods is an author who writes with a very special
warmth, wit, charm and intelligence."
—*New York Times* bestselling author
Heather Graham Pozzessere

On sale May 2000 at your favorite retail outlet.

Silhouette®

Where love comes alive™

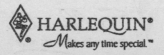